* * *

LOVE WILL COME LATER . . .

"Tell me," he demanded.

Emmeline threw back her head, her green eyes defying him. "Leave me alone," she said. "Have you not taken enough from me?"

Their son. "I will take whatever I want," he shouted. "Whether it please you or not. Damn you, you are my wife! And what are you hiding from me?"

He reached around her and groped across the table. He'd seen the gleam of gold. He lifted a pair of tongs, and some golden wire fell out of their jaws.

"The devil! Are you doing goldsmith's work here?" He picked up the wire. It was still warm, heated to form a filigree that would fit around a stone. "Show me." He took her by the shoulder and pushed her down on the stool. "Show me how you do this."

She sat with her back straight, staring ahead. The knotted head scarf exposed the smooth back of her neck with its tendrils of damp red curls. He suddenly wanted to put his fingers there. His wife was beautiful, delectable . . . and she hated him.

He reached for her, pulled her to him. Their lips touched and his mouth claimed hers, possessing her . . .

Books by Maggie Davis

writing as Maggie Davis

EAGLES
ROMMEL'S GOLD
THE SHEIK
THE FAR SIDE OF HOME
THE WINTER SERPENT
FORBIDDEN OBJECTS
SATIN DOLL
SATIN DREAMS
WILD MIDNIGHT
MIAMI MIDNIGHT
HUSTLE, SWEET LOVE
DIAMONDS AND PEARLS
TROPIC OF LOVE
DREAMBOAT

writing as Katherine Deauxville

EYES OF LOVE (Coming in 1996)
THE CRYSTAL HEART
THE AMETHYST CROWN
BLOOD RED ROSES
DAGGERS OF GOLD

writing as Maggie Daniels

A CHRISTMAS ROMANCE
(*also a CBS movie with Olivia Newton-John*)
MOONLIGHT AND MISTLETOE

THE CRYSTAL HEART

KATHERINE DEAUXVILLE

ZEBRA BOOKS
KENSINGTON PUBLISHING CORP.

ZEBRA BOOKS are published by

Kensington Publishing Corp.
850 Third Avenue
New York, NY 10022

First Printing: August, 1995

Printed in the United States of America

ONE

"That's the one," Gulfer said. "The big lad with the russet hair and the fine set of shoulders." He lifted his torch high to show they were friendly, standing there in the dark street, and not footpads or cutpurses. "The boy may be a tadpole still, but he overtops us both by half a head. And from the size of that great knot between his legs, it would seem we could not find a better one for our task."

They watched as two young men halted in the doorway of the inn, the light behind them. They were drunk enough to hang onto each other to keep from falling. The shorter boy began to sing.

The other knight shrugged, "Size isn't everything. My cousin in Lincolnshire has a shaft surpassing small, a wee mannikin, but he's sired twelve children with it, nevertheless."

Gulfer made an impatient noise in his throat. "Never mind that, just study the lad. Considering there's a lot of riffraff in the land because of this cursed war, we could do worse. I've been following this one for days in and out of Wrexham's alleys, and I say that of all I've considered—knights, squires, lordlings, even a few merchants' pups—yon redheaded gamecock is far and above the best for our purpose."

They saw a shadow come up behind the drunken pair. "Out, damn you," came the voice of the innkeeper, "if your money's spent. But in or out, stop the sodding noise!"

The door slammed behind them, shoving them out into the street. The taller boy kept his feet but the singer staggered, then sat down in the gutter.

"Sweet Jesu, Niall." He rubbed his head with one hand, helmet dangling from the other. "That's a fine way to treat us! A sennight in this hellhole and they still give us no welcome."

In the shadows, Aimery snorted. "I'll wager," he said behind his hand, "they've not a copper between them. Youngsters make little enough fighting for hire. And what they do they drink and gamble away."

"Aye, and so did you, at their age." Holding the torch high, Gulfer stepped forward. The redheaded boy was trying to drag the other to his feet. "Young sirs, by your leave," he called out, "I beg a boon. A matter of some small employment. At an excellent fee."

The young knight let go of the other, who promptly sat down again. "Keep your distance." His hand went to his sword hilt. "We have employment. We're Earl Robert of Gloucester's men."

"Just so, just so." Close up, the lad was even better than Gulfer had hoped: even-featured enough to be handsome, amber eyes to go with the russet hair, a long, arrogant nose, a mouth that indented gracefully at the corners. He kept his hand on his sword as his look slid past Gulfer to Aimery.

"Be at ease, young sir," Gulfer told him. "I solicit your services for a small devoir worthy of one—ah, of your youth and vigor. It is a task that will take only this night, in as pleasant as an occupation as one could desire. But with a most serious and worthy purpose."

The redhead looked down his nose at him. Beside him his companion got unsteadily to his feet. "Just what are you selling?" he asked, suspicious.

Gulfer had to smile. "Good young sir, empty your head of improper thoughts! Let me assure you, I seek only your most honorable services for hire." He paused and rubbed his chin with one hand. Then he told them what he was seeking.

When he was finished the two young knights stared at him. Then both burst out laughing.

Gulfer waited. It was only what he had expected. He pulled out a purse from a pocket under his mail and, handing the torch to Aimery, emptied the contents into the boy's palm. The torchlight picked up the glitter of coins.

"Two Flemish gold marks," Gulfer told him, "for only a few hours of your time."

There was a silence broken only by the raucous sounds from the tavern. The other young knight seized his companion by the arm. "Niall, come away," he pleaded. "We are hardly sober, and this can only be a devil's offer from some aged trull that lures young men to her bed. These old knights are her pimps, offering us tainted gold!"

The other eyes were on the coins. "Sweet Mary," he murmured, "but that's a lot of money."

Gulfer watched him closely. "Lad, I swear on the Holy Virgin that all is just as I told you. A rich, elderly merchant of this town has a young wife by whom he has tried to get an heir for these past three years. But after this long time it does not seem, considering that the poor man only grows more aged and infirm, that he can make a child. Yet he fears for his fortune if he should die and leave his wife alone with his wealth. I am sent to find a healthy, honorable young man who will give my master what he desires. In return, as you can see, it will pay well."

The boy tugged at his friend's arm. "God's mercy, Niall, come away! You are too drunken to know what you're doing! If you listen to this mad proposal you will find yourself robbed, assaulted, your body dumped in the river come morning!"

The redhead shook him off. "Peace, Orion, I have not said I would do it." His eyes narrowed. "If I say yes," he told Gulfer, "tell me just how all this is to be accomplished."

"You will be taken," Gulfer said promptly, "to a place I cannot name, except to say that it is the most proper of dwellings. You will be blindfolded so as to keep it all secret. You will be well and most courteously treated, then returned in the morning with your eyes covered to any spot you may name. At that time you will be paid."

The other gave him a sharp look. "Well and good so far. But all Christendom knows you cannot make a babe in just one night."

Gulfer spread his hands, shrugging. "Just so I have argued, bless me. But it is in God's hands. This night will be all that is required of you, for the pay you see before you."

The young knight's mouth turned up in a cynical grin. "Tell me, how many men before me has the lady called to her bed?"

The old knight scowled. "You misunderstand, tadpole. The lady is no wanton. Her intent is no more nor less than what you have been told." He shrugged. "It is too bad, the mistake is mine, I will take no more of your time."

He started off, Aimery following. The young knight stepped somewhat unsteadily in front of him. "Nay, I have a right to ask. This is a strange proposal."

He regarded him steadily. "Believe me, boy, I would not have it could I but disallow her of this fancy. But here I am."

The other stood for a moment thinking it over. Finally he said, "Show me the gold again."

Gulfer thrust out his hand. The redheaded boy picked up a gold piece and held it between thumb and forefinger. *"Louis rex Francia,"* he read. "With a sheaf of grain on the other side. This is French gold, my friend, not Flemish."

"So you can read." Gulfer was impressed. "And can you scriven, too?"

"Umm." He flipped the coin over his battle-scarred fingers. "By the saints," he said, abruptly, "why do we not let the coin decide?"

The gold piece spun through the air. He caught it and slapped it onto the back of his hand.

"I call it heads," he told Gulfer.

He took his hand away and Gulfer bent to peer at it. "Tails." He straightened up. "Aimery, fetch the blindfold."

The other boy threw himself in between. "No, no—this is madness!" he cried. "Niall, it stinks of—of—witchcraft, and treachery! Don't go, I won't let you!" He looked around, desperate. "Not unless—not unless you take me, also!"

Aimery pushed him aside. "No, lad, you stay here."

The youngster drew his sword, but his friend Niall caught his arm. "Nay, Orion is right, there should be two of us. To guard against treachery."

"Unruly brats." Gulfer glowered at them. "The whole thing's not worth a farthing, except that the blessed girl insists on it." He dug under his mail, then his padded underjacket. "Holy Jesus knows what does she thinks to get from this," he muttered. "Unless it's a miracle."

Aimery used the black blindfold on the bigger youth, Gulfer's own rather greasy kerchief on the other. When it was over the two young knights stood shoulder to shoulder. "We do not give up our swords," the big redhead said, fingering his blindfold. "Nor will you bind our hands."

"Aye, but keep them behind you," Gulfer warned. "We want no peeping. It is the end of it if you do."

They bent their heads together. The redheaded lad muttered something under his breath.

"Niall," the other boy whispered in answer, "I care not I only want you to remember that it is only your damnable, ever-ready cock that's getting us into this!"

Gulfer heard him. And because he knew they could not see him, he smiled.

Two

They were taken on foot through blind streets to a house with a wide doorway. They stumbled on the low step going in. Inside, from the smell of horses, they were in the wagon yard of a large house. Then a doorway again.

Niall bumped his shoulders against the wall as the old knights led him up narrow stairs. There were passageways filled with the heat and sounds and smells of a kitchen. Finally they stopped and Gulfer pulled off their blindfolds. "Wash, lads," he told them. "Then you'll have food."

Blinking, Niall looked around. The room perhaps belonged to a butler, or steward, as it had a table, a bed, and a roaring fire in the fireplace. A dinner was already waiting for them. Putting out a hot meal where they could see it was calculated to persuade them to scrub themselves skinless in record time.

Niall willingly shed his clothes to step into the huge black kettle of water. Orion came after him with a ladle of soft soap and some kitchen girl's scrub brush. Which only made Orion more loudly certain that they were there to entertain some lecherous beldame *a deux,* and not the story the old knights had told them.

Then, with only their underhose drawn up over their nakedness, they threw themselves down at the table to eat.

Niall finished first and pushed his shingle away, leaning back to belch. The dinner had been better than good: great slabs of roast pork and black bread, and an oat pudding doused in honey and butter, all washed down with an ewer of head-spinning Welsh ale.

"So she will want the two of us, Orion? Is that what you think?" Niall got up from the table, holding up his still-damp hose with one hand. "That it will take both of us for some palsied old Welsh marcher lady?"

"Don't make light of it," his friend said morosely. "I've heard stories—the old ones are the worst. I tell you, Niall, this is some wicked plot by an evil dame whose withered cunt cries nightly for the juicy shaft of innocent young men!"

"Innocent?" Niall searched about on the floor for the rest of his clothes. "Jesu, if I'm to crawl over some hag in her bed with you breathing down my back, you will need a more innocent nature than mine."

His friend broke off a piece of bread and threw it at him. Niall caught it deftly and stuffed it in his mouth.

So far the evening had not been bad, at least for two of Earl Gloucester's tired and hungry young knights. The hot bath had been as welcome as the good dinner; Niall's last trip to the Wrexham stews had been longer ago than he cared to remember. Now his skin smelled clean, if a bit soapy. And, thanks to the good meal, he was not as drunk as he had been. Nevertheless, he jumped when the bells of some church nearby clanged for compline. His hand went to his dagger.

Orion nodded, gloomy-faced. "Aye, and you'd better take your sword with you to wherever it is you're going."

Slowly, Niall let out his breath. By his reckoning they were somewhere in Wrexham's merchants' quarter. It was still possible—although God knows they had nothing of which to be robbed—that they could be ambushed here in an unknown part of the city while foolishly separated from Earl Robert's command. Even the dire things Orion suspected could still happen.

Niall tried to shrug off the feeling. God's wounds, he

was a knight, he told himself; he had come from Ireland with his sword for hire hoping for fame and reward, risking wounds, even death. The only thing he regretted as he picked his way through their mail and clothing on the floor was being so drunk at the tavern. Because only God in his wisdom knew how this strange business would turn out.

He bent to pick up his padded underjacket. "Have faith in me, Orion, I'll well earn my money, never fear. In spite of all the bawd houses you've dragged me to, my cock has never yet failed me."

The underjacket gave out a strong aroma of sweat. Niall thought about the condition of his clothes and a woman's sensibilities. Any woman's sensibilities. He decided it was better to leave it.

That left him clad in nothing but his underhose. Which was probably enough, if the night's work had been truthfully represented. That is, a matter of quickly into bed and just as quickly out, hoping, as Orion put it, that the woman was not too old and repulsive to dandle.

His companion was watching him, chin on hand. "You damned Irish think you can swive the devil's sister," Orion said thickly.

Niall looked around for his boots. "Nay, it's the gold that's captured my heart. What the old knight is offering is more than two years' pay in the empress's service."

"Hah. When we get paid." Orion lifted the empty ewer and shook it. "Tell me, of what damnable use is this war?" He looked morose. "You and I know that the empress will never sit upon England's throne, even with her brother Gloucester's help. England will not have a woman to rule, even if she *is* the old king's daughter."

Niall shrugged. "Ah well, they have a woman in King Stephen, haven't they? Stephen cannot make up his mind when to fight and when to forgive his enemies." He turned. "Are you sober enough for me to leave you?"

At that moment the door opened and Gulfer came in.

Niall knotted up the top of his hose, leaning over to pick up his sword.

Gulfer scowled at him. "Jesu, boy, put that down. You can't go to her like that. It's no battle you're waging, the lady's in her bedchamber!"

He held onto it. "My sword goes, or I do not."

The other reached into his jacket and pulled out the blindfold. "Now, youngster, consider what little you can do with your sword while wearing this over your eyes."

Niall hesitated, not wanting to leave his weapon. But the other was right. He was already cursing himself for having ever listened to this mad story. The more he learned the more stupid it seemed. *An old merchant's wife who needed to beget a child?* Only two drunken lackwits like Orion and himself would have been gulled by such a tale!

On the other hand, he thought as he studied the old knight, *there was the money.* The gold was real enough. He'd seen it and touched it. And when one came right down to it, there were very few things he would not do for two whole years' pay. "Give me your word," he said to Gulfer, "that this is not some treachery."

From the table Orion called, "Yes, make him swear on his mother's grave that this crone is sweet and winsome, and not queen of the Wrexham trolls!"

Gulfer's gaze was steady. "It is no treachery, boy. The lady is as I said."

Niall hesitated. Then turned and presented his back. The old knight reached around him and bound up his eyes.

They left Orion before the fire and went down a corridor in the now-silent house. Niall did not stumble as much as before, but his senses were alert to all that he heard and smelled: leather and wax, household dust, and the smoking mutton fat rush dips that lighted the way.

They came to a flight of stairs and he stumbled, cracking

his shins on the risers. He cursed under his breath. "Sweet Mary, tell me where there are stairs, will you?" he complained. "Or the next open pit where I might fall to my death?"

Gulfer put a hand on his arm. "Steady, lad, it is not far." He gave a gusty sigh in his ear. "Ah, you young gamecocks little know what treasures you have in your youth and your strength! I would give everything that I own, were I standing in your braies this night!"

He pushed Niall toward another flight of stairs. At the top they stopped, abruptly.

There was the sound of knocking. The old pensioner did not wait for an answer: Niall heard a door creak back on its hinges. Cautious, he held his hands up before him, feeling warm air. A prickling of his skin warned him that if some trickery were to come, it would come now.

Gulfer's hand in the small of his back steered him ahead. Without removing his blindfold the old knight went out, closing the door behind him.

Niall reached up to pull off the cloth and found himself blinking in sudden, bright candlelight.

The room was filled with tapers, dozens of them, enough to say high mass. He was in a bedchamber, its four walls hung with rich tapestries. There were brilliant woven scenes of boar and deer hunts, circles of maidens dancing in a forest, processions of nobles against vistas of walled and fortified towns. In addition, the room was furnished with velvet-covered chairs, tables, and chests of carved dark wood. Underfoot were sheepskin and goatskin rugs bound with scarlet braiding. A blazing fire burned on a white sandstone hearth. In the middle stood a great bed, its posts hung with curtains trimmed with red rope and gold tassels.

Niall blinked again. He'd been in castles and manor houses that were not as fine as this. It was hard to believe only merchants, and not the high nobility, lived here. He

almost did not notice the girl standing so still by the cano-
pied bed.

The merchant's wife. He felt a nerve in his cheek twitch.

She was medium tall, pale-lipped, with great blue or
green eyes. Against the velvet bed hangings her hair, unbound and flowing over her shoulders, shone like a copper
river laced with streams of fire. The embroidered robe hung
loose from her shoulders yet it was plain her form was
slender, her breasts full and high.

He couldn't help it, his heart leaped.

She was not only young, he thought, peering at her, but
beautiful. What had the old knight told him? Married three
years to an old merchant without getting a child? Most
girls of her class married at fourteen. Some at thirteen.

Seventeen, Niall told himself. Surely not a day more.

The next instant he could not help a sudden surge of
unease.

This was not the old harpy Orion had prophesied. Niall
supposed there were some who might not care for her short,
straight nose, the saucy set of her cheekbones, her catlike
green eyes, but to him she had a loveliness that reminded,
with her blazing hair, of the orange and red lilies one found
in the meadows in midsummer.

She was certainly not the cool, distant fair lady of the
troubadors' songs, he thought, studying her, but a golden
vixen, a blazing wood nymph, all cream and fire and emerald
eyes. She was so entrancing that he could not help, at that
moment, remembering Orion's warnings against witchcraft.

For a second a chill ran down Niall's back and prickled
the hair on his neck. Then he told himself he was a fool.
The girl was delicate as a tawny flower. Her lips trembled
uncertainly as she looked at him. It would be stupid to be
frightened of a maid whose only sorcery was her beauty.

She held the front of the embroidered robe together with
white, soft hands. She had graceful fingers, with pink, well-
kept nails.

He suddenly remembered that his own hands were blackened from hard duty and the care of weapons and horses. And he was just as aware of how he must look to her—a rough-appearing young knight, broad through the shoulders, with dark red hair that could never match the fiery blaze of her own. Wearing only his bedraggled hose. And in his bare feet, having left his boots and cross garters behind in the room with Orion.

Jesu, it was too late to think of all that. He was suddenly eager to get on with it.

Niall said, somewhat hoarsely, "I am—I believe I am the one you await, madame."

THREE

The candle flames had grown long and bright in the room's stillness, and shadows crept up the bedchamber's tapestried walls. Emmeline stood waiting, wrapped about in a China silk gown so stiff with embroidery that it rustled when she breathed.

This was going to take courage, she thought. More than she had reckoned on. She was finding that it was so much easier to plan, to think, to organize and arrange, than to deal with one's schemes when they were suddenly real.

Now, bursting into the room in his bare feet and wearing only a shabby pair of hose, the young knight Gulfer had brought to her bedchamber was *very* real.

She watched with astonishment as halfway across the floor he seemed to catch his toe on one of the sheepskin rugs. He lost his balance and staggered, flailing his arms. Emmeline caught a glimpse of tigerish amber eyes, high cheekbones, and a look of wild determination.

He came to a stop.

She couldn't take her eyes from him. From the moment he'd entered the room she'd been frozen to the spot, not able to move. For one thing, he was much bigger than Gulfer had told her!

Her husband, Bernard of Neufmarche, was small, elderly, gentle of habit and soft-spoken. Now Emmeline saw that what her old retainers had brought to her was a strapping, half-naked young buck in sagging chausses who strode to-

ward her on long legs, sprouts of dark red hair showing
where the hose did not quite meet his ankles.

Her mouth went suddenly dry.

Holy Mother, she thought frantically, for all his clumsy
charge into her bedchamber one could plainly see why
Gulfer had chosen him! He looked as though he could sire
a thousand—a hundred thousand—babes as lusty as himself! The red-russet hair was worn rather long and waving
to his shoulders. His golden skin had a silky sheen and he
was narrow-hipped, long-legged—in fact so powerfully,
youthfully male that had she not been rooted to the spot,
Emmeline would have bolted.

Her eyes found his groin where the damp cloth showed
the massive rod of his sex pressing against it. And which
seemed, while she stared, to grow even larger.

She felt suddenly dizzy. God in heaven, she could not
reject him, send him away now that he was there, it was
too late for that! Besides, what they were doing was too
dangerous—and not the least of it, in the eyes of the
church, a mortal sin.

She swallowed, tasting once again the stuff the nurse had
given her to assure that this night's work would not be in
vain. *Courage,* Emmeline told herself shakily. For better or
worse, there he was.

He stood before her, openly staring. She tried to return
that bold look, only too aware of the size of his arms,
shoulders, the bare feet. He seemed to fill the air with
muscular nakedness.

At that moment Emmeline no longer had any idea how
she had managed to persuade Gulfer and Aimery to help
her; it seemed a miracle now her husband's old knights had
even listened to her, much less found this towering young
gamecock somewhere in the town.

It was too late to change her mind, send him away. This
had been her own plan and she had her bounden duty to
it, may the good Mother in heaven forgive her. But the

realization that they had all night—that this might take all night—nearly unnerved her.

She fixed her eyes at a point on the far wall. Her face felt drained of blood, stiff as paper. Somehow they must begin. "Y-you—you know why you are here." Her words were almost a squeak.

When Emmeline lifted her eyes she found that strange, tawny gaze intent upon her like a shock. She told herself that at least he looked at one very directly; she supposed that was a sign of good character.

"Yes," he said finally, "I have been told."

She could not help it, the husky sound of his voice made her shudder. For all his boyish good looks he was still a stranger, one to whom she would have to give the most intimate use of her body. She quickly glanced at his hands. Dear God, they were nearly as big as his feet!

Her words came tumbling out in a rush. "H-how—how old are you?"

His eyebrows went up. He thought a moment before he said, "Four years a squire under my lord, Earl Robert of Gloucester. Now nearly one year a knight. I am twenty."

Emmeline clutched the front of the robe. *Twenty.* He was much too young, only two years or so older than she. Her mind was racing. The babe, if there was to be one, would undoubtedly be redheaded. And horribly big. If a little girl, she would be a tawny-eyed giantess!

She closed her eyes, saying a silent prayer. She could only cast herself on the mercy of the Holy Virgin and hope that all this would turn out well, but she was almost witless with apprehension. "Y-you understand," she managed, "that you will be paid in the m-morning?"

His expression changed. "Yes, I am in your debt to be reminded of that, mistress. That I will be paid." He stepped toward her, the same look on his face. "Shall we start now?"

Emmeline stepped back, bumping into the side of the bed. *"Now?"*

"The night grows no younger," he reminded her.

That was true. Looking into those golden-brown eyes Emmeline felt a strange sensation tingle over every inch of her skin. Curious prickling points of heat rose to the tips of her breasts. Her mouth was suddenly tender. She tried to take another step back, but the bed blocked her.

She made herself take a deep breath. God in heaven knew she was no coward; this might be the worst travail of her life but it was worth it, because she needed this baby so much! Not only for Bernard and the fate of his fortune, but for herself. She had yearned for a sweet little babe for so long that this was like a dream come true. If she could but get through this night.

She fought down her feeling of panic. It was well known in Morlaix town that the goldsmith's wife was headstrong and spoiled. That her old husband too willingly indulged her. But those same ones would also admit that she had been a good, obedient wife, and had made Bernard of Neufmarche happy.

She took a deep breath.

Yes, now, Emmeline told herself. While she still had the wits to do it.

She raised her hands and yanked at the tie of her chamber robe. It fell open, showing a white nightdress underneath laced with ribbons.

He had been watching her closely. She heard the swift intake of his breath. He reached out and pulled her to him.

His big, callused hands against her skin were warm, slightly trembling. "If this is a dream," she heard him mutter, "do not let me wake until I have had you!"

He bent his head and his mouth seized hers with an eager roughness. She gasped to be pulled so quickly against a half-naked body. To feel its heated power. Her fingertips dug into his bare shoulders. In response his arms tightened around her, nearly squeezing the breath from her.

Her head whirled. This young knight might seem impetuous, even clumsy, but he was more experienced than he looked. Insistent pressure poured from that hard, throbbing kiss into her lips. His hands held her tightly as the fire flamed into the tips of her breasts, then her soft, feminine places like rivers of liquid desire.

Emmeline tried to push him away. All this kissing was certainly unnecessary; she could feel from the huge evidence jutting against her that he did not need anything more to make him aroused. But he held her even more tightly while his mouth nuzzled her throat, the side of her face.

Right in her ear he rasped, "I never thought I would find such a wondrous treasure at the end of this night's journey. God's face, some magic holds me enchanted!"

"My arm," Emmeline managed. With some struggling, she pulled it out from where it had been trapped under his elbow. He did not seem to notice. His arms held her as his mouth trailed eager kisses across her face.

"I do not know how this has come about." She could hear the wonderment in his voice. "But I heartily thank the gods for whatever fate has smiled on me this night."

She managed to pry him away from her. All this impassioned talk was not what she wanted to hear; they had a task to accomplish. He looked down at her, amber eyes glowing, his mouth softened with his turbulent caresses.

She tore her eyes away. Dear holy mother, her body, her traitorous senses seemed to want only his lustful body inside *hers!* She was shaking like a leaf. "I-I will put out the candles."

He caught her arm. "Sweet mistress, I wish to bed you most tenderly, and—ah, with the successful outcome you desire. But do you not know that no babe can be made if a woman has no enjoyment?"

She turned to goggle at him. *"What?"*

"Yea, what we are about to do is no rutting act such as animals pursue. If a woman has no pleasure, there will be no babe."

She had never heard of such a thing in her life. She put her hand to her throat. "I must have pleasure?" she said faintly.

There might have been a glint of mischief in his eyes. "Even the church fathers assure us this is so," he said solemnly. "Only in the most pleasant physical transport between man and woman can new life be created."

She regarded him, openmouthed. His words, uttered in a faintly lilting accent she could not place confused her. And yet left no doubt of their authority.

Certainly the holy church preached that the pleasures of the flesh must be used only for procreation, the getting of children, and *not* to satisfy lust. Although it was common knowledge that most people, married or unmarried, paid little attention to that.

Emmeline licked her dry lips. It seemed so much easier to get into the bed, do the act, and get it over with, as she did with Bernard.

"Are you sure?" she whispered.

She saw him smile. His big hands quickly covered her breasts, stroking the nipples through the cloth of her gown. "Let me prove it to you," he murmured.

She leaned to him, knees suddenly weak. His heavy, caressing touch sent a feeling such as she'd never experienced before rippling through her. While she swayed, captive in the grip of it, he bent his head and pulled down the neck of the nightdress. The white flesh of her breasts swung free, high-tilted and firm. Then his warm mouth was on them, tugging and teasing, rolling the tender buds between his tongue and his teeth.

Emmeline's hands clutched his hair. She tried not to scream. Her nipples had hardened into aching knots that were connected to a blaze tearing through her body down to her toes. While his mouth sucked and nibbled his hands were on her bottom, kneading and caressing, pulling her to him.

She sobbed out loud. Holy Mary, she was being marvelously assailed, strangely tormented! At the same time her legs and hips writhed against him as she slid her body up and down against his legs and groin like a randy cat. Bernard, her poor husband, had never brought her such demented torture in all the years he had bedded her!

His hands carefully pulled hers from his thick russet hair. "Hush, my beautiful sweeting." His voice was oddly strangled. "My precious, passionate love." He brought her fingers to his lips and kissed them hurriedly. "I swear I will pleasure you, my heart. But you must give me a moment to do it."

She looked up at him, wild-eyed. "Why is it taking so long?"

She heard him sigh. His wide mouth gleamed in the candlelight. He bent his head and his lips went to her other breast, his hand cupping it while he pushed up the hem of her gown. Before she could stiffen his touch slid between her thighs, pushing them apart.

Emmeline moaned. This was much, much more than she had expected to endure. She was not even sure, in spite of all that had been said, that he understood the bargain. Or if Gulfer had clearly explained it. That is, that he was to try to get her with child. A simple, even tedious act. And not, dear God, what he was doing!

His hand had found its way toward the soft, furry cleft of her sex. She fell back in his arms as with a quick thrust, his fingers were inside her.

In the next instant he had pulled her down upon the bed. "Don't be afraid," he told her as he rolled over her and pressed her down into the coverlets.

Afraid?

She felt like shrieking. Over her, he was a fury of driving, passionate strength. Her back arched, her hips writhed, greedily following the burning, pulsing touch that had invaded her. She clutched him, not knowing what to expect. Or even what she wanted!

"Oh my sweetheart, my little golden goddess!" Roughly, he showered her face and throat with kisses. Emmeline bucked and thrashed, the stroking fingers driving her wild.

Dimly she remembered that she had planned to get her babe most quietly and carefully this night, in the safety of her own bedchamber, while her husband was away on his journey to York. She had thought to lie there in the big bed as she always did and endure the necessary thing with some young man that her knights would find for her.

Now, she realized as she stared up at the wildly flapping bed hangings, she was in the grip of a strange madness. It poured from this amber-eyed knight and his lithe, powerful body. His no doubt brothel-learned lust.

Why, this big, handsome young buck had told her she could have no child without proper fleshly pleasure! Now she was acting like a madwoman, a crazed roadside doxie, her breasts aching for him, her hips frantically chasing the tormenting caresses of his big hands. Wanting nothing else but the moaning, whirling release he could offer.

"That's my honeycake," he rasped in her ear as the bed bounded wildly. "Ah, dearest one, hold nothing back!"

Emmeline had never felt anything like this in all her years with Bernard Neufmarche. She was horrified. Abandoned. Debauched. Unashamedly wanton!

In the back of her fevered mind she knew there was yet time to throw him off, to spring from the bed before he could stop her and run from the room. Gulfer was somewhere about, guarding the hall; she could run to him and tell him to pay this redheaded young stallion the two gold marks they had promised, and send him away. Dear God, then it would be all over!

Emmeline shut her eyes. He was breathing in great gasps, fingers sliding in and out of her hot and slippery center. "If this be a dream," he croaked, "then as God is my witness, I say that at least for tonight I can make you all mine!"

She felt his shaft suddenly pressing against her flesh. He gripped her tighter, both hands under her, moving her legs apart. Then with a sudden jerk of his hips, one fierce plunge, he was in her.

She swallowed a shriek. Shuddering, he covered her mouth with own.

She was wet and ready, he had seen to it. But he was still so big Emmeline lay stiffly under him, feeling him throb and pulse within her. She drew a loud, sobbing breath. When she looked up his golden eyes were right in her own. "Kiss me," he whispered. "My angel, give me your lips." He smoothed her hair with a big hand.

Their lips touched, and his mouth claimed hers, drowning her, possessing her. After a while he began to move.

Emmeline reached up and locked her hands behind his neck and twined her legs around him, hearing his shuddering groan when she moved against him. He pounded her with all the strength of his big frame. She could not help shrieking. Several times it seemed that he would throw them both from the bed with his frenzied bucking. She clung to him with her legs wrapped around his hips, her bright hair flailing. She reached a hard, shaking peak such as she had never imagined, and wailed.

He hardly paused. He took her in his arms, lifted her out of the bed, set her on her feet and propped her against the bedpost. Drawing her leg up to his hip, he thrust into her while they stood there.

Emmeline's body clenched in fiery shock. She moaned into his lips as he drove into her repeatedly. Then with a shudder he bellowed out his release.

When it was over he lifted her and carried her back to bed and rolled her onto her stomach. Then, kissing her back from her shoulder blades to the curve of her bottom, he moved himself over her and entered her as she was, pressed on her elbows and knees.

He had grown hard again quickly. The feel of him was almost too much to bear. She moaned when he sank his teeth lightly into her shoulders and neck. With his fingertip between her legs, on the fleshy bud of her sex, she rose on her knees and bounced him wildly. The room reeled. He pounded her across the bed to the edge. As they slid off and onto the rug-strewn floor, they both convulsed in ecstasy. For a long moment after it was over, neither could speak. The floor smelled of dust, and dogs; Emmeline turned her face away, heaving for breath.

With trembling hands he reached for her and rolled her over on her back. He leaned over her and pulled the wet mass of her hair back from her face. They were naked and drenched with sweat, sprawled on the floor, their tangled hair wild. He looked down at her and burst out laughing. Gasping, Emmeline laughed back. She lay naked under him, her long legs tangled with his.

"My beautiful, passionate witch." He was flushed and looked very young. "Fate has brought us together in spite of the cruelty of your husband. You are my true love, you know I can't leave you now."

Emmeline stared up at him. It was almost impossible to think with her mind and her body so lustfully plundered. But he was speaking of love. She could hardly believe her ears.

She pulled wet strands of her hair out of her mouth. He was saying that he could not leave her.

"No, wait," she tried to say. Her mouth was so swollen from his impetuous kisses she could hardly move it. "You are mistaken. My husband is—"

He put his finger to her lips. Then, putting his arms around her, he lifted her up into the bed.

"You do not have to speak of him." His amber eyes adored her. "Ah, sweetheart, you know nothing of me. It is true I am poor, and have little of this world's goods, but that does not keep me from loving you. I am not base born, be assured of it, I am the son of a knight and my father is the son of an earl, although his birth is not legitimate. But I will take care of you, I will rescue you from this damnable place, and no thing such as this—this"—he looked around the room—"such as this—*ill-treatment*—will ever be forced on you again."

Emmeline raised herself to her elbow. Her arms shook with weariness. There were red marks on her skin that she supposed would be bruises, even though he had tried to be gentle. She stared at him, not knowing what to say. He was so young. He looked at that moment, beside her in the rumpled bed, as though he would fight the world for her.

She was beginning to have a terrible headache. "God's face, what are you saying?" She sounded more cross than she intended. "There's no mistreat—"

His big hand gently covered her mouth. "Shhh, have no fear, your husband's old watchdogs are no match for me, and they know it." A sudden thought struck him. "Do you worry that because your husband is still alive the church will not sanction our love? Is that it?"

He sat up in the bed and ran his hand through his sweaty red hair. "We must marry," he told her. "But the barrier to our happiness is that you already have an accursed husband."

Emmeline reached out her hand to touch him, then let it fall. She was stunned with weariness and her body ached almost as much as her throbbing head. She almost cursed the moment she had thought of this terrible scheme. She had wanted a babe—perhaps would even yet get one. But what, she thought, looking at the young man beside her, was she to do with *him?*

With us, she thought, suddenly.

Dear God in heaven, part of her desired only to put her arms around his neck and cling to him, this impetuous,

savage young knight who spoke so confidently of love, and
marriage. As if love and marriage for them could have any
meaning!

Yet, she thought, staring at his naked back and shoulders,
any woman would be mad not to want him. His body was
beautiful, his eyes full of love and amber fire. Worse, he
sounded as though he could do all that he said he could
do!

She nearly cried out when he jumped from the bed. She
saw him stride across the room to the table with its dishes
of cakes and ewer of wine.

"We must gain help from somewhere." He picked up a
cup and sloshed some wine into it from the pitcher. "I will
petition Sir Robert of Gloucester, my liege lord and commander. Or perhaps the church." He scowled. "Although I
am hard to put to think of any friends I might have there."

Her leg was tangled in the bedcovers. She struggled to
free it to get out of bed and go to him. "Wait," Emmeline
cried, "don't drink that!"

He wasn't listening. "God's face, it cannot be borne that
someone as young and beautiful as you should be chained
to a foul old brute who demands—" He tossed back the
wine and put the cup down on the table. "Who demands
what no decent Christian man should from his wife!"

She covered her mouth with her hand and sank back on
the bed, shoulders drooping. God's face, he had drunk it!
She watched him wipe the drops of wine from his lips with
the back of his hand.

He thought Bernard, her husband, had forced her to do
this. She watched as he filled the cup again and drained
it.

It was too late. There was nothing she could do now.

He came and sat down beside her and lifted his hand to
stroke her cheek. "My blood turns cold to think that you
might have found some other this night," he told her.
"Some other knight to put in my place."

She made no resistance as his lips touched her mouth in the gentlest of kisses. She lifted her hand and stroked down his back, feeling the muscles under smooth flesh, hard as stone.

"We must make a plan." His voice was muffled against her hair. "As there may be a child from this. But first I want to love you again. We have all night, sweetheart, to pledge each other."

He let her go, threw back his head and stretched. "Jesu, my heart, I remember—I do not even know your name!"

She turned away. "It does not matter."

"Yes it does. I must know the name of my love." He yawned, then fell back against the bedcovers. "In the morn," he said thickly, "before the sun is up, I will take you from here."

He closed his eyes.

Emmeline waited, but she could see he was not quite asleep.

"In the morning," she said.

In the morning.

Niall could remember the words, but nothing after it.

He woke and found his arms around her, holding her close, but the bed was damnably cold. It was like lying on ice.

Groaning, he opened his eyes. It was gray dawn light, there was a bad taste in his mouth, and his head ached fit to split. He told himself he could not have drunk all that much, to feel so foul.

He raised himself on his elbow.

He was lying, he saw, squinting around him, in some back alley street on cold, muddy earth. The body he'd clasped so tightly in his arms was his friend Orion lying beside him and snoring like a horse. The sun was just coming up, the air was filled with mist.

There was, Niall discovered with a feeling of dread, something in his fist.

He lifted his hand and squinted at it through the uproar in his pounding skull. When he opened his fingers something fell and bounced off his chest and landed on the ground beside him.

It was a small leather purse.

He did not have to open it to find out what was in it. He had already heard the telltale clinking.

Niall lay back against the earth and took a deep breath. Knowing, with a burst of helpless rage, a silent scream that almost blinded him, that the night was over.

She was gone.

And he had been paid his two pieces of gold.

MORLAIX

FOUR

A spring gale blew into the valley and roared through the town. The noise of the wind from the Welsh mountains was loud enough to drown out the sound of a troop of horsemen coming at the gallop through the winding streets. Fortunately the vintner, Jermyn Villers, who was carrying a pair of wineskins of some of his best Burgundy vintage, heard them in time.

Grabbing the wine to his chest, the merchant broke into a trot, shouting to his assistant, who was struggling under the weight of a small rundelet of Sancerre, to get out of the way. Mounted knights had little respect for townspeople, pigs, dogs, or anything else they might encounter in Morlaix's narrow lanes. If one wanted to live to see another day, alive and uncrippled, one ran.

Moments later the horsemen were upon them.

The Welsh boy jumped into the nearest doorway. Jermyn Villers suddenly found himself sprinting for his life in front of thirty mailed knights coming two abreast in the street.

The vintner ran as though all the hounds of hell were at his heels. At the corner, he slipped and fell. The leading horseman, a tall knight in a steel hauberk, reined in his destrier. Those behind him skidded to a stop, mounts rearing and plunging.

The leader leaned down and grabbed a handful of the vintner's jacket and dragged him to his feet. Villers had only a glimpse of amber-colored eyes behind helmguard

and nasal before he was let go. He promptly dove behind
a rain barrel at the butcher's door, and collapsed.

The column of knights milled for a moment. The leader
shouted something. Then with a jingling of arms and spurs
the troop trotted on past the wool factors' storehouses, the
church and churchyard, wheeled right, then disappeared on
the road to Morlaix castle.

The wine seller got to his feet. Gasping, he leaned
against the wall. One wineskin had burst when he'd fallen
on it. A puddle of red was spreading over the roadway. The
other skin he held clutched to his breast was still whole.
But his good clothes reeked.

His apprentice stepped into the street, wide-eyed. "Jesu,
Master Villers," the boy wanted to know, "are you hurt?
Was that not the lord himself what picked you out of the
gutter?"

Under his breath Villers cursed all of Chistendom's
knights, especially those of England's new king. The recent
war was not so long past that one forgot that nobles would
ride down common folk and never look back. Little did
they care, the murderous devils, as they did not have to
earn an honest living!

"It's wine, not blood," he snapped. "Although no thanks
to that foreign trash that I have missed my share of broken
bones!"

The boy shifted the wine barrel to his other arm. "Are
you steady enough to walk, or shall I go ahead to the goldsmith's and ask for a litter?"

Just above them a shutter flew open. "Hah, Master Wine
Seller, it was him, wasn't it?" a woman's voice cried. "The
new lord?" She laid her arms on the windowsill. "I saw
you fly over the rain barrel and I said to Harry, look at
that what they're doing to Master Jermyn Villers, poor man!
They're devils, them knights. I told Harry that if the new
master of Morlaix King Henry just give us hadn't pulled
in his horse with a hairsbreadth to spare, we'd have no

wine to speak of in the town, for our little vintner'd be dead by now!"

The assistant looked up. "They do it for sport," he called, "trying to run poor folk down in the streets. It gives knights pleasure to make you take a tumble and spill whatever you're carrying!"

Jermyn Villers jerked at his arm. "Shut your mouth, boy." Enough had been said. The middle of the street was no place to complain of the new lord.

The woman leaned out to look down at them. "They'll be going up to the castle now to see what the war has left," she called. "Left *him,* that is, the new lord. It ain't a pretty sight, now is it? We'd best pray the saints give him a bit of luck to make the most of our poor ruined land if he can!"

Jermyn motioned his assistant to shoulder the casket of Sancerre, and they started for the goldsmith's house. A few doors down, the boy put aside the rundelet to knock.

They did not expect Emmeline of Witherow herself to answer, but the goldsmith's widow had apparently heard the commotion in the street. She flung wide the wooden door.

At the sight of Jermyn Viller's torn and wine-spattered figure she stifled a cry. She promptly stepped into the street, looked up and down, and then threw the door wide, calling out for her servants.

"Do not be alarmed, fair lady," Villers told her shakily. "It may be I only cut my knees when I fell."

"Hush, save your strength." Mistress Emmeline was dressed for the guildsmen's meeting in a blue gown embroidered with gold thread. Over the bodice was a nice display of goldsmiths' work: gold and silver chains, some with pearls and polished gems, enameled brooches. An engraved circlet in three colors of gold was set on her brow in the Saxon style. But even the jewels paled beside the gilt-streaked blaze of her red hair, braided and pulled up in thick loops beside her jewel-green eyes. "Were you set upon by thieves?" She stepped to one side to let them in. "I thought the new watch we hired was to put a stop to all that!"

He sighed. "Yes, thieves, but not of the usual sort. Only those the king has sent to rule us." In spite of himself the vintner's knees suddenly gave way. Half a dozen kitchen knaves followed by the steward had just run into the hall. They caught him just in time and lifted him up.

Emmeline led the way. "Gently," she ordered. "Take Master Villers in by the fire."

As the kitchen boys carried him, the vintner reached to seize her hand. "It is good we have this meeting today," he said in a low voice. "For I have seen him, the object of our speculations. It was he who kept his horse from trampling me."

Before he could say more, the boys entered the manor hall. A fire was roaring on the hearth. The trade guild members were waiting, warming their backsides.

"Hah, Jermyn," the big smith exclaimed. "What ill-luck has struck you down now?"

As the boys lowered Villers into a chair, he said, "A troop of knights on their way to the castle. And the new Lord of Morlaix, I am sure of it. A big man, iron-faced though young. They say the old empress owed him much, he was one of her bravest commanders. I hear he is Irish."

The guild members crowded around. "Nay, he is Norman *and* Irish," the tanner declared. "My brother the clerk in the archbishop's offices says that fitzJulien is kin through his father, a bastard son of the old earl, Gilbert de Jobourg, may he rest in peace. He has a claim of sorts to Morlaix."

The wool factor frowned. "Jesu, half-Norman, half-Irish? Would Henry give us the bad and the mad all rolled in one? And a bastard to boot?"

They laughed. "There is precious little left in England after King Stephen and the empress have fought over it," someone said. "But there is no shortage of nobles' bastards."

"Better our own bastards than someone else's," another voice put in.

Emmeline sent the knaves back to the kitchen. "The new lord is not a bastard if his father was properly married," she pointed out.

The guildsmen of the trades and burghers of the town stood around the vintner, dressed in their good clothes. Not all the guilds were represented, as Morlaix town was small and supported only one sizable company, that of the woolmen, which included spinners, weavers, clipmen, and the fuller. But there were also two tavern keepers, the smith, the saddlemaker, armorer and ironmonger and the two bakers, husband and wife.

Watris the smith said, "Whatever he is, Norman or Irish, we must petition him to curb his loutish French knights that are billeted on the town. Not only does the riffraff take up our beds, but they fight and drink and will not leave decent girls alone."

Emmeline waved to the maids coming in with cloths and pans of hot water. She knelt herself by the vintner's side. "Ah, your poor knees, Master Villers!" The gashes were deep but had bled freely, which was to the good. There was an open drain in the street into which chamberpots were emptied, and its poisons were notorious.

"Norman or Irishman," the wool factor said, "he will want money. Now that we have a lord again, king and taxman will levy us until we bleed."

Emmeline gave the bowl of bloody water to a scullery girl to empty. Viller's Welsh apprentice had opened the small rundelet of wine, and now hurried around filling cups. There were groans of pleasure. More servants came in from the kitchen with platters of food. The winter had been hard and it was still a long time to harvest; Emmeline had told her steward to give the guildsmen only oatcakes and salted cabbage, of which there was still plenty.

The vintner's boy came to offer her a cup of the yellow Sancerre. He blushed furiously and almost could not bring himself to look at her. She smiled, amused.

She knew the apprentices made bets that she was even better-looking than other young widows elsewhere. There was even a rumor the rowdy tanners' boys had paid some wandering singer to make a song of her. It was flattering, Emmeline supposed, that the apprentices thought her, even at her advanced age of twenty-seven, passing fair.

"At least he'll keep the Welsh from the valley," the butcher was saying. "We do not need Prince Cadwallader to rule here."

The young fuller had been watching Emmeline as she bound up the vintner's knees. Now he said, "The Welsh do not rule, they only fight among themselves. If the Welsh knew how, they would have a king. And not a country full of nithing princes."

A voice said softly, "The Welsh are not the only danger. What if this new lord comes to ferret out those who were traitors to the empress, our young king's mother?"

A silence fell.

"Poor King Stephen is dead," the little vintner murmured, "may God rest his soul."

Emmeline gathered up the wet clothes. "Surely there will be no more vengeance. Merciful God, the war has been over three years and more!"

Those at the hearth looked at one another. During the long years of the war the Empress Matilda's forces had seesawed through the valley, and King Stephen's armies had taken Morlaix not once but several times. They had tried to forget how their loyalties had changed with each side.

Jermyn Villers had turned pale. "Let us pray to God that the new lord will let bygones be bygones."

Croc the armorer turned. "Speak for yourself, vintner. I was the empress's man from the first."

Emmeline said quickly, "Don't let us argue that again."

The big smith nodded. "Yea, let them search for whoever they think was on the wrong side. I tell you what is important is the taxes. No one has money this year. The new lord must listen to reason."

"Reason?" The young fuller looked sour. "What new word have you learned, Watris—*reason?* This town is not Stamford, nor London where the burghers are treated equal to barons, and merchants are as near noble as knights. We are here in the Welsh borderlands, squeezed between Chester on the north, Hereford to our south, and Cadwallader in the west, and have no reason nor rights save what the robber knight in that damned castle squatting there on the hillside gives us!"

Several spoke at once. The smith said grimly, "Unless you wish to see the inside of the bottom of yonder castle, fuller, you'll keep a watch on your words."

The handsome young fuller flung himself into a chair. "Tell me what part I have said is a lie. FitzJulien is the shoeless son of old Gilbert's bastard, a half-Irish cur that knows naught but fighting for hire. The old empress loved him because he was as merciless as she."

Emmeline motioned to the servants to collect the empty bread plates. Several guildsmen shouted at the fuller to be quiet, that he would have them all hung for traitors if he did not close his mouth. She knew that many agreed with him, although they were afraid to say so.

She got up, taking her basket of sewing, to move to a stool by the roaring fire. Helrud the baker's wife moved over to make room for her and smiled. Helrud had been head of the bakers' trade guild in Morlaix and also the small town of Wychden to the south, but the Bishop of Chester had preached against women holding office, or even belonging to guilds, and had made Helrud give up her place to her husband, Wulfer.

Emmeline shifted her stool a little away from the heat of the fire and stitched a yellow flower in the center of the altar cloth she was making. She was glad she had no husband to whom she could be forced to give her goldsmith's seat. Goldsmiths were the richest of the guilds and kept their affairs very quiet; no one really knew all that they did.

A weaver was saying, "Merchants and traders have more rights now that England is growing. Look at all the towns that are springing up."

The baker said, "In the old days we seldom saw a copper coin, it was all barter then. There's many alive what still remembers that where we sit this day in Mistress Emmeline's fine hall was once a butchers' shambles—and the town not much bigger than the old miller's tavern and the Irish fathers' chapter house."

"Times have changed," the vintner put in, "but we have been blessed."

"Hah," Nigel Fuller put in loudly, "we have taken care of ourselves, that's what's happened. It was merchants and the towns that kept England alive through the war. And not King Stephen and the empress and their armies what destroyed everything in their path!"

The butcher looked at his feet. "We should forget those harsh times, friends, except for those generous ones who helped save us such as Mistress Emmeline. If you sing anyone's praises, sing hers."

She lifted her head. They were all looking at her. " 'Twas my husband's gift," she said softly, "may God and the angels see to his eternal rest. He would have done the same, not wanting any of us to suffer."

As far as she was concerned it did no good to remember the bad years when King Stephen and the empress had fought each other across the width of England with neither strong enough to defeat the other. Beside her the baker's wife whispered, "Does the young fuller think to woo you? He never talks like this."

Emmeline lifted her embroidery and bit off the thread. She watched the fuller out of the corner of her eye. She thought the whole town knew she was not interested in marrying again. The fuller came from Wrexham, and had gone to grammar school. He was always talking of York and London, and even far off Flanders. The wool guild was large if one included clipmen who sheared the sheep, factors who brokered the clip, the spinners and weavers, and fullers who shrank and finished the cloth.

The talk at the hearth had turned to the coming Feast of the Ascension. "The villeins ask to be given feed for their oxen," the smith said, "or they will not come." He looked around. "Country people have little enough this year."

The baker's wife leaned to Emmeline and whispered, "The fuller *is* interested, see how he stares. What is that you are sewing?"

She held up the altar cloth for her to see. Nearly every guild prepared a wagon for Morlaix's Feast of the Ascension with a stage and canopy, and played out scenes from the Bible according to each guild's work. It took the whole day for the procession to make its way up the hill to the castle, for each wagon was required to stop at guildsmen's houses where, after a gift of food and drink, the players would perform.

The feast had not been held much during the fifteen years of the past war. But in good years when there were no armies close by, the clothiers and the wool merchants had put on fanciful plays, making much of costly costumes, masks, even hired musicians. The butchers and bakers, not to be outdone, had not only plays but distributed samples of their sausages and meat pies.

One year, when King Stephen himself had come to Morlaix, the vintner, who had been one of Stephen's loyal supporters, hired mummers from Chester to give a rendition of the wedding at Caana. On the wine-seller's wagon had been a very believable Christ who had turned water into wine for the Biblical wedding guests. Unfortunately, so much wine was consumed that several of the disciples were thoroughly unsteady by sunset, and kept falling from the wagon onto the roadway. While the actor playing Christ, untypically merry for such a holy figure, was too overcome by giggles to deliver his speeches.

Emmeline looked at the richly dressed trade guildsmen standing around the room. People needed to be merry after so many years of hardship; this year would probably be a very boisterous feast. Their young King Henry had promised to keep the peace and bring back prosperous times. Everyone wanted to believe it.

She put the embroidery in her lap and bent her head, thinking she had much to give thanks for. She had come to this house when she was fourteen, a poor knight's daughter almost dowerless because of six other sisters at home, and with little but her looks to recommend her, married to a man old enough to be her grandfather. But she had learned to be prudent, and clever, and saving. Through the wars she had kept her husband's property intact and even made it grow.

There were not many who could say that.

They heard a sudden racket of watchdogs in the courtyard. Emmeline put down her embroidery basket and went to see. "No one has ever been paid for the use of the Ascension wagons or given feed for the oxen," she said as she made her way to the door. "In past times, all contributed freely to honor God."

Outside the early spring weather was sunny but not very warm. Half a dozen of the new lord's knights that they'd had billeted in the stable were teasing the dogs. Across the yard her own people stood bunched, their faces sour.

The big dogs were in a frenzy, yelping and plunging at the end of their chains. One knight who was taller than the others poked a stick at them, wanting the mastiffs to seize it. From their flushed faces the men had been drinking.

Emmeline stepped out into sun. "If you tease the dogs," she told them, lifting her voice over the uproar, "they will soon learn to yap at anything and give us no peace."

The tall knight whirled. The others nudged each other. They were Frenchmen from the south, the Languedoc, and spoke a dialect, but she heard the word, "widow."

The knight shrugged, then threw the stick into the air. It clattered against the sides of a shed before it landed at her feet. They strolled away, talking and laughing, toward the stables.

Her steward, Baudri Torel, came hurrying up. "Mistress Emmeline, the knights have been at the tavern," he huffed. "It grows worse every day to have them underfoot. They call the beanpole Serlo, that is he that you—"

She waved him to be still. She knew he had waited until the last moment to come to her. Her people were afraid of the knights; all of them remembered what they had endured during the war.

She turned to go back inside the hall and lifted her eyes to the antlered head of a stag cut in the lintel. Bernard of Neufmarche had brought the carving from Falaise; it was the sign of his goldsmithing family.

In the next to the last year of the war Morlaix had been seized by one of King Stephen's commanders, a cruel Fleming who burned the villeins alive for stealing grain, and did nothing when the soldiers raped and killed some weavers' women and threw their bodies in the river. After some months the countryside plotted their revenge: to kill Pers Lastels and all his knights, and seize Morlaix for the Empress Matilda and her young son, Prince Henry.

The guildsmen, especially the woolmen, had seen the folly of such an idea. Any rebellion would only bring down the ironfisted vengeance that nobles of both sides reserved for any uprising. Instead, Emmeline had opened Bernard's coffers, and they had offered a great bribe of gold and silver to the Fleming and his men. To their surprise, it worked.

Some months later Lastels was called to the midlands to help King Stephen in his last campaign. All of Morlaix had rejoiced and promptly prayed for the monster to have a particularly horrible death. But as far as anyone knew, Lastels was still alive. Most probably, now that it was peacetime, happily at home in Flanders.

Emmeline stood under the deer's head, the May sun beating brightly around her. She *was* thankful for the things that were precious to her: the fine, walled manor house in the middle of the town, her kitchens, her stilling rooms, her feather beds, the goldsmithing shop. Even though it took an army of servants to keep it up and protect it. More than once they had had to call out the porters and kitchen knaves and stable boys to hold the manor against roistering mobs of apprentices, or deserters from both armies.

God had allowed her to keep her house, her husband's businesses—her good *life,* Emmeline told herself. And her most precious treasure.

Magnus.

Her son was coming through the gate. He made his way past the stable, long-legged as a colt, his shoulders already broadening. A stable boy reached out and gave him a playful buffet on the backside. Magnus grinned.

It was always like this. He drew all eyes; one could not help loving him.

And he was filthy as a mudhen, as usual. Emmeline pulled him to her. "God's face, where have you been?"

"Don't, Mother, I want to go fishing." He gave her a dazzling smile. "You said I could."

"Not at the river. Look at you. At your clothes. Dear God, I am not raising you to be a ruffian!"

"Mother." Amber eyes, beautiful enough for a girl's, flashed at her. "The pond is for babies. Besides, Tom was with me."

She took him into the hall. The guildsmen, talking of the town's procession, smiled at him. She sat down at the table with Helrud, and Magnus leaned to kiss her on the cheek. She pretended to push him away. "I meant what I said. You are only nine, and Tom is no older. I don't want you at the river, it's dangerous." She smoothed his long, curling hair back from his face. It was dark, not red-gold like her own.

The baker was saying that although bakers always presented the scene from the Bible of the loaves and the fishes, this spring it would be difficult to provide enough bread. Bakers, unlike some other guilds he could name, were not rich.

The guildsmen were getting somewhat drunk on the vintner's wine. The weaver shouted that all the wagons gave something to the crowds, that was the custom.

Magnus put his arm around Emmeline's shoulders, fingering the veil over her braids. "The new lord is here, Mother," he told her, "Tom has seen him. He is very fierce-looking. A Norman knight, just as they say."

"They say he is Irish."

The baker was openly tipsy, trying to shout down the butcher. Helrud got up, looking disgusted, and went out.

The burly smith pushed the baker down onto the bench. "All the wagons give something if that is their custom. Bakers give bread."

"Ask Mistress Emmeline for a judgment." The fuller turned, hands on hips, to look at her. "She is our leader."

She lifted her head thinking he was handsome, but too bold. She was master of a guild, the only one there other than the woolman. But considering the times, she did not like to be singled out. They all knew that.

"Some of the guilds," Emmeline said, "give to the crowds

and some do not. The soapmakers, who have the wagon with the angels helping Christ ascend to heaven, have never given anything."

"Fagh, who would give soap?" The smith looked around. "Besides, all the crowd wants is to guzzle free wine."

"Don't forget our sausages," the butcher put in.

"Mother." Magnus rolled a finger around one of her gold chains. The tips of his fingers were rough; he was already working at the goldsmith's table. "Tom says if we fish in the river and not the pond that we will catch enough fish so that Cook can fix them for dinner."

"Fishermen always say that." She put her arm around her son's waist, and he bent to kiss her again. "We should buy feed for the villeins' oxen," Emmeline told the guildsmen. "It is not so much, and they are right, everything is in short supply this spring." She looked over her son's head to Nigel the fuller. "I will pledge," Emmeline said, "the cost of the bakers' bread."

FIVE

The column of knights took the road to the castle. The day was sunny and as the road dipped down into the bottom lands the air grew appreciably warmer. On both sides the weeds grew high and rank, but the rowan and beech were budding, making deep thickets of lacy green. Clouds of gnats were speckled veils in the air. In the sudden heat some of the knights threw off their cloaks and hung them over their saddles.

Niall fitzJulien slowed his horse to a walk. The signs of war were everywhere in the uncleared woodlands, the overgrown fields. My fields, he thought, surprised at his sudden burst of feeling. He made his face show nothing; he was not a boy to grin with sudden elation, there was a troop of knights he commanded cantering behind him. But the reward he had hoped and worked for in thirteen long years of service to the old empress and now her son, Henry, the new king of England, was all around him. Morlaix Castle, town and fief.

And by damn, it was his!

He'd heard of it, of course, all his life. Morlaix was the dream his father, Earl Gilbert's bastard son, had broken his heart over. When he was drunk Julien of Nessvile talked of it endlessly, how the heiress had renounced her inheritance to marry and go to live in a foreign land so that what should have been theirs—Niall and his father's—had slipped away, falling into old King Henry's grasping hands.

Now he sat watching the mud brown of the river through

the rowans. The false dream of having Morlaix someday
had spoiled their lives. His father had been an outlaw
knight with a large and needy family, hiring out for what
he could get to any Irish chieftain with a quarrel to settle.
Later, when he was himself a knight, Niall learned the
world was full of bastards of noble blood, almost all of
them poor. Almost all of them dreaming of fortunes they
could never inherit.

But now, impossibly enough, he had his father's dream
in his hand. After weeks of waiting about in London for
the chancery clerks to draw up the king's grant and affix
the seals, and England's marshal to assign to him the garrison of knights to hold it, he was finally going to see what
Henry had given him.

He suddenly wished his father was there.

He touched his spurs to his destrier's sides and the big
warhorse ambled into a rolling trot. He said to his knight
captain, "This low place is a prime spot for an ambush.
Take six men tomorrow and clear the brush away from the
road at least twenty paces. Farther if you can manage."

Young Walter looked at him. The Welsh were a score of
leagues away in their sodden mountains; the danger of ambush on the road to Morlaix was very small. "Milord, if I
can say so, it seems to gather some villeins to clear the
roadsides would be better."

They had passed the curve in the road that descended
to a stone bridge. Some boys were fishing in the shallow
river. When they saw the column of knights the boys threw
down their poles and scrambled onto the parapet to watch.

Walter was saying, "As you can see, we have been given
mostly southerners from the queen's levy, Gascons, Basques,
some Provençals. They spurn base work. I have already had
the devil's own time keeping them moderate with women
and drink in the town."

Seeing the boys perched on the bridge's rail, Niall's destrier snorted and shied to the left. The horse crab-walked,

tossing his head. Niall gave him another touch of his spurs. Walter raised his hand and the column of knights rather lackadaisically pulled into single file. On the greening hillside beyond the river an orchard of crab apple trees was in bloom.

Niall guided his horse onto the bridge. The boys were wide-eyed as the column, pennants fluttering, mail and arms jingling, passed by. They stared at Niall, in glistening steel mail from head to toe.

"They know you," Walter Straunge said.

Niall grunted.

He had soldiered since he was only a little older than some of the boys on the bridge. There were times when he had to remind himself that he was only a few years older than his knight captain.

Beyond the apple orchard the meadows opened, green and filled with tall weeds. The black bulk of Castle Morlaix stood above the valley, its back against the Cambrian mountains.

Niall reined in. There'd been a wood fort here, a Saxon outpost against the wild Welsh, for a hundred years before the coming of the Conqueror. After William, Normans had torn down the wooden stronghold to make way for a proper stone keep. During the rein of the Conqueror's son, William Rufus, another tower had been added, a kitchen house, and then a great hall. Finally, when Henry the First had come to the throne, the first earl of Morlaix built a fine timber manor house in the bailey.

Now the castle's curtain wall lay cracked and gaping like a broken eggshell. The Norman keep was still there, an old-fashioned, square-sided tower. It was hard to see the rest for piles of blackened rubble.

Niall's squire pushed his horse up beside them. "Oh, sir!" he blurted. "I mean, it is not too bad, is it?"

The castle had been taken two years ago by young Prince Henry. *Taken and secured.* Niall could still hear the king's words. He put his finger to his chin and rubbed it. Those who got rewards from Henry Plantagenet should learn to beware of them. What the king had not told him was that "secured" was—to Henry's mind—another word for "mostly destroyed."

The king had also made it clear to his new baron that it was his duty to see Morlaix made whole again. Niall touched his spurs to Hammerer's sides. "Let us have a look at it."

They cantered up toward the hill, the column following raggedly. They stopped at what had once been the drawbridge. Niall trotted Hammerer to the edge of the moat. From the drawbridge they could look past the portal gate and into the bailey. The fire-blackened old keep seemed intact but there was no longer a great hall, nor a manor house. The second tower was without a roof, open to the sky.

"The Breton, Alan of Brieuc, and his local Welsh ally," Walter informed him, "held the castle for a year. But Prince Henry marched up from Wrexham and besieged them. I am told the castle's fall was a great blow to King Stephen, who at that time needed greatly to hold what he had here on the Welsh border."

Niall remembered. By that time the war was all but over. Stephen was failing, his son Eustace dead, and young Henry, fresh from France, was gathering England's barons around him.

He walked his destrier along the edge of the moat. The water in the ditch was green with slime. Winter rains had filled it to the brim. A dead rat floated, caught in the limbs of a branch.

God knows he, too, was glad the war was over. A good part of his lifetime of soldiering was behind him. Now he wanted a good life here on the borderland. His reputation was such that German princes and the French king would buy his services if he were interested; his knight captain

and his squire thought him the greatest of heroes. But Niall
wanted what he saw before him. Ruined or not.

Walter was saying, "As you can see, we have not been
given a full garrison. There are only fifty knights billeted
in the town. Food here is scarce and the townspeople not
friendly—we had to break heads at some houses to get
them to take our men in."

Niall turned to look at the column behind them. The
Frenchmen sat hunched in their saddles, looking bored.

"They do not like the cold," Walter went on. "They complain of it constantly. But then knights are only as good as
their pay." He lowered his voice. "Which they have not
had in some months."

Damn Henry, Niall thought. They sat looking at the shell
of the castle. "The king has no money," he said flatly. "And
what little he has must go to buy the love of his English
earls. Who, as we know, would run as wild and lawless as
they did under King Stephen if he let them."

He leaned over the moat. The water was rimmed with
ice. Walter was right, they needed villeins with buckets and
shovels. Knights would not muck out a ditch that stank like
the jakes.

He straightened up. "In the meantime, I do not think we
will get the price of an iron pot from London."

Niall backed the destrier away from the moat's edge,
feeling his leg begin to throb. He had ridden from Chirk
that day without stopping. The old wound would bother
him until he could find some hot water to soak it. "We
will levy the villeins for the lord's share of their labor. Six
days for the castle, excepting only Sunday. And they must
bring their tools."

Under his helm Walter's face was bleak. "That is another
difficulty. It is plowing time. Local folk are sorely needed
in the fields."

"Christ's balls, what the devil has that got to do with
it?" Niall was in pain. When he mounted, it was like a

red-hot iron boring into his hip socket. "Look around you. They have not given the lord's share of work here for years." He yanked at Hammerer's head and the horse side-stepped, surprised.

Feeling savage, he pushed Hammerer off the road and out into the fields. The others waited while he cantered the warhorse through the weeds.

The damned leg. Not even the king knew how much it still hampered him. If it didn't heal soon the whole world would know.

The warhorse paced the length of the field. Niall wanted a moment to think. The gutted castle was a temptation to the Welsh to come down out of the hills and raid them. He had a hundred French mercenaries to garrison Morlaix but they were scattered in billets in town. And no foot soldiers, when one needed men-at-arms as much as cavalry here.

Hammerer lifted his feet in a heavy trot. The ground was soft and springy. In London Niall had read the descriptions of his fief in the old Conqueror's tally, the Domesday Book, it was now being called. According to it Morlaix's fields had grown wheat, barley, and oats, even some millet, and there was a plentitude of common land for cattle and sheep. Before the war Morlaix wool had been sent as far as the cloth-making towns in Flanders.

In London the king had also spoken urgently of revenues. God's face, *revenues!*

Niall guided Hammerer through some old hedgrows, flushing larks and a small hare. Unless he thought of something, Henry would wait for revenues a damnable long time. Even if he made the land pay this year, the Welsh were poised to strike; he had no doubt Prince Cadwallader had his spies.

He trotted Hammerer back to where his squire and Walter sat waiting. "Tell me of the town," he said. "There must be money somewhere."

Walter brightened. "I think it is richer than it looks. Although the grain storehouse was burned by the empress's forces and has not been used since. And oh, yes, they are having a procession for the Feast of the Ascension in a few days."

"Ascension? Why not Easter? Or Corpus Christi?"

"Ascension is the custom here. They say at the feast the townspeople will honor you. I suppose they will expect to take the fealty oaths. They will even give you gifts."

"Hah! They'll feel differently when they hear what I want from them."

They turned the horses and trotted back to the bridge. The boys were still sitting on the parapet. Behind them the river roared with the spring freshet. Niall guided Hammerer across at a slow walk. The children openly stared.

Niall stared back. No doubt he looked, in helm and mail and with the long shield slung at his saddle, as dangerous as the Devil himself. It was what he would have thought at their age.

A boy about eight or nine years stood poised on the top of the wall. The other boys jostled each other. The parapet was a dangerous place to stand.

Niall started to give the order to chase the boys off the bridge when they seemed suddenly to disappear. He pulled his horse to a halt. For a moment he considered that all the children had dropped off the side and into the river. Then he heard their voices. There was some sort of way along the outside.

Walter was saying, "From what I have seen, there is enough wealth in the town to lay a hard levy. If the townspeople have money enough for a feast they have enough for Castle Morlaix."

Niall kicked Hammerer forward. "I hope you have found me a place to stay," he growled. "I want to sleep in a bed for a change."

His captain looked relieved. "Yea, I can promise hot

wine, and a bed to share with me at the tavern. The
Angevins will bed down in the stable."

Niall looked around. The children were gone. Something
had caught his attention even though he could not now
remember what it was.

Not all that important, he told himself. But the handsome
boy, the one he had noticed, had red hair. For a few minutes, as they rode, he thought of his father.

Six

"You're twenty-seven, Mistress Emmeline, twenty-eight next year," the matchmaker said, "and you have a half-grown boy. There's not all the time left in the world."

"I know." She took the woman's empty plate and put another helping of the herring and black bread the cook had brought on it. The fat woman began to eat again, hungrily.

They were sitting just outside the goldsmith's shop in the wash yard. Around them the maidservants were hanging out the winter bedding. The sheets swung out straight on the line as the wind took them, snapping them with a sound like whips. The matchmaker was wearing a stiff linen coif. She clamped it to her head with one hand while she lifted the tankard and finished off her ale.

Cloris of York had not traveled much to the border country in recent years, the journey being uncertain enough with the presence of empress Matilda's and King Stephen's armies. It was still dangerous: the company of armed merchants the matchmaker had journeyed with had been attacked by a band of Prince Cadwallader's men just north of Chirk. They had been thoroughly plundered, spending a hungry, miserable night on the road until the new lord of Morlaix and some of his knights had ridden out and discovered them.

"Magnus is only nine," Emmeline said, taking the tankard to refill it. "Not 'half grown.'"

"Nine and nine makes eighteen, that's half grown, isn't it?" Cloris mopped up the last of the herring juice with a piece of bread. "Now be reasonable, puss. With your riches and looks you can have any man in Christendom. Just study the pictures I've brought of these fine gentlemen, and make up your mind."

Emmeline drew her cloak around her and bent her head to peer down at the portraits in her lap. In spite of the sunshine it was not warm. Under the heavy cloak she was wearing a high-necked, green woolen gown with a tunic over it, and a green woolen cap, close-fitting over her freshly washed hair.

Every time the matchmaker came it seemed there were reasons why she should consider some merchant or other who wanted to bid for her hand.

She turned the likeness on a piece of parchment over in her hands. This was a new practice, Cloris had told her, to send drawings of would-be mates. Even though she would readily admit the likenesses were probably not all that reliable.

"Not this one, then?" She reached to take the drawing from Emmeline's hand. Four times in the past six years the goldsmith Myneer Boogs of Ghent had sent the matchmaker across northern England to plead his suit. Cloris shrugged. "Well, Boogs has had his day, I'll not come back for him. I have a widow in Lincoln I can try him with." She tucked the parchment into her skirt. "Now then, dear, how about the other?"

The young Italian had sent an oil painting no bigger than Emmeline's hand. In the portrait he appeared as a very handsome, dark-eyed youth with curly hair. The limner had painted him in a gold-embroidered cap, red jacket, slightly smiling. His name was Giovanni della Forza. He, too, was a moneylender.

Emmeline held up the picture. "Sweet heaven, he can't be this pretty."

"Ah, but he is! I saw him myself when he came with his father to York to buy gold. A fine, handsome lad."

"In the letter he extolls his riches. And recommends himself as a dealer in loans to his prince in Turino."

"And why not? They are very clever, these Italians. It is said they outnumber the Jews now in London, and work to take the money-changing business away from them." She clapped her hands against her thighs. "Look, with this one you'd be marrying into the same trade, and it's always a good thing to keep like with like, I always say. You'd get a bold and experienced man, even as young as he is."

Emmeline turned the small painting over in her hands. There was nothing on the back, not even the limner's name. But then she didn't know what she'd been looking for.

The matchmaker leaned to her. "Not only that, della Forza's but twenty years old, strong and potent, not like what you had before, may God rest old Bernard's soul. It's the truth, don't look at me like that. I have had it from his father that the boy has had two mistresses, they start young down there, and sired a little girl. So there's the proof. Everyone knows the Italos are hot-blooded—I'd lay a pretty penny on it that he'd make your bed squeak!"

Emmeline kept her eyes on della Forza's sultry likeness. It was hard not to burst out laughing. She didn't want to hurt the matchmaker's feelings, as after all the woman had traveled far, and been robbed for her pains. But neither did she have a desire to marry a young Italian with two mistresses and a bastard child. Squeaking bed or no.

Inwardly she sighed. Cloris of York was not the only one who believed she was pining for the pleasures of the flesh. From what her maidservants told her, the whole town gossiped of it. But if the matchmaker thought to tempt her she was mistaken. She stared down at della Forza's portrait, not really seeing it. Allowing herself to remember what she had done one night over ten years ago with an unknown young knight Gulfer and Aimeric had taken from the streets.

Even now it was something so reckless, so foolhardy, she couldn't think of it without a pang of terrible guilt. Holy Mother, she'd been so young and impetuous, so sure of getting what she wanted! It could have brought disaster on all of them. Certainly she'd never entertain such a thought now.

Still, Emmeline thought rather wistfully, it had been mad but it had brought her the joy of her life, her son. So the miracle she had so foolishly hoped for had happened after all.

Cloris of York watched her with narrowed eyes. "What's the matter, girl, is it the boy's age? Is that it?" She patted Emmeline's knee. "Be easy, it is all the style now. Ever since young King Henry took his Eleanor away from the King of France and married her, it's been the vogue for the woman to be older. Of course the church didn't like it, him being only nineteen, and Queen Eleanor divorced and already thirty, and with two little girls of the Frenchman. Not to mention," she said behind her hand, "the consanguinity, for they're related closer than they should be according to all the church tells one about such things. But all that's fallen by the way, now that Queen Eleanor's given the young king an heir."

Emmeline sat silent. Cloris nodded vigorously. "I tell you, it does work! Young Henry's besotted with Queen Eleanor, and she brings him Aquitaine, half of France. Besides, he knows how it is, that boy. His own mother, the Empress Matilda, was married to his father when she was thirty, and the young Duke of Anjou was only seventeen. Of course, those two hated each other on sight, but that's another story. Now what we're talking of here," the matchmaker said, leaning back and clasping her hands in her lap, "is only seven years. That is, young Giovanni's twenty to your twenty-seven. That's no barrier to a good pairing, is it?"

She made it sound so reasonable, Emmeline thought, staring down at the little painting. One could marry this Italian popinjay and feel right in fashion with young King Henry and Queen Eleanor. Or even the king's mother and father, the Count and Countess of Anjou.

The journeyman goldsmith, Ortmund, came across the yard, wiping his hand on his apron. "Mistress," he called, "there are knights in the street asking another levy for the new lord. I told them we have paid."

She stood up. "What in God's name do they want now?"

"What they always want." He nodded to the matchmaker, his eyes curious. "This one, the young knight captain named Walter, demands food and beer for the laborers at the castle."

"Food and drink?" They were not supposed to come back, the lord's knights. The merchants had already paid two harsh levies.

She sighed. It was best not to argue. The town's burghers had already learned that if one protested, the levy was doubled. Fortunately, there was still a store of salted cabbage, and the cook had just baked a two days' supply of bread. Although God knows what they would have for evening meal, as they had a houseful of servants and their share of the lord's knights billeted in the stables, to feed.

She said, "Tell Torel to give them what we have. How often will they do this, anyway?"

He smiled grimly. "Who knows? At least they have not taken me up to the castle to work like some of the other guildsmen."

The matchmaker's head had swiveled from one to the other. "Is it true Morlaix's new lord works his villeins so that they have no time for their fields, and must then plow them at night by torchlight?"

Emmeline sent Ortmund away with a message to the

steward to give the castle knights what they could find in the kitchen.

"We have not had a lord in the castle here for so long we have forgotten," she said. "This one has not been here a sennight and already we have been levied twice. The second time he sent his knights to the door in the middle of the night saying there was another levy. The truth of it was he had to pay his knights or they would revolt. I had to go to the goldworking shop in my shift, and give them the raw gold from the strongbox."

Cloris set her plate on the ground by her chair. "Have you seen him? He is not bad looking, they tell me."

Emmeline pulled a face. "I see him riding in the town with the knights. With helmets and mail they all look the same."

The matchmaker said, "Well, as long as he is just."

"Just?" Emmeline stared at her. "Five of the southern riffraff they call knights got drunk in the town and raped a girl. He only gave them twenty lashes. The townspeople wanted them hanged." She held out the Italian goldsmith's picture. "My thanks, but I think not to marry. In all truth, I have enough to look after here."

The other woman took it and slipped it into her bag. "Old Bernard's spoiled you," she snapped. "The old man doted on you more like a daughter than a wife, that was your trouble. But remember this, Mistress Emmeline, I brought you from your grandfather's house in Wroxeter myself—a carrot-topped, pretty little thing, but still a pauper with no dowry. It was your good fortune that I found you someone like old Bernard. But do you think to remain as you are, a comely widow like you—with a fortune no one knows the true size of?"

Emmeline's mouth thinned. "I'm sorry if I offended you. But I will say again, I do not need to wed."

"Do not *need* to? Listen, girl, it's been years now you shut yourself up out here and hoarded old Neufmarche's fortune for the sake of his boy. But God and Saint Mary, you cannot stay this way forever! Times are changing, and you have too much money—there are many who would not hang back if it came to seizing you and carrying you off."

Emmeline smiled tightly. "It has been nine years since my blessed husband died, and nothing has happened to me."

"Bah, it was easy enough to hide out here on the edge of wild Wales with armies going up and down the land. But I tell you, things are different now."

"My son," Emmeline said, "is the heir here. He will get all that his father left him."

The other woman stood up. "My blessings on you then, if that's the way it is. As God is my judge, I never go against a widow's virtue. The holy mother church teaches us one man and one marriage is all that's allowed in God's sight and no more." She picked up her cloth bag and her cloak. "But none of us are saints. It's the living flesh what gets lonely and needs a mate. And that's what I seek to meet, and satisfy."

Emmeline walked with her as far as the wagon yard. At the gate she pressed some silver into the matchmaker's hand. The other woman's mood changed. "Bless you, dear." She grabbed her hand and kissed it. "Remember, it's not natural to live alone. If you change your mind you know where to send someone to find me."

She went back to the goldsmith's shop. A brazier with coals glowed in the corner and the smelter was lit, making the room pleasantly warm. The journeyman goldsmith bent over the table with her son and Tom, the apprentice.

"Mother, look at this," Magnus called.

Ortmund picked up a piece of molten glass from the smelter with the end of a pipette. He leaned over the table and pressed his mouth to the tube and blew, letting the glass curl down into the gold cup of a brooch, nearly filling it up.

He took the tube out of his mouth. "Now," he told Magnus.
Emmeline's son seized the thread of glass with pincers,
cutting it off. "See, Mamma? Watch what I'm doing."

When the glass in the small gold cup hardened it would
be ground down and polished until it made an even surface
with the goldwork. After the blue was done, Ortmund and
the boys would work on the stem, to be done in green. Of
all the enameling in the Christian world, the best was still
done in Britain. When finished the brooch would be sent
to London and then most probably to Paris, where all the
ladies loved jewels that were made like flowers.

Magnus suddenly looked up. "Mamma, it has a bubble
in it!"

Emmeline turned to the journeyman, who lifted his eyebrows. Sometimes this happened. The little apprentice
made a cluck of disappointment.

Magnus tugged at her sleeve. "We must do something.
Mamma, tell me something to do!"

She handed him a little copper pick and sat down beside
him. Emmeline looked down at the gold brooch in its metal
clamp. "First, be quiet. Nothing is done with a lot of yelling. At least not in here."

"You can't break the bubble," the apprentice said. "The
glass is too hard now."

"Shut up," Magnus told him.

Emmeline raised her head and looked at Tom. The boy
dropped his eyes. The journeyman went into the outer room
and sat down at the high counter to weigh out silver bars.

Magnus took the pick and poked it carefully into the air
bubble. They brought their heads together, almost touching,
to watch. The bubble split. There were now two glistening
pockets of air in the blue glass, shining like moons.

"I told you," the other boy said softly.

Magnus threw the pick on the table. "Didn't I tell you
to shut up?" The pick rolled across the wood surface and

fell to the floor. Magnus lifted his fist. "Mother, may I hit him?"

Emmeline leaned back on her stool. Apprentices' training had its share of beatings, kicks, and sometimes, with stern masters, going without meals. Most of which the guilds regarded as useful. She did not let Ortmund treat Tom Parry so. But the boy tormented Magnus.

She bent to retrieve the pick from the floor. When she straightened up her son was out of his seat, standing over the other boy. "Mamma, he always teases me," he burst out. "He's jealous! Most of the time my work's better than his!"

Little Tom jumped to his feet. "Mistress, that's not true! My work is better!"

She took the apprentice by the arm. "I am sick of the shouting. Do you want me to hit you? Go into Ortmund and help him with the silver."

When Tom had gone she sent Magnus out into the yard to look for the stable master and tell him he was to feed and groom his pony himself. Her son stamped off, shoulders drooping.

In the sudden quiet she sat back down and pushed the journeyman's tools, the hammers, pincers and gravers, to one side. The top of the table was deeply gashed, and stained many colors from spills. On a shelf above the table there were bottles labeled copper, silver, lead, borax, all used for alloys. She reached up and moved them so she could pull down one of the strongboxes.

She put it before her in the litter of the worktable, opened it, and lifted out the top tray that held the loose gemstones. She sorted through the amber, opal, topaz, amethysts, white crystal and chrysoberyls, thinking of Cloris of York. The bright little painting the matchmaker had brought of young della Forza was exceeding well done, a little jewel in itself. She would like to have had it in a frame to keep.

At the bottom of the strongbox she found what she was

looking for, a silver buckle shaped like the head of a wolf. The jaws opened to grasp the opposite side of the catch. It was an old piece, probably Saxon, heavy and well made, a princely ornament. If she remembered right, it was from Winchester; English kings had always had their treasury there.

The matchmaker had asked her what the new lord looked like.

There was no matchmaking business for her with him, Emmeline thought as she spread the polishing cloth and laid the brooch on it. Nobles arranged their own weddings, and all but a lowly few had to ask their liege lord for permission to marry.

As to the other, *she* could not say what he looked like. Few could, as the new baron busied himself from morning to night galloping from one end of his fief to the other as he rounded up men to work on the castle. They all knew he had little or no fortune; he'd had to levy the town again to pay his knights or they would have deserted and gone back to London.

It had been decided that the guilds would give the new lord gifts when they took their oaths. The saddler had brought his cousin from Wrexham to do the final tooling and gilding on the leather workers' saddle, to which the butcher and the tanner had given money. Even though there had been an argument among the guildsmen that money gifts made the town, in the eyes of the lord, seem too rich. That giving coin would tempt him to come back and levy them again.

The wool guild's gift was a length of handsome dark blue cloth, enough for a cloak, made by the weavers at Morlaix and then waulked and treated by the new fuller so that it was soft and beautiful, and shed rain better than any cowhide.

The great silver wolf's head buckle would look handsome. Emmeline knew, with the blue cloak. She held it up to the window light, considering some sort of gemstone for the wolf's eyes. She picked up the pincers and hammer and worked to extend the edge of the silver under the brows.

The smelter was still hot. She stuck the end of the steel pincers in the coals until they glowed, then crimped around the wolf's eyes, bending the softened metal into a rim.

She supposed if you talked of it, fleshly pleasures, it made some marriages seem more desirable. After all, the matchmaker's business was to bring couples together and earn her fee. Certainly lust was an attraction. There were men who used their wives every night. Or so the steward's wife said.

She wiped a drop of perspiration away from her upper lip with the tip of her finger, and picked up a round, polished piece of yellow beryl with ringlike markings.

On the other hand, it was somewhat hard to believe that men and women coupled every night. There were not many men who seemed that lecherous. Certainly not her fat steward, Baudri Torel.

Perhaps his wife was talking of someone else.

She dropped the yellow cat's eye beryl into the rimmed collet she had made, and leaned over to look down. Of course, she of all people could hardly judge that sort of passion. Kind and gentle though he had been, her husband Bernard was old, and often his member too weak to do what he so greatly desired to.

The beryls' markings made them opalescent, like real wolf's eyes. She picked up the pincers and began to close the silver around the stones.

When it came to that, she could admit that she sometimes thought of that night in Wrexham. She was not a slave to the memory, but when she was alone in bed and the dark wind howled, and the whole world was restless, burning—*aching*—the mystery of what had happened that night long ago would not leave her alone.

Emmeline knew enough of her own body now to give herself satisfaction, quietly, not disturbing the maids who slept around her. She could do it best when she allowed herself to think of when the young knight had been brought to her, how the blaze of candles lighted his beautiful body. The murmur of his heated words. His clumsy desire. And oh, how he had loved her! she thought with a delicious shiver. Even now she could feel her moist, private places clench sensuously.

She put down the pincers and closed her eyes. God in heaven, these daydreams became too vivid! It was best not to think of them. After all these years what had happened was only a story such as the troubadors sang about knights on pilgrimages for a lady's love. Of wandering princes who could become enchanted lovers.

That night it had seemed her dream would have no end. But it had, disastrously, and far too soon. He had drunk the drugged wine before she could stop him. Old Gulfer, may God now rest his soul, and the pensioner, Aimeric, had carried him out.

Emmeline opened her eyes. Ortmund had come to the door of the shop. The sun was going down. He had come to remind her of the evening meal.

She struck a light from the tinderbox, then took a candle, lighted it, and put it in the lantern. The candle glow made the worktable a place of glitter. In the center of the polishing cloth the wolf's head buckle watched her with gleaming, feral eyes.

She decided not to go to dinner. She liked the shop in the evenings when it was quiet. She sent Ortmund away to find Tom and Magnus and see to it they were fed, then went back to the task of cleaning and polishing the brooch. When that was done she took a soft cloth and jewelers' clay and buffed the chrystoberyls, making them look even more like animal eyes.

All the beryls, sapphires, and rock crystal were some of

a store that the Neufmarche goldsmiths had brought with them when they left France. She found a small cedar box and put the buckle into it to be carried in the Feast of the Ascension procession. She tidied up the worktable, put a stone lid on the smelter, and found the failed enamelwork of the afternoon. Time passed as, absorbed, she reamed the blue glass from the gold flower petal with a pick, to put it aside for Ortmund and the boys to fix on the morrow. She was so intent on what she was doing that when the candle in the lantern guttered it was a moment before she looked up.

One of the stable boys stood in the door. The porter had sent him to say there was someone at the gate, asking for her.

Emmeline got up, picked up the lantern, and followed the boy out through the wash yard, then through the stables. The moon was high, shedding a bright, silver light. From the quiet of the house around them everyone was asleep.

The porter held the outer doors ajar, muttering about the late hour. Whoever waited for her was outside, in the street.

She stepped beyond the manor gates. He was pressed against the wall, a shadow in the moonlight. The moment she saw him she knew who he was.

"Mother of God," she said, taking him by the arm, "I thought I had lost you." He was dressed as a friar this time, cowl pulled up, his hands in his sleeves. "That you were with the merchants that were attacked on the Wrexham road."

"I don't travel with merchants begging to be robbed. They even had a litter carrying some fat woman from York."

Emmeline knew who the fat woman was; she had spent all afternoon with her. She guided him into the shadows of the gateway. "Come to the shop. I will get you some food and drink."

"No." He seemed uneasy, which was unusual for him.

"I can't linger, I want to get out of these holy rags and into other clothes. I've been five days on the roads and I thirst for wine, and a woman. Which I can't get dressed like this."

He pulled back from her and reached under his friar's skirts. She saw a glimpse of hairy white skin as his hands worked at the straps that held the leather bags to his leg. "Be careful," he said, as he handed them to her, "the last part of the journey into Wales is the most perilous."

She hauled the bags behind her, against her skirts. "When will you come again?"

She saw the flash of his teeth. "When the prince needs more. And we can get it. This gold does not come from France this time, it comes from the lords about Henry." The words died suddenly on his lips. He seized her arm. "Listen, what do you hear?"

"Hear?" She heard nothing. Behind them the porter came to the gate and stood looking out.

Emmeline put her hand to her throat. At first it was only a whisper, a faint noise that might have been anything.

"Holy Jesus in heaven," the gold courier said under his breath. He pulled back from her, flattening himself against the wall.

They heard the sound of horses in the town's center streets. Above the rooftops a ruddy stain like false dawn began to appear in the sky.

"Mistress," the porter called.

"What is it?" She called to the man she could no longer see. Her heart was beating as she dragged the bags of gold under her arm and groped for him in the darkness. But he had moved out of her reach.

His voice came to her from some distance. "Can't you see? They are burning the castle."

She cried, "What?"

But he was gone.

SEVEN

The church bell began to clang. Niall jumped out of the bed, reaching for his sword, as Walter, tangled in the blanket they shared, fell out the far side with a thump and a sleepy curse.

"Get up," Niall snarled, "that's the alarm!" Shouting horsemen galloped past in the street outside. He groped over the floor on his hands and knees, seeking the box with tinder and flint.

Below them they could hear the uproar in the common room as the knights came awake. No one had a light down there either to judge from the shouts and crashes. Walter groped at him in the blackness, found his hands and the tinderbox. "Here, milord, let me do it."

Niall gave it to him just as someone came running up the stairs, calling out that the castle was being attacked. The squire, Joceran, burst in. Walter finally got a spark to drop into the tinder and light flared. Niall sat down on the bed to pull on his chausses. His captain lit a candle and held it high. In the street crowds of people were shouting the alarm.

Niall, scowling, ran his hand through his hair. "Find my damned hauberk," he shouted.

Three knight serjeants came up the stairs looking for orders. Niall bellowed for them to go back down again. Naked except for his sword, Walter raced down after them.

Niall put his arms through the mail that Joceran lowered over his head. He said, muffled, "Tell me what's going on."

"One of the knights at the c-castle is below." The boy was jittering with excitement. "He's hurt. Oh, here he is."

The commander of the castle guard stumbled in, his face and arms bleeding. The candle flickered. "Milord, Gotselm and the others hold the keep," he gasped. "Helpo and Theobald are dead." He staggered to the edge of the bed and leaned on it. "I escaped by swimming the moat."

Cursing, Niall picked up his sword. He waved away Jocelyn, holding his boots.

"Then they set fire to the new gate." The serjeant picked up the edge of the blanket and tried to stanch the blood from his arm. "It's the Welsh. Their accursed prince, Cadwallader, is raiding us."

Niall started for the door. When he reached the tavern's common room below, Walter shouted that he had sent knights ahead to scout the castle road.

The stable yard was full of horses, with knights trying to catch and saddle them. Outside the townspeople were milling in the darkness, pointing to the pink glow of the fire in the sky.

Walter came up leading Niall's destrier, Hammerer. The warhorse danced and snorted, smelling a fight. "God's wounds, do you intend to fight naked?" Niall yelled at him.

Walter grinned, showing white teeth. "Yes, probably." He pushed his way back through the crowd to get his horse.

Niall hauled himself into the saddle. He pulled a gonfalon with the Morlaix griffon from the hand of a knight who came trotting up. "Follow me," he shouted, waving the banner. He spurred his horse through the gate. The townspeople fell back out of the way.

Yelling, yipping Gascon knights poured out of the stable yard. The moon was full and bright. The horses broke into a thundering trot. At the market square another group of knights nearly ran into them. Someone among the Gascons shouted that there were more knights billeted in the gold-smith's house.

It was too late to send anyone after them. Niall turned Hammerer in the direction of the castle road. As they galloped past the churchyard a thrumming sound like grouse being flushed struck among them. One knight fell into the road, pierced in the chest. Several knights slumped over their saddles.

Shouting a warning to Walter, Niall jumped his destrier over the churchyard wall. The overhanging trees hid the moon; it was pitch dark under the branches. The big stallion faltered, uncertain of the footing. Niall spurred him, hard. Hammerer reared, then plunged ahead, toppling tomb-stones.

The Welsh bowmen suddenly broke cover in front of them. Niall chased them among the graves, leaning from the saddle to swing his sword. Behind him his knight captain jumped his horse over the wall. The Welshmen retreated, zigzagging through the gravestones before they skinned over a far wall. For an instant the bright moon revealed half a dozen savage little men in furs and hides before they ran into a wood.

Niall reined in his destrier. "Goddamn them, they planned this well enough, even down to the ambush!"

Walter leaned from the saddle to pick up the fallen gonfalon. "Cadwallader seeks to humble you."

Niall laughed, harshly. "He'll learn better."

They wheeled the big horses together and jumped them back over the churchyard wall. The Gascons were galloping full course for the river road, yelling their war cries. A group of Prince Cadwallader's knights met them at the bridge.

The Welsh fought off the Gascon knights' first ragged charge. When Walter and Niall came racing up Cadwallader's forces were trying to drive the Morlaix knights into the river.

Niall charged, flailing his big sword over his head. Seeing him coming, the embattled Gascons howled like banshees. Niall drove Hammerer into the middle of the Welsh. They held their ground for a moment under the bright moon. On the hill behind them Castle Morlaix, repaired with new timber, burned brightly.

The Gascons ploughed screeching into the melee around Niall. The Welsh began to give way. Niall drove Hammerer at them, and the huge stallion rammed a little Welsh horse and sank his teeth into its neck.

Suddenly one of Cadwallader's men blew a horn. At its sound the Welshmen wheeled their mountain ponies and galloped for the woods. Like the bowmen in the churchyard, they seemed to melt into the night. The howling Gascons plunged their mounts into the thickets after them.

Niall pulled Hammerer to a standstill. Some Morlaix knights had dismounted to tend to their wounded. Two horses on the ground thrashed in their death throes. Beyond lay the still body of a Welsh knight.

Joceran limped into the road, unhorsed. Niall leaned from the saddle, breathing hard. "Are you hurt?"

Dazed, his squire shook his head. Some Gascons galloped their horses around them in circles, yelling, still wanting to fight. Walter Straunge cantered up, long hair like silver in the moonlight, naked except for his billowing cloak.

"Jesu," Niall said, staring at him. He realized his own feet in the stirrups were bare. He rubbed his face, slick with sweat, and found his helmet straps were undone. For all their haste, the Welsh had hit them hard.

The dismounted Gascons began to gather around him. Niall looked down into their grinning faces, not understanding what they were telling him in their strange French.

Walter came up and seized Hammerer's bridle. "They're calling you Satan with an invincible sword," he explained. "They talk like that."

"Do they." He slid down the stallion's side stiffly. The

Gascons crowded to him, slapping his arms and back, showing their teeth. Niall's leg was torturing him. He stepped back when one of the Gascons fell to one knee and seized his hand.

The knight pressed Niall's hand to the rim of his helmet and held it there. "Lion of courage," he cried in his thick accent, "God has favored us, to give us such a true hero. You fight like a Gascon!"

Walter said out of the side of his mouth, "Perhaps now they will forgo the rest of the pay we owe them."

Niall grunted. The castle guards had come to the far side of the moat and were shoving boards over so they could cross. The new drawbridge they'd just built had burned and fallen into the moat. The portal gate was only charred wood hanging from the hinges.

Niall made his way in his bare feet to the far side, followed by Walter and Joceran. The castle guard, Gotselm, waited for them with a handful of smoke-blackened knights.

They followed the serjeant into the bailey. The chattering Gascons crossed the moat. The damage was not bad in the inner yard, if one did not count the timber. The old tower was still intact.

"They sent fire arrows over, milord," Gotselm said. "We lost Helpo and Theobald getting water from the moat."

Niall nodded, making the sign of the cross. They should have had a full garrison at the castle by now. He did not have to be reminded of the lumber they had hoarded to rebuild the kitchen house, and the roof to the knights' tower.

The stink of smoke hung in the air. Most of the fires were out. Two knights went about with buckets, dousing embers. The French knights strolled about the bailey, kicking at stones.

Niall watched them. The raid was meant to discredit him with his knights and the people of Morlaix. It hadn't worked with the Gascons; since they'd seen him fight he could pass for the Holy Virgin. But he would have to drive the Morlaix villeins back to the castle with whips to start work over again.

He looked around the bailey. He needed stone masons from Chirk. He needed to move the garrison knights into the Old Keep and show the Welsh that he was there to stay.

He rubbed his face tiredly. If he taxed the townspeople a third time he would have a revolt. It seemed the only ones who loved him were the bloodthirsty Gascons. And that wouldn't last long if he couldn't give them the rest of their pay.

"What is this?" He bent and picked up a broken board.

"The platform, sir." Gotselm wrinkled his brow. "One of the knights, Osmer, saved most of it."

"Saved it?" Niall propped the board against a wall. "A platform for what?"

The castle guard shuffled their feet. Gotselm said, "Milord, have you not heard? This is the platform where you will sit on the morrow when all the town celebrates the Feast of the Ascension. This is where you will receive the oaths."

He straightened up slowly, his bad leg shooting spears of pain. He had forgotten all about the accursed feast. He looked around, at the faces of his knights. Regardless of fire, the raid by the marauding Welsh, or that Castle Morlaix was somewhat a ruin, on the morrow the people of his fief would have their Ascension procession. Where, Gotselm had just reminded him, they would pay fealty to the new lord.

Jesus God. Niall rubbed his hand across his face again, smearing soot.

He needed a miracle.

It had started to drizzle, not unusual in marcher country in May. A little before dawn the guilds that had not put

canopies over their stages tumbled out of their camp in the
meadows, cursing and half awake, to try to do something
by torchlight.

The passing rain soon died. At dawn the sun came up
in a misty sky. A sign, the country folk said, that the day's
weather would be warm, and fine. By the time Emmeline's
household had collected itself the town was already filling
with people. Magnus had wanted to march with the butchers' and tanners' apprentices. Wearing a fine silk shirt embroidered with silver thread to mark the goldsmiths, and a
green velvet cap with a long white feather, he was so
sweetly handsome Emmeline could hardly bring herself to
deny him anything. Except, of course, the company of notorious rowdies.

He was still arguing as the steward brought up her mare.
"Mother," he pleaded, "let me go. The other lads mock
me, always riding with you like a baby!"

"No, I said. The weavers' apprentices are bad enough,
but the tanners and the others are worse." She tried to catch
him to smooth his hair, but he skittered out of her way.
"You don't remember, you were too little, but one year the
butchers fought and overturned wagons. It was a disgrace."

One of the stable knaves gave Emmeline a boost into
the saddle. She turned her mare through the stable yard
where her kitchen people, dressed in their best clothes,
stood waiting. She bent down to say to her steward, Torel,
"See that all the girls wear cloths to cover their hair. I
don't want to hear that some foreign knight has mistaken
one of them for a common whore."

Magnus followed her, leading his pony through the gate
and into the street, his face stormy.

"Holy Mother, do you have to look like that?" Emmeline
snapped. "Ride your pony behind old Aimery, then. I want
to know where you are."

The smith came pushing through a crowd of country
people, calling to Emmeline. The players on the bakers'

wagon, where Jesus distributed the loaves and fishes, were
complaining that the guild had shorted them. They had only
two sacks of bread to give to the crowd. They were threatening not to move until they got more. They said when the
bread ran out the villeins would turn on them.

They were probably right. Emmeline wondered what
Wulfer had done with the money she had given him to buy
flour and lard.

One of the guildsmen from the weavers came up on the
other side to grasp her stirrup. "You should not have given
the baker the money," he told her, "but bought the bread
yourself in Chirk. If there's trouble we'll have a riot here,
with so many of the wild country folk come in."

She moved her foot away from his hand. He meant the
shepherds and the people of the forest, like the charcoal
burners and bird netters, who were seldom seen except on
feast days.

Emmeline sighed. Something always happened at the last
moment; it had been so long since they'd celebrated the
Feast of the Ascension they'd just forgotten.

The meadow was full of wagons and oxen, crofters and
their families, the shepherds with a huge straw image they
carried at feasts that was supposed to be an ancient spirit.
Some said it was a heathen pig goddess called Henwas
Hwych. The Old Servant. There hadn't been so many border people in one place since the end of King Stephen's
war. They had come not only for the Ascension procession,
but to see the new lord.

The baker's gaunt wife came running up. "Thank God,
Mistress Emmeline, you'll put things to rights! The players
say we haven't bread enough to use the whole day." She
glared at the men sitting on the edge of the stage. "What
they say is a lie. There was enough bread last eventide. I
saw the sacks put on the wagon myself!"

Emmeline dismounted and led her mare up to the grinning players. They had been drinking. Two were not much

more than boys, but one had a beard and a slovenly paunch. She looked at him closely. She would swear that years ago he had been the drunken Christ of the vintner's Wedding at Cana.

He leered at her. "Bread?" He turned to the other two. "Why are we talking of bread, boys, when here's a tasty little meat pie we can sample right here?"

Behind her the baker's wife gasped. The player reached out for her, but Aimeric came lumbering up. Emmeline waved him back. "We have a harsh lord here, and he makes harsh punishments." She was a guild master; drunks did not frighten her. "Are you ready to play the part of a one-handed man?"

The boys knew the punishment for robbery when they heard it. They quickly slid off the stage and ran off. A woman came out from behind the wagon and stood with her hands on her hips.

"We only put it aside to have some to spare," she whined. "The sacks are down by the river."

"Nay, they took the bread to sell, mistress," Aimeric said behind her. "Mummers are a thieving lot."

Emmeline bit her lip. It would do no good to chase off the actors, it would spoil the bakers' drama. But she thought of all the sacks of bread going to waste. "Get up," she told the bearded Christ. He got to his feet, adjusting his robe, and regarded her sullenly. "You will play the Christ for the loaves and the fishes, and do it well, or I will tell the new lord of Morlaix you are not only a thief but a blasphemer, as you tried to steal the bakers' guild's holy bread."

The woman thrust herself in between. "Don't do that, mistress! Odo will give you a good play, a dear drama of the Christ what fed the multitudes. You won't have nothing to complain about, I swear it."

Even as she spoke the bearded man hurried about the stage, straightening the curtains, picking up the wooden

fishes, calling for the boys to come back. Emmeline watched
for a few moments, then turned away, telling Aimeric to ride
with the bakers and keep an eye on them.

The other wagons started to move. Villeins prodded the
short-legged oxen with the heavy oak staffs they also used,
sometimes, as weapons. The wine merchant's wagon passed
with fine-looking players who would perform the miracu-
lous changing of water to wine. The old deaf priest, Father
Wilbert, led off, followed by the younger priest that nobody
liked, carrying the Ascension banner from the church. Morlaix lacked a true relic, such as the famous finger bone of
St. James in a crystal monstrance that was carried in Wrexham's feasts, but they had attracted a sizable crowd in spite
of it. Ragged tumblers and musicians had appeared from
somewhere. A man and a woman strode along, playing
drums and singing, another herded a troop of dogs walking
on their hind legs. Acrobat boys cartwheeled alongside the
road. And everywhere there were the lord's foreign knights,
fully mailed and armed, riding in their midst, black eyes
avidly looking over the village girls from behind their steel
helms and nasals. Emmeline pushed her mare through the
crowds, looking for Magnus.

Along the road the poorer people, many clad only in a
coarse long shirt, fell to their knees as the wagons passed,
their hands clasped. Seeing their piety, Emmeline thought
of the mummer who had tried to steal the sacks of bread.
She was glad, now, she had set Aimeric to watch him.

The sun grew warm on their heads and shoulders. The
first stop was the marketplace. Emmeline pushed her mare
up to Aimeric riding behind the bakers' stage. "I'm looking
for Magnus," she told him. "Have you seen him?"

The old knight shook his head. The crowd surged forward to watch the fishes and loaves miraculously multiply.
A roar went up as the bearded mummer playing Christ
tossed out the first pieces of bread.

Emmeline took off her cloak and laid it over the pommel

of her saddle. The little wooden box holding the gold-smiths' gift was tied to her leather girdle. As she rode, it bumped against her thigh. Townspeople surged up to the wagons to watch the acting out of the Bible tales. She recognized the group of sober-looking woolmen with their families, and the good-looking fuller, who tried to catch her eye. Three knights carrying a wineskin climbed into a hay wain filled with giggling villeins' girls. Gangs of apprentices roamed along the edges of the crowd waving willow switches that they used to slash at each other. But she did not see Magnus.

By the slant of the sun it was still early. The next stop would be the church, where those who could crowd inside would hear old Father Wilbert and the new priest say a special mass for Ascension Day. After that, the procession would make its way through the town, stopping at the guildsmen's houses, before it started up the hill to the castle.

Emmeline wiped the perspiration from her face with the back of her hand, wishing the feast were over and done with. Then she spotted Magnus without his new hat, leading his pony in the midst of a crowd of apprentices. She turned her horse and started after him.

At the moment the sexton climbed the church tower to ring for nones, the procession emerged from town and straggled out onto the road to the castle. Sometime after midday the vintner's wine had run out, so that those who wished to keep on with their drinking had gone on to spend the remainder of the afternoon at the taverns. A more sober crowd trudged among the oxen and the wagon stages, some praying, some singing old country hymns and psalms. Father Wilbert gave up walking and went to ride in one of the hay wains. His new curate, his face and nose somewhat sunburned, strode on in his place at the head of the procession carrying the church's banner. In the midst of the mob of shepherds

the giant, big-breasted figure of the pig goddess teetered
along, wagging its hay-stuffed arms and legs.

Emmeline took Magnus's reins, and in spite of his protests that he wanted to ride with the other boys pulled him
along behind the leather workers carrying their gift saddle
for the new lord. All the woolmen, weavers, clipmen, and
the fuller walked behind their guild head, Master Avenant,
who carried the length of fine blue wool that was their gift
for the lord's new cloak. After they had passed the bridge
Emmeline dismounted to walk with the guildsmen, and
made Magnus do the same.

They could see the young priest with his banner had
almost reached the platform set up on the near side of the
moat. The Lord of Morlaix sat in front of the burned-out
portal of his castle, flanked by a score of his knights in
glittering, newly polished mail.

The horses and wagons raised a fog of dust. In places
one could hardly breathe. Emmeline took off her gold and
silver circlet, and then the green silk veil that covered her
hair. When she shook it out she tasted the dust on her lips.
It was too hot, she thought somewhat crossly, to walk so
far in layers of her best silk clothes. Under her surcoat and
white bliaut, sweat trickled down her shoulder blades. The
red-faced, perspiring burghers around her looked no better.

She decided not to put the veil back on and tucked it
into her belt. The woolmen went forward to swear loyalty
to the new lord, the leather workers carrying their gift saddle crowding in behind them. The lord's knights in a half
circle partly blocked her view, but Emmeline could see the
top of his head as he bent forward. He had taken off his
helmet. His waving hair was dark red, wet with the heat,
sticking to his skull. She heard him say something to the
wool master, Avenant, and place the guildsman's hands between his.

Something about those big hands, even blocked partly
by a knight's back, gave Emmeline a start. She couldn't

say why they bothered her. She listened to the wool master's low voice repeating the oath to his lord. She had a sudden, strange feeling that Niall fitzJulien, Morlaix's new lord, would change their destinies. Just as the new young king, Henry Plantagenet, and his wife Queen Eleanor of Aquitaine, had changed England's.

Half-Norman, half-Irish. The son, it was rumored, of the old earl's bastard. All of Morlaix wondered how this man, the king's rewarded hero, and his French knights, would rule them. Most of the world regarded the Irish tribes as savage, barbaric.

Somewhat nervously Emmeline turned to Magnus and smoothed his hair back, brushing the dust from the front of his velvet jacket. Without looking up, he pushed her hand away. At that moment the tall captain came up, saying they would be next. Emmeline had seen him before: he was the blond knight who rode from house to house collecting the levies.

He stopped in front of her. "The goldsmith? You are the goldsmith?" He looked around for someone to correct him, then looked slowly and thoughtfully at Emmeline from the top of her hair, a copper color in the burning light, down to her embroidered slippers.

She stared back just as forthrightly. "The goldsmiths wish to give a gift to the lord." She held out the box.

He was now staring at Magnus. He couldn't seem to drag his eyes away. "What?" He looked down at the box she held out to him. "No, no, I don't know—put it in his hand, I suppose."

Frowning, he hurried away. The woolmen had stepped back. Emmeline craned to see. Niall fitzJulien leaned from his seat to hand the folded blue cloth the weavers had given him to a knight. The sun sent sparks from his polished mail.

They were right to call him a big man. Over his mail hauberk he was wearing a white woolen tunic, his long, muscular legs in neat cross garters. What one noticed were the shoulders, powerful and broad for swinging a great two-handed sword.

She came forward quickly, holding Magnus by the hand. A knight handed the lord a cup of wine. She watched the muscles in his brown throat work as he drank from it thirstily. He gave back the cup and the blond knight bent to him, whispering in his ear.

Emmeline tugged at Magnus to make him go to his knees. She sank down beside him. The sun was too hot. She knew her face was flushed, and she already felt rumpled and dusty. The strange unease that had begun when she saw the wool master swearing his oath a few minutes ago would not go away. She held out the box in both hands, and looked up into the lord's face.

She was close enough to see the fine lines at the corners of his eyes. Close enough to note the long nose, the hard slash of his mouth, the strands of slightly curling, dark red hair that hung over his brow. She had expected someone older.

Somewhere, she thought, staring up at him, she had seen eyes that tawny color before.

His expression changed as he looked at her and he leaned forward, hands suddenly gripping the chair. Then his eyes widened as he looked to Magnus. Then back to her again.

Behind Emmeline the saddler and his cousins whispered something. One of the lord's knights coughed.

Still staring, the Lord of Morlaix made a strangled sound in his throat. *"You!"*

Emmeline blinked, watching his face tighten with some unknown emotion. His lips twisted.

Something was happening. All those gathered there for the oath-taking could not move, their eyes riveted on their new lord as he was seemingly gripped by what very much looked like a dread demon possession.

A whisper rode the air as far back as the wagons in the road. Emmeline grabbed Magnus's hand. Before she could spring to her feet the man in mail had lunged forward. His arm shot out, the fingers of his big hand closing about her throat.

"She-devil!" the new lord of Morlaix bellowed. "Foul betrayer!" He held Emmeline, one hand about her throat. She gasped, her eyes bulging. "He's mine, isn't he?" he roared.

"Mother!" Magnus hurled himself at his mailed arm, trying to pry open his grip.

But Emmeline had fainted.

EIGHT

"Sweet Mary's tits," Niall swore, "she has half the countryside east of Wales in debt to her!"

Through the open door of the shop they could hear the late-night song of spring frogs in the wash yard. It was past midnight; the manor's stable yard was dotted with torchlight as knights moved from the house to the waiting wagons and back. The goldsmith's widow, her hood of her cape thrown back, her hair like new-melted gold in the hectic light, stood by a wagon piled high with her household goods, her arm around the boy. She was still weeping angrily.

Too bad, Niall told himself. He had little sympathy for her. As for himself—he had prayed for it, and now he had his miracle! From what he could see old Neufmarche had left not only the goldsmithing business, but a tidy moneylending trade as well. One that reached far and wide in the west of England. And the devil's vixen he had for a wife had apparently, since the old man's death, built it up even more.

He stood up and reached over the worktable and pulled down another strongbox, using the tip of his dagger to break the lock. He had opened four. The fifth was the same as the others, the bottom filled with neatly stacked bags of gold and silver coins. On top lay the rolled parchment records of the moneylending accounts, and the names and locations of the debtors.

The records were a marvel of neatness and precision, as
were the varying rates of interest. Reading them, one could
see loans had been made to merchants in the Welsh border
country, most particularly Morlaix and Chirk, but some
even as far as Wrexham. There were also modest sums lent
everywhere to craftsmen and skilled laborers, physicians
and lawyers, seasonal hay workers, even a rat catcher. She'd
overlooked nothing.

"The old moneylender," Walter said, holding up a vellum
roll, "left all his fortune to yon luscious widow. Who it
seems continued to lend it most profitably."

Niall grunted. From the looks of the accounts she'd kept
the widow had dealt in property loans and notes of hand,
tripling old Neufmarche's rate of lending. And almost that
much with profits.

No wonder, he thought, the miserable town was prosperous. The craftsmen and farmers hadn't lacked for the best
funding outside London since the goldsmith died.

He reached over and turned Walter's parchment around
in his hands. "Try right-side up. You'd do well to learn to
read."

The other shrugged. "I do well enough. I can cipher
numbers, can't I?"

Niall was in no mood to argue. If anything, he was sa-
voring his triumph. After all those long, bitter years of wondering what had become of her, she'd stumbled into his
hands with more wealth than any heiress at court! What a
piece of luck. He'd bet there was a stock of gold and silver
in her strongboxes equal to any fortune in the north. She
not only dealt in raw gold and silver and foreign coin, but
also lent money to a third of the border country. As far as
he could tell this had been going on for a good seven or
eight years. All during the Anarchy.

And no one knew about it.

Just the thought sent a cold feeling down Niall's spine.

He looked through the open door and saw her standing with her arm protectingly around the boy.

Christ crucified, he had never thought to see her again in this life! He didn't even know her name. He had begun to think she had never existed.

There had been times, as when he'd been wounded at Stafford and lay in a three-day fever, that he had dreamed of her so much he'd had to tell himself that she had been naught but a twenty year-old's passion-filled fantasy. Never to have happened. Even long ago in Wrexham when he was Robert of Gloucester's ardent young knight.

When he thought about her in years since, the reality faded even more. Her red-gold hair, that face with its soft, pouting lips, the unearthly beauty of her body that he had held that night in his arms, had all been so perfect that he had told himself that no flawless woman like the one he had made love to in Wrexham had ever drawn breath in this living world.

No, there'd been nothing real in it. Except the very harsh reality she'd dealt when she'd finished with him. He would remember waking up in the stinking mud of a Wrexham alley for the rest of his life.

Ten years, he marveled. It had been that long. He had been twenty then. He was near thirty-one now.

Today, as he had looked down into her face as she knelt for the oath-taking, he'd heard a great ringing in his ears, a dizziness, a blackness in his mind like the onset of death.

God's face, she was there! She *was* real.

Another shattering blow. She had their son with her. He knew at once the boy was his. How could one miss it? Looking into the boy's face was like looking into a mirror!

Now he stood at the doorway of the shop watching as one of the servants came up to her, holding a torch high, and said something to her. She dashed the tears from her eyes with the back of her hand, and shook her head, no.

He scowled. Damn her, it would do her no good now to

shake her head "no" to anything. But she had been defiant from the moment he'd seized her scrawny neck.

The household around her was a shambles. The servants were wandering dazed as his knights took furniture out and loaded it on wagons to be carried away. Surprisingly, the servants had been loyal. The old pensioner knight had done his best to defend her before the Gascons had disarmed him. Then her angry stable boys and kitchen knaves had had to be driven off. He studied her agonized expression as she gripped the boy tightly while their belongings were carried out and piled into the wains.

One could almost feel sorry for her if one did not know her black, evil heart. Jesu, he thought, what did you call a woman, anyway, who preyed on knights who were no more than mere boys? If he remembered right there was some sort of demon who took a female form to do that.

Succubus. That was it. The devil fiend in woman's shape that crept upon a man in the night when he was sleeping and stole his breath. And his seed, if it could.

Niall rubbed his hand across his chin, watching her. He could well believe it. Had she not stolen a child from him, this flame-headed hell's whore? No one could look at the boy and not know he was his. He was even the image of his grandsire, Julien of Nessville.

For a moment Niall wished he had his hands around her neck again. If it had not been for Joceran and Walter finally dragging him away from her, he could not say what would have happened.

"Milord," Walter was saying, "there are boxes of gems. We—"

"Take everything." He shut the strongbox with a bang. "Load the gold and silver and coin in a wagon and set a guard over it. The precious stones I will carry myself."

He was well aware that what he was doing was confiscation of the king's property—since everything in England was Henry's—without order or writ. And seizure under

King Henry had to be defended in most cases as a matter of right. Except, of course, when it was the king himself.

He pulled out the leather pouches of gems from their boxes and stuck them into his belt, tossing the remaining few to Walter.

Henry, he told himself, was the great danger. The king could take every scrap of Neufmarche's fortune away, carry it off to London, if and when he discovered it. Niall had not stopped thinking about the king from the moment he laid eyes on the hoard.

It was no secret that Henry Plantagenet was hard-pressed for money. Fifteen years of war had drained England, and the kingdom's quarreling, disloyal nobles had dined on the land's suffering flesh for all but a small part of that time.

And would feed on Henry's, too, if they could pull him down. As for Queen Eleanor, she was wealthy, but there was just so much one could get from her lands in Aquitaine. The king, Niall was well aware, needed the Widow Neufmarche's fortune as badly as he.

Walter had gone out to fetch some knights to carry out the strongboxes. When Niall looked up, Gotselm was at the door. "There are merchants in the street," the serjeant told him. He looked around the goldsmith's shop. "They know you have the widow here, and they are asking to speak to you about her."

Niall got up and followed him out into the stable yard. At once she stepped into his path. "I beg you." Her voice was hoarse with weeping. "Please let me speak——"

He shook her off. God rot it, he did not have to answer to her, he owed her nothing. He took the boy by the hand. "What do they call you?" he said, pulling the child along.

The boy looked up at him with wide eyes. In his mail and helmet Niall was a towering figure.

"Please, sir." He looked back at his mother. "Please, sir, my mother wishes to know what you will do with us."

He steered him toward the gate. "Never mind that, I will

speak to her later. First you must tell me what they call you."

He hesitated, still looking back. "Magnus. Magnus Neufmarche." His voice was loud but it trembled.

Niall looked down, feeling a curious sensation. Even in the dark stable yard his son was the image of his grandsire with those eyes, the ruddy hair that was brighter than his own. "I will call you Julien," he said huskily.

The boy looked surprised. He opened his mouth to say something but Niall jerked him toward the goldsmith's front gate. The knights there saluted when they saw him, their eyes on the boy.

The porter ran to open the gate. A small crowd waited outside, burghers and town merchants and a big man in a leather jerkin who looked like a smith. Behind them a larger group of townspeople had gathered in spite of the dark and the hour.

"Milord, we ask a boon." Hat in hand, the little fat man Niall recognized as the wine seller dropped to his knees. The rest stayed on their feet, faces set. A stiff-necked lot.

"Milord," the wine seller said, looking up, "we come to ask on behalf of the guilds." He stared at the boy by Niall's side. "What has the—what has the goldsmith—" he stammered. "What have the—"

The big smith shouldered his way forward. "What Villers wants to say is if there be offense to you by this household. And why its goods are being put into carts and carried away."

"It be lawless confiscation," someone muttered.

He could see they were afraid to ask what he intended to do with the goldsmith's wife. They didn't mention her, only the property. He hooked his hand in his belt. "The household goods go to the castle. As does the widow and her boy."

They looked at one another. The boy clutched his hand

tightly. Niall said, "It is not confiscation, I claim it all as her dower. Before the night is up I will marry her."

He heard their gasps. Someone shouted out, "She does not desire to be married! Ask any one of us."

The wine seller said quickly, "Milord, Mistress Neufmarche is a guild member. Many suitors have sent the matchmaker here from York and would like to—"

"She will wed me. There's no more to say of it." Niall pulled the boy back and motioned for the porter to shut the gate. It closed in their faces. Outside in the street there was a sudden silence. Then someone banged on the door.

He strode away, dragging the boy by the hand, shouting for Joceran and Walter. Some knights came out of the manor house, staggering under the weight of a bed. They had not stopped to take it apart but carried the whole thing, blue velvet curtains flapping, at a trot. They ran up and dumped it sidewise in a hay wain. One of the serjeants went after them, shouting.

Niall stopped. He stood holding the child's hand as, entangled in gold rope and tassels and bed curtains, his knights strained to set the frame upright. It was a big bed, an elegant one that no doubt generations of goldsmiths had prized.

He suddenly realized he knew it. How could one forget it—or the night he had spent in it? Not here in Morlaix, in Wrexham. But it was the same.

For a brief, wild moment he felt like laughing. It was only justice that he take the damned bed with him!

Walter came up with Joceran trailing. "Get the priest," Niall told him. "The young one, he looks corrupt enough. Bring him to the castle." He put the boy's hand in his squire's. "He says he has a pony. Put him on it, and keep him with you."

"Sir," the boy said. He stood with his back straight, his lips quivering. "I would like to stay with my mother."

Niall paused. He put his hand on his son's head and held

it there for the briefest of moments. "You see," he said to Joceran. "Don't take your eyes from him."

He walked off across the yard to talk to her. Or at least tell her what he was going to do.

In the street, Watris the smith hauled the vintner up from the dirt. The leather worker and his cousins stood with their arms crossed over their chests. "Blessed Virgin, did he say marry her?" Villers cried. "Well, it is better than nothing."

The young fuller pushed his way through the crowd. "You think that? He had her by the throat at the castle!"

The guildsmen looked at one another, remembering the boy. "There is more here than meets the eye," one of the saddlers from Chirk said.

The big smith shook his head. "For all that he says he will marry her, he is pulling down old Bernard's household and carting it away. Young King Henry swore to the guilds in London that there would be no lawless confiscation. That he would protect commerce."

"Bah, the king says what he has to!" The fuller looked around him for support. "Holy Jesus, have any of you seen her? Has he beat her, mistreated her? God rot him, he is holding her prisoner!"

One of the weavers touched his arm. "Easy, fuller, we do not wish to begin a quarrel."

"Yes, who knows what the true story is?" the vintner said. "He had the boy with him, by his side. The likeness was remarkable."

They stood in silence for a moment. The townspeople in back pressed forward to hear.

"There is one way to find out," the smith said finally. "We can send to the goldsmiths in Chester, and tell the guild masters there what has happened."

NINE

The bride had to be dragged before the seedy young priest, screaming her protests so loudly that it set the boy to struggling and howling as well. Niall took her by both arms and shook her until her teeth clicked.

"Do this," he snarled, "or as God is my judge, I'll send the boy this night to the Earl of Chester's court to train as a page."

She gave him a wild look. But she swallowed her sobs long enough for the priest to proceed. The ceremony took place in the castle bailey before the Gascon knights and the Neufmarche servants who had accompanied the household goods. It was almost dawn. As the priest pronounced the final words a thunderstorm opened up, sending sheets of rain down on them. After a few halfhearted cheers the knights scattered, some to haul the wagons to shelter, others to run for their quarters in the still mostly roofless knights' tower.

Walter Straunge escorted Morlaix's new lady to the chamber in the Old Keep, dragging her most of the way. He returned almost at once to report that the bed being carried up to the bridal chamber would not fit the stair, and one of the servants from the Neufmarche manor was needed to show the Gascons how to take it apart. Cursing, Niall found the goldsmith's steward, Baudri Torel, hiding from the storm under broken thatch by the dog pens, and routed him out to fetch men to fix the marriage bed.

While this was going on Joceran carried Magnus off, still struggling and wailing, to spend the night in the knights' barracks. Unrelenting, the storm battered the castle with gusts of rain and bolts of lightning that danced across the top of the towers. It made a lake in the ward, the water black from the recent fire.

Niall went to help the knights pushing the goldsmith's wagons under the overhang of the portal gate. As the last wain rolled in Walter Straunge came splashing up.

"Rain at a wedding is a good sign," his captain shouted. When Niall answered obscenely he only grinned and pressed something into his hand, a large iron key. "Rejoice, milord, I have seen that the wedding bed is up, and the bride safely locked in to await you."

Niall wiped the rain out of his eyes with the back of his hand. *The bride locked in to await you.* A happy prospect. From the faces of the Gascon knights around him they plainly thought him a bold and clever man to snatch a wealthy widow from the town to marry. They had cheered when the priest pronounced them man and wife.

Walter lifted the cover of the nearest wain. "Although your bride's dowry is somewhat worse for the downpour."

Niall grunted. "There's more where that came from." They had not a quarter emptied the splendid manor house, while the castle was still not fit to live in. At least the bed was up for his wedding night. Joceran appeared out of the rain. "God's wounds," Niall growled at him, "what now?"

His squire had a strange expression. "The boy wants you. He will not stop his squalling. It is keeping everyone awake."

Niall worked at the ties on his hauberk. The leather had swelled with the rain into rock-hard knots. He gave them an angry jerk.

He saw the squire and his captain exchange looks. Jesu, the whole world knew about the boy. Or guessed at it. He followed Joceran across the flooded ward to the Knights'

Tower. As he bent his head to go under the lintel, familiar odors assailed him: horse dung, sweat, moldering straw, oil for the armor. He had spent a lifetime in places like this.

Saddle blankets had been thrown across the ceiling to make a shelter but the rain poured through anyway. There was a lantern on the floor. By its light he could make out knights sprawled everywhere. Some of the old barracks' bed frames had survived. The boy sat on one with two Gascons flanking him, a blanket around his shoulders. He had been sobbing when Niall came in, but he quickly wiped his nose with the back of his hand and jumped up.

"I want to see my mother, sir," he cried.

"Tomorrow." He had a feeling he should say something more. After all, he had changed the boy's life with this marrying. There was no place to talk unless he pulled him out into the ward and they stood in the rain. But in there they were being listened to by fifty or so interested Gascons.

"Come," he said, taking him by the hand.

Once outside he meant to hold his cloak over him, but the boy pulled away.

He is only a child, Niall thought, looking down at him. He remembered all the times he had stood like this before his own father.

"I want to see my mother." Tears wobbled in his voice.

"Holy Christ, is that all you can say? Stop sniveling or I will take you back inside."

The boy's head snapped back. He drew himself up, fists clenched. "I know what you are going to do," he shrilled. "I know what men do to w-women when they wed them."

Ah, so that was the trouble. He bent to the tear-swollen face. "So you know what happens when men and women bed, do you?"

The boy returned his look bravely. "Sir, I—I have seen horses," he squeaked. "And bulls with cows. It is—I have been told it is like that."

Joceran came to the door of the tower. Niall pointed with

his chin. "See, there is my squire, Joceran. He sees me into my clothes, and out of them. If you ask him he will tell you I am modestly gifted, but of no stallion size. Nor yet a bull."

The boy thought it over. He whispered, "It is the same, though?"

Niall scowled. Confound it, why were little boys so concerned with their dams? He dimly remembered feeling something of the sort when he was his age.

He said gruffly, "As God is my judge, you do not need to fear. I give you my oath that I will treat her well enough." He gave him a shove toward the squire waiting in the doorway. "Tell Joceran to find you a dry place to sleep."

The child seemed to hesitate, then turned and ran full speed through the rain. Niall started through the ward, yanking at the fouled straps of his mail. The accursed night seemed endless. The storm was moving away, the thunder now in the distance. He looked up and saw it was almost light.

The stairwell in the old keep was ink-black and, like everything else in the castle, smelled of fire. He brushed his hand along the wall. At the top he found Gotselm the serjeant standing guard with a candle.

"Go below and get some sleep," he told him. He used the iron key Walter had given him to unlock the door, and stepped inside.

The bed was set up in the center of the room, its blue curtains and gold tassels wetly dangling. But it was the same bed, he would know it anywhere. One could even imagine it the same room, and that nearly ten years had not passed. The sense of it was so strong he passed his hand in front of his eyes.

The mood was gone quickly when he stumbled over clothing piled on the floor. There was a jumble of furniture. A chair. A low table with candles burning on it. A harsh screech made him jump.

"Where is my son?" His new wife rushed toward him from the far side of the bed, still wrapped in a rain-sodden cloak.

"God's wounds," Niall shouted, "is there no end to this?"

"I am not going to sleep with you!" She threw back the hood. In the dim light her hair was a red gold mass, raveled in bright strings about her face. Green eyes blazed at him.

She hurled herself at him, fists clenched. "This is no marriage, you only want my money! You said when you forced me into this that you would not take my son from me!"

Niall grabbed her to keep her from pummeling him. When he pushed her, she tripped over a bundle of her clothes and fell. She lay there, panting.

He sat down on the edge of the bed and worried the wet leather straps some more with his fingers. He needed Joceran to help him out of his mail. But Joceran, he remembered, was with the boy.

She rolled to her knees. "You must let me go to see my son," she begged. "Magnus is not used to being parted from me! He will be frightened!"

He said without looking up, "He is going to be called Julien. After my father."

She gasped. "You are mad! Your father? I have never seen you before in my life!"

She was lying; he could see it in her face. On the other hand, he supposed he had changed. Yet she seemed as young and beautiful as ever.

He pulled out his dagger. At the sight of it, she screamed and scrambled backward on her knees. "Don't you touch me!"

He put the dagger to the side of his mail and, twisting his head to see, sawed through a leather strap. He hated to cut the ties; it made him even more angry to know it would take Joceran a full day to replace them. But he was sick of being trapped in his own mail.

The problem was that the world knew his son as Neufmarche's. A merchant, not base born, but not noble, either. Something in between.

God rot her, he thought, putting the knife back in his belt, she had made this mess with her infernal scheming. It was monstrous—*inhuman*—to steal a man's seed, then pass his child off as another man's son!

He leaned forward to pull the mail coat over his head. No decent woman would do what she had done—send into the streets to do the thing with any man she could find!

"He's mine," he said, laying the hauberk on the floor beside the bed. It would do the lad good to sleep with Joceran and the Gascon knights in the barracks; before the age of eight most well-born boys were in pages' training. "The boy's mine, as you know full well. He will be called Julien."

While she stared at him openmouthed, Niall shrugged out of his padded gambeson, then unlaced his cross garters and threw them across the room. Then his boots.

"Jesu," he muttered. He wiggled his cold and cramped toes. "Get into the bed," he told her. He hiked forward on the edge of the bed to peel off his hose and drop them on the floor.

He heard a faint, gurgling sound. When he looked up she stood with one hand clutching her throat, staring at what was between his legs. The expression on her face made him swear again.

"Holy Mother of God," she whispered, not moving her gaze.

He stood up and swung his arm toward the bed. "Come, dammit, will you get in, or shall I throw you in?"

She lifted those blazing green eyes. "Nay, I am not married to you! It is no marriage when a woman is taken from

her house by force, under threat of having her son torn
from her! The law says—"

She broke off with a shriek as he reached out and
grabbed the front of her cloak. "The devil take the law,"
Niall bellowed. He was naked, the room was cold, the night
had been hellish and he wanted to get to bed. By jerking
his arms up and down he managed to shake her out of the
cloak. She reeled back, staggered, and fell onto the bedcovers.

He moved his body over her quickly. Under the cloak
she wore a richly colored gown of silk and wool. There
was a sparkle of gold chains around her throat, gold ear
bobs in her ears. She looked opulent, beautiful, even as
bedraggled as she was.

Holding her down with one hand, he jerked off the silk
bliaut, then her skirts. She fought him all the way, broke
free and rolled across the bedcovers, spitting like a redheaded cat. He hauled her back, hand over hand, to wrestle
with her shoes, then the hose.

"Villain, perjurer, thief!" She was wild-eyed, her hands
clawing at him as he got rid of the rest of her clothing.
Niall fought her off. He would say one thing for her, she
had courage. It was within his rights as her husband to
beat her soundly for the trouble she was causing him. Her
hair came down from its braids and tumbled like red fire
over her naked shoulders. He could not take his eyes from
it. Nor, God's face, her breasts.

She was naked now except for the gold necklaces and
the dangling eardrops. Her bare bosom was firm, lightly
spangled with gold freckles, rosy-tipped and lush. Below,
her dainty waist was narrow, her hips curving, her long,
perfectly shaped legs delectable. Even the curls in her feminine places were ruddy. He knelt on the bed, looking down
at her.

You could not tell she'd had a child; her body was in
no way marked. She was exquisite, flawless, all creamy

skin and emerald eyes and blazing copper-gold hair. At the sight of her lying under him, that jeweled look glaring up at him, all the old memories flooded back.

He felt his breath thicken in his chest. You would not think that it was possible to go back and have sweet revenge, but by God's grace it had been given to him! He had found her. And he was remembering every moment of that dreamlike night and how he had given her his boy's heart those long years past, in this very bed. And how, damn her, she had trampled it in the mud of a Wrexham alley.

Slowly, he bent his head and touched the tip of her breast with his lips. He felt her shudder. "I will give you anything," she moaned, "only stop! Listen to me, I have wealth that you do not know—"

Her voice trailed away as he lifted his head. "Anything," she whispered.

His hands stroked the full curve of her breasts, flirting with the tight buds of her nipples. She groaned, turning her head away.

"Nay," he said huskily, "not just anything, sweetheart, but *everything*. I will have it all from you this time. And more."

To show her what he meant, his mouth lowered to hers and plundered it in a way that made her gasp. His tongue thrust in.

She tried to resist him, but Niall held her down and kissed her thoroughly, then let his lips caress her silky breasts, the beating pulse in her throat, the small, tender lobe of her ear. At the same time his fingers stroked the trembling flesh of her inner thigh.

Then very slowly, very carefully, his touch explored the soft, moist cleft between her legs while she squirmed. When her body was slick with sweat and trembling, he moved over her, letting her feel his weight, his strength, the straining hardness of his shaft against her. Then he kissed her again, long and hard, until she stopped fighting. He took handfuls of her tangled hair and dragged her face-down against his stomach. "If you bite me," he muttered, "I will strangle you here in the bed."

When she jerked her head up and tried to pull away, he brought her back again by her hair. He thought he would have to do more, at least threaten to hit her, but with a loud sob she surrendered. The first touch of her lips nearly undid him. His quick, tortured thought was that this, at least, she had not forgotten.

He held onto her, one hand gripping her shoulder, the other in her tangled wet hair. The heat of her mouth took him even as he heard her smothered angry sob.

But she was doing what he wanted her to.

And by the tripes of St. David, he thought, dazed, how she was doing it! He barely held onto his sanity as she first ran her tongue around the rigid tip of his straining shaft, then lowered it to lave and suck him with her hot, deliciously wet mouth. She must have known how much this tortured him, for of a sudden her hands cupped under him and gently squeezed as her mouth moved up and down on his flesh.

An agonized growl burst out of him. He teetered on the edge of demented ecstasy. It was he who surrendered first, seizing her by the arms and hurriedly dragging her up across his chest.

He was in a frenzy to have her. He turned her on her back, pushed her knees up and entered her in a rush, heedless of her choked squeals.

Ah, sweet heaven, but she was tight, sweetly burning, clasping him with all the strength of her protesting body! Yet he was true to his vow to the boy. He did not use her roughly.

As he plunged into her yielding softness Niall remembered to slip his hand between them and press on the little nub of her desire. She jumped in his arms and cried out, but he stroked on. Finally she put her hands on his wrists, nails digging into his skin.

His stroking of her feminine nerve peeled away the last of her resistance. She began to thrash under him, moaning. He gathered her hips in his hands, held her up to him, and plunged again and again into her.

Above them the bed shook, tasseled curtains swaying as they had that night long ago. Niall bucked with a violence that nearly threw them over its sides. Then, with a bellow, he raked her a final time and sprawled on her, gasping.

There never had been, he knew dimly, another woman who roused him so. She was all flame-haired devil, evil and conniving as the day was long, but when he held her in his arms it didn't matter.

And now, God help him, she was his wife.

While he lay sprawled on her, she suddenly pushed him with both hands and rolled out from under him. She turned, raising herself on her elbow. She looked down at him.

He knew with some certainty he had not hurt her. So he was taken by surprise when the next thing he knew she had lifted her fist and rammed it into his face.

Niall jerked upright in the bed, his hand at his nose. He stared at her, amazed. She glared back at him, sobbing loudly.

Jesu, the bitch had struck him! And just when he was priding himself on having done it all without resorting to beating her!

With a backhand sweep of his arm, Niall knocked her across the bed. She went tip over naked arse on the far side and hit the floor. She sat there, surrounded by her scattered possessions, looking stunned.

He rubbed his nose. It was, he saw, incredulous, bleeding slightly. She had a respectable fist for a small woman. But by God he didn't intend to give her a chance to do it again. He reached over the edge and took her by one arm and pulled her back into the bed. He had to drag her; her damp, gleaming body with the gold chains and dancing ear bobs was limp, unresisting.

He settled her down beside him. There was a cover somewhere. He sat up again and reached for it, and pulled it over them. He lay back with a groan.

The storm's wind roared around the stones of the Old Keep and banged at something loose in the ward. The room was damp, even chill, as summer always was in the marcher country. They would have to get the fireplace fixed when the masons came.

The woman beside him whimpered.

Wife, Niall reminded himself. He turned his head and saw her staring up at the blue hangings over their heads.

The heat of their naked bodies was finally warming the damp sheets. He felt a sharp, burning twinge of pain in his wounded thigh. But to lie there and listen to the pounding rain was suddenly quite satisfying. A thousand times more so than sharing a blanket and fleas with Walter.

Somewhere beyond the mountains the Welsh prince, Cadwallader, waited to pounce on all he now held as his fief in the valley. Add to that the garrison's Gascon knights biding their time, expecting the rest of their pay. And in London, King Henry impatiently awaiting his share of future profits.

Niall put his arm across the bed, his hand curving down to touch her bare shoulder. He let his fingertips rub against the smooth skin. For now, he told himself, he had more than he'd ever thought in his life to have: Castle Morlaix and its land that his father had broken his heart over, the flame-haired witch who had haunted his years'-long dreams. Her untold wealth. Even a son.

After all the starved years of his childhood and youth, and the war that had made him the young king's ruthless, famed knight commander, it was all *his.*

The thought was like a triumphant, bursting light in his head. A flaming star deep in his soul.

And now, Niall told himself, it was his unholy task to try to hold onto all of it.

And all manner of men that live by meat and drink,
Help those who win your food to work stronger.

Serfs' plea, 10th-century English

TEN

"No, no!" Walter Straunge shouted. He waded into the fray, thrusting out his arms to separate the combatants. "Slash, not poke! You'll get naught from jabbing a sword like that except a fouled blade."

The taller boy stepped back at once. "I was doing as you said, sir."

"The devil you were." Walter took the wooden swords, stuck them under his arm and gripped Magnus by the shoulder. "I have eyes to see with, boy. You fought like a kitchen knave armed with a roasting fork!"

It was plain the smaller lad, Tom, was no match for the lord's new stepson. It was not so much a matter of size but that like most of the town boys, he had no heart for a knight's style of fighting. Oak staves and thrown rocks were the apprentices' weapons, not swords. On the other hand, Magnus made too many excuses. In some other place, such as an earl's household, he would have his whiffling beaten out of him.

Now, Walter noted, the boy stood with hands at his sides, facing him bravely even though he plainly expected to be cuffed for lying. That much he'd learned, anyway, in the past few weeks.

Looking down into those tawny young eyes he was struck once again with the likeness to Niall fitzJulien. Everyone knew there was a story there; the whole garrison buzzed with it. If the lord of Morlaix ever wanted to deny this young sprat was his, he'd be hard-pressed; it was like looking into a mirror.

However, whatever else could be said about the hasty marriage to the goldsmith's widow, it had provided in the nick of time for all they now had. The masons had come from Wrexham almost at once when they'd heard they'd be paid in silver coin. As did the carters and the joiners who now made such a racket, night and day, about the place.

Walter handed the wooden sword back to Tom. The boy was halfhearted about starting again until he explained what he wanted. "For lying to me about parry and thrust," he told the apprentice, "your foe must now defend himself without a weapon."

Both boys stared at him.

Tom looked at Magnus and licked his lips. "Thee gives me leave to whack him in fair fight, when he hadn't no weapon to whack back?"

Walter touched him on his bare shoulder. "Ah, lad, you go to the heart of it, don't you?"

He left them regarding each other warily and walked back to his seat on the stable yard barrel. The sun was hot. The year was approaching its zenith, midsummer's day. Near the stalls the odor of horse dung was strong.

Across the bailey a line of wagons came up the castle road and in through the portal gates to be unloaded, then made their way out again with much noise and raising of dust. The ward was busy with the builders and their barrows, squires grooming horses, and the hurrying, sweating goldsmith's servants unloading the new lady of Morlaix's household goods. The goldsmith's manor in town was slowly being emptied. The bailey had taken on the look of a place filling up with the plunder of war. Iron cressets now lit the ward by night, wains with grain sacks stood waiting by the newly built kitchen, and the grass was overrun with chickens waiting to be cooped. There was even bedding in the knights' barracks, something almost unheard of even in the best of times.

Walter leaned back to watch both boys, who had been allowed to strip off their shirts. They circled each other in the hot sunshine, skinny chests like plucked cockerels.

Tom promptly charged Magnus, who flung his hands up and took a series of blows on his forearms and shoulders. "Ow, ow!" he screamed, flinging Walter piteous looks.

Wildly encouraged, little Tom landed several hard blows on the top of Magnus's head. Each time Magnus yelled. Out of the corner of his eye Walter saw his new liege lady leave her maidservants and start across the ward. He knew why she was coming.

He would have wished for just a few moments more for the combat to settle itself. But Magnus, with a lump on his forehead and a little blood flowing from it, finally pounced on Tom and wrenched the wooden sword from his hands.

"By the c-cross!" The taller boy was red-faced and spluttering. "You would *hurt* me, wouldn't you, y-you little rat? All you want is unfair advantage!"

Tom tried to stand his ground. But, swinging the sword like a scythe, Magnus charged him, hitting him across the ribs.

"Stop! Boys! Stop!" As Walter had expected, the lord's new wife came running up in a swirl of skirts. "Holy Mother, who told you to set them at each other? Look at Magnus, he's bleeding!"

She wore her hair wrapped in a white cloth, but drooping red-gold curls escaped about her forehead and cheeks. Even without the goldsmith's money that came with her, only a blind man could have resisted the lord's wife.

She stamped her foot, furious. "Tell them to stop! I do not want my son to learn swordplay. He is training to be a jeweler!"

"Milady," Walter said, "I do what the lord of Morlaix tells me to do."

Tom and Magnus pressed their half-naked bodies against her restraining hands. The young apprentice had tears in his eyes, having a taste, now, of what his true lot in life would be like. The other boy, panting and triumphant, was getting a glimpse of *his*.

She managed to part them, and put her arms around her boy, murmuring to him, stroking his sweaty hair. Walter had noticed that when she could spirit him away from Joceran and the garrison knights she brought him cake and fruit and tried to coddle him. Joceran was under the lord's orders not to let her.

Walter crossed his arms over his chest and leaned back on the barrel. He felt rather sorry for her. The boy wasn't a baby, although she went on treating him like one. He supposed she had little other use for her affections, and certainly was not likely to find any in their ironfisted new lord. Who at that moment was not too far away in the outer bailey with his squire and the farrier, helping shoe his warhorse.

"Mamma!" Magnus shrilled, "look what he's done!"

She had been trying to press a simnel cake into his hand. Tom had taken the moment to land a kick on Magnus's shins. When the apprentice turned to run, Magnus started after him, sword swinging.

"I'll kill you!" Magnus screeched.

She managed to catch him by the sleeve. "Dear God, don't say that! Tom Parry is your fellow apprentice, your friend!"

He glared at her. "Not now! Don't you understand? Not *now* he isn't!"

The other boy had run between the wagons into the outer bailey. "I'm not going to be an apprentice anymore," Magnus was yelling. He shoved her away. "Never! I'm going to be a knight!"

Walter stood up and brushed at his padded gambeson. "Knights obey their lady mothers." He took him by the ear. "Make your apologies, sprat."

She grabbed Walter. "Let him go! You're hurting him! Holy Jesus, do you want to wrench his ear off?"

At that moment the Lord of Morlaix appeared, followed by Joceran and the Chirk farrier. He was bare to the waist, wearing only hose and boots. He led his stallion up to them, growling, "The devil take it, what's all the squalling about? Have you nothing else to do? They can hear you all the way to the town."

Magnus broke away and ran to him. "Oh sir, I was beating that little rat of an apprentice, but he ran away!" He brandished the wooden sword. "Ask Sir Walter. He gave me punishment, but I was brave and overturned it!"

Niall looked over the boy's head to Walter. "Where is the apprentice now?"

Magnus looked scornful. "Run back to town, the weasel. He hit me when I was unarmed! Oh sir," he begged, "let me go after him!"

His mother hurried up, her coif fallen down around her shoulders, her flame-colored hair tumbling free. "Holy Mother, don't set him on poor Tom, he's had enough!"

The Lord of Morlaix shouted, "Damn you, don't interfere!" To Magnus he barked, "If you started it, finish it."

Magnus gave a screech of joy and raced away.

"Dear God, why did you do that?" She held her hands to her flaming cheeks. "It's bad enough I never see my child, but now you are teaching him to be like the foreign riffraff that hangs about this place!"

"What drivel are you talking? Do you want me to order the boy to the goldsmith's shop to make the other one a confounded gold ring?" He took the rag Walter offered him and wiped his sweaty chest and arms. "Julien is going to be a knight, not some puking merchant!"

For a moment she held her breath. Then she burst out,

"He's not a puking merchant! I am a knight's daughter of *lawful* birth. Although that estate may be strange to you! I know why you are doing this. You think you are revenging yourself!"

He hurled the rag back at his captain. "God's wounds, keep it up, and I will send the boy to London, to the king's court. Henry will be glad enough to have him."

She stepped back. "You can't do that!"

He bent forward to shout in her face, "*Can't do it?* By Jesus, I am lord here! Unless King Henry say me nay, I do what pleases me. And if you think on what I get in bed of you, madame, you will know the damned truth of that!"

She gave a low, humiliated cry. Walter Straunge stood to one side. By now the whole castle could hear the lord and his wife shouting at the top of their lungs. One would think they hated each other.

Certainly, Walter couldn't help thinking, the lord tormented her about her pampered boy. But what the Lady of Morlaix had said about lawful birth—since all knew Niall fitzJulien's father was an earl's bastard—was not calculated to soothe him, either.

He saw her expression suddenly change. She lowered those blazing green eyes. "I beg you, milord, I ask only for a little kindness. Not for myself—"

He shouted, "Hah, I give you as much kindness as you give others. In back alleys! Shall I say to you now in front of all those who can hear me what sort of 'kindness' yours is?"

Her eyes lifted to him for a second, as though she would say something. Then she clamped her lips together, lifted her skirts, and started back across the ward.

Walter watched her go. The words about what the lord got from her in bed hung in his mind as he contemplated the sway of her hips under heavy skirts. "The boy is strong," Walter said, absently, "and has a good arm. Mother-coddled as he is, it may be that his training is best done here."

The man beside him did not give any sign that he heard as he stood watching her retreating figure. Then without a word to Walter, he turned and stalked away.

One of Emmeline's maidservants met her with an armful of basins and pillows. The girl cried, "Oh, mistress!"

"Hush," she told her, "give them to me." She took the pillows from Hedwid's arms. She told herself she wasn't going to weep there in the ward with half the castle looking on. The girls followed, murmuring sympathetically. Emmeline kept going. To the Old Keep, up the tower stairs, the maids trailing her. Once inside the lord's room she dropped the bundles on the bed and sat down on the edge, willing the tears to come.

They wouldn't come. She was still too angry. She leaned forward and held her head in her hands. Blessed Jesus, she had only herself to blame! Cloris the matchmaker had tried to reason with her, warning her she'd waited too long to marry again. All the woman had said had come true. She'd been seized and forcibly wed by a ruthless lord who'd wanted her money. Now she was trapped. So was her boy. Niall fitzJulien could make good his threats by sending Magnus away to the earl's court at Chester. Or to London to King Henry. He could even be put into a monastery as an oblate, a child gift to God, to become a monk!

She rubbed her burning eyes.

God take him, the Irish lout who held them captive believed he was her son's father! But this fight-for-hire adventurer who had forced her into marriage, dismantled her household, stolen her strongboxes and the fortune in them, was not and never could be the yearning young knight who had held her in his arms in this very bed years ago, and made love to her! Never! She rejected it with all her heart!

She threw herself back against the covers, her fists at her mouth. Oh, Blessed Mother, that night in his arms had been a sin against God and nature. She had willfully taken it into her own hands to have a child with someone other than her lawful husband. And that, everyone knew, was the mortal sin of adultery. God was punishing her. If, during all these years she'd ever confessed her horrible crime to a priest she knew he would have told her that she would live with her punishment forever. Not just in this life, but beyond.

She choked back the sobs that rose in her throat. Yet much as she tried, she couldn't feel repentant. Dear God, even now!

Worse, Emmeline thought as she looked up at the tasseled curtains above her, she had dreamed of that night for years. It had never seemed such a dreadful thing—to have made a child with a young man she remembered as so beautiful, so ardent, so tender.

She couldn't stand to lie there any longer thinking about it. She rolled over and flung herself out of the bed. The candles had burned low and the room was growing dark; she looked around for more, but the girls had not yet brought them up.

She had to escape. She could not bear to live with this crude and baseborn Norman-Irishman, who above all else that he did, corrupted Magnus, her beautiful, gentle boy who had been happy learning the goldsmith's trade. He would try to make him another knight. Another murdering brigand like himself.

And God and the saints knew, Emmeline thought as she paced the room, his incessant desire for rutting made her very flesh rebel. He would not leave her alone. He craved to bed her every night of the week until she prayed for her monthly flux when she had an excuse to go and sleep with her maids.

She knew what he wanted, she told herself as she turned and paced the room again. He needed children, heirs, and to get them as quickly as he could. That was all men of his class thought of.

Worse, she could not always refuse him. With his soldier's brothel-skills he knew how to raise her passion until he could make her moan like an animal in his arms, wanting whatever he could give her, begging him unashamedly for her release. Niall fitzJulien saw to it that she was forever in thrall to him.

She turned and paced to the window high on the side of the tower, built for the old lords to look out over their desmesne. She rested her elbows on the sill. The shutters were open, the afternoon air still warm.

From the old keep the castle overlooked the valley the Welsh still called Llanystwyth, although it had long been known by its Norman name of Morlaix. The window gave onto the west and the hill country, cut by the glistening thread of the river. Below on the castle lands the wheat and barley were ripening, gold-green against the dark of newly plowed fields. In this wet country, mist streamed from the mountaintops like smoke, and when the sun came out after rain it spawned a sky arched with rainbows.

The Welsh marcher country was green and fertile. The country folk and townspeople, if left in peace to work the land and trade its bounty, grew prosperous, well fed. Only kings and nobles and their knights wished to rip it apart with their warring.

She raised to her toes to lean far enough out to see a line of wains returning from town, crossing the bridge below, carrying more of her household goods.

She wished she were not so filled with despair. But to escape she needed somehow to get her money. With enough gold she could take Magnus and go north to Chester and take a ship to Scotland or France. Along the way she was sure the guild of the goldsmiths, at least, would help.

She bit her lip.

Niall fitzJulien had her strongboxes filled with gold and

her accounts. And God's curse on him, she did not know where they were kept! Even if she did, she couldn't think of a way to get to them.

But somehow, she thought grimly, she had to save Magnus and herself. Dear heaven, if she stayed here, if he forced her to live with him, she knew that sooner or later she would have to kill him.

Later that afternoon a band of peddlers came up from the village. The hawkers had first to go the burghers of the town to get permission. The merchants had looked into their packs to see that nothing that could be made in the valley was to be sold by them. Then the peddlers made their way out the river road and the castle.

When the packmen came through the portal gate they were greeted with squeals of excitement, especially by Emmeline's maids and the scullery girls, who fell on the ribbons and fancy combs and the salves for the skin, and ointments for thicker, more beautiful hair. Baudri Torel, now seneschal for the castle, came out with the bailiff to look over kitchenware. Even the knights wandered up, following the girls, and stood chaffing and flirting with them by the kitchen door.

The cook bought blocks of salt, and looked at small cloth sacks of spices: cloves and cinnamon brought from the Holy Land by way of France, dried garlic, rare herbs from Venice and Malta.

Emmeline bought a featherweight of Toledo steel sewing needles, ordinary bone needles, and some handsome black silk frogs for fastenings for a cloak. She had no money of her own; she had to send one of the knights to the lord of the castle to ask for some, which annoyed her. It was the first time she'd been without her own money.

Torel drew her to one side of the young spice peddler. "The prices are too high," he told her in an undertone.

She didn't doubt it. Everything was scarce, still sky high even though the war was more than three years past.

The peddler protested, "Cinnamon alone is worth its weight in gold! Come close and listen." He beckoned her to sit by his pack spread open on the grass. "I swear to you, gold is the counterweight when both cinnamon and clove spice are measured out."

He took her for some dull-witted Norman man-at-arms' wife. She leaned over to see his face.

God and St. Mary—he was not a monk this time, Emmeline saw with a shock. But he made a very convincing peddler with lopsided grin, a jaunty green cap over his brown curls. She quickly waved her steward away. "I will see to this myself."

The peddler took that moment to break a stick of cinnamon into fragments, and pressed them into her palm. He rubbed them back and forth with his finger. The pungent odor rose at once.

"What in God's name are you doing here?" she whispered.

He grinned at her. "Ah, if you will but smell it and taste it," the gold courier said, "you will see what I mean. It has come a long way this day." He fixed her with his bright blue look. "From far, far over seas."

Emmeline touched her tongue to the cinnamon fragments. Far, far away meant France. He carried gold this time from King Louis in Paris to pass onto the Prince Cadwallader of Wales.

At that moment, the dusty taste of cinnamon filling her mouth, Emmeline realized how far she was caught in their schemes. She was the lord's wife now, virtually a prisoner here in the castle. Would he understand that if she tried to tell him?

She carefully brushed the crushed cinnamon bits back into the fabric bag he held for her, trying to think.

This was not her plotting, but that of her dead husband's,

may God rest his soul. Until he died Bernard Neufmarche had received regular deliveries of gold from the French king to send on to Wales. The money, at least in the early years of the war, went to help King Stephen by having the Welsh attack the empress's castles in the marches. Sometimes, Emmeline found, it went to bribe the Welsh prince, Cadwallader, to do whatever he thought best to serve his own interests. Which often meant not giving his support to either side.

When King Stephen died and the empress's son, young King Henry, at last ascended to the throne the gold, to Emmeline's surprise, still passed in through the eastern ports, transported by a new courier. From Morlaix, the goldsmith's house gave it to shepherds to carry across the mountains. In the past few years though, there was not only the bribe from King Louis in Paris but now also gold and silver secretly sent by King Henry's own English enemies—a few of his own seemingly loyal nobles who wished to keep the Welsh strong and rebellious. Among them was the powerful Hugh Bigod, once the prince's supporter, who now more or less opposed Henry Plantagenet.

"The shop," Emmeline said, picking up another small cloth sack and sniffing at it, "is closed now."

The courier's eyes were hooded. "Tell me where to leave my burden. It must go over the mountains soon, as it is expected."

She handed him back the packet of spice, not knowing what to do. Then the thought struck her that the gold the courier carried, meant to buy the favor of Prince Cadwallader, was just what she needed to rescue herself and Magnus.

God's face, what a wicked thought!

She stared at the courier a long moment, her mind full of raging temptation.

It was dangerous even to think such a thing! If she stole the gold, if she did not pass it on to the shepherds to take into Wales but took it to buy passage from England to Norway or Denmark for herself and her child, they would come after her to kill her.

Emmeline gnawed at her lip. On the other hand, perhaps not, if she got an early start before it was missed.

He had been studying her closely. "Must I take it back?" he asked. "It will be the first time in all these years that my packages not go where intended." He shrugged. "If that is the case we will have to find some other—"

"No, no," she whispered hurriedly. She picked up pouches of cinnamon and cloves and handed them to Hedwid, who had just come up. "Find someone to pay for this," she told her.

Just let me think.

Tomorrow she could go back to the manor house with the wagons with an escort of knights. She would give the excuse that the almost empty house must be straightened up. That she needed to find caretakers; it was too fine a house to let it stand unoccupied.

"In the marketplace in the square," she told him as Hedwid came back with the coins. "At noon, on the morrow."

The gold courier nodded. He picked up his pack from the grass, stuffed the spice bags into it, and ambled off into the ward. Emmeline, trembling a little with her excitement, left the maid to collect her purchases.

ELEVEN

The boy knelt in the rushes on one knee, holding up the platter rather shakily. Thomas à Becket looked down at the page, not unaware of the squire hovering in the background, waiting to ward off disasters.

"May I serve you, milord?" the child piped.

England's chancellor studied the platter of roasted doves and onions the boy held up at eye level. Becket's mouth quirked. He was finding Castle Morlaix infested with redheads. His informants had told him some days ago that the boy was Niall fitzJulien's new stepson. Although, as his spies had also pointed out, the unusual resemblance indicated something more. He couldn't help thinking that King Henry, a connoisseur of good stories, would love it.

Down the high table the gilded little beauty, watching them while trying to listen to the Cistercian prior at her side, was the redheaded child's mother. She, too, had hair the color of new-polished copper.

The new Lady of Morlaix, the chancellor had been told, was a knight's daughter and granddaughter, her grandsire being the venerable Simon of Wroxeter, famed scholar and old King Henry's close friend. But there was no money in the family, as was so common with lesser nobility. So, dowerless, the girl had been married into the merchant class, to an elderly goldsmith now long dead.

Thomas studied the redheaded boy for a long moment.

"Take your thumb out of the dish when you serve it," he said. "Its presence in the sauce offends me."

The squire heard him and immediately jumped forward. Thomas à Becket waved him away.

"Are you listening to me?" Overawed, the child could barely nod. "I do not know what rude upbringing," the chancellor went on in the same pleasant tone, "they give to young pups here in the wild marches of Wales, but when training to serve your betters some thoughts should be uppermost in your head. Such as, a thumb as sooty as the one you possess belongs at the *edge* of the plate. And not in the gravy."

He was making his point as he usually did, softly and with a delicate edge. The child actually shivered. Beside him Thomas heard the master of the woolmen's guild chuckle.

Thomas allowed himself a chilly smile. The truth of the matter was that although Archbishop Theobald had elevated him to the post of England's archdeacon a few months ago, Thomas himself came from merchant stock. The Becket family were prosperous provisioners and chandlers on London's docks.

"A likely lad, young Magnus," the guild master offered. "The new lady here——" He hesitated. "That is, the lord's wife, Lady Emmeline, thought to apprentice her boy to the gold trade of his father, old Bernard Neufmarche. But now—er, Sir Niall seeks to train the stepson for a knight."

"Hmm." Thomas picked up the wooden spoon from the platter and helped himself to another roast pigeon. He was sensitive to rough provincial fare and always traveled with his own cooks. But from the steamy odor wafting up from the birds he detected a glaze of honey and cinnamon. Perhaps the Lady of Morlaix had already put an educated hand on her new kitchen.

Around the grassy ward, for they were dining outside since the castle's great hall had yet to be completed, were the chancellor's retinue of men-at-arms, knights, cooks, grooms and horse boys, and his small army of personal servants. Flies and gnats drifted in from the moat, as well as the usual stinks. The servers carrying food from the kitchen house had to step over masons' barrows and lumber to get to the tables. But the evening sun that slanted down from the castle walls was golden, and the diners had grown somewhat merry. Only the Cistercian monks the archbishop had sent to Morlaix for the new chapter house, were making a frugal dinner of black bread and salted cabbage.

Thomas studied the monks over the rim of his cup. In escorting them to Morlaix he was acting in his capacity as England's archdeacon, rather than King Henry's chief minister of state. The Cistercians were a formidable order now dominated by the monk, Bernard of Clairveaux, and it was said they were dedicated to prayer and the mortification of the flesh, including fasting and the wearing of hair shirts, like their leader. As a result they were in constant pain, their backs and ribs perpetually frayed and bloody and peppered with running sores.

Thomas sighed. He was far from an admirer of ascetic orders; his own luxurious way of life was testimony to that. However, the archbishop was undoubtedly wise to use the Cistercians to reestablish the mother church there in the borderlands. From all reports the country people were still prone to various heresies, backsliding and heathenism. And one could not rely on the Celtic churches of the region, Welsh or Irish, that were wild and undisciplined, and favored odd theologies. Their half-civilized priests often married. That is, when their private lives were not even more scandalous.

The chancellor drew his dagger from his belt and deftly sliced the meat from the dove's breastbone, using its point to carry the piece to his mouth. Another page came up, offering fresh plums cooked in whey. Thomas shook his head.

A burst of applause broke from the high table. Beyond

the wool factor sat the Earl of Chester's bailiff, and beyond him, the king's new marcher sheriff, also from London. On the far side of Master Avenant was one of fitzJulien's shabby-looking vassals, Hugh de Yerville. They were applauding a group of well-dressed servants who suddenly appeared and herded some villagers onto the greensward before the tables. At the same time two bagpipers and a drummer came forward.

The chancellor sipped his wine, stifling a smile. To try to provide some sort of entertainment in spite of the castle's disordered state did not go unappreciated. He could see there was to be more after that. Waiting across the courtyard were a handful of archers carrying the famous Welsh longbow. They were to have a shooting exhibition as well. A prime enjoyment.

It was more, actually, than Thomas had expected. Perhaps, he thought as he wiped his mouth and leaned back on his bench, the Irishman hadn't been a bad choice to hold Morlaix after all. He was well aware fitzJulien was somewhat deficient in bloodlines for all that his father had been an earl's bastard. The mother was Irish—an unstable, unpredictable race.

At court, it had been widely thought that Henry had been too generous to make fitzJulien a baron. The old empress's famed boy commander had, after all, been no more than a rough-and-ready adventurer. But the king was fiercely loyal to his mother's supporters, and one could not help but admire fitzJulien's first moves here at Morlaix. Lacking money and men, he'd acquired a rich goldsmith's widow and with her, the chancellor's spies had told him, some appreciable treasure.

God knows, he thought, looking around, the man was diligent. The castle curtain wall and the kitchen house had gone up in record time aided by the new lord himself, who was not above lifting a timber or pushing a barrow when it made a good example.

Becket signaled for the redheaded page to refill his cup. It was too bad that he had arrived when fitzJulien was away pursuing Cadwallader's raiders, who had recently burned a village. But it gave him time to observe the discipline and good order, the work proceeding well on the rebuilding. Even the villagers, now jumping about on the grass of the ward like frenzied oxen, he found in better condition than in some of the king's other districts.

Of course, there was also a muted air of discord that one eventually came to notice. The new wife was plainly unhappy that the squire and fitzJulien's captain were never far from the stepson. For all her yearning looks, they never let her boy out of their sight.

One would never mistake such close surveillance for commonplace duty. Were they keeping the boy from her? Was the new Lord of Morlaix, as the goldsmiths' companies complained in London, holding the stepchild hostage, to assure the mother's obedience in an outlaw marriage that had confiscated most of her property?

Thomas's body servant came up with a skin of his favorite French wine. He gestured for the man to offer some to Master Avenant, and leaned forward to look down the table again at the Lady of Morlaix. She was a toothsome little piece; no doubt fitzJulien had fully enjoyed her. On the other hand, confiscation of a guildsman's property was a serious matter. The guilds had grown strong during the anarchy of King Stephen's reign, and were now quite adamant about their rights. Henry had sent word from France to his chancellor that whatever this complaint was about fitzJulien's wife, he wanted no trouble with them.

Thomas à Becket told himself that the goldsmith's treasure must be a large one to have tempted the Irishman to marry without first asking King Henry's permission. FitzJulien had a reputation for being brash, but one could see the widow's money had aided him greatly; one had only to look about the castle to see what it had accomplished. But he was aware such a rash act as marriage meant a large fine. The affection in which the king held him—Thomas was mindful that fitzJulien had saved young Henry's life at the siege of Atliers—would hardly help him in this.

He took a sip of wine and rolled it about on his tongue. Beside him the wool factor was watching the villagers stamping through their country dance. He knew Master Avenant was impatient to get down to business.

The archdeacon had been overseeing the razing of some of King Stephen's supporters' illegal castles when he'd received the petition the burghers had sent. That is, about the forced marriage of a woman guild master to the local lord, and the lord's appropriation of the goldsmiths' property.

Now, he thought, watching her, the widow was safely married so there was no tinkering with that. The goldsmith's fortune was what needed settling. Thomas told himself King Henry would want at least half as the fine for marrying without permission.

The serfs finished their cavorting and went trooping out of the ward, followed by the bagpipers and the drummer. Men-at-arms came forward to set up the archers' butts. Thomas noted the castle steward, in rich black velvet and gold chains, who came to the high table to converse with his lady.

She frowned, then stood up and leaned across the board to tell him something, apparently about the archers. Thomas's servant bent forward with more wine for his cup.

"You will enjoy the shooting, milord," Avenant said. "They be masterfully skilled, these longbowmen. The bow itself what stands as tall as a man, will drive a shaft through six layers of wood at a hundred yards."

Thomas murmured something. He was watching the Lady of Morlaix. She wore a green woolen bliaut, her red hair braided and twisted with gold and silver links studded with gems. No doubt fitzJulien prided himself on his good fortune; she was a sumptuous little doll, delicate but well curved. He suddenly tried to imagine them together.

Thomas had never seen a woman naked. The whole court knew he was chaste, and proud of it, like so many of his clerkly profession. There were many clerics and accountants in the service of the archbishop—as the chancellor had been—who elected to obey the laws of chastity for the sake of God and, in most cases, their careers. The archbishop looked favorably upon those who were strong enough to deny the hungers of the flesh. Thomas was blessed, also, to have deeply loved his devout mother who had guided him and taught him, and died when he was only twenty.

However, he *had* seen lewd pictures. He thought of them sometimes when he was looking at elegant women like the Lady Emmeline of Morlaix.

The paintings he had seen had been crude, luridly colored scenes limned on panels of wood, kept carefully shuttered and locked by the priests, and opened only for the instruction of young men on the terrors and temptations that led to eternal damnation in the depths of Hell.

Now the pictures of whores and harlots suddenly came back vividly as he watched Lady Emmeline talking to her steward. Thomas stared, fascinated, as she lifted a hand to brush back a strand of copper-gold hair from her brow.

The women in the terrible German paintings had been positioned with legs wide to show their places of female lust. The harlots and whores, lounging back on chairs and pillowed couches, their pale bodies with knees spread apart, showed their shockingly strange genitalia. Thomas had found it impossible to take his eyes from the red and pink folds, pale, fleshy mounds, all framed in dark hair. Rather, he couldn't help thinking, like hungry, gaping mouths in a beard.

Even now he could not say whether the sight had alarmed or shamefully aroused him. He remembered only the spellbinding ugliness. The memory still burned in his mind.

"If you want my thoughts on it, milord," Avenant was saying, "what it's come to now is lord's rights against guild rights. It wasn't her choice to marry, it was *his*. We were all there to witness, we saw how it was. He jumped at her at the oath-taking and put his hands around her neck, he did. With all due respect to the new lord, he saw what was to be gained." The woolman took a deep breath. "But she is still one of us. A goldsmith and a guild master."

Thomas à Becket turned to him, eyebrows lifted. Some heads of guilds in England's west country were women. Although the church was vigorously opposed to the practice, and worked to stamp it out.

The Lady of Morlaix sat back down in her seat. A herald picked from among the garrison knights lined up the Welshmen with their bows at the far end of the ward.

England's chancellor leaned back to enjoy the shoot. He was not born of the warring class, and far preferred archery and wrestling to bloodier sports. Some of which had become even bloodier with the growing popularity of tourneys.

What they first needed to do, Thomas told himself, was determine the size of the goldsmith's treasure.

Before they began to divide it up.

From the high table Emmeline watched the Morlaix bowmen form a line to shoot. She was glad she'd asked Torel at the last minute to shift the targets so that the archers faced at a wider angle away from the table. There were still many in the borderlands who owed allegiance more to Cymry princes than the young Norman king; no one wanted to see King Henry's handsome, blade-nosed chancellor take a sudden stray arrow "accidentally" through his heart. That was the way the first Norman King Henry had found his way to England's throne.

More importantly, Emmeline didn't want the hue and cry raised for someone's murder, when she took Magnus and slipped away.

She would have to hurry now, she thought, looking around. The shadows were growing longer as the sun sank behind the castle wall. A courier had already left for the Welsh hills to find Niall fitzJulien and his company of knights and tell him that the king's chancellor, Thomas à Becket, had arrived at the castle. So the Lord of Morlaix would be coming back before too long. How long, she couldn't really be sure.

She looked down at her hands knotted together in her lap. *Dear Holy Mother, she had not planned her escape to happen so soon.* She did not know if the guildsmen in the town who had said they would help her, in particular Nigel, the young fuller, had even received her message.

The sheriff sitting next to her, a Saxon from Wessex, called her attention to the first flight of arrows. All had landed center target or close to it.

"Ah, milady, a fine display!" The big sheriff turned to her, nodding approval. "Verily, to make a contest now, they will have to move back the targets."

She gave him an absent smile. Walter Straunge had already sent men-at-arms running across the ward to move the butts farther back. As soon as it was twilight the chancellor surely would end the feast and take his secretary, the bailiff and the sheriff and his army of servants and retire to his elaborate camp in the meadow. The Cistercian monks had asked for shelter inside the castle, in the stables; Baudri Torel had seen to them after getting Walter to move out some of the grooms and the men-at-arms.

Once their guests were retired for the night, she would go to her chambers, tell one of her maids to find Magnus and somehow spirit him away from his caretaker, the squire Joceran.

Shouts and applause resounded as the bowmen made a

spectacular hit. Emmeline rubbed her forehead with her forefinger and thumb. She had to pick one of her maidservants who could keep her head and think of some good excuse to send her to get Magnus away from the squire. A spot between her eyes throbbed painfully. All she could think of was the ruse of calling Magnus away to the jakes. One of the maidservants would not come to do that, not unless he was sick. So some one of them had to be sick.

Dear Jesus, she was not good at this sort of thing! Emmeline closed her eyes. Noisy acclaim for the Welsh archers beat in her ears. She still had the gold King Henry's enemies expected her to send on to Prince Cadwallader. It amounted to quite a sum.

If her courage did not fail her this was what she planned to use to travel north to Chester, then take a ship to Scotland or Denmark. When she left Morlaix, she would undoubtedly be pursued not only by Niall fitzJulien but perhaps Prince Cadwallader, too, when the Welsh prince realized that his gold payment was not going to reach him.

"Milady, you look pale," the sheriff shouted. "Have some French wine!"

Emmeline managed a smile. When she left Morlaix she would leave behind all that she had known since her girlhood: memories of her husband, the comfortable life he had offered her, her valuable manor house in the town, her servants, the trade she had so painstakingly learned. Even the bed where she had borne her son.

She would leave all this carrying a sack of stolen gold, fleeing for her life. Her stomach churned painfully at the thought. But she would not live here at Castle Morlaix with a man who abused her, took her son from her, stole her wealth—forced her to lie with him! She knew if she failed and he caught her he could bring her back, imprison her, or even kill her.

She swallowed, hard.

The guilds would not allow the king to let it happen,

Emmeline told herself. It was for Magnus's sake, anyway; she would do anything to save him from being a murdering beast of a knight.

TWELVE

"I don't want to go anywhere," Magnus cried as she dragged him down the path to the river. "I want to stay here and be a knight!"

"Hush," Emmeline told him. "Have you lost your wits? That madman who thinks he has married me will turn you into a murderer. And beggar me, besides!"

She saw the white blur of her child's face as he looked up at her. She was in a frenzy to get away; at any moment Walter or Joceran would discover Magnus was missing. She told herself she would explain everything later. In her hurry she stumbled over a root in the path, almost dragging them down. It was well past compline, and most everyone had gone to bed, which had aided them greatly in their escape from the castle. But it was dark as pitch along the river bottom. They careened into bushes and vines as it began to sprinkle rain. Every few moments there was a flicker of lightning that showed a storm was coming down from the Welsh mountains.

She was looking for Nigel the fuller. She had been so occupied with getting Magnus out of the castle that she had not considered the guildsman might not answer her summons. Or that she might not be able to find him there in the blackness along the bottoms.

Ahead they saw the ruins of the Lady Chapel. Emmeline gave a sob of relief. When Magnus tried to hang back she panted, "Come, we must escape this accursed place!"

He pulled at her hand. "I don't want to! I want to be with Joceran and Walter. And the lord!"

Near the ruined nave a shadow separated itself from the other shadows. "Holy Mary, I could hear you coming half a league away." He stepped into a patch of moonlight. They saw the handsome fuller with his short-cropped beard and glinting eyes. He held a brown cloak over his arm for Emmeline. He frowned at Magnus. "Why did you bring the boy?"

She stared, surprised. "God's face, why would I not? Where are the horses?"

"There are stories that the boy is fitzJulien's and not the old goldsmith's," he told her. "If that is true, the lord of Morlaix will come after us and kill us."

She tried to peer around him. Why hadn't he brought the horses? "He will come after us and try to kill us, anyway. Are you afraid? All you have to do is take us as far as Wrexham. The goldsmiths' guild there will help us."

The fuller stepped toward her. "Mistress Emmeline, I am the only one to answer your message, the others would not come. They say you are married now, and that if you want justice you must appeal to the king."

She turned to look at him. "What are you saying? I sent a message, I know the guildsmen along the way will help us."

"They will if you send the boy back." His eyes were on Magnus. "Perhaps then the Irishman will be satisfied and not pursue you. As for me," he said, his voice suddenly husky, "believe me when I say I will risk all I have to help you. But in the name of heaven, you must say you care a little for me."

Magnus dragged at Emmeline's arm. "Mamma, don't go. Let us go back!"

She glared at both of them. "God's wounds, be still, both of you!"

The rain began to pour around them. They had gone

nowhere yet, and she was already soaked through. Now, no horses, and a lovestruck fool who wanted her to leave her own son and go away with him!

Moving slowly from the weight she carried, she hauled Magnus around and pushed him toward the river path. "Sweet Jesu, how can we go anywhere on foot?" She was very angry. "I bribed half the castle to get us out, and now look at us!"

The fuller hurried up behind her. "You know I care for you. Holy Jesus in heaven, will you listen to reason? Where are you going?"

"There's no ford here, we will have to use the bridge." When Magnus dug in his heels, she dragged him on. "On my oath, no one is going to keep me here, not after all I have done to leave! I am going into town to get horses."

"You are mad." They were out of the cover of the trees. "Look behind you," the fuller pleaded. He trotted to keep up with her. "They have discovered you're gone at the castle. They have opened the drawbridge."

Across the river, someone was approaching from town. In the dark they could barely make out a column of horsemen, stray sparks of light from arms and mail.

"Mamma!" Magnus cried, "it is Lord Niall coming back! Look—"

She slammed her hand over his mouth. They ran for the bridge that way, lurching from side to side. But she held onto him.

They did not make it across. Lightning zigzagged in the sky. In the brightness the leading horseman saw them, spurred his mount, and raced toward them. On their side of the bridge he reined in. The big destrier reared, whinnying. The Lord of Morlaix shouted, "Where in fiery hell do you think you are going?"

The rain suddenly came down in sheets. There was another deafening roll of thunder. Magnus struggled to break away, but Emmeline held him by the back of his jacket.

"I won't go back!" she screamed.

Knights came cantering up. One kicked his horse into a gallop to chase the fuller, who was running back the way they had come.

Emmeline knew they would kill him. She threw herself at Niall fitzJulien's stirrup and locked her hands around it. "Let him go!" she begged. "Nigel Fuller did nothing. He was only helping us!"

In the heavy downpour the destriers shouldered one another. She grabbed at Magnus to keep him from being knocked down. A knight, his mailed collar pulled up to cover the bottom of his face, reached down and took Magnus by one arm and lifted him up onto his saddle.

Emmeline staggered. She couldn't recognize anyone with helmets and long nasals covering their faces. "Listen to me," she shrieked.

The big horses milled in the road. The Lord of Morlaix shouted orders. The knight came trotting back, the fuller tied by a rope and dragging on his belly. The fuller's face was bloody.

"What are you doing?" she screamed. "Don't punish him!"

The fuller, yanking on the rope, tried to get to his knees. Emmeline would have run to help him up but Niall fitzJulien moved his big destrier to block her. He leaned down to shout, "Shut your traitorous mouth!"

He reached down and took her by the arm and would have dragged her up on his horse before him, but instead he suddenly remained that way with one hand on the pommel, leaning into the air, not able to budge her.

She looked up and saw his tawny eyes widen under his helmet. "What the devil!" he growled.

He slid out of the saddle. A group of knights moved their horses around them. "What in Satan's name is this?" His big hands in mailed mitts prodded Emmeline's shoulders, then her waist, then shoved up under her soggy skirts. "Gotselm!"

The knight serjeant dismounted and handed his reins to one of the knights. "Don't touch me," Emmeline cried. Gotselm held onto her as she twisted.

"Damned if I could lift her," Niall fitzJulien was saying, "she's heavy as a millstone."

He rucked up Emmeline's wet skirts to her hips. When he bent the rain poured off the rim of his helmet. His groping hands found the bags of Prince Cadwallader's gold bound to her thighs with leather straps. The same way the gold courier had carried them across England.

Kneeling in the mud, Niall fitzJulien untied the straps. He hefted the leather bags in his hands, weighing them. The knights leaned from their saddles to watch.

"Gold, by the cross! No wonder lifting her was like trying to shoulder an ox." He got to his feet, breathing hard. He stuck his face in hers. "Is there more treasure you're withholding from us, madame?" he shouted. "Perhaps hidden somewhere between your tits? In your crafty money-lending little cunt?"

Before she could move he ripped the cloak from her shoulders. When he jerked at the top of her bliaut copper and gold pins flew off as the cloth parted. The pelting raindrops suddenly beat upon Emmeline's bare breasts.

She screamed. She lifted her free hand to strike at him, but he seized her wrist as his hand grabbed her belt and ripped it away. Then the soggy mass of her skirts.

She shrieked curses, trying to claw him with her free hand, but that iron grip was locked around her wrist. Now she was almost naked. Still he would not stop. His hand raked the pieces of the shift that still clung to her. Her cloak, her skirts lay on the ground in the mud.

Gotselm stepped forward. "Milord—"

"Goddamn her," he roared, "she has hidden hoards of gold all over her! Where's her lover? Do you have him?"

Emmeline screamed, "He's not my lover!"

He whirled on her, lifting his hand as if to strike her. But instead he stopped, bent, and picked up some leather bags. "Carry this," he told Gotselm, "hand the rest to me when I mount."

The serjeant picked up the sodden cloak and threw it around Emmeline's nakedness. She couldn't stop sobbing. The Lord of Morlaix swung himself into the saddle, then reached down and dragged her up before him.

She felt Gotselm's hands on her leg, pushing her forward. The rings of the mail dug into her back. She knew Magnus was somewhere behind in the column of knights. It was all that sustained her.

She closed her eyes, telling herself she did not care what became of her; she would be better off dead if it were not for Magnus. She wondered what had become of Nigel Fuller. If he were still alive. She twisted in the saddle to look up at Niall fitzJulien's face. "What will you do with me?" she croaked.

"Shut your mouth." He tightened his arm around her. "We have King Henry's beloved ferret, Thomas à Becket, camping before us."

The king's chancellor. She had almost forgotten.

She squinted through the rain, realizing he wanted them to pass to the castle without rousing Becket. They started across the bridge. The tents stood silent in the dark and rain. They went on up the road to Morlaix Castle.

At the curve the chancellor's picket challenged them. When Gotselm answered the knight raised his spear in salute. "Milord Morlaix, God welcome, I hope you have had good hunting."

"Tolerable." Niall inclined his head toward the rear and the Welsh prisoners. "A few of Cadwallader's birds who will not sing so sweetly for some while." He kicked his horse ahead and the column moved. "Godspeed to you, sentry, and hope for a dry morning."

The horses' hooves were loud on the boards of the drawbridge. The portcullis gate was open, torches flaring under the arch. Walter Straunge was waiting. Garrison knights ran forward to take the horses' bridles. Walter came to Niall's stirrup. He looked up and licked his lips. "Milord, I swear I did not know she—"

Niall hit him on the side of his head with his fist. The knight captain reeled back. Then, saying nothing more, the Lord of Morlaix rode on into the bailey.

THIRTEEN

Dragging her by the wrist, Niall mounted the stairs, shouting for someone to bring him hot water. At the top, the guard knight rushed to open the heavy wooden door. Emmeline sank to her knees, but it made no difference: with his big hand still locked around her wrist he skidded her through the doorway and did not let go until they were in the middle of the room by the bed. She sank down in the rushes, huddled in the fuller's brown cloak.

Walter was right behind them, followed by the serjeant, Gotselm.

"Milord," Walter said. He held his hands outstretched, pleading. "She sent one of her maids to entice Joceran while she made her escape. The boy's not used to that sort of thing. While he—"

At the top of his lungs, the Lord of Morlaix relieved himself of a prolonged obscenity. His captain winced. Gotselm hurried to help Niall out of his long mail coat.

"Walter, you consummate ass," Niall shouted, "for all the good you have done me this night I might as well get a begging bowl and take to the road as a monk! Christ Jesus, in the last few hours I have force marched over ten leagues in the damned Welsh mountains, harried by every sheepherder and pig tender with a hunting bow, to get here before the king's spy master Thomas à Becket confiscates my very bed and board from under me." He yanked off his sweat-stained padded underjacket and threw it at him.

"And you have proved yourself worthless when you cannot keep your eye on my treacherous wife. Who, I now find, will run off with any passing peddler unless I can properly chain her!"

Walter swallowed. "Nay, sir, I do not think Lady Emmeline was dandling the fuller, if that's what you mean. I think he—"

"Goddamn you, do you know how the chancellor will relish telling all this to the king?" Two menservants with buckets of hot water and a washbowl rushed into the room. Niall sat on the edge of the bed as Gotselm knelt to pull off his boots and cross garters. "Thomas à Becket will report most gleefully to our glorious sovereign that he found me off in the mountains chasing Cadwallader's thieves while my wife was cuckolding me, fleeing my castle in the company of a local tradesman, her skirts full of my gold!"

Emmeline shivered, listening to him shout. The cloak the fuller had given her was soaked through, her teeth were chattering. She closed her eyes, thinking this day was yet something more she would have to atone for in hell. Her sins would not be forgotten; she was certain she would go there.

In her sinful wickedness she had stolen the money intended for Prince Cadwallader, and now it was in the hands of the one man who should never have it—his enemy, the Lord of Morlaix. Worse, Niall fitzJulien plainly regarded the gold as part of old Bernard's fortune, since he'd found it on her, and therefore rightly *his!*

She held her head in her hands, wanting to weep. Was there ever a woman so thoroughly cursed? At the very least, her husband could throw her in Morlaix's dungeon and leave her there to rot.

Or he could kill her right there.

That was more likely, she told herself. He thought she was an adulterous wife, and death was the usual penalty. She felt a sob rise in her throat. It was her own reckless will that had gotten her into this—as it had in the beginning, when she had plotted to have a child. Her fate had been sealed years ago by the one rash act that had brought Niall fitzJulien into her bed.

She would acknowledge now in the depths of her miserable sins that, pride-cursed, she had not chosen to be like other women, the ones the priests held up as models of virtue. Obedient women, agreeable and spiritless and accommodating, who left the running of important affairs to men.

Instead, she had done what her demon will wanted, and had her child by a stranger. It was not important that Magnus had brought her boundless pleasure and comfort; she was not supposed, as a woman, to fly in the face of God and nature by doing such things. Now God was punishing her.

Or perhaps, she thought, watching as the Lord of Morlaix stepped out of his braes and dipped a rag into a bucket of steaming water, it was punishment by the Devil.

Naked, Niall fitzJulien bent and washed his legs, first one, then the other. Battle scars crisscrossed his back. A newer scar, the skin around it still inflamed, ran slick and pink across his hip and onto his thigh. Gotselm the serjeant knelt to towel him off.

She bit her lips. Surely he was going to kill her. It would be easy: he was a big man with his broad shoulders and narrow hips, bigger than either Gotselm or Walter. Far bigger than any of the men servants who were hurrying in and out to light the fire and bring dry clothing. With a shudder she watched the muscles in his back coil powerfully as he lifted the dripping rag to scrub his neck.

She knew that body far too well. Those powerful swordsman's arms that could hold her helpless when he wanted her. His knobbed shaft, thick and long, with an equally large sac below. In bed he rode her with driving, insatiable lust, satisfying himself more than once. Unless he was so tired working with hay gangs that he fell asleep after his first release, flopping on top of her.

She told herself she could not bear it any longer.

But a small voice in her head reminded her that he had Prince Cadwallader's gold. Emmeline truly could not help it; she sobbed aloud.

Walter turned to look at her. Gotselm was using a linen rag to dry Niall fitzJulien as he stood, still naked, drinking a cup of wine. The servants moved around the room, taking away the water buckets, and his sword and mail for the squire to clean.

Walter said something that she could not hear. With a scowl the other man turned to look at her. "No, I am not going to kill her. Not with the king's chancellor roosting in the meadow, eager for any tales of misrule to carry back to London." He handed him the empty cup. "When Becket leaves will be soon enough."

Gotselm and Walter shot her startled looks. Both wanted to speak, but he herded them to the door and saw them through it, then slammed it shut.

Emmeline jumped to her feet. She had only a little while left if he was going to kill her when Thomas à Becket departed. She thought of Magnus, of leaving her orphaned child. Of trying to arrange now for some sort of horrible revenge on Niall fitzJulien to take place after she was dead.

"You can't punish Nigel Fuller," she cried, "the guilds know he is innocent! Even if you kill me the wool guilds will keep on with the matter, for the fuller is their man. They will petition even the king!"

He whirled on her, snarling, "God rot it, your mouth flaps all the time and does not know how much my fist itches to close it! Where is the rest of the gold? How much more of your fortune have you hid from me?"

She stepped back. "The—the rest of it?"

He stalked her, fists clenched, a sheen of perspiration on his bare shoulders. "You were going north to have your pleasure—where, after you left me? Rutting in an inn in

Chirk for a sennight? Entertaining your clay-handed pimp in a bawd house in Chester?"

Her mouth fell open. She backed away. "I was going to the guild houses in the north, to ask that they help us. The fuller was not going with us, the gold was only for Magnus and me!"

Rage fairly burst from him. "Damn you, the boy's mine!" He reached out and before she could duck he had grabbed her around the throat with both hands. "Try to take him away again," he shouted, "and I will come after you and kill you— on my word!"

Emmeline pried frantically at his hands. His fingers dug into her neck. The muddy cloak flapped around them. With an oath, he tore it from her shoulders and threw it off into the room.

She sank to the floor, rubbing her throat. He was going to strangle her next time; that was how he would kill her. He strode away from her, kicking pieces of clothing across the floor. She watched him favoring his wounded leg.

"Cripple! Beast!" she croaked. "I know why King Henry has only given you only a borderland fief. It is because you are not a whole man!"

He stopped stock-still. Then he turned. When she saw the look on his face she screamed, "Kill me now and have done with it!"

He stormed back to stand over her. "I'll kill you when I'm ready!" He was shaking with rage. "As God is my witness, I knew from the moment I set eyes on you that I was cursed. You used me for your foul purposes that night in Wrexham when I was blindfolded and brought to you. I was nothing but an innocent boy—"

"Innocent? You whoremaster! In that very bed"—she pointed with a furious, trembling hand—"you were hardly innocent! In all truth, you taught me such coarse, lustful acts as I'd never dreamed of!"

"Be still," he thundered. "I have title and fortune now,

damn you. I will lock you in this room and keep you here
before I will let you wreak havoc on what I have!"

"What you have?" She jumped up and followed him
across the room. "It is my gold you're spending! You would
not have this castle without it, your precious knights would
leave you! Did you forget to tell your lofty king's chancellor that?"

He turned and seized her wrists. "I tell Thomas à Becket
nothing, and neither will you. Hellcat you may be, but you
are my wife." He started toward the bed, pulling her.
"God's wounds, my wife you are until I say nay!"

He flung her on the bed. She scrambled away from him
on all fours, long hair flailing.

"Get back in bed," he roared as she slid to her feet on
the far side.

"Never!" The bed was between them. Panting, Emmeline
ran around it toward the door. She was almost as naked as
he; only a few tatters of her shift clung to her. She reached
the door. "Take my money and be damned to you!" she
howled. "May God curse me forever if you get anything
else from me—unless I am dead!"

He reached her before she could open the door. "What
a vile-mouthed hellcat you are, to call me crippled!" He
seized her shoulders and shook her. While she was still
reeling he picked her up and dumped her over his shoulder.
He strode across the room, limping.

He dropped her on the bed and naked, male flesh rigid,
he rolled in on top of her, jerked up her legs and thrust
into her.

Emmeline gave a scream of outrage. She thrashed under
him, clawing at his back, trying to gouge at his eyes, no
longer caring that he would certainly kill her.

In return he held her down with the weight of his body
and battered her, his great shaft bucking into her and filling
her up as though he would possess her, conquer and subdue
her through the sheer force of his strength. She saw his

contorted face over her, his red hair hanging in his eyes, his mouth parted, the sound of his frenzied gasps—*uh, uh*—filling the room.

She tried to scream for him to stop but she did not have the breath. She wanted to kill him as much, she realized, as he wanted to kill her!

Suddenly she found herself moving with him, inflamed by their anger that licked like bright, scalding fire around them. She grabbed fistfuls of his sweaty hair and yanked with all her might. She took the force of his raking thrusts, met them by locking her legs around his body. She reached up for him, her fingernails boring into the smooth skin of his shoulders.

She heard him grunt.

Then he lifted her bottom with his hands and thrust so deep and hard into her that she cried out. The old bed danced with their frenzy, the tassels flapping. They went mad, taunting each other with raw desire. The coverlets became tangled around them, trapping their legs. Still they did not stop.

Suddenly with a loud groan he bent his head and seized her mouth roughly, thrusting his tongue inside. It muffled Emmeline's shriek as her body stiffened, then convulsed with a peak that was like hellfire and blackness. Like the world come to an end.

Her scream mingled with his bull-like roar as he bucked and thrashed with his own peak. Suddenly it was like a landslide, a mountain moving down on her as he let his body go slack. His sudden weight was punishing. She gasped for air.

While she quivered, her own passionate tide slowly ebbing, he lay on top of her with his fingers threading her tangled wet hair, his breath at her ear. Still groaning.

Emmeline closed her eyes. Dimly she thought how much she hated him. He had stolen all that she had: her child, her house, her money—her thoughts were beginning to be filled day and night with desperate plots of how to regain what she'd lost. She felt nothing for him; it was unholy lust that brought them together like this in such violent, shameful pleasure.

She felt him shudder. In the soft, sensitive center of her womanhood his flesh stirred, wet and reluctant, and slowly slipped out of her. She heard him take a ragged breath. His arms tightened around her.

His face was pressed into her neck and shoulder. The odor of his sweaty big body, musky and sensuous, filled her nostrils. For a moment her hatred wavered. Suppose he had already gotten her with child?

A traitorous rush of tenderness filled her; she quickly fought to put it out of her mind. She tried not to think of babies, marriage, a happy and comfortable life such as other women dreamed of. That was not for her.

Lying there under his wet and still throbbing body, Emmeline told herself she would go somewhere out of England with Magnus. That was still her plan. If she had to kill the Lord of Morlaix to do it, then she would.

He had not moved. His hand was still in her hair, stroking it. She turned her head away.

She felt him stir. "Go put out the candles," he said.

She lifted her hands to push him off. He rolled away to the other side of the bed, untangling the covers about his legs as he went.

Emmeline put her feet over the edge and stood up. She did not bother with a covering; God knows he had seen her naked enough times. None of her clothes were about, anyway; he had torn them to shreds in his fury at the bridge and there, later, in the lord's room.

The warmth of the day had faded. She shivered as she padded to the candle stands. As she put out the flames one by one with her thumb and fingertip the room grew dim. She carried the last taper to the table by the bed, blew out the flame, and got in beside him.

She did not know whether he would want her again. At least he had not rolled over to put his back to her. He watched her; she saw the gleam of his eyes.

She pulled the covers up to her chin. Her bare body ached from his strength, from her own passionate responses. What he had put into her was still sticky between her thighs. She thought about a child again, uneasily.

She tried to keep awake by thinking of ways she could murder him. One could cut a belly strap on his saddle so that it would break at a full gallop and he would pitch forward and die under the hooves of his own stallion. That was a not-too-uncommon accident.

When he went deer hunting in the forests in August, the "grease-time" of the slaughter of the young bachelor stags, he could be shot through the heart "accidentally." That, too, was not uncommon. Although she knew the problem would be finding someone to do it. At King William Rufus's death in New Forest, everyone knew Walter Tirel had killed the king that way, even though he managed to flee England safely and live out the rest of his life in France.

She pressed her knuckles to her mouth, wondering why she felt so much like weeping. She hated Castle Morlaix. She would do anything to be away from there.

Beside her, in the darkness, he said, "I'm sending the boy away. He is going to someone, a friend of mine, who has a proper castle garrison, and will see to his training for knighthood. Joceran goes with him."

She lay still, hearing his words, so anguished that she could not breathe. He was going to do what he'd threatened. To take Magnus from her.

She told herself it was useless for the time being to fight him. When she could speak, Emmeline said hoarsely, "Where?"

There was a silence.

Then he said, "You are not to know."

FOURTEEN

Joceran and Magnus left long before dawn light. Almost no one except the portal gate guards saw them go. Emmeline had no chance to make any sort of goodbye, to even see that Magnus carried the right sort of clothing away with him, or to give him a final tearful mother's hug and kiss. Nothing.

Later Gotselm brought her the leather folder of Magnus's goldsmithing tools that had long lain, the serjeant told her, under one of the barracks' beds in the knights' tower.

"Pax, milady, the boy wanted to be a knight." Gotselm plainly meant to be consoling. "And not a craftsman as you can see, since the tools have been so long forgotten under the beds. The boy's a fine lad. His spirits were high when the squire led him off on his pony. I heard his voice piping in the dark all the way down the castle road. It was questions this, questions that, where were they going, how long would it take to get there, would they stop at an inn on the way?"

Unable to bear any more, Emmeline shut herself up in the tower room and wept all morning. Her servants going about their work pulled long faces in sympathy, although some had expected the lord to at least beat her senseless and shut her up in the bottom of the donjon where the prisoners were held. The serving maids from the manor house thought fitzJulien would put her aside, and send her to be confined in a convent. However, when the girls came in at noon with a meal of a cup of ale and some meat and bread and saw the lord's clothes scattered about and the rumpled bed, their faces suddenly beamed. Merciful God, he had already forgiven her!

They got Emmeline out of bed to dress her. "Ah, now what you need to do is fill that up," Hedwid said, patting her mistress's stomach. "With the boy gone, bless his little heart, you need a new babe to take up your time."

The thought of Niall fitzJulien's child inside her filled her with violent feelings. *Never,* she told herself. She did not regard this as a true marriage, only robbery and imprisonment! How could someone like him father her child?

He had fathered Magnus, a small voice reminded her.

She stood despairing while her maids bustled around her. It was useless to deny it any longer. The night in Wrexham was no dream; the clumsy, impassioned young knight Aimery and Gulfer had brought to her and this unfeeling, ruthless man, King Henry's new-made Lord of Morlaix, were one and the same.

A wave of bitterness so harsh swept over her that she began to weep again, great tears rolling down her cheeks.

The next day the Lord of Morlaix went off with Gotselm and a troop of knights to chase Cadwallader's sheep thieves, leaving Walter in charge of the workmen on the outer walls. Emmeline shut herself up in the tower bedchamber to grieve over losing her child, and to plot how she could find out where Magnus was. But after a steady stream of Baudri Torel, the cook, her servants, even the stable master mounting the tower stairs with complaints of what chaos there was with only the foreign knights in charge, Emmeline gave in and came down.

In the ward, Walter came up to her, grinning through a mask of soot, even his long blond hair streaked with black.

He had been helping the gang of joiners lift away kitchen roof beams burned in the fire.

"You have a gift," he told her.

She didn't want to talk to him. He was as bad as the rest, wooing Magnus away from her with his swordplay and his so-called knightly arts. She started across the ward to the kitchen, where the cook was fighting with the kitchen knaves. He kept up with her, still grinning. "You don't want your gift now, after all the pleading to be allowed to keep up your fine house?"

A pair of hunting dogs ran up, glad to see her after a lapse of a few days that they jumped at her, pawing her skirts. Emmeline pushed them down.

"The whole castle is marveling that he did not kill you," Walter was saying. "Now, an even greater marvel—he gives you what you want. The women are here."

"The Beguines?" She nearly tripped over the hounds. She had asked for caretakers for the manor house. But she couldn't believe it. "Holy Mother, don't tease me! Where are they?"

"Where would they be?" He cocked a mischievous blond eyebrow at her. "Where you want them. In the town."

She didn't wait to thank him. Walter deserved no thanks, Emmeline told herself as she picked up her skirts and ran toward the stables, calling out for someone to saddle her mare. She heard him shout, "I told you it was a gift. Remember that."

The two Beguines consisted of a strapping aunt, very much the big, fair Fleming lowlander, and a willowy niece with a sculpted face, downcast eyes, and the palest of fine gold hair.

Emmeline could have danced in her excitement. Both women looked able-bodied enough to do what their contract promised: the very best of household management including all cleaning, cooking, spinning, weaving, stilling, dairying and buttermaking, egg and poultry and dovecote production, the pickling and smoking of other foods and, of course, management of servants.

When Niall fitzJulien had given his permission to bring the Beguines up from London, she was sure he did not know all that it would entail. But she was finding that unlike many fighting men of his class, he did have some grasp of property. The house in town was much too fine to let it go to wrack and ruin. To finally have the women there to look after it was pure joy.

They were not cheap. The older Beguine usually asked a wage of two copper pennies every fortnight, and the girl one penny. To get them to travel north to work in the Welsh borderlands she'd had to offer three pence for the elder, and the younger, one and a half. But, Emmeline told herself, they would be worth it. The Cistercian monks had left the goldsmith's manor, where they'd been staying until they put up their chapter house, some weeks ago. The place was quickly showing signs of disuse.

It had been Emmeline's hope that no matter what happened she could keep the manor intact. The Beguines had the highest of reputations, being devout—although not an order of the church—observing a chaste, hardworking life of piety. Everyone had heard of them, even in the far west of England. It seemed to Emmeline that in a world where women had little choice but marriage or the church—or whoring—the Beguines provided something even better. They did not marry, they led chaste lives independent of men, and made their profession of the oversight of households a high art. They were already famed for the quality of their stilling and brewing, especially their fine Frisian ale, and preserved foods such as ham and pickles. From all accounts their numbers were growing in the Flemish lowlands, where their contracts for household management were little interfered with by the church.

The same was not so, unfortunately, in northern France. There the Bishop of Rheims had issued an order to the city burghers to warn their citizens not to hire Beguines on the grounds that they violated, by working outside the home, their Christian role as women as laid down in the Holy Bible.

Of course the same charge was often leveled at women in the guilds, even those who had merely taken over their husbands' businesses when they'd been widowed. Most women who were members of craft guilds, or even masters in their own right, gave heavily to the church to avoid trouble.

Now she looked around the manor yard, thinking about the changes the Beguines could make. The household had had its share of problems with the castle knights billeted in the stables, then the monks living there while they built their chapter house. Already so much had been taken from the inside of the house and carried to the castle that it looked barren and shabby.

"I will have horses here and a wagon shortly," Emmeline told the Beguines as she led them across the courtyard, "for you will need them for hauling. The kitchen is also quite bald now, but I will have pots and kettles and other things brought down from the castle."

Her knight escort lounged by the stables, talking. The gilt-haired Beguine, Berthilde, walked at a pace behind her aunt, eyes on the ground. When they saw her the young knights fell silent.

Emmeline unlocked the doors and stepped into the hall. Downstairs smelled musty from fireplaces that needed to be scoured and bleached. The older Beguine wrinkled her nose. "Lime vater," she muttered in her thick accent. "Needs lime vater und hog bristly brush."

Emmeline showed them their rooms off the pantries, windowless cubicles that would be warm in winter back of the chimneys, but that were hot now in the summer haying season.

Looking around, the big woman gave a grunt of approval. She dropped her bundle on the floor and bent to punch the bed's mattress. Behind her, Berthilde was silent. The younger Beguine kept her eyes so steadfastly on the floor that Emmeline was not sure of their color.

At that moment the girl looked up.

They were blue, she saw with a start. And what a blue! Wide and dazzling as the July sky.

"She no has much Norman French," the other woman offered. She crossed her arms, her coif like a large white sail around her head. "In a little while I teach her some, maybe."

Emmeline was struck with how beautiful the younger woman was with her blue eyes, silver hair, and milk-white skin. The world from the Danish kingdoms to Norman-held Sicily regarded such coloring as the only true beauty. Why, she wondered, would such a lovely girl want to dedicate herself to piety and endless drudgery, no matter how skilled, for the rest of her life?

She supposed she knew the answer. These were peasant women or came from families of lowborn city workers. If they married the men of their class they would soon meet a worse fate. That is, the bearing of children in addition to the backbreaking labor of their lot—if the younger one did not attract the attention of some noble lord first.

She left the Beguines to put away their bundles and explore the kitchen and went out into the courtyard. The old porter came up to her.

"There are things that happen here in the night, in the street, with the house empty," he complained. "We have thieves and robbers now. Mistress Emmeline, you should see to it there are castle knights stationed here to protect your manor house."

He still called her Mistress Emmeline. Many of the townsfolk did. She had always been a good friend to them, especially those who had borrowed money from her; she didn't think they did it to slight her. God knows they had no love for the Lord of Morlaix who drove them so.

"Eudo, you are right, it is the lord's duty, now, to keep the streets safe." Before, the guilds had all contributed money to hire their own armed watch.

She crossed the yard to the goldsmith's shop and pushed open the door, surprised to find it unlocked. She was even more surprised to see young Tom seated at the workbench in a beam of sunlight, hammering out some silver coins. Ortmund the journeyman stood at the window, his elbows on the sill, looking out into the alley.

"Mother of God, what are you doing here?" She hadn't paid their wages since she'd been married. She'd never expected to find them there.

Ortmund turned to her. "Milady." He looked her up and down from her crimson veil held by a silver circlet on her braided hair, to her tight-fitting russet linen gown that trailed on the wooden floor cinched by a belt of silver links. "We have," he said simply, "no place to go."

She sat down on the bench with the apprentice. *God's love. So they had kept working.*

On the shelves behind the table were rows of completed work, finished and locked away, and therefore missed by the lord and the castle bailiffs. The afternoon light lit a silver cup with decorated gold rope around the rim that was intended to go over the mountains to Wales to be used as a monastery's communion vessel. They had all worked on it the past year. Chased silver beads lay in a wooden plate waiting to be strung on a chain for a Chirk merchant's wife's necklace. A hunting horn newly bound in gold and copper bands for the Earl of Chester's court. Too many objects to count. All finished. She supposed Ortmund had not known what to charge for them.

And all this time she had been held virtually a prisoner

in Castle Morlaix, she thought, exasperated. Without even enough of what was once her own money to pay their wages!

"What are you making?" she said to the boy. She picked up a silver coin, hammered flat. "Have we no other silver, that we must melt down currency?"

Little Tom shook his head. "The silver is all gone, mistress." He had inched closer to her on the bench. "The lord's men came in and took everything. They scraped our silver boxes clean."

She fingered the piece of flattened coin, remembering no one had seen Nigel the fuller since that fateful night down by the river. There was a rumor the lord held him in the very depths of the castle, in the prisoners' hole. But she had no way of finding out. All was secret, now; no one spoke to her of anything.

"Take these." She scraped the rest of the coins into a pile and held them out to Ortmund. "This will be more than the wages I owe you. Not forgetting Tom's penny."

He stood in a shaft of sunlight, squinting at her. "What shall we do, mistress? Command us."

Little Tom pressed tight against her. He whispered so low that she almost could not hear, "Mistress, I am sore lonely for Magnus."

The journeyman stiffened, shooting a look at Emmeline. "Now hold your tongue, boy—"

"Nay, leave him." She put her hand on Tom's tufty hair and stroked it. "It does not hurt me to hear from Tom what I feel myself."

She knew they wanted to hear about Magnus, but she could tell them nothing. She was being punished for attempting to leave Morlaix by being deprived of her child. It was a punishment that brought Niall fitzJulien what he wanted, anyway—to have Magnus trained in some lord's court as a page, then a squire.

All the guildsmen in the marcher country knew that in

retaliation for her attempt to leave him the Lord of Morlaix had sent her son to some far place, and now would not tell her where he was. From what her maids told her, indignation about the matter was widespread. A delegation of goldsmiths had appeared before Niall fitzJulien's overlord, the Earl of Chester, protesting the confiscation of the Neufmarche property. But the earl was wary of young King Henry's hero and had dismissed the burghers without a hearing. In all, though, many guilds had pledged to pass on any news they might hear. But it had been weeks, and there had been nothing.

"With this much finished, we must send it out and get our wages," Emmeline told them. "I know the Welsh monks have waited months for their chalice. I will come tomorrow and prepare the tally for each."

Ortmund usually rode his mule to deliver the finished work. The communion cup would go over the mountains to the Welsh monastery with the shepherds. If they could find them.

She looked around at the journeyman and the apprentice, their faces solemn. Yes, all this was their work but the money from it belonged to the lord. Who had already stripped their shop so that there was little left to work with.

"With what we make on this," Emmeline said, "we will buy more metal. We are low on copper and silver, especially."

She saw them exchange looks. It would please them to hold back the money for the completed work for their metalworking supplies, but it was dangerous. She had no idea what the Lord of Morlaix would do to them when he came to claim his profits.

If, she thought wickedly, he ever discovered them! Looking down at the hammered pieces of silver she was reminded that she had forgotten the gold courier. She had not seen him in months.

She could not keep back a tiny shiver. Could the courier,

traveling back and forth as he did from England to France, have any way of knowing whether the last portion of gold had been delivered to Cadwallader or not? Or did the Welsh prince have some way of letting the courier know that the gold had not been forwarded to him from the last stop, from Bernard the goldsmith's in Morlaix?

She rubbed her finger across her mouth with a slightly trembling hand, smearing the acid metal dust. Old Bernard Neufmarche could not have known what evil he'd sown when he first began to deliver King Stephen's gold to the Welsh princes so many years ago. And then later, after the war, when the gold began to come across the channel from the French king to pay those same princes to harry his former wife's new husband, young King Henry.

Now, Emmeline realized, she had deliberately broken this deadly chain. There was no way she could think of, since the Lord of Morlaix now had the gold, that could mend it.

"Mistress?" Ortmund said.

She looked at him, distracted. The gold had not served its purpose anyway. Which was to buy her and Magnus passage from England, because now Niall fitzJulien had it. If only, she thought, looking down at the silver spread across the goldsmith's table, she had Magnus there. She could face anything if she only had her child by her side.

"Let us go back to work," Emmeline said.

They still had time to make a little money. While she tried to think of a plan.

After leaving the Welsh borders the king's chancellor, Thomas à Becket, had gone north to visit the court of the Earl of Chester. Who was not King Henry's friendliest magnate, but certainly one of his most powerful. Then the chancellor took the road back south again to Morlaix.

It was the feast of St. Anne, a hot and airless day, the sun overhead a beating white disk. But the peasants in the fields

sang as they worked, as it was fine weather for the hay harvest. Soon they would be scything the ripe corn, then gathering the beans and peas planted in the spring. Now, lacking
hail, or downpours of rain, it looked as though it would be
a fat year.

The long line of the chancellor's household, monks,
knights, scribes, bailiffs, horse grooms, a pair of troubadors, mules and wagons, and a seemingly endless crowd
of servants stretched at a leisurely pace along the road,
and spent long siestas under the trees in the heat of the
day, where the serfs and villeins brought them fresh water,
red and yellow plums, and ripening crabapples for refresh-
ment.

Becket had not expected to find villeins harvesting a
millet field on the outskirts of the town. Nor the lord himself, Niall fitzJulien, and many of his Gascon knights, all
working stripped to the waist. Such a rustic scene was
drolly amusing. The chancellor called a halt to his column
to enjoy it.

Thomas à Becket had known the new Lord of Morlaix
at court in London. Time had not improved his original
impression of the old empress's wild Irishman, but he knew
of his prowess on the battlefield, the rescue of the young
Prince Henry at a siege in Normandy, and his reputation
in the tourney lists. Now, Thomas saw, somewhere the Lord
of Morlaix had also learned to swing a scythe.

He watched the muscles under the tanned skin bunch
and pull as the new baron rocked the scythe's wooden handle. At the same time his rather harsh voice floated over
the fields, urging the workers to put their cursed backs into
it the way he was showing them. To the rear of the wagons
some kitchen knaves and cooks tittered.

The Gascon knights were the first to notice the chancellor and his party watching from the road. Some dropped
their scythes immediately and struggled through the hay

field, feigning nonchalance, pulling on their gambesons as they came. Snickering among the Londoners broke out.

"Hush," Becket reproved his people. "Where the lord leads, his faithful knights must follow. Even to do battle with a field of ravening corn."

There was outright laughter. At that moment Niall fitz-Julien emerged from the wheat looking like a sun-bronzed pagan god even to the stray stalks of grain sticking in his hair. When he saw Thomas à Becket his face turned rigid.

"God's blessing on your industry, Morlaix," Becket said. The archdeacon of England made the sign of the cross, his lips quirking. "The Holy Book tells us God truly blesses His gatherers of the fruits of His earth."

The Lord of Morlaix was not listening. With a growl he grabbed the nearest Gascon, driving his fist into his midsection. The knight collapsed, sprawling on his back in the earth. The others hesitated. Then in spite of the roars of laughter from the chancellor's train they picked up their scythes and dove back inside the waist-high grain.

FitzJulien turned to face the man on the horse. "Welcome back to my demesne, milord archdeacon. We lost two ripe fields to rain yestereen, and are using all hands to harvest. You must forgive our rude tasks."

"Tut man, don't be testy." The chancellor stopped smiling. "Our gracious king would regard your—ah, diligence as noteworthy. Morlaix, I need the hospitality of your meadow once more to camp ere I make my way back to London."

"It is yours." His tone was barely cordial. "And my table for the evening meal, and whatever else big or small milord desires."

"Hmm." Thomas gestured to his captain, and the column started up again.

The mailed knights, then a bailiff passed by, followed by the grooms and servants, and finally the wagons. In the last wain a singer holding a viol across his knees looked directly at Niall and caroled in a lilting voice about the joy of the lord and his good peasants bringing in a happy harvest time, hey-nonny-nonny-o!

Niall flung an oath after him.

In spite of the fact that Becket carried fodder for his beasts and delicacies for his own table, his guzzling crowd's stay last time at the castle had sorely taxed them. Even victualers with outrageous prices in Wrexham and Chirk had a hard time keeping that traveling army of poppinjays and sycophants supplied.

Niall wished to hell the king's clever minister would go back to London and stay there. They could ill afford the extra mouths to feed as the new grain was not yet in, and the old corn stores were running out; the cook had been relying heavily on marrows and dried beans.

In the distance, on the road that skirted the town, Walter Straunge and a troop of Morlaix knights were coming at a gallop. The reapers in the field had gone back to work. Niall waited, wiping the sweat from his chest with his balled-up shirt.

When he was close enough to shout, his captain wanted to know if that were the chancellor's party ahead. Niall caught his bridle as Walter reined in his foam-mouthed stallion.

"Yes, it is that sweet-smelling ass, Becket, who else?" Under his helm Walter's mouth curved. "Who else crosses England like a satrap's hareem going to a wedding? They have gone on to the castle to make camp for the night."

His captain made a face. "Why does he come back here?"

"Because Morlaix is on the road south."

"Nay, I swear it must be more than that." Walter swung himself out of the saddle. "King Henry does not send Becket to the borders of Wales and back merely to sample the pickled cabbage his loyal subjects will feed him. It is something more, I would bet you a ha'penny."

"We have nothing here for Becket to covet."

"Huh, do not be too sure of that. This accountant is too clever a fellow. It is said Queen Eleanor hates him."

Niall said, "No woman loves her husband's best friend."

"Is that what he is?"

He smiled. "Believe me, I have campaigned with Henry, prince and king, and his appetite is insatiable, but all of it is for women."

The rest of Walter's troop came cantering up. One carried a rough-looking villein, his hands tied up behind him.

"Another pig worshiper," Walter explained. "Usually it's women, middle-aged and fat, who claim they give service to the old goddess and can make charms and spells for the barren and lovelorn. But now there are many like this fellow here. They have blossomed like fleas since the damned Midsummer's Eve, when in spite of your order they had the usual mummery with fires and naked dancing. We have four in the prison hole that preach against church and castle and what they call the robber lords of England."

Niall looked up at the shaggy-haired villein. The man's face was bruised and cut; he had put up a fight before they had taken him. "What say you, man," he said in Norman French, "are you a worshiper of old Cerridwen?"

He had mentioned the local name for the goddess. There was a feral black gleam of eyes from under the tangle of hair, but no answer.

Walter snorted. "If it was me I'd give them the right to worship what they please—pigs, rocks, horse dung—it's all the same as long as the brutes do their work. But they won't be content with that, will they? It's shocking to hear what they say against the nobles."

Niall said, "Put him in the prisoners' hole until our new monks can find some reason to bring him to church trial."

He turned to go back into the field but his captain caught him by the arm. "She is at the manor house again," Walter said softly. "It is the second time this sennight, always at the same hour."

Niall stared at him, the words taking a moment to sink in. "What knights are with her?"

"The most trustworthy. But milady goes into another part of the manor house and closes and locks the door. Jehan and the others are then made to wait. And it's hours while she's in there."

Niall whirled, already shrugging into his shirt. "Get me a horse. I want you to come with me." As one of the knights jumped down and handed him the reins he grated, "No, stay here, I have changed my mind. If I find her with a lover I don't want the whole damned world to know." He hauled himself into the saddle and looked around. "Is it the journeyman gold worker? I'll kill her. The lout is old enough to be her father."

Walter moved to seize his bridle. "Stay, Niall—milord, you do not know—it could be innocent, it could be nothing! Do not let my words inflame you. Since these women, the Beguines, have come, she goes many times to the house."

"Jesus, that's worse! She spends her time locked alone with the foreign women?"

Walter looked harried. "Nay, nay, I did not mean that! I told you, she is in another part of the house, and she makes the knights stay at the stables."

"God's wounds, do you call that innocent?" He turned the horse's head, kicked the stallion hard enough to make him rear, and then started at a gallop down the road toward the town.

"Now he is going to kill her," the knight with the prisoner up behind him said.

The others agreed.

FIFTEEN

Niall galloped down the road and into the town, catching the old priest out for his evening stroll and making him lift his robes and sprint wildly for the safety of the churchyard. At full course he jumped the borrowed destrier over a wine cart at the vintner's door, Viller's housekeeper screaming to God and the angels, then drove the lathered stallion straight through the gate of the goldsmith's manor and into the stable yard, where he reined it to a skidding stop. A troop of garrison knights playing at dice scrambled to get out of the way.

"Milord!" Jehan cried. They goggled at his flapping shirt, his hair full of hay, as he slid from the saddle.

"Where is she?" he croaked.

They lifted their hands to point. *Somewhere on the other side of the house.* He strode off, cursing the pain in his leg which a hard gallop now set to raging.

Damn her! He knew she deliberately set herself to defy him for sending the boy away. She couldn't see it was in the child's own interests; the boy needed to be trained now as a noble, not a craftsman, so that he could fight for whatever he would inherit some day.

No, she wouldn't see that, he fumed. Flouting him like this with her lovers before his own men—before the whole town. She was daring him to kill her!

He wrenched at the handle of a door and it swung open, revealing storerooms at the back of a kitchen. He slammed it shut. She had to be somewhere. She dared not take her lover into the manor house, into the bedchambers; those Frisian women she had hired were there. He saw a face framed in white at an upper-story window. It quickly drew back.

Revenge, that was it, Niall told himself.

She would rather have him murder her, bring down scandal on all of them as her vengeance for the forced marriage and taking the boy away. Ah, she thought herself so clever! King Henry, himself newly married to an heiress and a fiery one at that, would regard the Baron of Morlaix finding his faithless wife with a base-born lover and having to kill her as stupid and clumsy. No one ever lived down the ignominy of being cuckolded. The townspeople would feel the same way.

He dragged open a very small door. It led to the street and barrels of refuse from the kitchen. He kicked it shut.

But God rot it, what else could he do? The world would think him a yellow coward if he didn't strangle her as he found her, beside her lover! He'd been a fool not to have put an end to it days ago, when he'd caught her running away with the good-looking fuller.

The door to the goldsmith's shop was locked. Niall charged it and rammed his shoulder against it and the bar broke. He reeled inside, the force taking him halfway across the room. His bad leg buckled. He grabbed a worktable just in time. He heard a shriek.

He turned, panting.

Jesu, his wife was not in bed with her lover, she was standing with a small hammer in her hand screaming her head off!

As he looked around, Niall realized he was in the goldsmith's shop. Which had no bed, only tables and shelves, furnaces and tools and boxes and buckets.

"What the devil are you doing?" he shouted. "Who is in here with you?"

The place was blazing hot. She was wearing a thin linen

gown with sleeves rolled up and the neck pulled down to
show the damp, milky flesh of her breasts and throat. A
leather apron, he found, staring, did not disguise the lush
curves of her body.

"In here with me?" She stared at him as though he was
a gibbering madman.

He stepped toward her, favoring the agony in his leg.
Her hair was bound up in a white cloth but wet, copper-red
strands escaped to drift about her flushed cheeks. Her lips
trembled, whether with fear or guilt, he could not tell.

"Yes, the gold worker, the old man, where is he?"

An odd look came over her face. Her green eyes widened. "You mean you meant to surprise me here in the
company of all my lovers?"

He scowled, not liking the way she said it. "Hah, you
admit it, then!"

"Admit it? Is that why you burst in here, tearing down
a good door and frightening me half out of my wits?" She
put down the hammer on a metal stand and turned to him.
"Alas," she said, suddenly sweet, "it is not my wish to
disappoint you, milord, but there are too many of them,
you see, for such a small space as this. It is, after all, only
a goldworker's shop. So I have to make my lovers wait,
taking their turns in the wash yard. Stay where you are but
a moment, and I will call them."

She started for the open door, but Niall grabbed for her.
He stepped on something that had fallen to the floor when
he first charged in and crushed it. He managed to catch
her arm.

"Damn you, do not mock me!" He dragged her to him,
at once feeling the warmth and softness of her body even
in the damnable heat. "You still have not told me what you
are doing here."

She threw back her head, green eyes defying him.
"Leave me alone! Have you not taken enough from me?"

The boy. He'd been right about that. "I will take whatever

I want," he shouted, "whether it please you or not. Damn you, you are my wife! What are you hiding from me?"

He reached around her and groped across the table. He'd seen the gleam of silver, when he'd thought the place had been stripped. He lifted a pair of tongs, and some silver wire fell out of their jaws.

"The devil! Are you doing goldsmith's work here?" He picked up the wire. It was still warm, heated to form a filigree that would fit around a blue stone in a clamp. "Show me." He took her by the shoulders and pushed her down on the stool. "Show me how you do this."

She sat with her back straight, staring ahead. The knotted head scarf exposed the smooth back of her neck with its tendrils of sweaty red curls. He suddenly wanted to put his fingers there. His wife was beautiful, delectable—and she hated him. It was a dispiriting thought.

He saw her shoulders droop, heard her sigh. She picked up the tongs and held the wire before an open vent in the clay furnace, skillfully rotating it. The workroom was quiet except for the popping and cracking of the flames.

She knew what she was doing, he thought. He saw the deftness with which she laid the wire on a stone slab and shaped it with the little hammer. To one side lay a collet, a rim that would hold the sapphire, its edge ragged with little teeth that could be pounded down to hold the gem in place. After a few moments she became so engrossed in the brooch she did not seem to be aware that he was standing there.

Looking down at her, at her slender hands moving so confidently, Niall felt a stirring deep inside him. Old Neufmarche had taught her goldsmithing work, an old man with a wife hardly more than a child, the two of them whiling away their time together back here in this workshop. The goldsmith had not been able to give her a babe, so he had given her this.

He knew little or nothing himself about the goldsmithing

craft, but he could see her skill. A master of anything had that rapt, single-minded look: he knew he had it when he was working at practice with his sword.

Ah God, it was better than thinking she was giving herself wantonly to men! He reached down and gave the knot in her kerchief a sharp tug. She jumped up instantly, the table rattling. "What—"

He pulled her up and took her in his arms in spite of her struggles. There was only one way now to explain away his mad charge into the manor before Jehan and the others. His hands gripped her thighs and he lifted her onto the worktable. He murmured, "Don't fight me."

Her eyes widened, cold and green as winter seas. "No, stop!" She struggled harder. "You fool, you will burn yourself!"

"Then don't move."

With one hand he shoved the furnace back on its stone slab. Then the tools with it. Once he had settled her on the wood surface his hands found what he was looking for under her skirts, the slit of her underdrawers and through it the hot, furry opening of her sex like some hidden jewel. Exquisitely tight, clenching sensuously as his fingers invaded.

She could not escape him, trapped on the littered table with its ovens and sharp-pointed instruments. He held her with one hand while he stroked her with his fingers, hearing her gasps of protest. He still held her as he untied his braies and moved between her knees and pushed himself into her.

She sheathed him with hot, reluctant softness as he dipped in and out. He smothered her angry sobs with his mouth. It was sweet, it was as heading as a dozen cups of wine to take her like this; she had never been so responsive, so luscious. So conquered. As her body quivered Niall was remembering that in spite of her devilish scheming she was smart and practical enough to be a good craftsman. Almost like a man. Something in him wanted to possess and conquer that, too.

He held her carefully as they both reached their peak—a quick, breathless torrent, a flood of scalding sensation. So wonderfully intense it left him staggered.

When Niall opened his eyes she was glaring up at him. He put his mouth against her throat and muttered, "When are you going to give me another child?"

She gave a low cry and pushed him away. "Get away from me! Let me go!"

He was tempted to let her fall back on the smelting ovens. But he released her and straightened up and pulled at his hose. Then he reached out to pull her skirts over her knees.

He limped to the door and said, "I will tell Jehan and your escort that you will be leaving."

Niall made a great show of tying the drawstrings at the waist of his hose as he crossed the yard. He saw the nudges and knowing grins the knights gave one another. Their faces said the lord had been in a raging temper when he first burst in, but now—having plainly swived his wife to good effect—he was in great spirits coming back.

The little charade did not make him feel any better. He did not bother to continue to look the satisfied husband as the Gascon's horse was brought up and he mounted and rode it out the gate.

In the street outside he nearly ran down the figure of a musician carrying a viol. The sun was setting, the light not good enough for him to be sure, but Niall thought it might be the same cocky troubadour he'd seen singing in Thomas à Becket's vanguard that day.

But when he turned to look, he was gone.

* * *

"The Welsh cannot win," the chancellor said, "because they follow their princes and not a God-given king. And their princes, being many and quarrelsome, agree on nothing. Owainn of Gwynedd, Rhys of Deheubarth, Cadwallader—they sit in endless council arguing when to raise their armies, or whether to trust their allies. The only thing they know is that their enemy is England."

A voice said farther down the high table, "Sometimes, milord, that may be enough."

"God knows it has taken years to subdue them," the chancellor's bailiff put in.

Morlaix's steward, Baudri Torel, stood behind the high table in the great hall, directing the flow of servers to the kitchen and back. Now he bent over Niall's shoulder and said something in his ear. The Lord of Morlaix shrugged him off.

"The Welsh are never subdued, much less vanquished," Niall growled. "If that is the thinking now in London, then it is wrong."

The bailiff sniffed. "Yes, Morlaix, we have all heard how Cadwallader pricked you hard, right here at the gates of your own castle. Which, I believe he also burned." When Niall glowered at him, he smiled. "Oh, bad fortune, to be sure. No doubt you are more ready for him now that you have gotten the outer walls up."

"Eustace," someone said.

"Nay, I only wish to point out that our glorious king fought in these marches when he was but a fuzz-cheeked prince, and had no trouble whipping the Welsh most properly."

Thomas à Becket said, "Peace, Banastre, this is not wisdom, to twit Morlaix. He has been undermanned since he came. And with Gascons, no less." One of his lackeys was passing a dish of smoked, jellied eels brought from London. Becket helped himself, then pointed to Niall, who declined with a shake of his head. "Our worthy Lord fitzJulien," the chancellor went on, "was Prince Henry's commander in those years you speak of. And if Cadwallader nurses a peculiar ire, it is because he well remembers the trouncing Prince Henry's forces gave him. And the commander who was the cause of it."

"Milord, the king—" the bailiff began.

"Has a dislike for bloodshed, Banastre," Becket put in. "Few know it, but for all that he has bravely seen his share of battles, Henry Plantagenet far prefers discourse and parley to rude warring."

Niall muttered, "Aye, the butchering he leaves to others."

No one had heard him; he leaned forward on the bench to look down the table to see his wife sitting on the other side of Becket. She was looking into the platter of eels the server held for her. She picked up a piece with her fingers and put it on the board, her bright head, braids stuck with dangling gold hair ornaments, bending to examine it.

Even though some of the wives in the chancellor's retinue were exceeding pretty and fashionable, she was still the best-looking woman in the hall. They had been drinking all evening and Niall was feeling it, as witness his remark about the king leaving war's slaughter to his commanders. But he suddenly found himself wanting to be alone with his wife. He watched those bright gold pins twinkling in the torchlight, the curve of her cheek as she studied Becket's pickled delicacy with a wary expression. God's wounds, but he wanted to leave the crowded, noisy hall and the company of the king's lackeys! He wanted to be out of his silk jacket and hose and the Spanish leather shoes he'd never worn long enough to make them feel comfortable, and stretch out beside his wife in their own big bed, perhaps with a good fire going in the fireplace. And a pitcher of wine.

The fancy gripped him so strongly that for a long moment he could not force it from his head.

These days there was damned little privacy to be found in Morlaix. It seemed to him that he never sat down at his own table anymore without wondering how many more

days and nights they would be obliged to entertain the
king's first minister. Who, in spite of some prodding, never
really enlightened them as to what brought him so far in
Welsh border country except the announced reason: that
while King Henry and Queen Eleanor were in Normandy
their chancellor traveled England as their rightful agent,
tearing down illegal castles, appointing sheriffs and bailiffs,
and holding king's court.

Niall knew Henry too well for this to be all of the story.
There was bound to be something else.

Torel the steward came from behind the high table with
a group of kitchen boys acting as ushers. They cleared a
space for the chancellor's troubadors. The Londoners were
devoted to entertainments, and the popularity of singers and
poets was truly amazing. There was a new favorite every
month in the city who captured the public with some daring
song or other, or the way he looked, or the style of clothing
he made fashionable. And there were more with dazzling
reputations coming from France constantly.

Night after night the chancellor's company could not seem
to get enough of them. At the lower tables some of the Morlaix knights got up and went out to the midden pile to relieve
themselves. Niall knew they would not be back.

The two troubadors brought stools and sat down and adjusted their instruments, a viol and a shawm. Niall watched
them glumly. His guest, Thomas à Becket, was undoubtedly
a fountain of wit, a wizard of learning and intellect, but
he still had the cares and duties of his own fief to look to.
Torel the steward had just told him that a delegation of
villeins and sokemen from the hamlet of Wycherly, north
of the river, waited on him in the outer bailey.

Niall knew what they wanted.

All the Morlaix villeins labored together at the hay harvest. The crews chose their own leaders. Perhaps because
of this the haying went quickly, with few failures and disputes. But Thomas à Becket's visit had thrown the summer

awry. The chancellor's horde of knights and servants not only drained the countryside of provisions, but took away good people from the fields to cook and serve at the castle. The result was that the hay cutting had all but stopped. And many fields stood waiting.

The men from Wycherly wanted to speak of the haying, which should be finished in order to begin harvesting the corn. The weather was what one would expect at that time of year: hot and thunderish, with random showers that had already spoiled two fields. Wycherly was the farthest north sector of his fief; all they needed up there was a thunderstorm to lose their hay for the year.

Niall looked around the hall. Crops were the villeins' great worry, while the chancellor's party enjoyed themselves with dicing and hunting and horse racing. That is, when they didn't sit at what seemed like their damned eternal feasting.

He turned to Becket and said, "Milord, a pardon, but there is a matter I must see to in the bailey. In the meantime, command my servants as you would your own, and my lady will pledge my gracious best."

He looked over the chancellor's head and caught her eye. That much she could do for him. He got to his feet and made his way behind the arras and out through the back of the hall.

He crossed the grassy outer yard packed with victualers' wagons. The men of Wycherly were hunkered down under an overhang of the stable roof that afforded some cover from the sun. They were weathered, sun-browned men, their long shirts and ragged trews and bare feet all the same color. When they saw him they sprang up. He could tell they had not really expected him to come.

He stood before them, fists on his hips. He had driven these men hard, taken them day after day away from their fields to rebuild the castle. Some he recognized from the curses they had flung at him from the hedgerows as he rode past.

"We come to talk abaht the hay," someone muttered.

A huge grizzled villein in the back said, "I ha'ant got enough hands for no haying, both me boys is up here at castle carrying and fetching."

Niall said, "What are their names?"

"Little Rhys, Gwern."

It had the ring of truth.

"Big storms are bound to get us this late," another said. "We done lost hay already."

The others made a rumbling noise of assent.

Niall looked around. A few dropped their eyes, but most stared back boldly. He said, "When time and weather's as chancy as this, pray to Lady Luck. And use an old soldiers' trick."

There was a dead silence.

"What's that?" someone said finally.

"The gang masters," he said, "draw lots for the hay fields remaining. And cut hay in that order."

It was hard not to laugh at their startled looks.

"Trust to the tossup? Old Cerriddwen's call?" They looked at one another. "We thought we didn't do the heathen thing no more."

"It's fair," a voice said. "Fairer than what it were before, when our fields waited after the lord's."

"Yea," the big man burst out, " 'tis better for far Wycherly to take a chance on the toss than be last!" He turned to Niall. "We need our men you have waiting on yonder guests at the feast."

Niall said, "Good hay hands will be out of the castle by nightfall. I will see to it myself." He told himself that was one way, at least, to get rid of the chancellor.

"Milord!" the big man said huskily. There was a rustling among them. Niall sensed he had won them; they were about to drop to their knees. He turned away.

"And continue," he told them as he started back across the bailey, "to pray mightily to the Holy Virgin that, until we get the hay in, it does not rain."

Inside the hall, the troubadors had launched into a pretty melody, their voices blending in Provençal harmony. One singer was tall and handsome with well-shaped, muscular legs he displayed in diamond-patterned hose. The other, a slightly smaller man, wore a short capelet and hood. As he bent over his viol it was hard to get a good look at his face.

Although the chancellor's people laughed and applauded at what must have been a very entertaining performance, Emmeline couldn't understand a word. Thomas à Becket leaned to her and tapped her lightly on the back of her hand with his forefinger.

"What you are listening to is the *languedoc,*" he explained. "They are singing in the language of Aquitaine and Provençal, Lady Emmeline, that is called Occitan. It makes a strange sound for Anglo-Norman ears such as yours and mine, does it not? But now all the poetry and songs of the great troubadors are in that tongue. One can choose from the Occitan of Auvergnat, Limousin, Provence, and Languedoc. Or Gascon. I see you have Gascon knights here from that part that is Queen Eleanor's own Aquitaine. The Gascon dialect is very different from the others."

Emmeline sipped her wine. From the faces of the Normans and Welsh, they seemed as baffled by the troubadors' songs as she. All this southern minstrelsy might be the latest fashion, courtesy of England's beautiful new queen, but the lands bordering Wales were accustomed to the singers that came from the north of France, *trouvères* they called themselves, as opposed to the Provençal *troubadors.* The trouvères sang in northern French, the *langue d'oil,* their songs mainly of the conquerors such as Charlemagne and William the Bastard, and thrilling victories and bloody battles. And sometimes, but only incidentally, romance.

The Provençal troubadors on the other hand, sang of little

else. Mostly about young knights who fell unrestrainedly in love with their liege lord's lady, but could not consummate their passion because of their knightly vows. Or something. It was never quite clear. To Emmeline the tales skirted thin ice. The things that the lovers expressed in the songs, the things that the lovers *did* hardly seemed that innocent, no matter what the troubadors said. And would surely have brought about their murder at the hands of an angry husband in England.

Yet the troubadors seemed to rival the king himself for public attention. All England had heard of the *courts of love* where Queen Eleanor and her noble ladies listened to tales about married beauties, lovelorn young knights, and so-called chaste passion.

One of the things one noticed at once about these strange southerners, Emmeline thought, pushing away her piece of jellied eel, was that the worship of the Holy Virgin was very strong among them; they constantly called upon God's Mother, calling her The Dove, The Star, God's Jewel, rather than invoking God the Father, or the Heavenly Christ. It was almost as if they preferred a woman, too, as their deity.

"Gervais Russel." The chancellor pointed out the long-legged singer playing an intricate solo on the shawm. "Russel is a great favorite with Queen Eleanor. But as a troubadour he cannot compare, of course, to the great Bernart de Ventadour, who was troubador to our beautiful lady when she was Queen of France. You will be interested to know that despite Ventadour's name he was not a nobleman. His mother was but a lowly kitchen servant of the Ventadour family in Limousin. But there is a tradition of *gai saber* in the family, lowborn or not." He smiled at her puzzled look. "Occitan words for the 'poet's gift.' It strikes both high and low, and in Aquitaine they generously accommodate it, wherever the troubadour's art is to be found. Of course, there was the scandal—"

His voice trailed away. She looked at the big troubador,

who had put aside his horn and was now, accompanied by the other on his viol, singing some long account of a knight's love for a lady named Alweyn locked in a tower by her cruel husband.

In all the weeks the chancellor's party had been in the borderlands, Emmeline was still amazed at their love of rumor and gossip. If anything, she was told, the king's court was even worse.

She was not naive; after all, she was a widow, a mother, and a guild craftswoman. But the stories the chancellor's people brought with them made Henry the Second to be as much of a lecher as his grandsire, the notorious Henry the First who had boasted that he made more bastards than any man in England.

His daughter, and the present king's mother, who had called herself the empress, was married first to the Emperor of the Holy Roman Empire, then to the present young king's father, the handsome Duke of Anjou, when she was thirty and he but seventeen. And what a family the Angevins were! Even in the border countries of England and Wales people had heard of the terrible Counts of Anjou. Fulk Nerra the Black, their blood-drenched warlord ancestor, had married a ravishingly beautiful evil spirit, Melusine, whom the priests swore was the daughter of Satan himself. And who, after bearing the count's children, turned into a bat in church before the eyes of the whole congregation and flew straight back to hell!

From the gossip, Queen Eleanor and her family in Aquitaine were no better. Eleanor's grandsire, Duke William of Aquitaine, was a prankster and roistering fighter and Crusader, a fine singer and poet who named himself the first of the "troubadors" and abducted a neighboring count's wife, curiously named Dangerosa, raped her, and put her in a tower and kept her as his mistress. He died excommunicated by the holy church. Eleanor's father, Duke William the Tenth, plundered monasteries and menaced abbots and bishops and was excommunicated many times before he died. Queen Eleanor herself was, of course, shockingly divorced from her first husband, King Louis of France. But she had then quickly married young Henry of Anjou, eleven years her junior.

"Many of these troubador fellows feel they must declare real love for their noble lady," the chancellor was saying, "as a matter of form. If one is dedicated to the courts of love, one must be in love. Or so they reason. But Ventadour overstepped his bounds. King Louis, for once, put a stop to his queen's young admirer and Ventadour was punished somehow. I have heard he never came back to France."

The troubador had finished his song and now stood, bowing, to accept the applause. Thomas à Becket clapped heartily. "Of course," he said raising his voice slightly over the noise, "this was while Queen Eleanor was still wife to Louis of France, and before she married our beloved young king."

Emmeline hardly heard him. The things Thomas à Becket was saying about the king and queen made her fearful. She thought of her own scandal: that she had borne a child of one man while still married to another. And that man, the Lord of Morlaix, had taken her now as his wife. It sounded as awful as the Londoners' tales!

She saw that fitzJulien had come back to take his place at the high table. The sun had sunk beyond the castle walls. Servants were bringing out candles and lanterns to set on the table before them.

Emmeline looked down the table at her husband, filled with the terrible feeling that sooner or later she would be forced to tell him about the Welsh money. She had stolen it, she did not deny that; certainly someone would be sent, eventually, to get it back. But just the thought of how he would receive this news made her heart pound.

Niall fitzJulien would never believe that she was innocent. He would see the matter of the gold as pure treason.

Inwardly, Emmeline moaned, feeling she could bear anything if only she had Magnus. She thought of him every moment of the day, worried whether he was well cared for, whether he had a good bed to sleep in, enough to eat.

Her husband was talking with the chancellor's bailiff. Candlelight touched the line of his jaw, the shadows of his eyes, the rather reddened knuckles of his big hand as he gestured.

God and the saints, if it would soften his heart she would throw herself at his feet and beg to have her child back! But she knew it was useless. He never spared her; he thought her some sort of whorish monster for what she had done years ago.

Both troubadors stood up and bowed to loud applause. Emmeline had hardly heard their last song, a duet. The smaller man turned and bowed in turn to the nobles at the high table: the bailiff, the Lord of Morlaix and his lady, the high chancellor of England, Thomas à Becket himself. His hood slid back a little.

After the first shock she knew that he had wanted her to see him. She sat frozen as the gold courier, in his troubador's garb, turned his head and stared right at her.

Cadwallader, Emmeline thought, trying to keep her teeth from chattering, had let them know he had not received the gold, after all.

SIXTEEN

It was the other troubador, surprisingly, who sought Emmeline out, and not the gold courier.

The meadow was a tangle of mounted knights, wagons, and servants, all vying for the one single road that led into town. Thomas à Becket had already taken his leave of the Lord and Lady of Morlaix and ridden away, pleasantly engaged in the company of the Wrexham sheriff, his friends and their wives. But the vanguard they left behind strongly resembled a battlefield rout.

Niall fitzJulien hurried off at once to the hay fields. Emmeline came down into the ward to help the seneschal, Baudri Torel. Some of Becket's stragglers had hitched up a wagon to a pair of mules, claiming it was theirs, and were trying to drive it away. The troubador came up and stood beside her as Torel and some Morlaix knights unhitched the mules in spite of the Londoners' protests.

Gervais Russel smiled. "This is nothing—it is far worse when the king travels. King Henry is devoted to knowing every city and hamlet in his kingdom, but nothing is arranged ahead of time except the lodgings for the sovereign and his lady queen. Everyone else forages as best they can. The magnates, the ministers, the high churchmen fare passably well, but for the rest of us it is anarchy, and the devil take the hindmost. I have seen knights with drawn swords fighting it out for a place to sleep in some byre or hedgerow."

Emmeline said nothing. Becket's men seemed to be close

to blows over the wagon, which was plainly one from Morlaix. She remembered seeing it, its sides painted with clouds and angels, in the Ascension procession. A crowd had gathered. Gotselm, jamming his helmet on his head, came running out of the barracks, shouting.

"It's not theirs," Emmeline said, turning away. She was needed in the kitchen where the cooks were in despair over what was left of their food stores. "Plainly someone has stolen their cart, and they cannot leave without one."

The troubador followed her. One of Becket's servants ran up and took him by the arm, saying they were late and the chancellor looked for him to sing while they traveled to Chirk. Russel shook him off. "Milady," he said, catching up with her, "a word with you."

She gave him a sidewise look. She didn't want his company, she'd been on edge all morning looking for the gold courier in his minstrel disguise, dreading his coming to question her about what had happened to Cadwallader's gold. But there'd been no sight of him. She could not imagine what this other one wanted.

He planted himself in front of her. "I-I, madame—milady—I have heard you have some skill in goldworking."

She stopped, thinking it was some sort of joke. She didn't doubt the gossiping Londoners made fun of her, the Lady of Morlaix. The goldsmith's former wife.

He said quickly. "Nay, my profoundest respects, this is a matter of great importance to me. I would not seek you out, Milady Emmeline, if I did not need to ask your generous aid."

She wondered what he could possibly want from her. Russel was a head taller, his bold, lively face topped by thick black eyebrows. He was quick-tongued, confident; all the women courted his favors.

Now he pulled her into the shadows of the curtain wall by the armory. "I beg you," he said somewhat hoarsely, "before you refuse me, let me show you something."

She wanted to back away, but he reached into his green satin jacket and pulled out a gold chain with something attached to it. He seized her hand and put into it the chain and a piece of crystal. "You cannot know how much this means to me. I broke it, it was an accident, and now I am at my wit's end to find anyone who can restore it to what it was. I cannot wait until we get to Wrexham. Besides, there are reasons—"

Emmeline picked up the pendant. The crystal was particularly fine, of the kind mined in the mountains of Bohemia. There were several in the Neufmarche gem boxes. Flawless crystals, even big ones like this, were not all that rare, but were popular in the courts of Spain and southern France. When cut and polished the blue-white gems were like sparkling chunks of ice. And they could be faceted, the new art of cutting gems that made them much more brilliant and interesting than the old round, polished cabuchons.

This crystal was large, about half the size of her palm, and had been cut heart-shaped, with faceted edges. It had popped out of its setting, a gold filigree collet set with rubies and garnets.

She turned it over, thinking it was worth money, perhaps a lot, but it was too gaudy for her tastes. If Neufmarche's shop had made it they would hardly brag on it.

Still, it was valuable by its very modishness. Half the ladies in court would give their best baubles in trade.

The ladies in court, Emmeline thought. She was sure it was some love gift. "You wear it around your neck on this chain?"

He nodded, eyes downcast.

Her fingers had found the place where the crystal's irregularities fit into the encircling collet. She snapped it back. "It is loose," she said, handing it back to him. "You will have to have it fixed, or the stone will drop out again."

He couldn't believe it. He gaped at the pendant as if she'd just accomplished a miracle. "Is that all?"

She tried to push past him to go to Gotselm and her servants. "Yes. Was that what you wished to ask of me?"

He was still staring. "It was—this, the jewel was broken, I saw for myself!" He held it in his hand, his face contorted with gratitude. "Ah, dear lady, how I cursed my own clumsiness these past few days! I despaired of ever seeing this jeweled heart that is so precious to me—that was given to me by beloved, saintly hands—ever restored!"

"Well, the gem will pop out of the setting again unless you get Bertram in Wrexham or some other goldsmith to solder it."

He still stared down at the pendant. "I cannot tell you what I owe you. You have held my life in your hands, verily." He abruptly dropped to one knee before her and seized her fingers and brought them feverishly to his mouth. "I vow to you that from this day forward I will cherish my love's token with my life. For you have been heaven's own angel to me, saving that which I prize more than breath itself. Milady Emmeline, I shall never forget this."

"Yes, yes." She tried to shake him loose. How people went on about their broken jewelry!

"Call upon me, dear lady, should you need me," the troubador said. "I am your eternal slave. Ask of me anything!"

She ducked past him, teeth gritted. "Nay, I am pleased that I have been of some help."

When she got to Gotselm the chancellor's drovers were still hanging stubbornly onto the wagon. "Are they the last?" Emmeline meant Becket's people. The serjeant nodded.

By the look of their wares, the pots and pans and bedding, the Londoners were peddlers, a ragtag lot. Their wagon, if they truly ever had one, was probably a nothing. "Tell them to give us two blankets and some big stewing pots," she said, "and trade them the wain in return."

The crowd around them gasped. She was all but giving the cart away, unless the packmen possessed something worth bartering. Gotselm barked his orders. The peddlers eagerly began to unload their wares. Torel came up to look them over. Emmeline walked away.

The troubador, Russel, had evidently taken his leave. From the portal gate they could still see the line of Thomas à Becket's party on the town road, traveling between hay fields newly shaved of their crop.

Emmeline felt as though the terrible biblical sword of doom was hanging over her. She hoped the gold courier had gone with them. She had expected him to approach her about Cadwallader's missing gold before the chancellor left. But other than that one look while he and Russel were singing, there'd been nothing.

The seneschal came up behind her, wanting her to look at the pots the peddlers wished to trade for the wagon. Some, he told her, were probably not as good as she wished.

With a sigh, Emmeline turned away.

The weather stayed hot and dry except for one thunder-shower that raked the corn in the eastern part of the fief with hailstones, but did not do all that much damage to the rest.

Midsummer, harvest time, was the best of the year. Day after day a brazen sun rode high in a blue sky. Morlaix held a wool fair the end of July and factors came from London and Flanders. The clip brought such good prices the shepherds stayed drunk for days. The warm, wet spring had made the millet and corn higher and thicker than many could remember. The reapers worked from the hour the sun grew hot enough to burn the dew from the grain heads until the dew began to fall again at dusk. After the first weeks in the fields everyone in Morlaix had a sunburned look.

Emmeline thought constantly of Magnus. The summer before she had gifted him with his first pony, and it had been a battle to keep an eye on him and not let him go off roving the far country lanes. Now she remembered his excitement riding the summer fields with his little mount. The sound of children in the castle ward drew her to the nearest window; she listened without thinking for the sound of her own child's voice. She tortured herself that he was growing up without her. She constantly wondered whether he was in the north, in the country somewhere near York, or if he had been sent south, perhaps to a castle such as Chepstow. Someone, especially among the knights, surely would know. She was dying to ask them. And knew they wouldn't tell her.

Walter was unusually sympathetic. "Don't fret, milady, the boy's all right. I know my lord, and there is no braver, truer knight. He wants only the best for the boy. Perhaps"—he paused—"perhaps some day not too far away he will allow a priest to write a letter so that you will not yearn so much for the lad. Why do you not ask him?"

Ask him? She had enough to bear without crawling to the Lord of Morlaix to beg to have her child write her a letter! It would probably be a false one, telling her nothing. She knew it was a boon he would not grant, anyway.

At night her melancholy moods only seemed to rouse his lust. He wanted another child; his actions said a babe would make up for the loss of her boy. But several times, after his caresses had brought no response, he turned his back to her and fell asleep.

It was at times like these that Emmeline lay awake listening to the harvesters at the threshing floors, celebrating late with dancing and drink in spite of the hard day's work they faced on the morrow. The villeins hurried to bring in the sheaves so that they could thresh the new grain to make

flour for the first bread for Lammastide, the first of August.
A day some still knew by the name of *hlafmasse—hlaf*
being the old Saxon word for loaf. The first loaf at Lammas
brought luck, a good harvest and fat winter. All the roadside crosses would be decorated with flowers and the new-
made loaves of bread, to be blessed by gods both Christian
and pagan.

On the nights when there was a near-full moon traffic
moved late on the roads. It was not uncommon in the summer to have hardy peddlers walking in the nighttime with
packs on their backs and their wains. The past two years,
since young Henry had been their king, there had been not
only packmen and merchants, but preaching friars from as
far away as Paris and Italy, even traveling bands of mummers and musicians who made a meager living in the ham-
lets. Following them came Saracen traders with rugs and
brasses, Italians with beads and cloth, even a few shaggy
Norsemen selling furs.

In spite of the tradesmen there were still outlaws from
the long war who lived in the woods. They were numerous
and strong enough even to attack those travelers with es-
corts of armed knights. The Earl of Hereford's constable
with two hundred mounted knights had launched a foray
against outlaws' dens in the south, took many prisoners,
and held a mass hanging in Leominster. And then there
was a steady stream of fighting men from the Holy Land,
some looking for the king's new baron at Castle Morlaix,
to see if he needed good swordsmen to fight the Welsh
prince, Cadwallader.

Walter Straunge and Niall fitzJulien sat almost daily in
the great hall to talk to these knights. Many were turned
away. One knight was found to have leprosy, which he'd
tried to conceal. One was a former Templar. Niall rejected
him out of hand. "He's a fine-looking man," Walter said,
watching the Templar leave the hall.

Niall made a noise under his breath. "They never let go

of them, the Templars. He may think he is running away, but the Grand Master's men will come after him one day, wherever he is. Besides, I have found there is always something damaged there. If broken Templars pray night and day it is not piety but some unholy sin which they think torments them. If they don't pray that's worse. Then for sure they've gone over to the Devil."

Emmeline was watching the kitchen girls scalding the vats for the new crop of pickles when one of the serjeants, a bandy-legged Gascon named Jiane, came to fetch her.

As she came into the hall the joiners were sawing a frame for the last door; she could hardly hear what Jiane was trying to tell her. The Lord of Morlaix sat at a table with Walter, his long legs stretched out in front of him, his linen gambeson open in the heat, showing his sweaty chest and curls of dark red hair. A strongbox was on the table in front of Walter Straunge, one of the account books open before Niall fitzJulien. From the look on his face she could tell he didn't know what he was reading.

"What is it you want?" She let her shoulder touch his as she reached over him and turned the thick, yellowed page. There was Bernard Neufmarche's familiar fine, weblike script across the top, her own, darker, stubbier hand below.

Three Crusader knights, one a raw-boned Saxon with pale hair and skin like saddle leather stood in front of the table. They eyed her, suspicious, as she bent over her ledger.

"Where the devil is the sum that should be here?" Niall poked his finger at the page. "No one's paid it."

She looked up at the knights. "Why are you paying these men now? They've done no service yet."

He looked annoyed. "Look, here, none of these people are paying their debts! Damn them, they're hiding, waiting for us to ferret them out, before they'll render what they owe!"

He was talking about the loans that had been carried for

more than a year. "Well, you can't collect this instant." She sat down and made him slide over on the bench so there was room for her. The Crusaders looked at one another. They were lean as hounds, their clothes full of patches, but their mail and weapons were clean, polished to catch sparks. All three wore the cockleshell badges of Outremer.

She reached in front of Walter and pulled the strongbox over to her. "What are you issuing these men money for? To buy arms?"

He observed her under half-lowered lids. "Full gear." He watched her pick up the quill, dip it in the ink pot and make an entry. "And loans for better horses. They are riding nags."

Emmeline opened the latch of the strongbox and looked inside. "You have been paying money out and not making note of it in the books. But that has nothing to do with how people are paying their debts."

Walter made a small sound of protest. Her husband studied her with a strange expression. "No, let her do it. It's her genius. I know for a fact she has a ledger book where another woman would have a cunt."

The three Crusaders barked their laughter. When Niall looked up they stopped. He put his hand on the ledger and pulled it away from her. "Let Walter pay them. Afterward take the ledger yourself and study it, and tell me which of these people we can dun."

Emmeline did not look up. He did not have to tell her they were already short of money.

Fifty knights, a levy raised by the king in London, arrived on St. James's day, the last week in July. Most of the new knights were English, from the eastern shires. Walter drilled them in the bailey with the Gascons and the Crusaders. Niall and Walter and the serjeants sat long hours in the great hall talking of strategy, how to attack Prince Cadwallader before the first frost.

"Something to hurt him," Walter said. "Since our Welsh friend has been boasting all up and down the west how he has pricked us stealing sheep, and burned down our very castle gates."

The plan was a foray into the Welsh mountains to the Welsh fort at Glyn Cierog. A bold move was called for, and an attack on Glyn Cierog would please the king. They were no longer under strength now with the new knights and a small cadre of seasoned Crusaders. A horse fair that had come to town had supplied them with more destriers. And the harvest was almost done; they could bring some of the villeins with them as foot soldiers.

Talking about it filled them with energy. The practice yard was filled from early light to after dark. The armorer worked late, by torchlight. Emmeline found it hard to sleep. When her husband reached for her, running his hands up under her shift, she pushed him away.

"What is the matter with you?"

Emmeline turned her face away. He leaned on his elbow and looked down at her. She waited for him, as she always waited, night after night, to say something about Magnus. That her child was all right. Or even to hear that Walter had talked to him as he'd promised. That he would try to get a letter from Magnus for her.

But he lay back down in the bed and turned away from her, and went to sleep.

To live with a woman without danger is more difficult than raising the dead to life.

St. Bernard of Clairvaux

SEVENTEEN

Niall fitzJulien, Lord of Morlaix, Walter Straunge and ninety-five mailed, mounted knights and seventeen villeins equipped as men-at-arms marched out of Morlaix Castle, warhorses stamping and pulling at the bit, bright gonfalons fluttering.

Emmeline and her maidservants leaned from the castle wall walk to watch as the column passed over the draw-bridge and down the road to the river. Her husband rode straight-backed and tall in his gleaming ring mail, holding his helmet in the crook of his arm, the sun striking his russet-red hair. The girls around her squealed at how hand-some he was. All along the castle walls there were loud cheers. It did not seem to matter that by nightfall the Welsh would know the Morlaix army was coming. And that they headed for Prince Cadwallader's great fort of Glyn Cierog, to burn villages and scatter tribesmen as they went.

"It is a madness," Emmeline muttered under her breath, "this going to war. It will only use up all our provisions and arms that we've worked for all the year."

Torel was standing beside her. He looked disapproving. "It is necessary to subdue the Welsh," he said piously. "It is God's will."

Emmeline snorted. One could not find a man in all of Morlaix who did not want to attack Cadwallader. But she had lived with the Welsh all her life and had never seen them really conquered.

By the next day the wounded began coming in. There had been an ambush at Maidenwell and some of the young knights King Henry had given them had unwisely charged bowmen hidden in the trees. Six of them were carried into the great hall and laid out on the trestle tables for their wounds to be bound up. Three looked as though they would recover but two had taken arrows through the lungs.

Emmeline sent for the nurse, Gaeweddan, wife to John Avenant, head of the wool guild, a stout, able woman and a good midwife. There were two barber-leeches in the town who were fairly skillful, but their patients too often died of fevers after their surgery.

Gaeweddan looked at the two boys with lung wounds and shook her head. "Sometimes they bleed and sometimes they don't," she said. She pulled back the knight's red-stained shirt, indifferent to his pleading looks. "See how the blood bubbles in and out of the hole the arrows made? If they don't stop bleeding, they die."

Feeling a little sick, Emmeline turned away. But the nurse was right. The two southrons died at sunset and Gotselm set the garrison knights to digging graves on the hillside. By the next day the others had been moved to the cramped barracks' quarters in the Knights' Tower. Soon after that the master builder, whose men were just finishing up the last of the work on the great hall, came to Emmeline to show her what he'd found.

"There was once a small chapel inside these walls," he told her as he led her outside. "I remember hearing of it, the castle chapel. Before the Lady Chapel was built down by the river."

As the builder talked his fingers probed the stones of the wall. A small piece of a carved stone rose came up and there was the click of a latch, then the sides of a pillar moved to show a black, vertical gap.

Emmeline bent to peer at it. It was a hole big enough

for a person to slip through. "Holy Mother of God, where does it go?"

The builder scratched his jaw. "Ah, that's the clever part. Yestereen me 'n the mason, Cob, and the joiner Mat Watson, we slipped inside and found there's a tunnel what goes down the sluices from the cistern. The castle well and cistern what supplies the castle is under us here. They made a water defense from it against sappers."

She straightened up. "I've never heard of such a thing."

"Bless the saints, milady, it is something you should know, should you ever need it, like. When the castle is under siege the foe will send sappers to dig under the castle walls and undermine them. When the walls is breeched and falls down, in comes the enemy and takes all. Here at Morlaix the old builder put down a gallery of sluices what can be flooded from the water in the cistern. Then the sappers is trapped down there underneath us and drowns and dies."

She shuddered. According to the master builder, men burrowing into the castle would drown in water tunnels under their feet. "I have never heard of Morlaix besieged."

He took off his felt cap, white with stone dust, and scratched his bald head. "But it has, milady. The last siege was laid by poor King Stephen, may God rest his soul, when he was fighting the empress." He stuck the hat back on his head. He reached out and passed his hand over the pillar and released the stone latch. When the column turned he put his shoulder to it and pushed it back into place. "It mought yet be good to know this for sommat in the future. Peaceable times don't last. And wars is hardly ever over, now, is they?"

She thought of the young wounded knights in the tower, the dead ones on the hillside below. He was right. The war was over, and yet the war went on.

"What you need to know," he said, "is that the old water defense is still there, could you take time to find the wheels and gates to open it when and if it was needed, God forbid."

Emmeline had no idea how to search for the water gates the builder talked of, no one went down there. She didn't think the cistern, which sometimes sent up moss and green tendrils in the water buckets, had been cleaned in years.

"And that's not all," he went on. "We did not stop there, me'n Cob and Mat, but went down the sluices ourselves and found where all them tunnels come out."

Her face went blank. "Out?"

"Aye." He nodded. "The tunnel come out right there on the bank down by the river."

She gaped at him. "Do you say there's a secret way out of the castle?"

"Milady, there usual is, you know," he assured her. "Few knights what has their wits about them would close themselves up in a keep or a tower without a way out, if they could." He turned back to examine the old wall. "With all respects to you, milady," he said in a new, brisk voice, "you might think a bit about building up the old chapel again. 'Twould be a good thing to have a little church inside the walls as it was before."

A chapel inside the castle did not appeal to her. It was usual to have one for the lord and his family and the garrison knights, but now they had zealous Cistercian monks in their new chapter house. Who had already asked permission to preach in the town market square on Sundays and in the hamlet of Wycherly on Wednesday eves.

If she had a chapel inside the castle, Emmeline told herself, the Cistercians would want to send one of their order to hold masses and be their confessor. And she didn't want that. Cistercians were notorious for preaching against women. The order's leader, Bernard of Clairvaux, taught that the only vocation for virtuous Christian women was not as mothers and wives, but as chaste nuns enclosed in convent walls.

"You could make a right pretty little oratory," the builder insisted, "like a Lady Chapel. And keep this column what opens into the secret way underneath right where it is."

Such a bijou would cost a pretty penny; she suspected the builder was thinking of his fee. Although, Emmeline thought a little wistfully, she could almost see it. A white and pink sandstone nave, delicate columns to hold up the roof, and a carved stone screen for the altar. They were all the rage in France.

She shook her head. She could see he was disappointed.

But later when she thought about it she wondered why the builder had waited until after Niall fitzJulien had gone to tell her about the secret way out.

The castle felt empty. It was still full of people: the serjeants drilled the new garrison knights in the practice yard, Torel and the servants were sacking up the summer's crop of corn at the back of the kitchen house, the stable knaves exercised the destriers that had been acquired at the July horse fair, and each morning there were packmen and country people waiting at the portal gate to come in with their wares to barter in the ward and kitchen yard. But no one could forget the Morlaix men marching in the west. The guards on the wall walks kept their eyes on the blue, faraway mountains of Wales. They heard there had been a battle at a river somewhere in north Glamorgan. The Morlaix forces had been victorious, and had pressed on for the fort at Glyn Cierog.

In a few days the wounded made their way back to Morlaix. They were in sorry condition. Niall fitzJulien's army in its haste to pursue the Welsh prince had not had the time to provide them with any sort of escort back over the mountains. The exhausted wounded were lying about the open ward when Walter Straunge came galloping back up the castle road with empty supply wagons.

"Jesu," he said, looking around, "so few?" He was bareheaded, blond hair blood-spattered and flapping about his shoulders. "There were half as many wounded on the road. Did they not make it back?"

Emmeline did not have time to answer him. She and Gaeweddan had marshaled the chambermaids and the scullery girls, but there was little shelter within Morlaix's walls except for the stables and the Knights' Tower. And both places were crowded, dark, and dauntingly filthy. She did not want to put wounded men in there.

She grabbed Walter Straunge by the arm. "You will not leave until your wagons have taken these men down into the town, to the goldsmith's house." The Beguines could help. She could not have men dying all over the ward. "We will use it as a hospital."

"Nay, there's no time." He looked around, scowling. "We are loading the extra arms now, Lord Niall is waiting for them."

"Then let him wait more." She went to a wagon and began to pull pikes and shields out of it and throw them on the ground. Walter's men stopped what they were doing to stare at her.

He strode to her. "Leave the wounded where they are. They are knights, they are used to it. I need to return to the battle at Glyn Cierog. Don't you know what's happening?"

She pulled a battle-ax out of the wagon and threw it down at his feet.

"Now listen." He was white-lipped with anger. "The goldsmith's house is no longer yours to use for anything! It belongs to my lord."

"Get out of my way." Emmeline hauled herself up into the wagon seat and picked up the reins. Castle people stood around them in a circle, their mouths open. She wore an old apron and her hair bound up; it was hard to command Walter when she looked like a slavey herself. But she was not going to have the castle piled high with sick and dying. She leaned down to say, "If you will not help me, then I will take the wounded down myself."

For a moment they glared at each other. Then Walter turned from her, cursing. He flapped his arm at his knights. They looked at one another, then began to throw the rest of the weapons out of the wagons and onto the grass of the ward.

The weather continued dry. It was good for the corn harvest, but the pastures were dead. Without the green grass the cows were not giving much milk.

"Always sumt'ing," Mainsant said. The Beguine was sitting on a bench in the wash yard with her niece, shelling peas. Emmeline had come out to sit with them and rest from the heat of the goldworking shop. "They complain all the time, serfs do," the older woman observed, "it is the same everywhere. What is good for the corn, *ja,* is not so good for the milk."

She ripped open a pea pod with her thumb nail and let the pellets fall to the sheet spread at their feet.

"But very good for peas," the younger woman murmured.

Emmeline shot her a quick look. Berthilde seldom spoke. The corners of that graven, perfect mouth turned up as their eyes met.

"Ja," Mainsaint said, oblivious. "Good for peas."

Emmeline smiled back. So there was more under that smooth expression, those downcast eyes than one would suspect.

Beyond in the stable yard some of the boys were fetching water for the wounded knights who were lying out in the sun on their cloaks and straw pallets. Matters had been quieter since she'd brought kitchen knaves down from the castle to nurse the wounded knights, and kept the maidservants away. Now, Emmeline saw, their eyes avidly followed beautiful Berthilde.

The two Beguines had been shelling the new crop of peas for days. When each sheet was full they carried it to a stack of flat wicker baskets, where they took one and emptied a shower of peas into it. After several vigorous shakes to settle them they placed the basket on the roof of the chicken coop. In a day—two at the most in such hot dry weather—the wrinkled yellow peas would be dry enough to store in sacks. In the wintertime the thick pease soup the cooks made with turnips and a mutton bone was a prime treat.

Watching them work, she marveled at the speed of their hands. Rip! went the pea pods as the little globes spilled down onto the sheet. Flip! went the empty pods as with a flick of the wrist they sailed into a sack placed between that would be carried away to be fed to the hogs. There was no dirt; everything around the two women was scrubbed until it gleamed. When the sheet that caught the peas grew dusty it was bundled up and taken away to the wash pile and another clean bedsheet brought in its place.

Emmeline closed her eyes, lifting her face to the scalding summer light. When she dreamed of anything other than having Magnus back once more, she thought of how fine the Beguines had made the manor house. The storerooms were a miracle of cleanliness and order. Onions and herbs hung in the rafters with hard sausage and smoked meat, cheese ripened under cloth next to eggs and salted butter, and now there were sacks of peas and beans for the coming year. The bedchambers smelled sweet with fresh rushes and newly turned straw mattresses, and linens made smooth with lavender and something the Beguines put into the wash water.

She yawned. Now wonder they were expensive. They made a house perfection. So much so that Emmeline had toyed with the idea of making the Neufmarche manor house into an inn with the Beguines to run it.

Well, why not? she thought idly. All of England was a ferment of prosperity and trade these days under the young king, and there were more travelers on the roads than ever before. The more she thought about it the more the thing took her fancy. She knew both women were very frugal; they had hardly spent any of the wages she paid them. She could tempt them with becoming, as hard as they worked, quite extravagantly rich.

Her mind raced ahead. With the manor as a decent, well-run inn, and the work from the goldsmith's shop she could live and work comfortably, profitably. Peacefully. Not having to worry about the gold she'd tried to use to escape Niall fitzJulien. That he was now using to make war against the very one it was intended for—Prince Cadwallader.

Dear Holy Mother in heaven, how she longed to think of a way to get away from Castle Morlaix and its grasping, bloodthirsty lord! Who wanted nothing, now, but to rut on her night and day to get her with another child.

"I bring water."

Emmeline opened her eyes. Berthilde stood up, lowering her end of the sheet and folding it back so as not to spill the peas.

"It is hot," the girl said. "I bring water to drink."

She watched her make her way across the yard in her plain gray dress and wooden clogs, her slender body swaying, the long gilt braid hanging down between her shoulder blades. The wounded knights in the outer yard stirred, eyes following her.

Mainsant said, without looking up, *"Ja,* and the monks come here, too."

She could only mean the Cistercians. Emmeline said, "Why would they come here?"

"Her." She wagged her head in the direction of Berthilde, intently watched by the knights as she drew a bucket of water from the well. "Me they do not worry about so much, I am old. But they want Berthilde." Her gray eyes,

irises black-ringed, met Emmeline's. "You ask why, maybe?
To make a nun. They come all the time to seek out women
who work and do not marry, those monks, to talk that it
is only good in the eyes of God for you to live the life of
a nun in the convent. Hah." She scooped peas from the
opened pod into the sheet with her thumb. "That Berthilde.
They pray over her much, I think."

Emmeline felt a ghostly finger run down her spine.
"Give the monks food, that's what they come begging for.
Don't let them in."

"My sister, Berthilde's mother, has only girls," the other
woman said stolidly. "No boys. Berthilde, she is bringed
up among women always, all her life, nine sisters, two
aunts, and mother. My sister loses her husband before Berthilde is born. Berthilde is a good, hardworking girl, happy
she is, she knows nothing of men. My other sister and me,
we pray hard to join Beguines, praise God and heavenly
Son, work in other places and make money. But not to be
nuns."

Emmeline watched the girl at the well. Berthilde moved
and spoke in a calm, gentle world. She could well believe
the girl had hardly known the company of men.

"And that other one." Mainsant's big fingers ripped open
a pea pod. "He come, too."

The journeyman appeared in the door of the workshop
behind them. "Mistress, I have brought the silver."

They had searched high and low for some silver to buy
or trade. Ortmund had found some in Chirk in exchange
for a handful of the Neufmarche beryls and other stones
they had managed to salvage from fitzJulien's plundering.

"I am coming." Emmeline said in a low voice, "Tell me,
who else comes here to talk to Berthilde?"

"Talk?" The woman gave a scornful grunt. "That he
would like to do. To talk. Yes, talking to her, he would like
that. But he only sits outside, in the street, and watches.
When he does not come with you."

Emmeline had gotten up from her seat. Now she looked down at her. "Walter."

The Beguine reached for a handful of pea pods. "The young one with the yellow hair. Down from the castle he comes and rides about the town and sometimes he does the lord's errands at the smith, and the tavern, but always when he is through he comes here, to this street. And sits on the horse outside and waits to look. For Berthilde."

Emmeline turned from her. She was angry. Walter Straunge had no right to bother her workers. She knew what was behind it, you could see it in the eyes of the wounded knights lolling about out there, who never took their gaze off the girl. What was in their filthy minds. God's wounds, she would put a stop to it! Even if she had to talk to Niall fitzJulien. Whenever he got back from his war.

The wind blew down the funnel of the Welsh valley and then curled back, right in their faces. So would the smoke, Niall knew, when the sappers set their fires.

He rode his destrier down the lines of the Flemings, calling out to them to make sure they moved well back when the tar barrels were lighted. The soldiers that King Henry had sent him rested on their mattocks, grinning back at him through masks of dirt.

There was a threat of rain over the mountains, the sky dark as a bruise. They needed it to stay dry, and bring the damned siege to an end, Niall thought wearily. He trotted his destrier along the ditches to meet Walter.

"Well, let us burn it," Walter called, cheerful. "They've sat behind their pile of dirt long enough. And given us enough dead and wounded in return for it."

Niall didn't answer.

Above them on a half-league-long earthen mound stood the Celtic fort, older than the Normans in Britain, perhaps even older than the Saxons who had fought the Welsh here many times, circled by outer raths, then the wooden stockade, then the timber towers inside. Glyn Cierog had resisted their assault for four days. They had battered the stockade and towers with siege towers and catapults relentlessly. They could see the damage, even standing out of arrow range.

He almost hated to begin. The Welshmen inside had put up a valiant fight. He had wanted to see them surrender rather than be forced to set fire to the old fort, an ancient tinderbox from the looks of it. With a sigh he pulled on his helm, straightened the nosepiece so that he could see around it, and pulled up his mail neckpiece to cover the lower part of his face. Walter would take his position on the right flank, bringing the siege tower up to the walls after the fires had started. The main thrust, Niall's own charge, would be for the portal gate.

All up and down the line the Fleming sappers were ready with their torches. They suddenly saw furtive heads appear against the sky at the top of the fort, then withdraw. Niall wondered if the Welshmen inside knew what was about to happen. Unless they were blind and noseless they could see the torches, smell the damned pitch.

Niall lifted his hand, then dropped it with a jerk, the signal for the Flemings to light the tar barrels and start them toward the fort. Down the line a catapult flung a lighted barrel streaming flames like a comet over the walls and inside. The siege tower rolled up with its cargo of mailed knights, ready to breach the walls. Suddenly everything seemed to go wrong. A black pillar of smoke rose from the center of the old fort. Rivulets of flame raced along the top of the wooden stockade wall. There was a low noise, a massive moan, like the groaning of the tidal sea. Then screams tore the air.

Jesu, not the usual male battle screams of pain and rage, either.

For a moment Niall was baffled. The shrill shrieking made his hair stand on end. One of the Gascon knights came racing up. With their convoluted language he couldn't understand what the Gascon was shouting.

Children? More Gascons now, shouting around him. The damned stupid Welsh had counted on holding Glyn Cierog forever. An impregnable place. At least they believed it—as though there were no such things as tar barrels and Norman siege towers and catapults. They had filled the accursed fort full of women and children!

Niall spurred his destrier down to the drawbridge, which was burning fiercely. The inside of the fort was like a huge bonfire, spewing smoke and red flames. The shrieking set his teeth on edge.

Walter came galloping up. "They are throwing them over the wall," he bellowed. "The children."

"Get a hook," Niall roared.

The sappers had already attached a chain to the burning drawbridge and were trying to break it apart. Those inside hadn't released the mechanism to the gate. Over the howling they heard sobs, small children wailing.

Niall fought Hammerer, who was almost unmanageable that close to fire. Walter came up with some of the sappers. The boards of the drawbridge were burning under their feet.

"God rot them, God rot them," Walter cried. "They could have parleyed a truce for the children."

"That's not the way they fight." *Not the way we fight, either.*

The sappers had their hook in place. The drawbridge was too hot to stand on, they moved back, dragging the chain. Someone was shooting arrows down on them from the parapet. One of the Flemings fell. Two of his friends dropped their section of chain to drag him off. Walter jumped down and picked up the chain again.

Fire ate through the boards. The drawbridge burst apart. Half fell in the ditch.

Someone inside had found the wheel that opened the gate. The shrieking and wailing beat on their ears. The doors opened a crack. A horde of women and children and men squeezed through like ants spilling out, some missing the smoldering boards of the drawbridge and falling off into the deep ditch. The door opened wide and a mob of wild Welshmen pushed through. The tribesmen attacked the sappers with spears and short swords. Some of their clothing was on fire. The Fleming sappers fell back.

Niall tried to force Hammerer across what was left of the drawbridge. A howling mob surged around him waving their arms, clutching at one another, some tottering, screaming and falling into the ditch. Maddened cattle stampeded through. The inside of the fort was still burning, the roof thatch on buildings like torches. People were jammed in there. Smells of burning flesh filled his mouth and nose.

In the jostling mob someone screamed at him. A woman with a red, burned face held up a charred dog or a pig in both hands and howled something. Then Niall saw the charred thing was a baby.

The burned woman had a long knife or a sword. As he tried to back Hammerer to get away from her she lunged at the stallion and buried the knife in its shoulder. The horse reared, squealing.

Niall lost his seat and pitched off, still clutching the reins. Into the crazed mob of Welsh. And under Hammerer's hooves.

Hedwid came into the lord's chamber carrying a candle. With the light, Emmeline was instantly awake, but the maidservant touched her on the shoulder anyway. The girls who were sleeping around the bed raised up on their elbows, whispering sleepily.

"They are coming back," Hedwid whispered, bending over her. "And they are bringing the lord."

That didn't sound right.

Emmeline shook her head to clear it of sleep. The dim-

ness of the one candle, Hedwid there in the middle of the
night, gave her a strange foreboding. Emmeline threw back
the covers and sat up in the big bed. The sound of rain
beat all around the tower room. The weather had finally
broken. She threw back her tangled, unbound hair from her
face and said, "Why is the lord coming back?"

The girl looked away. "There is a messenger down in
the ward. That is all he said. They are coming back and
they are bringing the lord."

God and St. Mary. With her heart pounding she pulled
a blanket from the bed to cover her and started down the
stairs, the maidservants trailing and talking.

One could not go outside, it was pouring. The grassy
ward was already a lake. In the rain the red glare of torches
at the gatehouse shone like jewels. A long line of dark,
bundled shapes wended its way up the road to the castle.
Men and horses. The men of Morlaix returning from Wales.
Emmeline stepped out into the downpour. She was barefoot; the water was ankle-deep.

Walter was in the lead. He reined in. She hardly recognized his white, fierce face, eyes puffed from lack of sleep.

"Walter!" Behind him the knights were silent. She
splashed up and took his bridle. "God has sent you safely
home. Where—"

Something made her stop. They were like stone men in
their sodden cloaks, their mail and swords, sitting there in
the rain. She saw Walter held the reins of a mottled gray-
and-white stallion with a black, tightly wrapped shape face-
down across its back.

The darkness seemed to reel. She swallowed, seeking
Walter's eyes. He looked away.

She wanted the truth. "He's dead, isn't he?" she whispered.

It was a moment before the ringing in her ears cleared
enough for her to hear his answer.

EIGHTEEN

"His horse trampled him," Walter said, "on that same bad leg that always bothers him and won't heal. I sent for the barbers as we passed through the town."

Two knights carried the cloak-wrapped form of Niall fitzJulien up the winding tower stairs to the lord's chamber. The maidservants, caught with knights stinking of sweat and horses, squeezed against the wall. The knights reached the top of the stairs and shifted the body sidewise to get a better grip. The bundled man groaned again. The chambermaids darted ahead into the room to fix the bed.

"There was no way he could sit in a saddle," Walter went on, "so as you see, I wrapped him in his cloak, tied all together with his belt and put him over his horse on his belly to ride that way. But after a while the jouncing made him puke."

Emmeline felt a sinking in the pit of her own stomach. She had not expected to see her husband brought home in a state close to dying. The whole castle knew there was no love lost between them. But what was she going to do?

The big knights smelled of smoke, and rain. She got out of their way as they swung Niall fitzJulien into the bed. From somewhere in the cloak's sodden wrappings there came another deep moan. The knights gathered around, worried, shuffling their mailed feet. Walter bent over to worry the straps of the cloak.

She pushed Walter out of the way. Looking down into

her husband's face she hardly recognized that scowling vis-
age that was now pinch-nosed, seemingly lifeless. He
looked like nothing so much as a corpse wound in a filthy
shroud.

Walter rubbed his jaw. "He was alive at the pass. I got
down from my mount and turned him over to see if he was
still breathing, but by then he did not know me as he was
in a deep swoon."

She put her hands on her husband's face. It was clammy
cold.

"The leg is bad," Walter said. "I think it is broken."

She wanted to scream at him to stop talking. One of the
maids brought a knife, and she used it to cut away the
cloak's fastenings. When she had him partly uncovered she
motioned for the knights to turn him, to get him out of the
cape. He was not awake, but he cried out hoarsely in pain.

Damp prickles of perspiration broke out all over her
body. She stepped back. Underneath the cloak he was in
his mail. The chain links were smeared with blood, but she
could not tell where he was bleeding.

*Holy Mother in heaven, what if he should die now while
they were only trying to undress him?* Would she be blamed
for his death? "Walter," Emmeline said. Her hands were
shaking.

"Milady." He stepped forward. "Leave this to us."

He moved her aside and the knights got the mail hauberk
and chausses off. Niall screamed again in pain. Emmeline
paced to the window, trying to shut out the sounds. There
were footsteps on the stairs. Two barber surgeons came to
the landing just outside the door, carrying their tools in a
sack.

"Ah, there you are." Walter left the knights and went to
them. He spoke at length, stopping now and then to look
over his shoulder at the man on the bed. The barbers kept
looking past him to Emmeline. They had oiled, ringletted

hair and dirty fingernails; she had never liked them. She could guess what they wanted to do.

She turned her back and told one of her chambermaids to go downstairs with a message to Gotselm. That he was to send one of the Gascons into the town to fetch the nurse.

The girl made a round O of her mouth. "Mistress, do you want to do this? Master Avenant will not let his wife go into the streets at this hour."

Emmeline's nerves screamed. She gave the girl a push that made her stagger. "God's face, do you want me to beat you? Tell them it is the Lord of Morlaix who needs her!"

Sobbing, the maidservant turned and ran down the stairs.

Walter had been watching, his expression blank. Looking down, Emmeline saw she had put the blanket somewhere; she was wearing only her short white bed shift. Anyone could see her nipples, the outlines of her breasts and legs. She was too tired to do anything about it. She went and stood by the side of the bed.

Niall fitzJulien, the Lord of Morlaix, lay fully naked, arms flung out and long legs sprawled, the great rod of his sex fallen to one side, half erect among his groin's ruddy curls. He had a stubble of rusty beard. His body, which gave off an odor of smoke and wet, was unusually pale except for the great purple, yellow, and red swelling that ran from the back of his left hip down to the knee. His feet were muddy and there were streaks of dirt on his arms. When she looked closer she saw that his hands were burned.

The maids had brought basins of water. Emmeline took a rag, wet it with the tepid water, and wiped his face.

His skin was feverish, she could feel the heat through the cloth. She started when he opened his eyes, no more than slits behind which the irises gleamed. He closed his fingers around her wrist. Even wounded and sick, his grip hurt.

"Don't take off leg," he said thickly. The tawny eyes pinned hers. "Die with it. But not—off."

She sat down on the edge of the bed, held by his clutch on her. Walter came over to stand beside them. She did not have to look at Walter. She already knew how he felt as he had brought the surgeon barbers.

She kept her gaze on her husband's chalky, rigid face. Without his leg Niall fitzJulien would have little chance to hold his fief. King Henry could afford to be generous to a knight who had saved his life in battle, but holding the borderland here between Chester to the north and Hereford to the south, took an able-bodied man.

Sweet Holy Babe, she thought wearily, if she had wanted revenge she supposed she could not have thought of a better one! If they took his leg off and he lived, the king might give him some post such as the castellan of a royal castle, a sheriff of revenues, a constable of a town in the midlands. But cripples were still cripples. He would have to get about on a crutch.

"He has no chance of saving it," Walter grunted.

The grip on her wrist tightened. She looked down into feverish, gold-colored eyes. They glared at her, threatening her silently with everything under heaven and earth.

They threatened, but they did not beg. What did he want of her? she wondered. He knew how much she desired to be free of him in any way she could, short of murder. Perhaps even that. Hadn't she stolen money to try to make her escape? Run away with a guildsman? If he kept his leg, if the rotting thing killed him, then even he should know she would finally be free of him!

He made a dry, rasping noise in his throat.

She motioned for one of the girls to bring a cup of water. She bent over him and held the cup to his lips and he swallowed painfully, most of the water trickling out of the corners of his mouth and down onto his neck. So close, their eyes locked.

The fever-cracked lips moved. "The boy," he croaked. The knights around them bent over, listening. Walter looked at her. Emmeline could not move, imprisoned by that iron grasp on her wrist.

As she stared at him a great revelation told her what he was trying to say. *Only he knew where her son was.* Merciful Christ, if she wanted Magnus back, she would have to move heaven and earth to see that Niall fitzJulien lived!

Beside her Walter said, "Milady, shall we turn him again? The leg will rest easier that way."

She stared down at the man on the bed. If she had ever pitied him, held some small, stunted affection for him, or passion for him in any marital duty, it was over now. She gave her hand a violent wrench and he let it go.

He thought to bargain with her: the saving of his foul, suppurating leg for the only thing she loved in life, her son! She could not imagine anything so base. So cruel.

"Milady?" Walter reminded her.

She sat back. Oh, he would keep his leg, she would somehow find a way to do it. Because if Niall fitzJulien died, she would never find where Magnus was being held.

She bent to him so that the others could not hear and said in a low voice, "I promise, the barbers won't take off your leg." His lips twitched disagreeably. She knew that he trusted her no more than she trusted him. "Nay, I give you my oath, if that is what you wish. I have sent into town for Gaeweddan, Master Avenant's wife. She is the nurse. The midwife."

His eyes widened.

Hah, let him think the worst! She could not resist saying, "Howsoever, the barbers are outside, and ready to take the leg, if that is your desire. You have only to say it."

She knew he wouldn't call in the barbers.

Why couldn't he show some mercy now that he was sorely wounded? On the brink, mayhap, of life and death, he had only to utter the words to tell her where her child was. A merciful act whether he lived or died, a credit to his soul in the eyes of God when he rose to heaven. She knew he would not do that, either.

He closed his eyes. Walter bent over him. "My lord? Niall?"

She said, "He has swooned again. He does not hear you." Emmeline picked up the wash rag and began to bathe his face and shoulders. She called out for the maids to bring more water and begin on his legs and feet. He had been in the field for days. He smelled rank.

Walter stood by the bed, gnawing his lip. "You should not have told him that, about the nurse."

Emmeline pushed her long veil of hair back from her face. "Sir Walter, take the knights out of the bedchamber and tell the cook to feed them. Have the grooms see to the horses. Then send Baudri Torel to me with a pitcher of wine and some food. I wish to break my fast."

She didn't think that he would let her order him about like that. But he only pulled off his helmet and ran his hand through his flattened hair. Then without a word he turned and signaled to the knights to follow him, and left the bedchamber.

It continued to rain. Both the old priest and his young assistant came up from town to administer extreme unction. Emmeline told them the lord was not dying yet, and sent them away. Gaeweddan the nurse arrived, dragging her herb satchel up the tower stairs, groaning. Emmeline helped her off with her cloak and put it before the fire to dry.

"Ah this weather," the nurse exclaimed. "We are finally getting water now, bless be to God and all His saints, if He does not see fit to drown us in another Flood. The river's a torrent."

She brought her a cup of spiced wine and led her to the bed. The nurse bent over the body, pressing his belly at length, sniffing at his lips, listening with her ear pressed to Niall fitzJulien's feverishly pumping chest. Then she looked at the leg. Afterward she pulled up a stool and sat down on it.

"What do you want me to tell you? That you should send away the fancy beard-trimmers out there and we'll save the lord's leg? Is that what he told you he wants?"

Emmeline got the pan from the fire and poured her more hot wine.

Gaeweddan said crossly, "Hnnnh, that's what I thought." She took a sip. "They'll burn me, girl, for witchcraft if the leg poisons his body and he dies. Not you, though, you'll be a widow. The king will find a husband quick for a pretty thing like you.

"Now if I was to advise you," she said, "I would say send for the physician from Wroxeter, he's good, a Jew like his grandsire, old Ha Kohen. I like them better than the Italians. And then you'll be assured of the best care, and no one can blame you."

Emmeline gave her a bleak look. "It will take two days to get to Wroxeter and back. By now the roads are a quagmire."

The other woman held her hands out to the fire. "He's had the wound for a long time. It would have troubled him, horse or no. But a fine strong body like that is a wondrous gift." She lifted her hands, making gestures in the air. "In all of us good and evil humors run in a great flow from head out to the arms and hands, like so, then down into the trunk and to the legs and feet and back again, as we know when we see the blood coming out. When the flow is damaged it dams up and putrifies. He has had putrifaction there for a time."

Emmeline looked away. "The wound has never healed."

"Hah." The nurse leaned back, arms over her breasts. "Well, the barbers would take his leg off. My thinking is that would kill him, too."

Emmeline could not stand on her feet any longer. She sat down on the bed and put her head in her hands.

"Old Ha Koen, may God rest his soul," the nurse went on, "had good luck with opening putrid humors. He had the finest steel lancets from Toledo to drain them of their devil's poisons. Not as one would open a carbuncle, you understand. Putrefaction must be cut out, then packed with hot meal, mayhap well-boiled onions also to draw out the rot until it is clean."

The seneschal came in with kitchen boys carrying platters of wine and food. Although she had asked for her breakfast Emmeline could not stomach even the smell. She offered it to the nurse, who drew her stool up to the table, picked up a spoon, and began to eat a dish of sausage. The seneschal stood over her with a tankard of ale and poured her a cup.

Emmeline closed her eyes and swallowed. The rain and heat of the fire made the room muggy, the air hard to breathe. She said, "Cut open his leg and drain it of the poisons, but promise me you will not cut his leg all the way off."

Gaeweddan put down her spoon to pick her teeth with a fingernail. "There's risks. The cutting around the putrefaction oft makes it grow, like digging around a vegetable patch in the spring. Then there's nothing to do. The whole body will take the miasma, and death comes swift. That is why so many who call themselves surgeons think best to leave old wounds like this alone." She pushed the plate away from her and wiped her mouth on her sleeve. "But your lord's evil flesh won't stay the same, it will get worse now from the horse falling on him. You can tell that from the fever."

Walter came back into the room. He had taken off his chain mail and wore his padded gambeson. Rain had washed his hair clean, but there were weary circles, dark as soot, under his blue eyes.

Emmeline said, "Walter, get four strong knights to hold Milord fitzJulien down."

The nurse stood up. "Tell your steward I need four buckets of boiled bran with the steam still rising. Clean rags, from your bedding cupboards, mistress, not the kitchen if you please. I have my own knives, but I would look at what your cook has, also."

The barbers came in from the landing. Both bowed and smiled. One reached into a sack and took out a fine, polished steel saw and held it up.

They heard a protesting groan from the bed.

So he was awake, Emmeline thought. She wished she could think of something cruel, make him think the barber surgeons were ready to begin. But she was too tired.

"Do you have tuppence?" she asked Walter. She still had no money of own. "Give it to the barbers, and send them home." She thought of the storm beating outside. "No, pay them and send them to the kitchen for something to eat."

He gave her a strange look. She leaned her head against the bedpost, her eyelids drooping. The nurse was already bustling about the room, poking up the fire.

The knight captain said, "You will try to keep the leg, then."

Hoarsely, Emmeline laughed.

The leg was not broken. That much could be seen when the nurse, with four knights holding Niall down, cut into his thigh. A great globule of pus and blood immediately burst through the flesh and splattered them all. The man on the bed roared once in agony, then fainted.

From the opened wound came a stench that made their eyes water. The maidservants ran up and down the stairs, bringing wool battens and stacks of clean cloths to mop up. Others changed the bloody bedding. Baudri Torel came in with the cook. They stood talking about the proper way of cutting into muscle while the nurse, Gaeweddan, worked, throwing pieces of morbid flesh into a wooden bowl. From time to time knights came up the stairs from the ward offering wine and ale for Sir Niall in case he should need it, but the man in the bed remained in his deep swoon.

Emmeline sat on a stool at the end of the bed, her face propped against a bedpost, listening to their voices. She was dozing when the cook, leading a line of kitchen knaves, came in with buckets of steaming wheat bran and peeled onions. A cowhide was slid under the lord's hip, then a layer of sheepskin still with its fleece. They rolled the leg in it from ankle to hip to hold the boiling hot poultice. He howled when the mixture was poured in.

"Hold him!" Walter cried. The four knights threw themselves on the man on the bed. It was all they could do to hold him down as he thrashed and screamed. The stink of putrefaction came back.

The nurse walked up and down, wiping her hands on her apron. Her face shone with sweat. After a while she went to the bed and helped the kitchen boys open the cowhide and take out the bloodstained sacks of bran and replace them with fresh ones. Niall fitzJulien's leg down to his toes looked like a boiled joint of beef.

Emmeline went to sleep sitting on the stool. When she woke it was still dark but it had stopped raining. Some of the candles had been taken away; the room was quiet and dim. Her maids had tied up their skirts and were raking up the wet rushes and putting down clean ones. The rotten smell still lingered.

Gaeweddan was sitting by the fire. She got up heavily and came to the bed, standing with her hands clasped under her apron as she looked down at the man there. Flushed with fever, he muttered something and flung back the covers. She put them back, pressing them down against his chest and shoulders. "The poultice will draw out the poisons, but a long fever will weaken him," she said. "Keep him well bathed in cool water."

Emmeline hauled herself up from the stool. "I will send two knights back to town with you."

The other woman looked grateful. The road was dark; it was not yet dawn. They walked to the door. The nurse turned to her, gray eyes sharp. "Tell me, girl, why do you want him alive?"

Emmeline gaped at her. She said quickly, "So be it, if there is a hearing I will say you did all you could for him, like a loyal wife."

Gotselm had stationed a pair of knights on the landing. Emmeline shut the heavy wood door but did not bother to bar it.

She went to the fire and banked it, the room was still overly warm, the rain had not cooled the air. Her shift was stained and damp. She stood before the fire and shrugged it over her head and dropped it on the hearth. In the dancing firelight her body suddenly felt smoother, freer, lighter. She touched her arms and belly, cupped her breasts with her hands, then stretched. With her hands flung high she caught her hair and dragged her fingers through it, catching the snarls. Her long red mane had gone unbound the whole night and it was tangled and sticky.

She turned and padded barefoot back to the bed and lifted up the bedcover and slid in. The coverlets had been changed but still smelled of onions. She burrowed away as far as she could to her side of the bed.

A pulse throbbed in Niall's head. His face was stiff, burning with fever, and he could only see the bedchamber through half-closed eyes. Worse, something imprisoned his leg in a leaky vise so that he could not move it. He was in great pain. But he had just seen a faerie vision dancing in that very room, naked in the firelight, her elfin hands flung above her head. Her hair was long. When she moved it lifted and whirled and flamed in the light.

He licked his fever-cracked lips. He was sick, sorely wounded, but far from dying, he told himself. And this trick of his senses was less an angel than some enchanted creature that haunted a man's more lusty dreams. She moved, and his eyes lost her.

Then she suddenly appeared beside him in a golden light. Glowingly naked, she pulled her fiery hair in a rope across her shoulder, lifted the covers, and settled down beside him in his bed.

When Niall tried to move, to try to touch her, the swamp under his leg and hip shifted perilously. His hip hurt as though demons with red hot swords were attacking it. But he knew the slender, naked faerie being was in bed beside him; he felt the jiggle of the bed ropes as she turned.

Someone, he thought dazedly, had sent her to look after him. He could almost feel all that bright, lively fire in that slender form breathing life into him by being there beside him. He closed his eyes. And in spite of his hammering, throbbing fever, Niall slept.

On the other side of the bed Emmeline lay with her eyes open, studying the shadows the firelight cast against the walls. A moment before she was so tired she felt she could not drag herself into bed. Now she was wide awake, for she had forgotten something.

She had meant to ask Gaeweddan for a dose of pennyroyal and rhuet before she left. And she had forgotten it.

She knotted her hands together under the coverlets, trying not to wiggle the bed and waken the man beside her.

If Niall fitzJulien lived, there was a hope she could find Magnus. But she did not need another child. She would be trapped.

NINETEEN

Walter Straunge watched all morning for her. Although as captain of the line of knights that stretched all the way from the castle portal gate to the town market square, he was not supposed to let his thoughts, or his eyes, wander.

The garrison knights made an imposing sight as they sat stiffly on their mounts, eyes straight ahead, each holding a white and green Morlaix banner. Eager crowds surged and milled behind them. Hundreds, perhaps thousands of people, Walter told himself, all gathered to see King Henry and his queen. But *she* was not among them.

He knew that it was the devil's own task to single out just one girl from a mob that equaled that of any Christmas or Easter feast. Not only were there villeins and other country folk from miles around but many from as far away as Chirk and Wrexham who had trudged the roads all night to get a sight of the king. Walter had tried to tell himself that in spite of everything the face and slender form he was looking for would stand out from the throng. God knows in his dreams she appeared to him as real as though she were there in his arms. In his bed.

Yet for the past few hours he had been sitting his mount in full battle regalia of helmet, ring mail hauberk, gauntlets, and chaussures, holding the fluttering green and white standard of Morlaix at salute, and there'd been no glimpse of anyone like her. He felt as though his eyes had strained out of his skull, looking past the long steel nasal of his helm, trying to find her.

The old bulldog of an aunt has not let her out of the manor house, he thought, not even to see the king and queen.

He did not know what to make of the Beguines. One would think if they desired piety and good works they would choose to take the veil and dedicate themselves to Christ in a proper convent. But that, apparently, was not their way.

They, of course, had not spoken to Walter. Even if he had wanted to inquire of their mode of living they had not, by so much as a flicker of an eyelash, acknowledged his presence on earth, no matter how often he had appeared at the manor house or ridden by in the street. He doubted that Berthilde even knew what he looked like. Other than that he wore mail and helmet like other knights, and carried a sword.

He had asked in the barracks, especially of the Flemings, and had learned that the Beguines' order—if one could call it that as they took no vows and had no superiors—encouraged only the finest of freeborn, unsubject women to give themselves over to strict rules of prayer and work and simple living, and good deeds, especially to the poor.

What was to him oddest of all was that although they were not nuns, they appeared just as serenely satisfied with their nunlike condition, perhaps even more so. And did not seem to need men.

He could not understand it. Especially with someone as beauteous as the younger one. Now, looking around the crowd, he couldn't believe the two had so little womanly curiosity they would not come to see King Henry and his queen, Eleanor. God's wounds, even *he* wanted to see if Eleanor of Aquitaine was, as everyone seemed to believe, the most beautiful woman in all of Europe.

A blatting of horns shattered the air, the signal that the

king was soon to arrive. The crowd surged out into the
narrow street as the first column of King Henry's escort
made its way from the Chirk road. The burghers of Morlaix, the woolmen, the leather workers, the butchers, clustered together on a high wooden platform at the market
cross, looking splendid in their best clothes, their lavishly
dressed wives standing in a group behind. Walter recognized the smith, Watris, in the back row, his huge bulk
squeezed into a tunic of black wool over bright purple hose.
From their looks, the guildmen and tradespeople had all
prepared welcoming speeches.

A gust of wind blew over the rooftops and fluttered the
banners. Gotselm the serjeant, who had been trotting up
and down the line of knights, moved his destrier up beside
him. The vanguard of the knights of Anjou, from King
Henry's own duchy in France, came trotting down the street
three abreast. The Angevins wore silk tunics in orange and
red. Their conical helms were decorated with waving
sprouts of black cock feathers.

"I have heard there will be a tourney," Gotselm shouted
over the trumpet blasts.

Walter nodded. The Angevin knights looked very fit. No
doubt there were good men among them. England had become as tourney-mad as France. Knights who were not
sworn to any lord roamed the land in the summertime calling themselves champions and looking for any challenge
at fairs and feast days. Some even made a decent profit
from it. The usual tourney was two days of melees, mock
battles in which knights fought to take one another captive
for ransom.

Walter was thinking enviously one could make a good
bit of money that way. As one of the younger, poorer sons
of the Count of Couteme-Lassey, he could be eligible by
noble birth to fight in the king's melee—that is, if he could
bribe someone. But not Gotselm, who was part-German,
and as a knight, not much above a mercenary.

He sent the serjeant back down to dress the lines of the Morlaix guard again. Their knights had been in place since sunup and the horses needed watering. He'd considered sending grooms down with water buckets but by then the purple banners of the bishop of St. Botolph's knights were approaching.

The bishop's knights were as colorful as Italian mummers in their gorgeous tunics. The crowd surged against the rear of Walter's destrier, wanting a view. The big horse snorted, and moved out into the street, where it relieved itself of a long and noisy piss. The crowd laughed. Walter turned the stallion back in time to get out of the way of the king's cojusticiars, Robert de Beaumont, Earl of Leicester, and Richard de Lacy, who rode side by side engaged in conversation in the midst of their knights, hardly heeding the cheers.

Suddenly Walter thought he saw her. Berthilde, in her plain gray dress and a white kerchief on her hair, the telltale long silver-gilt braid hanging down her back. Moving through the crowds opposite with her swaying walk, graceful, taller than most women. Almost as tall as some men.

For a moment it was all Walter could do to keep from spurring his horse out of line to go after her. If only he could catch her! Stop her, make her talk to him. The frantic blood pounded in his head.

But when he looked again, she was gone.

On the other side of town Baudri Torel and a few of his reeves were having trouble with the king's Angevin and Provençal-speaking cooks and kitchen lackeys. They were supposed to turn over seventeen stags the royal party had hunted on the Earl of Hereford's lands the day before and brought in wains for the feast that night.

Getting into the town to claim the game had been difficult enough. The progress of the court, with hundreds of

men on horseback and on foot, along with servants and
knights and Queen Eleanor's ladies, and clerks and nobles
of the church and their baggage, had clogged the Chirk
road, straggled off through the newly harvested fields, and
even wandered off to be lost in Morlaix's streets. It had
taken Torel hours to get the wagons through to their meeting place in the butcher's shambles.

Once there, the seneschal and his men had found the
king's people spoke a language no decent Norman understood. From what they could make of it the suspicious royal
servants did not believe that he was the seneschal of the
castle, and treated them as though they had come with wagons to steal the Earl of Hereford's deer.

"Bunch of jabbering thieves," one of the Morlaix reeves
growled. "That's what they expect of others."

The Frenchmen waved their arms, shouting that even if
they turned over the deer, all the king's food must be prepared by Angevins or Provençals. The king, or perhaps it
was Queen Eleanor, did not trust local northern England
cooking.

The Morlaix people were outraged. Any Norman En-
glishman could not help but resent this great, arrogant gag-
gle that followed King Henry and, as all well knew, would
soon run out of provisions and then scour the countryside
for what they could use. The castle kitchen had heard that
the king's court could turn a prosperous fief into a plundered wasteland in a few days.

Tempers flared. Both sides loudly denounced one another
and their ancestors for several generations. A few blows
were traded. Holding his bleeding nose, King Henry's steward ordered his men to load the stags back in Hereford's
wagons.

There was a sudden silence. Then the voice of Luc, the
head Morlaix cook, rang out demanding to know if those
who prepared the king's dishes could devise an entire venison *au courant* in spiced turnips, dumplings and gravy, with

hooves, head, eyes and antlers fully restored. To be carried into the hall and presented for the king's pleasure.

"Turnips?" The king's cook sniffed. "Never with dumplings. What kind of dumplings?"

Both sides studied each other. Roast peacocks served with their feathers put back on, sometimes with the wings extended as though about to take flight, and tiny braised suckling pigs tastefully arranged in lifelike rows at the spitted sow's tits were culinary triumphs reserved for the grandest banquets. A full-grown stag, weighing as much as three men even when cooked, was the ultimate triumph.

The Frenchmen looked at one another. "Of course, it can be done perfectly," one Provençal *saucier* said. "It is one of our glorious king's favorite dishes. But we ask—can you?"

For a moment no one said anything. A full-grown stag on a bed of turnips and onion dumplings, roasted to perfection with its antlers and even crab apple eyes, restored to almost lifelike appearance? The Morlaix staff's expressions said that King Henry's lackeys might think the Welsh marcher country ignorant and barbarous, but by the tripes of St. David they had yet to observe the wonders its castle kitchens could produce!

Far away, in the streets by the market square, roars from hundreds of human throats greeted the royal party. The King and Queen of England had arrived.

The seneschal heard it, realizing that he was missing what he had most wanted to see. Queen Eleanor, the woman they called the world's most beautiful.

Then he remembered the queen would be at the feast. His heart leaped at the prospect. With luck, he could find time from the madhouse of kitchen and feast hall to stand and watch her as she sat at the high table with Morlaix's lord and lady and England's greatest magnates. The elaborate banquet the castle had prepared would be nothing short

of superb. He and his staff would pledge their very souls
to it.

The roast stag, in a way, was nothing.

Thomas à Becket was also thinking at that moment of
food as he followed the justiciars and their company of
bailiffs and knights. It was noontime, and he was growing
hungry, but he supposed there was little hope of breaking
his fast. Young King Henry was notoriously indifferent to
meal times, either when on horseback, or reading a book.
And his provisions, the chancellor remembered, were somewhere in the rear with baggage where he could not, at that
hour, get to them even if he wanted to. With a sigh, Thomas
resigned himself to waiting until the court made it up the
hill to make camp in the fields surrounding the castle.

He also hoped that by that time the quarrel that the king
and queen had begun that morning at Hereford's hunting
lodge would have somehow worn itself out. But he doubted
it.

He kept his eyes on the royal couple riding ahead.
Henry's stocky, muscular body slumped ungracefully in his
saddle, but he was not as bored as he appeared. The queen,
tall and lissome, was surrounded by Gascon and Provençal
troubadors and hangers-on vying for her attention.

In spite of the fact that the king that morning had flung
himself without warning on his horse and galloped off to
set a breakneck pace for his followers, his lackeys had managed somehow to worry him into a satin tunic and plumed
hat. He looked less disreputable than usual, although
Thomas knew he still wore his scuffed and filthy hunting
boots. After the late drinking party with de Lacy and
Leicester, Henry had slept in them. At the last minute one
of the braver valets had flung a miniver-trimmed cape
around his shoulders. Now mounted pages rode their ponies
behind the king, each carrying a corner.

The procession filed into the town's market square. The packed crowds cheered and threw wildflowers under the horses' hooves. The queen pulled her horse abreast of the king's. Thomas knew there was bound to be some sort of welcoming ceremony with fitzJulien, the local lord fresh from his bloody Welsh triumphs, and the townsmen. As far as anyone could tell the king and queen had not spoken since leaving the crossroads. But as Christ and the saints would testify that cold silence was better by far than their screaming matches.

Inwardly, he sighed. If only England's twenty-three-year-old sovereign would forgo not only the queen's ladies, and wives and daughters of his nobles, but also common villeins' daughters, kitchen maids, even the nubile, shaggy-headed little things barely out of their childhood one saw gleaning the fields. The queen had a right to be infuriated.

On the other hand, one had to consider the king's detestation of most of the queen's court of singers, philosophers, scholars, and poets. A great number of whom went out of their way to be outrageous and provocative both in dress and manner. The queen was noted for her impish sense of humor; he'd long suspected some of the more bizarre oddities she kept in her court were meant as irritants aimed at her spouse. King Henry's rank-and-file English subjects, unfortunately, found the collection of flamboyant beings who orbited the queen surpassingly hard to take.

One of Thomas's young chancery clerks reined in his horse beside him. The boy held out a small wineskin and half a loaf of crusty bread that was still warm, fresh-baked somewhere in the town. The chancellor took the wine and bread gratefully. "God's blessings, Earnwig," he said. "For this Christian gesture I have just appointed you lord archbishop."

The clerk blushed. Because of the press of men and horses following the king they slowed their horses to a walk. Ahead of them Gilbert Foliot, Bishop of London, had dismounted to make some sort of invocation. It was still somewhat gusty; the wind carried the bishop's voice away across the wide square.

Thomas studied the back of the queen's head. She wore her hair bound in a silk scarf with a gold fillet topped with a row of *fleurs de lis* studded with rubies. Even in the saddle she sat slender and tall.

He worried, with good reason, that she was overtired. When Henry, in a fit of temper had set his horse at a gallop the queen had called up her mare and raced after him in the same sort of mood, matching his pace mile for mile. If anything, Eleanor rode as well as the king. And, God help England, she was just as reckless! Racing full course on country roads was sheer folly, especially since the court gossiped that she was carrying again. As well as Thomas could remember the last baby, Prince Henry, was but three or four months old.

He finished the last of the wine, and handed the bottle to Earnwig. It was then that Thomas à Becket remembered his last visit here, at Morlaix. It had been rather pleasant in spite of the brash Irishman, whom he did not especially care for. But he'd liked his enchanting little golden vixen of a wife.

Niall dismounted before the Bishop of London, keeping the new destrier between himself and the crowd as his leg was not quite healed. He still moved awkwardly in and out of the saddle, and as a consequence tried to expose himself to public view as little as possible.

Holding the reins in one hand, he reached for his wife with the other. It was a gesture not of sentiment so much as it was to keep her by his side. Knowing Henry, the king was not finished with him. The writs levying a heavy fine for marrying without his sovereign's permission had arrived some weeks ago. The other, a royal claim of one-half of all his wife's possessions from her former marriage, had just come.

Holding his wife's wrist for support Niall lowered himself to one knee. A small dust devil of wind, a hint of the coming autumn, swirled past the Bishop of London who was standing on the first step of the market cross. Niall began the first words of his speech of welcome to Henry, by the grace of God Duke of Normandy and sovereign King of England.

The gust of wind had sent dust into Emmeline's eyes. Blinking, she scarcely felt the tug on her hand as Niall fitzJulien went down on one knee before the king and queen. As she knelt with him a groom had came up to take the reins of the queen's lathered white mare. The king eased one foot out of the stirrup and regarded his Morlaix vassals.

King Henry was not handsome, she thought, disappointed. She had heard all her life about his father, the Count of Anjou, a beautiful man who had hated his ugly wife, the old empress eleven years his senior. Their son must take after her. Henry Plantagenet was stocky with a deep barrel chest and the bandy legs of a horseman. A large round head, with a square, freckled face, bulging blue-gray eyes and close-cropped red hair and beard made him no prettier. She had heard he had terrible rages, where his face would turn purple and he would fall on the floor to kick and roar himself senseless. And yet Emmeline thought she had never seen a man with a look so keen, so intelligent. There was a power in that freckled countenance that reminded one that Henry had invaded England with an army when he was barely sixteen, challenging the old king, Stephen, for the throne, and that he had almost succeeded.

The king was saying something to Niall fitzJulien. Fascinated, Emmeline shifted her gaze to the queen.

There was certainly no disappointment there. Queen

Eleanor was ravishing, yet not quite what one expected. She was not blond nor blue-eyed like the ideal rose-petal ladies of troubadors' songs, but a willowy beauty with olive skin, a carved, perfect face with a mouth a trifle too wide, and melting dark eyes that held gaiety, laughter, temper, willfullness, and endless charm.

The queen wore a red silk coif held in place by a small crown of gold and rubies, but the long hair that showed at her back and shoulders was dark brown streaked with gold. Eleanor of Aquitaine possessed an assured, eternal beauty that dazzled. No wonder people talked of it.

Emmeline realized she was staring. The Bishop of London leaned to her and said something about the queen, and she nodded. She still held her husband's hand. The king was still talking. At that moment Emmeline looked past Henry and saw the two pages on their Welsh ponies holding the points of his fur-trimmed cloak.

One of them was Magnus.

Were the world all mine
From the sea to the Rhine
I'd give it all
If the Queen of England
Lay in my arms

12th-century German, Anon.

TWENTY

"How the devil could I know that the king would find him?" Niall growled. "I had Joceran take the boy to the constable of Wallingford. He is a friend, a fine knight with a family of his own. It was a good place to train him."

He thrust away a chambermaid who was trying to get him to step into his boots. The tower room was full of servants helping them into their feast clothes. Outside the landing was packed with messengers from the nobles of the court, all wanting something, with Walter and another knight holding them at bay.

His wife faced him, trembling, white-lipped. "The king knows everything," she said in a raw voice. "He is holding my child as a hostage!"

"What the devil's the matter with you?" He took his boots in his hands and sat down carefully on the bed, favoring his half-healed leg. "The king knows what I told him, that I found you and married you. And that the boy is my by-blow. According to the writ Leicester has served me with, I will pay a damnable great fine, too, for wedding without royal permission."

The excited maids had stripped Emmeline of her undergown. She stood shivering in her linen shift. "Your by-blow? Is that what you call him?" She twisted her hands together. "Oh, why didn't you let me go to him? There he was, my child, and I could only look at him, watch him ride off with the court!"

Niall scowled up at her. He had no idea what had happened to make her so terror-stricken. He'd held her fast by the wrist that afternoon, otherwise she'd have run to the boy to snatch him off the pony in front of Henry, the queen, and everyone.

Walter came in with a message that there was no longer room in the meadow and some of the more unruly elements of King Henry's court were spilling over into the town. The burghers and guildspeople, who were already at the castle for the feast, wanted to speak to him about it.

Swearing, hiking up his hose, Niall went to the door and shouted to the merchants to go on to the feast hall, that he would send someone to see to it. Walter came back in with him, and they slammed the door shut.

"Holy Jesus in heaven, after all this time you would think they would learn to look after themselves. But the king loves chaos." He took his linen gambeson from a chambermaid and handed it to the tall blond knight, who helped him into it. "Watch you, Walter, at the crack of dawn the king will throw himself on his horse without warning, at whatever ungodly hour he chooses and go off to hunt, leaving the rest of the court to grab their boots and braies and saddle their horses in a great cursing furor. I've seen it happen. Bishops and earls and baron of the realm, all scrambling after Henry to wonder what he will do next." The knight captain held the silken tunic embroidered with white griffons over his head, and he shrugged into it. "It took me years of soldiering with the prince to discover what it's all about."

Walter handed him a belt made of gilded leather held by a silver wolf's head buckle with beryl eyes, with an embossed sheath for his dagger. "What is that?"

"Ah, can't you guess?" He bent his head to the buckle, the light of the candles bringing out the red sheen of his hair. "Prince Henry is already a master of treating the great magnates of England and France with no better care than one would hunting dogs. Keeping them forever falling over themselves for his favor, then booting them aside when they fall out of it. Leicester, Hereford, Chester, de Lacy, even the archbishop—surely you've seen how the great men scramble in the king's presence?"

Walter adjusted the neck of the shimmering tunic, smoothing it flat across his shoulders. One of the maids handed him two gold chains and he lifted them over his lord's head. He said, softly, "The king does not seem to subject you to the same."

Niall touched the gold lying across his chest. "Hah, what the devil do you think we do now? We are rooting about before the king like pigs in a kitchen midden. And when he leaves we will be beggared and still on our knees. Still hoping we have won some small measure of grace."

The maids clustered around him, holding up a small mirror. He bent to squint in it, smoothing back his longish, curling hair with his hands. He quickly straightened up and looked across the room where his wife stood while her women adjusted her dress.

The gown, of a stiffened silk of a deep yellow color had a train, now so fashionable in London, and fit her tightly from her curving breasts and tiny waist down to her hips, where it flared in deep folds. She looked like a great yellow flower.

She had decided not to wear a coif or wimple like the ladies of King Henry's court, but had her hair brushed from a center part in the old style, to fall over her shoulders and down her back. Entwined in the fiery strands were strings of pearls. Braids by each cheek were laced with more of them, little moons of lucent white among the red.

Walter said something under his breath. Still studying her, Niall nodded. The frightened pallor of her skin had faded, pinched into a blush by the chambermaids' fingers. There seemed to be red shiny salve on her mouth, a blue color above her eyes. Standing there, a faint frown on her

beautiful face, his wife was no less than wondrous. Only
the queen could be more beautiful.

Of a sudden Niall remembered the days of lying in bed,
the leg draining and stinking, and the nurse and her mess
of hot bran poultices. He supposed he owed his life to her.
By some good fortune his wife hadn't let the filthy-handed
barbers touch him.

He said wryly, "We had better put her in the outer bailey,
away from the queen."

Walter grunted. "Hah, put her somewhere away from the
king."

There was too much truth in that. Niall grimaced.

Emmeline listened to them discuss her as though she
wasn't standing there. She did not bother to lift her eyes;
she didn't need to. She knew too well what Niall fitzJulien
looked like and how her maids had fawned over him since
they had come in. Barefoot and standing only in his hose,
they had ogled the strong curve of his rump, the long legs,
the tight, grooved plane of his bare belly, and lingered
wide-eyed over the great manly bulge in his groin.

She supposed he was handsome. Not so much so as Walter, who was tall and fair-haired and made the maids sigh
and swoon. If anything, Niall fitzJulien reminded her of
the stone images of Norman knights in the crypt of the
village church, lying there in their helms and their mail
hauberks, holding their swords in both hands, stern and
strong and silent.

Except, of course, when he was in a rage.

He would never forgive her, she thought with a small
shudder. She carried the secret of the traitor's gold like a
stone in her heart, and felt every day that she was on the
brink of destruction.

From the moment she had first glimpsed the king's face
in the market square she'd known young Henry Plantagenet

was not a man to be ignorant of what his nobles were plotting. Those bulging, gray-blue eyes suspected everything, thought about everything. Just looking at him one could see why he was a leader of men when most of those around him were, at his age, just winning their spurs.

It was why he now had Magnus, Emmeline told herself. It was no droll whim of the king's to pluck her child out of the knight's household where he'd been sent, and bring him back here. The only thing she could think of was that Henry was going to hold Magnus until he found out the truth about the courier and the gold. And the traitors who supplied it.

She tried to quiet her trembling. She didn't know how she could live through a royal welcoming feast when the king, if he wished, could expose her before everyone! Accuse her of being one of the traitors sending money and aid to his archenemy, the Welsh prince.

She stood with bent head thinking, *I have condemned fitzJulien and my son, too, who know nothing of this. We will all die horrible deaths.*

Her husband came forward and the maids stepped back, giggling. Side by side in their clothes and jewels the Lord and Lady of Morlaix were handsome, magnificent. Their servants' faces reflected it.

He looked down at her. "God of angels, if you are going to look like that they will think we are going to a funeral, not a feast."

Walter crossed himself. "Milord, don't say that, even in jest."

"Well then, get her to smile."

The servants rushed ahead of them to open the door. Baudri Torel in his good black tunic and great ring of keys and a crowd of kitchen people nearly fell inside. "Milady," the seneschal cried, "I must speak to you, it is of the utmost importance! There is a matter of milord of Hereford's stags—"

Walter pushed them all back out to the stairs. On the landing the crowd of pages and messengers stumbled back in haste.

Emmeline pressed her fingers against her husband's arm and lifted the back of the skirt and the train with her other hand. The tower steps were winding and narrow, and she was still trembling.

She was left with the desperate thought that the king could not accuse her of high treason there, tonight, at the feast. It would be something more subtle. There was still time to see Magnus, he was only a child. Surely the king could not think him guilty of anything.

They went down the stairs into the ward.

It was a fine, bright summer's late afternoon. The royal ushers were in the bailey before the great hall, trying to arrange some of England's greatest nobles into a procession according to rank. Most paid no attention, talking among themselves. The earls of Chester and Hereford, complaining that they were hungry and would not stand about like schoolboys, went off to find more ale. The king arrived with his silk jacket only partly buttoned, and grease stains on its front. Two clerks carrying vellum rolls flanked him; he looked harried. He shouted for someone to push the musicians ahead and get started. They went through the doors in a jostling mob in spite of the pleas of the ushers, and down the aisles, through the trestle tables. The castle's new feast hall still smelled of fresh cut logs.

The royal ushers rushed around seating important churchmen and lesser nobles at a second table just below the dais. Hereford and Chester climbed over it and settled on a bench at the high table beside Gilbert Foliot, the Bishop of London. The musicians, following some prior etiquette, circled the back of the hall, viols fiddling, horns tooting, until King Henry and Queen Eleanor had taken their places in their special high-backed chairs.

The royal couple sat apart, several places separating

them. The chancellor, Becket, smoothly slipped into one of the spaces along with his friend, Earl Patrick of Salisbury. They began to talk with the king.

The queen was a glittering vision of dark beauty in gold samite and a ruby-studded crown from which drifted transparent red silk veils. She leaned over the table to call to a troubador down among the merchants' tables to come and pull up a stool opposite her. He did so, bringing a companion.

Walter came to stand behind Niall at the high table. He bent to whisper in his ear, "The queen is in contrary spirits. Look at the king."

Niall looked. Eleanor of Aquitaine was playing a dangerous game. Henry had been drinking since morning; his face was flushed, heavy-lidded. The two handsome young troubadors sat down before the queen with their backs to the crowd and engaged her in conversation. Eleanor's silvery laugh rang out.

King Henry watched them, elbows propped among the wine cups. Beside him Thomas à Becket began to talk, discussing Aristotle, with the Bishop of London joining in. Morlaix servants and the king's lackeys rushed about with wine ewers and bread and wheels of cheese. The cojusticiar, de Lacy, on the other side of Emmeline, fidgeted, making some remark about the difficulty of having Angevins and Provençals in the same court.

Niall took his wife's hand in his. She turned and looked at him. Walter Straunge bent and whispered that the queen had put up her own tents in the lower meadow, leaving the king just outside the gate in the company of Thomas à Becket, with the Bishop of London and Archbishop Theobald of Canterbury camped nearby. All the Gascons and Provençals of the queen's party were in one camp, the king's Angevins and Normans in the other.

Niall raised his eyebrows.

The laughter at the queen's end of the table rang out

again. One of the troubadors was standing, his foot propped on the bench, while he declaimed poetry. The queen threw her head back to look up at him, her face vivid. Quick as lightning, his hand went out to cover hers caressingly. And then just as swiftly withdrew. The churchmen at the lower table turned and stared at them. The other troubador sat down suddenly on his stool and began busily tuning his viol.

"Jesu," Niall murmured. He saw the king's head lower ominously, like a bull's.

Someone appeared behind Emmeline. When she turned it was Baudri Torel in a bloodstained apron, with two of the Morlaix kitchen knaves. While she stared at him the seneschal burst out, "Milady, in God's name, send someone to help us! The kitchen is no longer ours."

She turned on the bench. Two little king's pages came up, and tried to push the seneschal away so that they could offer a bowl of stewed fruit. Walter grabbed them by their collars and turned them around.

"The king's people have usurped our places," Torel cried, "At this very moment, Roberson and Dyce and some of Sir Gotselm's archers are even now defending the meat."

Walter was listening intently. "God is my judge, I swear I left knights in the kitchen in just such an event. The king's damned people will ravage anything."

Emmeline supposed she could go with Walter to mediate the trouble in the kitchen, but she doubted she would do any good. She was not at all handy with the castle staff, they still had a tendency to treat her as the goldsmith's wife. Which would never do before the king's Angevins. Who thought them all barbarians, anyway.

Beside her de Lacy poured himself a cup of wine, then filled hers. "The queen is, after all, greatly esteemed," he said in her ear. "One must not be deceived. Even the English like her."

Emmeline could not catch her husband's eye; he was

talking to the cojusticiar. She said to Walter, "Go to the kitchen and do what you can."

The king was no longer talking to Thomas à Becket, who now sat silent, twisting an empty wine cup in his hand. Queen Eleanor, her beautiful face animated, had taken a lute from one of the troubadors and was strumming it and singing. Someone called up the musicians. They threaded their way through the tables, took up a place before the queen and her troubadors and struck up an accompaniment to her song.

"Of course there is no doubt she has the *gai saber,* the minstrel's genius, also," de Lacy was saying. "It is a strong thing in that family. The grandsire, old William of Aquitaine, boasted that he was Christendom's first troubador, as well as his subjects' duke. They both doted on Eleanor, the grandsire and the father. You can see she is used to being adored. And then of course, Louis, the King of France, made no secret that he loved her to distraction."

He paused and looked to see if she were paying attention. "You know, do you not, that the older brother was supposed to marry her, but he was riding on the streets of Paris one day and a pig came out of the gutter and made his horse rear and throw him? He was killed on the spot. Young Prince Louis, who had been given to the church to be a monk, was taken out of the monastery at once to be crowned king and marry his brother's intended bride."

Emmeline nodded. She knew how fourteen-year-old Eleanor of Aquitaine had been given to the gentle, monkish brother who would be King of France. Who in England had not?

"Ah, but these troubadors and poets." De Lacy sipped at his wine, thoughtful. "Too many in England see them as a great affliction. But the queen loves them, as did her father and grandsire. As King Henry loves his law books, his studies, the philosophers in spite of his—er, more earthy tastes." He sighed. "They are quite different. While she

was married to Louis of France there was almost a scandal
over the troubador Marcarbru. And again over Bernard de
Ventadour, who was not only common-born, but developed
an extravagant passion for the queen that he made known,
alas, in some of his most public songs. But Henry Plantagenet is not gentle Louis of France—Ventadour disappeared. They say he is now at the court of Ermengarde,
viscountess of Narbonne, his new patroness. However, I
have it on the best authority that for a long while no one
could find him."

Emmeline was becoming used to the way the court gossiped about the queen. She suddenly remembered the
troubador who had been with Thomas à Becket on his first
visit. The broken pendant, his talk about his mysterious
love. What was his name?

She turned to ask de Lacy, but King Henry abruptly
leaned forward to shout at the musicians, who had their
backs to him as they clustered before the queen, and did
not hear. Angry that they had not stopped playing, the king
threw a piece of bread down the table. It landed in front
of the queen.

In the front of the hall everyone stopped talking. The
king pushed his wine cup away, overturning it. Swaying
visibly, he stood up in his place, eyes fixed on Queen
Eleanor and the noisy group around her. Thomas à Becket
put his hand on the king's sleeve, but Henry shook him
off.

The packed hall fell silent, all eyes on the king. Henry
Plantagenet had a hideous temper. In his rages he was
known to roll on the floor and bite at the rushes. Now as
those in the feast hall stared at the king's bloated, angry
red face, a ripple of dread seemed to run through the air.

At the same time Emmeline saw Baudri Torel and a
group of castle cooks and kitchen knaves appear at the
open doors carrying a wooden slab that, from its size,
looked as though it might have been a door taken from its

hinges. It supported a whole roasted, decorated stag with restored antlers, hooves, and crab apple eyes.

She could not see every detail, it was too far away and the aisles were filled with lackeys carrying platters of food. But two knights wearing the colors of the Morlaix garrison stepped forward, lifted their trumpets and blew a loud blast.

At the sound of horns the hall stirred. A few heads turned. Baudri Torel, more presentable now in his black wool and wearing his huge ring of keys, took his place in front, flanked by four cooks carrying their wooden ladles shoulder high.

Emmeline touched Niall fitzJulien's arm. He'd been watching the king and had not noticed the appearance of Torel and his men. He gave a start.

The procession started for the high table a little unsteadily, the bearers clutching the greasy edges of the board. A round of cheers greeted the sight of the traditional stag, a feature of the London court but fairly rare in Welsh marcher country.

It could almost immediately be seen that some odd trouble was developing. The great roast body of the stag lay in a lake of gravy that was beginning to slosh over the barrier of turnips and dumplings placed around the edges.

The procession quickened its pace. As the wooden platform jiggled slightly the gravy dripped over the fingers of the kitchen boys and cooks. The front end, bearing the weight of the stag's head and shoulders, slid a little in their grasp and began to dip forward. A ripple ran through the gravy as the stag shifted, its left antlers visibly dropping down and to the left.

The procession slowed, the bearers trying to get a better grip with their greasy hands on the huge board.

"No, no, don't stop," the seneschal hissed. He waved away one of the Morlaix knights, horn still in hand, who had come forward to help. "Lift up the front!" he barked. "Walk a little faster!"

The cooks at the front lifted manfully, but the stag had moved too far. The men in front were bearing most of its considerable weight. The seneschal was right, there was only one thing to do.

Walk faster.

However, by this time they were already proceeding at quite a rapid—if slightly wobbling—pace. As the Morlaix cooks came even with them, a bench full of the Earl of Norfolk's knights prudently vacated their seats. The stag, a crisp, toothsome brown bulk, responded to the greater forward momentum by lowering its head and sliding downhill a little farther. At that moment a portion of gravy broke through its wall of dumplings and splashed underfoot. A kitchen boy at the back stepped into the puddle and went down with a muffled cry.

The stag was going too fast to wait. The sweating cooks and kitchen boys staggered and their burden slid to the right and then back to the left, perilously. With a great show of strength they moved to fill the empty place of the fallen pot boy, and lunged on.

Niall had gotten to his feet. So had de Lacy. So had half the high table. The king leaned forward, powerfully drunk, his mouth slightly open, as the greasy-handed Morlaix people and their cargo bore down on them.

The cojusticiar cried, "Saint George save us, Morlaix, do you think the thing's run away with them?"

There was no time to answer. The panicked kitchen people were coming at a trot. The stag's head was already hanging over the front of the board, its chin dripping a line of sauce. Baudri Torel had dropped to one side, panting to keep up, screaming for his staff to stop.

There was no place to stop.

At the last moment, as they made an effort to veer slightly away from the king, one of the cooks cried, "Up, boys—hoist it!" in an attempt to get door and stag up among the dishes.

But that was not to be.

Their new direction aimed straight for the band of musicians and the two troubadors. Who looked up in time to see a lifelike arrangement of roasted stag supported by galloping kitchen workers bearing down on them with desperate speed.

The musicians screamed, throwing their instruments away as they dove for safety. The two young troubadors, after one terrified look, bravely hurled themselves with arms flung wide in front of Queen Eleanor to protect her.

The two front bearers made a last attempt to lift the edge of the board. But, now somewhat leveled, the stag shot out of its resting place and flew straight ahead in a shower of turnips. It hit the troubadors chest-high.

The first roar of laughter came from King Henry. Suddenly full of explosive good humor, he drew his dagger and jumped on the table, calling for all to come to the aid of Christians under attack by ancient enemies from the forest.

The hall sat in stunned silence.

After one look at the king shouting and brandishing his dagger, royal guard knights vaulted over the high table and hauled at the board to get the troubadors out from under it.

"Do you not see?" the young king bellowed. "Those we have hunted from time's beginnings now seek us out for their evil justice! The rebellion must be suppressed!"

A burst of laughter finally greeted this speech. The earls of Hereford and Salisbury, as drunk as the king, joined him on the table among the bread and overturned cups. The knights working to free the troubadors found the roasted stag in several pieces. The constable of the king's household lifted a haunch dotted with dumplings and carefully laid it before the king. Henry sat down beside it, wheezing with laughter, as Patrick of Salisbury ceremoniously accepted the head, minus the antlers, handed up by his knights.

Emmeline had come to her feet as soon as she saw the

castle kitchen staff racing toward them. Now she clung
somewhat shakily to de Lacy. The Lord of Morlaix had
vaulted the high table, and was among those lifting the
wooden door from the unconscious troubadors. Above the
struggling group Queen Eleanor stood up, wiped the spat-
ters from the front of her gown with a linen napkin, and
left the table, surrounded by her ladies.

"Excellent, excellent, my dear," de Lacy was saying in
her ear. "Our sovereign is restored to good spirits, thanks
to your people. Think of what you want, dear lady, for now
King Henry will grant any favor you ask."

TWENTY-ONE

Emmeline had put out most of the candles and was in her shift when she heard the sound of feet running on the tower stairs.

"Don't let them in," Niall said. He had sent the servants away and was sitting on the edge of the bed taking off his boots. "Feast or no, there's got to be a way to get some damned sleep around here."

The door banged open and Magnus burst in, followed by Joceran carrying their bundles of clothes. For a moment Emmeline stood frozen, unable to shriek her joy.

"Oh Mother!" He threw himself at her, wrapping his arms around her and nearly taking her off her feet. "Wait until I tell you! The places we have traveled, Joceran and I!" His voice squeaked with excitement. "Oh, yes, I'm to tell you we can't stay, Joceran says we must go down to the barracks right away and see if we can find a bed. But I was with the king, Mother! There is a master of pages, Sir Wulfran, he is very stern. My task was carrying helmets to be polished and replacing candles and other things. And yesterday and today I had to walk with the other pages and the squires of the court all the way from Chirk because there wasn't enough room in the wagons. But now Sir Wulfran says I am home to stay!"

"Sweet heaven, don't scream!" She managed to hold him still long enough to plant kisses all over his face. "Oh, dearling, just stand here and let me look at you!"

She was almost sobbing with happiness. After all these weeks she actually had her arms around him! If she had her way she would never let him out of her sight again.

He managed to squirm out of her grasp. "Motherrr, *don't!*" Joceran, over his shoulder, made a long face of disapproval. "You must stop kissing me now, I'm not a baby!"

She let her hands drop and stared at him. Magnus had been gone only a matter of weeks, but a terrible thing had happened. He was so changed she could hardly believe it. Someone had cropped his hair like a Norman knight's. It went across his forehead above his brows in a straight line and cupped like a bowl under his ears. He was dressed in the king's colors, and the small shoulder cape he wore had a sprig of broom pinned to it, the *planta genet,* the sign of the House of Anjou.

Even more telling, he had learned somewhere to stand straight, eyes ahead, with shoulders thrown back, hands turned in and palms pressed to his legs. The couriers, the garrison knights, all presented themselves to her this way. She could not believe she was seeing this miniature knight standing at rigid attention.

Yet the king had sent him back.

"My lady mother," Magnus said. He shot Joceran a look, as if just remembering, then dropped to one knee and took her hand. "May God keep you and bestow His gracious blessings."

He gave her a hurried kiss on her fingers, then bounded to his feet. He raced across the room to Niall, who had taken off his boots and was sitting there, watching them.

"My lord." He bowed from the waist, another new thing. "My lord," Magnus said solemnly, "my best wishes for your health and well-being. I am most glad to be here with you again."

Niall made a great show of looking him over. "It is good to see you looking well." His voice was gruff. "How is it you've grown so much in the short time you've been away?"

Magnus looked serious as a judge. "It has not been that short, sir, we have been gone most of the summer, have we not? As for growth—" He sighed. "They tell me that is a condition of my age."

Niall struggled to look just as solemn. "You are well advised. Remember your mother in your prayers, she has missed you sorely." He looked over his head to the squire. "You will do well to look for a bed below quickly. See Sir Gotselm. He has some well-guarded places put aside for our own."

The squire saluted. Magnus saw it and quickly did the same, knuckles to his brow. But Emmeline blocked their way.

"No, don't go so soon, you've just gotten here! Sweeting, pay no attention, our guests will still be at their drinking, let Joceran go downstairs." She tried to take him by the hand. "Come sit in the bed with me as you used to when—you were a little boy. I will get you something nice to eat, and you can tell me where you've been and all that has happened."

He looked at her with that same look. "Nay, my lady mother, I must obey my lord and go below." He drew a deep breath. "But I really would like to stay with you," he burst out, "I really would! Is my dog Rega still here? Has she had her pups?"

He gave a whoop, waved to Joceran to follow, and dashed from the room.

"Joceran," she said helplessly.

The Lord of Morlaix stood up and shed his braies. He nodded to the squire, who saluted again and went out.

She went to the bed and sat down on it, her mind still full of Magnus. The way he spoke now. The way he looked. "Why is Joceran cold to me?"

He lifted his feet, brushed them together and swung them into bed. "You undo all his good work."

She turned to look at him.

He lay back among the pillows, an eyebrow cocked, studying her. At the feast that evening he was more handsome and vital than many of the king's nobles around them. Perhaps, she thought, he knew about the traitors near the king who sent gold to support the Welsh. Perhaps he knew about *her*.

She turned her head away, knowing she was tormenting herself. Even her own boy seemed to worship him. Ah holy God, why not? Magnus was, after all, his child!

Emmeline sat staring with unfocused eyes, thinking that her life was closing around her, shaping itself of its own accord, regardless of how hard she fought. She was not mistress of anything now. Not her child, not her manor house nor even her goldworking shop. Any priest would tell her that it was due to her sinfulness, past and present. That she did not have the humbleness of spirit to accept what God had ordained for her.

But she still did not want to be Niall fitzJulien's wife, she thought with a burst of bitterness. From what she'd seen the past few days she disliked the king's court, its gossiping, quarrelsome lords and ladies and their constant striving to win favor, and the huge mass of clerks and priests and bailiffs and cooks and drovers and servants that held it up and moved the court along and gave it being. The sun and moon revolved around Henry, who, from what she had seen, could ruin any of them with a word.

She didn't want to live like that.

Dear heaven, she hated to think it might already be happening! Would she never have her good, solid life again with the tradespeople of the town? Or her snug manor house that was finer by far than anything in Morlaix Castle, the pleasure of the goldworking shop—and Magnus, and Ortmund, and Tom.

"What are you doing?" Niall wanted to know. "Put out the candles and come to bed."

She got up and went around the room looking for the candle snuffer. The castle was full of servants, but so ill tended things got lost all the time. These places were not intended to be lived in; they were, after all, but forts for soldiers. Servants struggled in them. She said, "What did the king say to you about the stag?"

She'd been too far away to see all that had gone on after the roast had landed on the queen's singers, but he had been down there with them. She found the candle snuffer in the rushes and picked it up and scraped off the wax with her finger.

He said, "The king gave your steward a purse. Of course Henry was drunk, but the whole thing had pleased him greatly. Thank the saints that your kitchen people did not fell the queen with that damned thing." He yawned, pulling the covers up to his chest. "If Eleanor were wiser she would get rid of her Acquitaine songbirds. There's been trouble before."

"Yes, so I have heard." She put out the candles with the snuffer, then licked her fingers and pinched them so they would not smoke. "De Lacy was telling me of a troubador who caused trouble when the queen was still married to the King of France. And one after she married King Henry. Both professed a great love for her and went around singing about it in public. I cannot fancy anyone would let troubadors be that bold." She carried the last candle to the bedside and put it on the table. "The justiciar is a great gossip. He said the queen's great weakness is that she is used to being adored."

He lay with his arms behind his head, watching her. "She is used to being rich and beautiful. She's known nothing else."

She turned slightly away from him. She knew he wanted to lie with her. She said, "I think she wants King Henry to love her. As the French king did."

He reached out with one hand and seized the edge of her shift and drew her down on the bed. "Henry loves her

in his own fashion. She has given him everything he
wants—half of France, wealth, and now two sons that Louis
could not make with her."

"That is not the same thing." She let herself be drawn
into his embrace. He pulled her over him and hauled up
the linen shift until he could reach her bare bottom and
stroke it, then the backs of her legs. His big hands covered
the curves of her buttocks and squeezed.

"And she is beautiful," she said a little breathlessly. "I
have never seen a woman so lovely."

She raised up on her hands to let him pull the shift over
her head. Her breasts swung free, rosy-tipped, as flawless
as the pearls in her hair. She felt the intake of his breath.

"You are more beautiful," he told her.

She lifted her head to stare at him.

"Come here to me." He seized the back of her head with
his hand and drew her mouth down to his. His lips were
soft and warm. His tongue thrust into hers.

With a soft moan she gave in, her thighs slipping to rest
between his. He was naked under the coverlets. Her legs
touched the hardness of his shaft, the rounded heat of his
sac nestled below. Breathing hard, his hand moved between
her sprawled legs and found her hot, wet center and his
fingers pushed inside. He thrust in, stretching her there,
quickly bringing a hurting, restless ache that made her
squirm.

"My fire witch." His hands kneaded her backside, "My
beautiful fire witch." She could feel him tense with the
force of his need. She shifted her body and moved her
mouth down his belly to do what he especially liked.

He stopped her. "No, stay, I want to look at you." He
seized her elbows to haul her over him, to straddle him.
He winced. "Be careful of my leg."

She had never seen him like this. He went slowly, kissing
her with painstaking gentleness on her shoulders and down
her arms, little nibbling caresses. He licked the tips of her

nipples as they swung over him tantalizingly, then pulled
her close so that his mouth could suckle her breasts, nip-
ping and biting until she cried out. Still that relentless hand
between her legs kept her pinned.

He pulled her head down, fingers tangled in her hair.
"Is this what it takes to make you happy?" he whispered
against her lips. "To have the boy with you?"

It broke the spell. She tried to pull away from him.

He held her tightly, frowning. "I tried to tell you that
night—with my accursed leg. That if I died Joceran would
bring back the boy to you."

She did not believe him.

"Damn you." His hands gripped her arms. "You would
have got the boy back as I promised. The king had naught
to do with it." He gave her a shake. "I want you to show
me your thanks."

In one way she supposed she believed him. That he
would have told Joceran to bring Magnus back to her if
he died.

She flung back her hair with both hands and looked
down at him. Back arched, her hips settled against his
darker, powerful body. She held her arms raised, pale hands
holding the shimmering mass of her hair up behind her
head.

She heard his swift intake of breath as she crouched over
him, naked as a pagan goddess. He held his cock in his
hand, huge and engorged, as Emmeline slowly lowered herself onto it. He seized her hips and pushed her down all
the way. She gave a shivering squeal.

He gasped as her flesh clasped him hotly. She moved
her hips in a small circle. He could not stand it for long.
Both his hands abruptly seized her hips and rotated them
against him, hard and rough. Emmeline shrieked; it was
almost more than she could bear.

Impaled on his body, she rode him wildly, her blazing
hair flailing around them. He caught it in his hands and

pulled her down against him as his big frame began to
thrash with his peak. The bedcoverings tangled around
them in their frenzy. He heard her cry out through the
crashing waves of his own release, and he seized her and
pulled her tightly against him until it was spent.

Emmeline suddenly burst into tears. Still straddling him,
she lay on his big body and wept.

Breathing hard, he stroked her wet, tangled hair.
"Shhhhhhh, it is all right. God's wounds, why are you
crying? You have the boy back now."

She wiped her mouth, wet with her tears, with the back
of her hand, but kept her face pressed to his still heaving
body. She did not want to move just yet. His big, bare
body under her was strong and warm. In the ward below
they heard a burst of noise, singing and the banging of a
drum and a viol; some of King Henry's highborn feasters
not ready to go yet to their tents, although it was almost
dawn.

She felt his shaft slip out of her, soft and limp and re-
luctantly moved her hips. She did not want to leave him.
She wanted for some reason to lie sprawled on him like
this, and cling to him.

"Emmeline," he said softly, right in her ear. "When are
you going to tell me about the babe?"

The drawbridge had been left open all night for the traffic from the feast to the king and queen and their court
camped in the meadow. The sun, as Walter cantered his
destrier over the boards of the drawbridge and out onto the
road to the village, was already a pale presence in a misty
sky above the trees. His eyes burned with sleeplessness,
but there was one more thing he needed to do.

In the meadow, a few servants were up and stirring,
building breakfast fires. The knight guards posted along
the road saluted him as he rode past.

At the stone bridge a fog lay over the surface of the leaden river. As the destrier crossed over, its hoofbeats muffled in the mist, Walter lifted his hand and crossed himself for protection against the water spirits, sprites, kelpies, and other ancient things that were known to haunt such places. He was stiff and tired from the night's duty at the feast, and the fog raised the hair on his head unpleasantly. At the far side he touched the stallion with his spurs. Surprised, the horse shot ahead, galloping halfway up the hill into town before it slowed. Walter grinned, the haunted spell broken.

He slowed his mount at the town gates. People here were up and about in the early light: a carter with a wagonload of vegetables for market, the town watch carrying his lantern high as he looked into corners for loiterers and thieves, the baker flinging open the doors of his shop and letting out the mouthwatering smell of fresh-baked bread.

They stared at Walter as he rode by. They all knew him, the lord's fair young captain in his heavy ring mail, gauntlets, peaked helmet, and long nose visor. The baker and the watch called out a hail.

He raised his hand. He supposed they knew where he was going. Enough of them had seen him in the goldsmith's street, spending a few moments stolen from some errand or other.

The big destrier almost knew its way. They passed the church, the stone wall surrounding the trees in the graveyard, then the block of wool factors' warehouses. The horse, knowing where they were, slowed and then stopped.

The manor house was surrounded by a high wall. But from the street one could see the upper stories, the shuttered windows of servants' rooms tucked under the thatch. There was a light in one of them. Walter saw a candle passing, throwing bright shadows on the walls.

They worked from dawnlight to dusk, he was thinking. Work and prayer. And yet the Beguines seemed happy. They laughed and smiled when they were with each other, in contrast to the way they were with other people. Then they kept eyes downcast, faces smooth, the briefest of greetings on their lips.

Someone came to the window, opened the shutters, and threw out a basin of water. Walter saw the silvery sheen of it, heard the splash. His eyes searched through the gloom for the face framed there. God and St. Mary, it was Berthilde! She had just washed, she was in a loose gown that showed the shapes of her young breasts. She had not put her hair up for the day. It flowed over her shoulders as brilliant as moonlight. She lifted her arm and he saw the motion of her arm as she began to brush it.

He sat there in the street on his mount, looking up at the window, transfixed. The sky grew a lighter color. Enough light now to see someone sitting a horse just outside the gate.

She looked down, yawned, and then saw him. He saw her start. Her eyes hesitated for only a moment. But that lightning glance, that wide-eyed look, seared Walter Straunge to the depths of his soul.

The next moment she had dropped the brush, reached outward quickly and slammed the shutters shut. Abruptly, the candle went out.

Walter had not moved. He sat his horse for a long time, still staring at the window, but there was nothing there but darkness. Finally he turned the destrier's head, and started back down the street.

It was more than he had hoped for. At least she'd known that he was there.

TWENTY-TWO

"Now may all the demons take me to rot in hell before I tell you there's anything good in what Henry Plantagenet's just given us!" Niall flung the wine cup he was holding across the room. It hit the wall and the wine in it splashed across the stones in red, spidery rivulets. The Earl of Hereford bent and picked up the cup and put it on a nearby table.

"At least the king gives you and Chester and Salisbury the courtesy of his counsel. But for me nothing, even as I've been these past months twisting in the wind with my cock hanging out for Cadwallader and half of damned Glamorgan to take their bites of it!"

Rannulf of Chester scratched his big belly. "Softly, Morlaix, the last time I saw that bludgeon of yours it hardly looked as though the Welsh had been chewing on it."

The Earl of Hereford looked thoughtful. "Yet Morlaix is right. Who could know that the king had sent Thomas à Becket to secretly parley with our friend Cadwallader? You see how Henry relishes surprises? It is his way of keeping us on our mark." He shrugged. "I think it was your attack at Glyn Cierog that turned them, fitzJulien. Some of the prince's own womenfolk were in the fire."

Niall shot him a burning look. "Christ's wounds, I would as soon forget that particular slaughter. It's nothing I'm proud of."

Hereford said, "Be easy, someone was a fool to put all those women and children in one wooden fort."

The door to the tower room was ajar but Emmeline had no desire to go in. She stood outside on the landing, able to hear most of what was going on. The news that the king would seek peace with the Welsh prince had come as a shock. How like Henry Plantagenet, everyone was saying. The king loved policy, politics, parleying; these were his element. That the news came as a surprise to his marcher barons was even more like him.

She had been with a delegation of guildsmen who had come to complain about conditions in the town when she first heard of it. There had been drunken fights and disturbances since the king and his court had been there, but what most worried the town was that virtually another had sprung up outside their gates, with traders and shopmen who had come from as far away as York and Chester. Not only were the strangers peddling food to King Henry's court, but one could buy almost anything now from a veritable army that offered iron mongery, bedding, clothing, jewelry, and even horse and mule trading.

The burghers' complaints had faded away when they heard that King Henry and Prince Cadwallader would meet to discuss a treaty of peace. No one knew what to make of it.

"Remember," Watris the smith said, "the old prince, Cadwallader's father, claimed this land as his own from ancient times."

The little wine merchant moaned. "Young King Henry has betrayed us. This is an English valley. We have always fought the Welsh here!"

It was not peace with the Welsh that worried Emmeline. Cadwallader would come there, to Morlaix, to meet with King Henry.

All those years couriers had carried the gold from France, and then shepherds had taken it across the mountains to Wales, only one gold courier had seen her. But surely others knew the Neufmarche house and how it had been used.

"Perhaps the peace will not come about," she told them. "Parleys go on for a very long time."

The guildsmen were still gloomy. They went back to have a meeting of the guilds and discuss whether to petition the king for a hearing. If they had to live with the warlike Welsh it was important that the king know their hardship.

She could not give into panic, Emmeline told herself. It was useless to try to run again, she had no money, no place to go; she could not help herself now if she tried. The guildsmen had come to her with their troubles because she was still a guildswoman, one of them, but more importantly, now the chatelaine of Castle Morlaix and the lord's wife. They looked to her to help them with her new influence.

It was almost too much. What influence she had, as of that hour, was that her seneschal and cooks had almost killed two of the queen's troubadors with a roasted stag.

A knight came up the stairs with a tray of bread and meat and clean cups and stopped when he saw her standing there. Emmeline took the tray from him and went inside.

The two marcher earls quickly stopped talking of the king and began to discuss the coming tourney.

"We'll have our work cut out for us, Morlaix," Hereford said. "The Welsh don't fight in tourneys, they hardly know the meaning of the word. Instead of taking knights' ransoms they'll be lopping off our heads."

Niall said shortly, "Then they can watch how the Normans and Angevins do it."

Chester finished off his ale, his small black eyes on Emmeline. "Ah, the Welsh are not as savage as you'd think. The prince has one or two who can mix in a decent melee. Daffyd ap Llandro was a year at court with French King Louis, was he not?" He put the wine cup down on the tray.

"Watch yourself, fitzJulien. I doubt they've forgotten Glyn Cierog. If captured your ransom would come high."

Hereford snorted into his wine. "If they bother to capture you at all!"

The Lord of Morlaix turned away. "I don't like tourneys. They're a waste of men and good horses."

Hereford laughed. "I will take you, Morlaix, if the Welsh cannot. I like the looks of your new stallion. The horse alone will make it worth my while. Too bad you lost the other one, though. What was his name?"

"Hammerer."

"Yes, good horse. I saw you fight him in France."

The earls went out. Emmeline stood with the tray in her hands. If there was a tourney everyone would be required to be there. The king, and Prince Cadwallader, certainly.

Somehow she had to think of a way. She said, "You can't fight in the tourney. If someone captures you, your ransom will take everything we have. They think we are rich."

Niall poured a cup of wine and tossed it off. He wiped his mouth with the back of his hand and looked at her. "God's wounds, I was expecting some piteous speech about not fighting in a melee for the sake of my poor wounded leg."

She said between her teeth, "Why would I make a useless plea like that? You will do what you want. It's the money I worry for! I am only trying to keep you from squandering what little we have left."

She longed to find out how much the Neufmarche accounts had been drained. By now, according to her figuring, they could be empty. Most of England's nobles who had had King Henry honor them with his presence would testify how much it had cost. Even bluff Chester had made some passing remark about his turn being next.

She watched him pour another cup of wine. He had been

drinking for hours with Hereford and Chester and was hardly sober.

"No one is going to capture me for ransom in any tourney." His words were slurred. "Jesu, but you have a poor opinion of my prowess. But then you haven't seen me fight."

God in heaven, she didn't want to.

She put the tray on a table. "King Henry is looking for girls in the town. Watris the smith told me he sends an older woman with two royal knights as her escort. She is in the town daily looking for young maids. Master Avenant the woolman has already sent his daughters to relatives."

"Christ in heaven." He stared at her, swaying slightly.

Emmeline bit her lip. She wanted to tell him of Cadwallader and the gold. That Cadwallader might at least have heard who she was and what part she had played in the passing of the gold, and that he might denounce her to Henry. But she doubted he was sober enough to believe such a story.

With a sigh, she said, "There are some who would like to have their daughters, even their wives—go to King Henry's bed. They can boast that they slept with a king. Some girls think that if they are lucky perhaps they will have a bastard of him."

He glowered at her. "Don't let him touch you. Do you hear me?"

She turned away from him. "God's face, is that why you never take your eyes from me when the king is near?"

"I know Henry." He poured himself more wine. "He would have had you by now, but he knows I am vigilant."

Only because he was vigilant. Her lip curled. It was useless to think she could explain about Cadwallader's gold.

In the beginning she had only continued sending the gold to Wales as her late husband had done. Now she was not so blameless. She had passed the gold on even when the courier had warned her it was coming not only from King

Louis of France, but also from some of King Henry's own
nobles.

God knows who they were. Perhaps some of them were
with the king here.

"What is the matter with you?" He was standing with
his hands hooked in his belt, scowling at her.

I am a traitor, Emmeline was thinking. No matter what
else I may have done, it is true: I stole the last gold the
courier brought, thinking to use it to escape.

Suddenly she felt light-headed. She had not thought
much of dying, but she could see that death might be very
near. Traitors died horribly. First they were tortured, then
dismembered, then their bowels drawn out, their arms and
legs lopped off. Finally they let the poor screaming
wretches hang.

The room seemed to waver before her eyes. Dear God,
he was right. What was the matter with her? Why did she
feel as though she no longer wanted to live if it meant this
constant state of terror?

"Emmeline. Wife." She heard his voice, rough with
worry, as if from far away. "The babe—speak to me. Are
you unwell?"

She could not answer. Her head spun, her mouth was
filled with brackish fluid. She felt as though she might
vomit.

Perhaps it was the babe after all. She had started puking
in the mornings, before she could get on her clothing. She
had never been sick like that with Magnus.

He picked her up and carried her to the bed and put her
down on it and bent over her. "Lie here." His voice was
hoarse. "I will go call Hedwid."

She did not want her maid, she wanted him to stay. She
needed someone to help her. Holy Mother, now of all times
she needed someone to help and protect her!

But she did not say anything. A moment later she heard
him go out, and close the door.

TWENTY-THREE

"Where the devil is Walter Straunge? Where is my captain? He was supposed to act as my squire."

Niall held his arms out as Gotselm tightened his mail chausses at the waist, then settled the bottom of the linen gambeson over them. He would sweat like a horse under it before the morning was up, but when one wore full tourney mail one could not do without thicker padding. He saw Gotselm had brought another clean underjacket, carefully hanging it from a limb of a tree nearby.

Out of the corner of his eye he saw the herald, an old Crusader by the name of fitzEadnoth, trot his horse across the tourney field, checking it for potholes and stones. A group of King Henry's Angevin knights had already set up their camps under the best shade trees. It was going to be a hot day. The sun was hardly up and the dew had already burned off the grass. The Welsh were making their camps on the west, keeping a distance from King Henry's French and English. Little Welsh servants ran about exercising the horses, sorting out gear and arms and laying it out.

To everyone's relief only a few of Prince Cadwallader's knights were going to fight in the melee, tourney veterans like Daffyd ap Llandro and his cousin, Meifod, who had spent some time at King Louis's court. There had been a rumor that the Welsh might take the field in force and fight together, which would have had the makings of a new war. Evidently even the Welsh wished to avoid that danger.

Those who had given their names to the herald numbered only a handful.

Prince Cadwallader himself rode up on his black destrier wearing polished mail that struck sparks in the sunlight, and a black tunic emblazoned with a silver dragon. He carried his helmet in the crook of his arm. His black-browed face was handsome, smiling. All the Welsh cheered.

Beside Cadwallader, stocky, red-haired, florid-faced young Henry would look plain as a spinster sister. And be at his most dangerous. If he fought the king, the Welshman didn't know how much trouble he was in for.

The field that fitzEadnoth had chosen for the tourney was in the flatlands next to the river, fairly level, and big enough to fight twenty or more to a side. The court servants that swarmed down to them had set up a pavilion with chairs for the queen and her ladies. It was decorated with rosettes of ribbons, and there were several brightly colored pennants on poles. Queen Eleanor had not yet arrived, but some of the other noble ladies were there, Chester's tall, fat wife among them. They stood to one side, talking. Niall looked for Emmeline and could not find her.

They'd had another row while he was dressing. It had ended only when she became sick and had thrown up in the chamber pot.

It served her right, he told himself, for having a damned tantrum over his fighting in the tourney. As though he could get out of it. With his reputation in France, and then under the old empress, he could no more fail to show than he could renounce the pope. But she thought somehow that he could.

She wasn't worried, either, about his leg. That annoyed him, for it was still healing and not as strong as he'd like. But she'd screamed like a virago about ransoms. That someone would capture him, probably a Welsh knight, and bankrupt them with demands for an outrageous fee.

It was the babe that was the cause of it, he told himself,

and that now she could not leave him. And not the fear of his being captured.

Hereford came up as Gotselm was helping him pull on his hauberk. "Where's young Walter? I thought you said he would squire you."

Niall swung his arms, getting used to the weight of the mail. He'd sent a groom back to the knights' tower and the boy had returned with the message that Walter had not been seen that morning. Nor, apparently, had his bed been slept in.

He said, "Will you ride in the first melee?"

The first combat of the day was usually full of new knights anxious to get into the middle of things. The veterans usually sat back and waited for the second after having noted the riders and especially the horses.

Hereford said, "No, the second. And you?"

"I'll go out in the first." He wanted to try out his leg. There was the possibility it might not last the day. In the afternoon the field would be churned up anyway; they would fight in a cloud of dust. Where the devil was Walter, anyway? He was seldom late. And then only with some good excuse.

Magnus came racing across the field, dodging horses, Joceran behind him.

"Oh, sir! Oh, sir!" The boy skidded to a stop and his eyes took in Niall in full tourney mail. Niall realized he had forgotten what blazing adoration looked like. That rapt expression as though one gazed on a being that surely was no less than the Archangel Michael.

"Oh, sir," his son breathed. He could not take his eyes from him. "May I—may I help? They say Sir Walter is late." He licked his lips, looking at Gotselm, who was strapping on Niall's sword. "I could—I could—"

Niall said gruffly, "See to my spurs. That they are safely put."

Gotselm leaned around to look into his face, eyebrows lifted.

Niall gave him a look that said he couldn't think of anything else. Magnus had dropped to his knees, examining each rowel with cupped hands, as reverent as a priest at mass. Joceran grinned.

After a few moments Niall took Magnus's shoulder and gently shoved him away. Then he dropped to one knee and crossed himself and muttered a prayer. He got to his feet and the groom came up with the new horse, a big bay, Jupiter. The stallion handled well, but had no experience in either battle or tourney. The horse stood rather tamely as Niall boosted himself up into the saddle.

The Welsh groom said, "He's a little lazy, milord. Good tempered, as it were."

Jesu, he didn't need that in a warhorse. "Well, I'm not."

He tucked his lance under his arm and gave the bay a touch of the spurs. The horse quivered, then broke into a fast trot.

Out into the field, Hereford on his big chestnut drew even. "FitzJulien," he shouted, loud enough to be heard into the trees, "I'll have Wycherly of you today, and five hundred crowns. How's your bad leg?"

The destrier suddenly stretched out his neck and tried to bite the earl on his mailed foot. Hereford drew back, cursing. Niall laughed.

FitzEadnoth stood under the king's banner at the head of the field. "Are you going out in the first?" he asked. When Niall nodded he waved him to the other side.

He knew fitzEadnoth watched him as he rode away. Under the herald's eyes he felt self-conscious, as though already beginning to favor his bad thigh.

Once he had crossed the field, Niall maneuvered the bay into a line of milling, shifting horses. At least on this side the sun was at their left shoulder, not yet in their eyes. The light danced on the chain mail, polished helmets, horse harness. Across the field some in the line of the knights there had painted their shields. He saw the White Horse of Chester, the Boar of Hereford, Cadwallader's Dragon.

A voice in their line said loudly, "There's a dip in the middle, covered with grass. Beware of it."

A second later the herald lifted the horn to his lips. Niall pulled the reins tight so that Jupiter backed slightly, then hit him with the spurs. An instant later the horn blasted. Mouth open, neck outstretched, the destrier bolted down the field.

The trick was to stay in front in the first charge. Six or seven of them had gained the front. Across the field about the same number were out ahead. Niall lowered his lance, set his shield and put Jupiter straight at Hereford's huge chestnut. They came together with a crash. All up and down the field the lines met with shouts, a cracking of lances and horses' screams.

Hereford's lance had glanced off Niall's shield, while he had managed an off-center blow that had lifted the other man in the saddle, almost unseating him. They passed, spurred their mounts, and turned to come back again.

A knight on a black horse suddenly loomed in between. Before Niall had time to make note of the face under helmet and nasal, the black knight swung a mace that Niall managed to catch on his shield. The blow jarred his arm to his shoulder.

He countered with his sword, slicing off a good portion of the other's shield. Jupiter crowded the black horse, forcing it back. They fought with great swings of their weapons, pounding one another. Hereford cantered back, took one look at their battle, then charged off into the melee.

The field surged with fighting men, some on horseback, some fighting on foot. Riderless horses galloped across the grass. At the edge squires tried to catch them and pull them off.

Niall spurred Jupiter and the destrier charged the black

horse like a juggernaut, chin in, spume flying from his jaws. By now Niall knew who he was fighting. From the fierceness of the sword blows, giving no quarter, he knew Cadwallader wanted to kill him right there. Rules of the tourney or no.

He dodged another swinging chop from the other's mace and turned Jupiter away in a circle, coming up on the other side. Niall swung his sword. Before the other man could turn his horse he hit him broadside across the back, knocking him over the stallion's neck.

Prince Cadwallader hit the ground and sprang at once to his feet, drawing his sword and dodging two knights on wounded horses hammering at one another. Niall drove Jupiter down on him, forcing him to back, and back again. The Welshman tripped and staggered backward, almost falling. He stopped, gasping, and lowered his sword, surrendering. Niall reined in and laid his sword briefly on the prince's black-clad shoulder.

Two fighters galloped around them, their horses' hooves kicking up bits of grass. The Welsh prince stepped out of their way and took off his helmet. His hair was plastered wetly to his skull, and his eyes burned like a madman's. Niall had no doubt Cadwallader had taken a vow of vengeance for Glyn Cierog.

"Name your ransom," the prince shouted.

"Your horse and armor," he shouted back. It was the least one could demand. Christ knows he didn't want money. Not after the slaughter at the fort.

The prince nodded. "I will send my squires to you."

Niall touched his helmet, and turned his horse toward the sidelines. FitzEadnoth had sounded his horn. Knights were riding, or walking off the field. A horse lay dead. Another, with a broken leg, was being led away. Under him the big bay, Jupiter, his neck and shoulders lathered, tossed his big head, not wanting to stop.

As Niall passed the ladies' pavilion he noticed that

Queen Eleanor had not yet arrived. For that matter, he'd not seen the king in the lists, either.

Joceran and the groom ran out to take Jupiter's bridle. Joceran said, "How did he do, sir?"

Niall dismounted and threw Gotselm the reins. "He's mad." The boy was bouncing up and down with excitement. He put his hand on his head and smoothed his red hair. "The damned horse is mad. It tried to bite Hereford."

The squire grinned. "He served you surpassing well in the melee. We were watching when you overturned the Welsh prince. Did you not hear the cheers?"

No, he hadn't. Once one was on the field and in combat one heard nothing. He looked around. "You have no news of Sir Walter?"

Another melee was being organized. Across the way the ladies of the queen's pavilion were in a clump, their backs to them, talking animatedly. A messenger in the king's colors broke away and left at a run for the castle road.

Niall pulled off his helmet. Inside his mail his clothes were steaming. His thigh was beginning to hurt; he gave up all thought of entering the melees in the afternoon. He could not shake a growing feeling something was wrong. The second melee was beginning, and the king should have been there. Hereford and Chester were in a group of magnates, talking, ignoring the herald's horn.

He saw Becket, the king's chancellor, making his way through the crowd. From the look on Becket's face something had happened. Niall felt the hair on the back of his neck rise and prickle.

Gotselm and the groom walked the lathered bay up and down to cool it. At Niall's nod Joceran pulled the boy away and sat him down on the grass to point out the lines of knights readying for the next melee, their lances at salute.

Thomas à Becket came up to Niall and took him by the arm. "Morlaix," the chancellor said urgently.

All that Niall could think was that it couldn't be the Welsh, they were there at the tourney. He braced himself.

"Walk away," the chancellor said, "so the others can't hear us." He took his arm and they strolled into the trees. "We have grave complications. The king has had a girl from the town with him these past two nights. Now your captain, Straunge, has abducted her."

At a little before noon the king came down from his camp to join the tourney. He fought in the fourth melee of the day on the side opposing Prince Cadwallader. The Earl of Chester actually engaged the prince, only to be soundly unhorsed and made to pay a stiff ransom, as well as give up his mount and arms. Chester was in a foul mood for the rest of the day, having prized both the sword and his new destrier.

King Henry fought both the Welsh knight, Daffyd ap Llandro, and the Provençal champion, Garibault, and acquitted himself well in two prolonged, well-matched battles. The queen did not appear to see his successes. The tourney seethed with gossip. Knights talked of it in the lists before the horn blew.

King Henry'd had a different girl in his tent for most of the nights the court had been at Morlaix. But a knight, variously named as one of the queen's Gascons, a Fleming in the king's service, or one of Morlaix's garrison, had abducted her. It was rumored Queen Eleanor was preparing to leave and return to London.

In midafternoon Thomas à Becket, the cojusticiar de Lacy, and Gilbert Foliot, the Bishop of London, met Niall at one end of the castle great hall. Archbishop Theobald did not come; he was still with the queen.

"She wishes to leave him," the bishop said. He wiped his sweating face with a small linen napkin. "The queen resists this great humiliation she feels the king puts upon her. Not only with this girl, but all the others. The disputes between them this morning were very public."

De Lacy snorted. "She followed the king from her tent out into the camp hurling curses, and threw an ale pitcher at him."

The bishop winced. "The queen is again with child and has the usual dyspeptic humors of her condition. One would pray King Henry would give it gentle consideration."

Becket said, "He needs to give more than this gentle consideration, but I fear he will not. I worry greatly about the Welsh treaty. It would be a mistake for Cadwallader to think Henry Plantagenet a fool." He turned to look at Niall. "Did the king say aught to you about sending after Straunge and the girl?"

Niall's conversation with the king that morning had been exceedingly brief. It was, after all, one of Niall's own knights that had committed this treason. He said, "No, milord, and I doubt anyone here knows where to seek them."

He had hoped the king would not ask him to send Gotselm with a troop of knights to run them to earth. Other than an occasional thought on what he would do to Walter if he had his neck between his two hands, Niall wanted no part of this until he could see his own position more clearly. The king had not dealt fairly with him in the matter of peace with the Welsh, but did not seem angry with him about Walter. Yet.

On the other hand, if Queen Eleanor left Henry, God forbid, she took half of France with her and another heir she might be carrying.

Becket started to speak, but de Lacy broke in. "If the queen leaves now, and takes her people and travels the length of England to London, half the world will know it."

The bishop said, "I fear half the world knows it now. Or will by the morning, given the tale-telling powers of our court. Milords, do not let us make light of it. It is not only a matter of the treaty with the Welsh, but England cannot suffer the king to be estranged from the queen."

Thomas à Becket pushed himself away from the table. "King Henry has forbidden Queen Eleanor to leave Morlaix. They are not estranged yet." He turned to Niall. "The king rode in the tourney this noon. How did he fare?"

"Very well, milord. He took on both Cadwallader's Llandro and the queen's Provençal, Garibault, trounced them, and extorted large ransoms. He seemed in good spirits."

As they left the hall the chancellor drew him aside.

"It would do no good to bring them back," Niall said before Becket could speak. "The king said as much. There would have to be a charge of treachery and treason over a trull he has had in his bed but one or two nights."

Becket walked him along, his arm in his. The ward was all but deserted except for a few servants and the castle guard at their posts. Everyone else was below at the tourney.

"Be easy, Henry loves you, Morlaix," he said in his rich, smooth voice. "You are his loyal marcher knight, not to be ruined this time." He paused as they made their way around a kitchen wain loaded with grain sacks. "Now if it were Hereford—"

Niall started. The chancellor smiled. "No, we do not need to bring back the knight, nor the girl. Your captain has caused enough mischief, but it is far more difficult than that. I did not want to speak before de Lacy or Gilbert, but the king is now filled with vengeful wrath, and seeks his defense before the queen as only he can. Which is, a bold attack."

They stopped at the smithy's yard. Becket let go of Niall's arm. For the first time he could see the chancellor's face without its calm, clever mask. "The king will not let the queen return to London until they have settled some matters over which they have quarreled before. The lady suffers greatly from the king's infidelities, while Henry most unwisely accuses her of the same with those members of her court he most detests, the troubadors. And in particular one Gervais Russel. Whom I believe you saw in my train when first I visited you."

Niall said, cautious, "He's not with the queen. If he is the blond singer I remember, I would have noted it."

"No, Russel is gone." The chancellor looked away. "Morlaix, you must know I am no favorite of Queen Eleanor's. I am too much her husband's great friend, and she is jealous of the time I spend with him. But she surely must know the church will not allow her another divorce, and an annulment is impossible. Besides, the queen has given King Henry two baby sons and it is said she now carries yet another child."

Niall frowned. "Milord, I—"

The other lifted his hand. "The king is demanding to see certain gifts he gave to the queen, which she has admitted to my lord Archbishop Theobald that she may have foolishly bestowed on some of her favorites. There were two. One, a ring, was given back. The other is missing."

Niall stared at him. Henry was indeed on the attack. Queen Eleanor was caught in her own trap if the king could claim his gifts were given as love tokens to some troubador. He said, "Is it anything that can be replaced?"

Becket shook his head. "It was a jewel the king thought most handsome when he gave it to her. And that the queen, not liking it that much, she now says, gave to Gervais Russel. Who, God help us in His mercy, now may be somewhere in Spain. Or perhaps even Italy."

"Jesu," Niall said under his breath. They were on the edge of Wales. Russel was too far away, even if one knew where he was, to send for him. He couldn't help saying, "How much simpler it would be if Henry just gave vent to his temper, and beat her."

Thomas à Becket smiled sourly. "Unfortunately the king will not settle for that. And one does not beat Eleanor, by the grace of God, Queen of England and Duchess of Aquitaine."

They stood in the half-empty ward, the sun hot on the back of their heads. The chancellor sighed heavily. "I have labored much for peace with the Welsh. I would not see this treaty slip through our hands over a king's weakness and a woman's folly. I am afraid those who love England and want to keep it from its enemies, must now pray fervently to God to preserve the future of this marriage!"

TWENTY-FOUR

Niall flung himself into the chair before the fireplace and ran both hands through his russet hair. "Christ in heaven, only now do they tell me, Gotselm and the rest, that he has been going to the goldsmith's house almost daily! Sitting in the street hoping for some sign of her, like any stupid, lovesick calf. The garrison knew, and damn them, not one would come forward to tell me!"

Emmeline stretched out the hem of the gown she was sewing against her knee. "It is not Walter's fault. The young king is a lecher. Like his grandsire, the first King Henry."

His head snapped around. "Don't talk like that. God's wounds, we are near enough to destruction as it is. I was a fool to let you bring those women here—they're devil's spawn, not wanting to be in a convent, like decent women."

She said evenly, "Yes, you remind me daily of my indecency."

That brought a snarl from him. "Holy Jesus in heaven, will I have this from you now? That you pick at every word I say?"

She shrugged. "That is what you said. That all decent women were in convents."

With a growl Niall got up from the stool and went to the table and poured himself a cup of wine.

While he was drinking it Emmeline said, "I, too, have had my losses, you know, but no one thinks of that. Mainsant, the aunt, has left. The guildsmen came to me and said that the priests in the church and the prior of the new monks have said both my Beguines are harlots, that Berthilde tempted men. They did not mention King Henry." She lifted the thread and bit it off, and smoothed out the edge of the gown. "So the guildsmen called on her. They brought me her keys."

"Good. From now on I will rent the manor myself." He paced up and down the bedchamber, around the stool where she was sitting with her sewing. "Damn Walter, how could he go off when I only have Gotselm to replace him? One can't pick a good knight captain out of the air."

He was fairly sure now that the king would not ask him to send a troop of knights after Walter and the girl. Attention was on the queen, who was thought to be confined to her tent in her encampment in the meadow. Although there was still talk of her leaving for London.

In the meantime, Becket had gained his treaty. There would be a great feast to celebrate the signing of a peace between England and Prince Cadwallader of northern Wales. A line of wains loaded with meat and wine had been coming down the Wrexham road since the tourney.

Emmeline stopped sewing and looked down at her hands in her lap. She said softly, "You know he will not marry Berthilde."

He stopped his pacing. "Probably not, if the king had her first. Walter's only a younger son, anyway he must do as his lord father says." He threw himself into the chair. "Worry about us if you must worry about anything," he told her wearily. "Henry may yet decide we are the cause of his troubles—you with your beauteous Beguine that his pimp woman handily found for him. And I with my fool knight captain so enamored of the girl that he carries her off virtually from Henry's bed. Jesu, who else would the king blame for the great scandal but us?"

He jumped up and went to refill his cup. "I tell you, it

is our good luck that the king seems to want to lay all fault at the feet of Queen Eleanor."

She opened her mouth, then closed it. "I had not heard that."

"Hear it now." He reached for the wine pitcher. "The whole court quakes with terror, fearing a schism in England if Queen Eleanor leaves the king—even to retire in a huff to London. By the cross, can't you see what will happen if her tribe of Gascons and Provençals decide to quit us and return to Aquitaine? Henry would never rule there again. He would have a Gascon revolt on his hands."

She said, "The queen has not left yet."

"No, he has forbidden her to. And so that her cause will be properly flanked, the king has ordered her to wear some jewel he gave her. Which she cannot. Becket tells me Queen Eleanor gave it to a love-stricken pet troubador before she sent him away."

His wife sat with her mouth open, her eyes fixed on him.

"However, the troubador is in Spain or Italy or some such far place, nursing his aching heart. And the jewel also, one must gather. No one knows where he is, or how to get it. God's wounds, you see how the king has won in this clever turnabout? Now he is the deceived husband, and not the adulterous villain! Queen Eleanor is a fair match for him in scheming, but this time I think he has checkmated her." He turned around in the chair to look at her. "God of angels, are you sick again?" She was white as a sheet. "What is the matter?"

"What is the troubador's name?" she whispered.

He got up. "If you are going to puke I will fetch the chamber pot."

"Stop." She held out her hand. "Did Chancellor Becket— did anyone speak his name?"

He frowned. "The troubador? His name is Gervais. Gervais Russel."

"Holy Mother." Her lips barely moved. "I have seen this jewel. He brought it to me to fix it."

There was rain in the night going northward through the hills, and the downpour on the slick, muddy track slowed them. Several times Walter stopped under the heavy-leafed trees to give the horses a rest and take a pause from the torrents that beat in their faces.

Since they'd left Morlaix he'd pushed his destrier hard, leading the girl riding the mare he had purchased at the horse fair some weeks ago. The little mount was a sturdy thing, and kept a good pace, but was no match for the stallion's speed and endurance. Walter doggedly kept the pace, telling himself that no matter what happened, he was not sorry he had taken her. Each time they stopped he leaned from the saddle to lift her hood and look down into her face. And each time, no matter how dark or raining it was, he saw the pale gleam of her smile that made his heart leap.

After a while, his hope that neither the king's forces nor troops from Morlaix would come to pursue them grew stronger. When the sun came up, he left the girl and the mare well hidden in a thicket of alders, and rode to a country inn to buy cheese and bread. They were just outside of Chester. His spirits rose when no one there seemed to have heard of a knight and a girl fleeing northward. Or anyone seeking them.

He began to hope that they would escape. That King Henry would not think it worthwhile to try to regain Berthilde. After all, the king rarely kept his girls for more than a night or two; he had counted on that when he had come up leading the mare and taken Berthilde as she was waiting near the king's tent for an escort to return her to the manor house. He had leaned from the saddle, picked her up and put her up before him and cantered away before any of the king's guards could stop them.

Niall fitzJulien, though, was another matter. Walter could not escape an awful guilt when he thought of how he had abandoned his post, breaking his knight's vows of faithful duty. The Lord of Morlaix was the one he had expected to pursue him.

But so far, their luck was holding.

He found Berthilde where he had left her, sitting on the grassy bank by the sun-spangled stream. She had taken her cloak off, hanging it in the branches of the alders, and had undone her long gilt-colored hair to dry it. Walter sat for a long moment before he dismounted, just watching her. She was still the most beautiful woman he had ever seen.

She turned to him, smiling. The blue gown she wore was still damp and clung to her, showing her rounded thighs, her perfect breasts with the outlined thrust of budded nipples against the cloth.

He slid out of the saddle, unable to speak, and walked to the bank of the stream and sat down beside her, handing her the lump of cheese and the loaf of bread he had bought in Chester.

She bent past him, brushing his chest with her arm, and pulled out his dagger from his belt and began to cut the bread.

Walter put his arm around her. He still could not believe that she was there, beside him. So much had happened—he had planned so much, risked so much in those desperate hours when he knew the king had taken her. Henry of Anjou was not brutal with women, he took too much pleasure in them, so he knew the king would not mistreat her. Yet the thought of her lying for her first time in another man's arms had filled him with helpless torment.

Now he had not thought much beyond this. To take her away and have her all to himself.

"Berthilde," he whispered into her hair. Surely everything would go well from now on. She was well worth his life, if it came to that.

She held up the tip of the knife with a piece of cheese on it and pursed her lips, wanting him to open his mouth. So close, her azure eyes filled his vision like the summer sky above them.

She was so lovely, so warm, leaning her soft body against him, that he swallowed the cheese almost without tasting it. Before he could refuse she put a piece of bread in his mouth.

He took it out of his mouth, not sure what he was going to say. "Ah, now—" he began huskily. He was somewhat surprised to find her hands at his sword belt, undoing the buckle. When it fell away, she leaned back, tugging at the bottom of his hauberk.

Walter started to resist. Then some reckless inner voice told him that it was safe enough there in the dreamlike sunshine. He needed to get out of his wet clothes and hang them up to dry, anyway. His padded gambeson under his mail oozed rainwater whenever he moved.

She helped him out of the mail hauberk and then his underjacket, smiling when his wet boots stuck and would not come off until she sat on the grass and braced her feet against him and pulled at them. He wanted so much to touch her, hold her. But when he tried to pull her into his arms she gave him another piece of bread to eat.

"Berthilde," Walter said. She spoke very little Norman French, and he did not know her language, Fleming or whatever it was.

She pushed him back against the grass and leaned over him. "I stay wid you," she whispered into his lips.

The very sound of her voice enchanted him. Those few words, he told himself, were actually a long speech in which she told him that she was glad that he had rescued her from King Henry, and that she believed they would live, and not be captured.

He put his hand on the back of her head and drew her mouth down to his, and kissed her.

The sun was hot where they lay. Somewhere in the long grass a bumblebee droned. The world seemed to be filled with sparks that flowed into their bodies, like a gold river into their veins, warm and delicious.

"Say that you are mine, Berthilde," Walter said as he touched her lips lightly with his. "No longer a Beguine, beloved, but mine."

There was no turning back for either of them. He was taking her home to Normandy, where perhaps his father would let him marry her. When his father saw her, he told himself, surely he would not be able to resist her.

She smiled again meltingly. Her long hair, still drying in the sunshine, dangled onto his face and shoulders. Her serene, blue-eyed loveliness took his breath away. "Maybe I be Beguine someday," she said. "If you make dead."

Startled, he saw her nod, the veil of her hair flying around them. "Vidows make Beguines," she explained. "Mainsant is vidow. Is not bad. But now"—her hand slid under his chausses, and her fingers found him, rigid and aching—"now I stay wid you."

"Berthilde," Walter managed in a strangled voice.

His mind was churning. He had risked both their lives to take her from King Henry. Perhaps she didn't understand. But he couldn't think clearly when her warm hands were on him, stroking him. He was suddenly drowning in a torment of ecstasy. And then he felt her mouth.

It wasn't going at all the way he had thought it would. Not that it wasn't wonderful—it was heaven. But it was strange, his angel-faced darling was not shy; she seemed to glory in what she was doing.

One night with King Henry, Walter thought. Somehow it no longer seemed to matter. Her long hair drifted over his legs. He heard her voice, muffled against his skin.

"I stay wid you," Berthilde murmured, "make you happy. I show you. Like your king show me."

The parchment had an odor of perfume. Emmeline put it on the worktable and smoothed it out with her fingers and leaned over it to peer at the sketch.

The queen had drawn it herself in greatest secrecy, Thomas à Becket had assured her, and had it smuggled from her tent by one of her court ladies.

Emmeline knew why she had not been summoned to take the drawing from Queen Eleanor's own hand with instructions and explanations. She would not want to explain it, either. Although now that she had met Gervais Russel she could believe that the queen was enraptured of her poets, but not guilty of infidelity. If anything, she wanted to think the imperious, reckless queen had given her lovesick troubador a final parting gift to ease his heartbreak. Just as Russel had said.

But she could see why King Henry was furious with her.

"It is not like this," she said. "My memory serves me better."

Thomas à Becket frowned. "You have only seen the jewel once, from what you say. The queen—"

She said without looking up, "The queen is not a goldsmith. I held it in my hand and examined it."

From behind him Niall said, "She knows the craft, milord. I have seen her work."

She shot him a look, but his expression was bland. Becket drew a stool out from under the worktable and sat down on it next to her. He watched her pull the ink pot to her, dip the quill and make a correction on the drawing.

Ortmund, who was standing behind her, leaned over to look. "That is dull work. I would have put rosettes there."

The chancellor lifted his head and caught the eye of the big journeyman. His mouth twisted ironically. "The king, although a brilliant man, is not a master of taste. You can see that in his daily attire. I have heard that although the crystal heart was his gift, Queen Eleanor never loved it."

Emmeline shoved the boxes of stones toward Ortmund. "This is what my gracious lord husband has brought back to us. There is a crystal shaped in an oval. Look to see what can be done to facet the top and the bottom so that it is made heart-shaped."

Ortmund sat down. Emmeline picked up the small bellows, opened the door to the smelter and blew the charcoal into yellow flames. If they worked all night they might be finished by dawn. She trusted Ortmund; there was not a better gem cutter in the west of England. If the crystal did not chip or break he might shape the heart in a few hours.

"You think it can be done then?" the chancellor asked.

Inwardly, Emmeline sighed. One could say "if the crystal did not chip nor break," but it was not so easily done. They had no spare crystals, at least not of that size. If they broke this one—

Ortmund had found it. He held it up between thumb and forefinger. By the light of the candles the crystal looked more than ever like a piece of clear, cold ice.

What worried them most was that the Neufmarche crystal had a slight flaw in what would be, if they were lucky, the upper right curve of the heart. The flaw was a tiny glint of light, an embedded crack no bigger than half an eyelash that one might look for and hardly find. But it was there. They could not even draw the filigree down far enough to cover it.

Emmeline picked up the hammer and a loop of softened gold wire and began the heart-shaped ring of the collet. It was very warm inside the goldworkers' shop. Crickets sang their loud night songs in the dark outside, but in the workshop it was quiet except for the occasional whoosh and hiss of the smelters as Emmeline worked the bellows, and the faint chink-chink of Ortmund's chisel against the crystal.

From his perch on a stool beside the journeyman, little Tom nodded sleepily. After a while the chancellor got up and went outside and the Lord of Morlaix joined him. They could hear them talking.

Emmeline listened to their low voices. She did not need to be told that Thomas à Becket was not happy conspiring with the queen, who had never been his friend. The chancellor was an exceedingly clever man; she'd known that the first time he'd visited Morlaix. He was clever enough to know that if King Henry found he had been tricked with a copy of the jewel he'd given the queen he would lose the king's trust and friendship forever. But Thomas à Becket also believed England faced a great peril with King Henry and Queen Eleanor so at odds over their marriage.

It was just as well, Emmeline told herself, as she had plans of her own. The opportunity to make the queen's jewel had fallen like a gift from the sky. It had taken time to persuade first Niall fitzJulien and then the king's chancellor that it could be done. But if it worked, she would have powerful friends. And, as God was her judge, she needed them!

She had felt Cadwallader's gaze on her more than once these past few days, even though she had taken pains to stay out of the Welsh prince's way. And the thought of meeting the gold courier again haunted her dreams.

The gaudy jewel, and she remembered it well, was not so difficult to make with Ortmund's help. It was the small amount of time they had, barely a night's work, that was daunting.

Dear Holy Mother, she murmured under her breath, *let me succeed.*

Ortmund looked up inquiringly.

"Nothing," Emmeline told him. "I was only thinking that I do not believe anyone on this earth is happily married."

* * *

Thomas à Becket took his leave, riding out of the manor yard, accompanied by a sleepy-eyed clerk on a jennet. The church bells were tolling for matins, which the Cistercians in their monastery outside of the town now observed. Dawn was still three hours and more away.

Niall had seen the chancellor out the manor gate. When he came back into the workshop he nearly fell over the small child sleeping curled in a knot on the floor. His wife and the journeyman goldworker were still bent over their work. The late August night was still warm and the small furnaces made the room even hotter. Even the shutters were closed to keep out the clouds of moths that collected around the candle flames.

He bent and picked up the boy, curled into a bundle of bony arms and legs. Failing to find any place to put him, he sat down in the chair by the fireplace. The child's head lolled back on his arm, still sleeping soundly.

He heard the journeyman goldsmith make a small sound between his teeth. "It's madness, to work this fast. Look at that."

"I see nothing," Emmeline said. Their heads were so close they were almost touching. "It looks the same to me."

Niall shut his eyes, hearing talk about a flaw in the stone that he could not quite catch.

He was sorry now that his wife and the goldworker had been dragged into this, even though they had agreed to it willingly. If they lived through this the journeyman would have to be rewarded somehow. Not only for his skill, but for risking his life. He should probably buy the man's master's certificate from the guild. Lack of money was probably all that had kept him, at his age, from getting it.

As for his wife—

He opened his eyes slightly to see her. By the blaze of the candles she was a sweetly curving figure in spite of the big leather apron, her elbows propped on the worktable and the sound of her hammer tap-tapping gold wire into

filigree. The light caught the fiery streaks in her tumbled
red hair. A splotch of perspiration stained her gown between her shoulder blades.

A fine lady of the castle, he thought. My goldsmith wife.

He was surprised at a rush of feeling. And the thought
that he would strike anyone else who used those words to
mock her.

He doubted she fully realized the danger of what she
was doing. The queen could not protect them if King Henry
discovered the truth. Yet she had pledged herself to it most
bravely.

She *was* brave, he thought. He had married her by force
and taken her money, her house, her boy, and she had not
been conquered. She was so much a part of his life now
that he did not know what he would do without her.

That was God's holy truth, Niall knew with a sinking
feeling. His wife sewed his clothes, sat beside him at
meals—she had nursed him back from hell when he feared
losing his leg. She lay beside him in bed at night and gave
him comfort just with her warmth, not to mention her body
when he desired it. He owed her an honorable reward as
much as he owed the journeyman goldsmith.

More. For he loved her.

He sat quite still, thinking about it. *He loved his wife.*
Somewhere in the days they had lived together, only toler-
ating one another, this prideful, prickly, golden vixen had
stolen his heart.

He shifted the sleeping child in his lap. Trickles of perspiration ran down his thighs where the boy sat on him.
All he could think of was that he loved his wife. It made
a great, hollow place inside him. For he knew that to give
her what she most desired, he would have to set her free.

He could hardly bear the thought of it.

If he let her go she took his son and the new babe with
her. It was worse than anything he had faced on the battlefield. He would lose all of them.

There was one thing he could do. He could send her to her grandsire's, old Simon of Wroxeter. Even with the heavy fines he'd had to pay King Henry for his marriage there was still enough money left to set her and the children up comfortably under the old man's roof. There was irony in knowing how surprised she would be to find her precious fortune was not as gutted as she had thought. That there was still much of it left.

God knows he couldn't much blame her. Morlaix was all he had ever wanted, thanks to his father's dreams, along with enough wealth to maintain it. Now, for being a consummate fool, for being hard and unloving and grasping, he would have to give his wife her freedom. His honor would let him do no less.

Damn her, though—when he finally found what he wanted, she was taking it away from him! The thought of losing her made the rest of his life stretch out before him empty, and unbearably dreary.

He shifted the sleeping child again and considered putting him down and going outside for a breath of air, but found his body too tired to respond.

Somewhere in the night outside there was a rumble of thunder.

Just before dawn Emmeline closed the vents to the furnaces, snuffing out their fires, and leaned over the table to blow out most of the candles. They had worked so long the table was spattered with candle wax. Ortmund stood up and leaned over to open the shutters. The night breeze blew in upon them, cool and damp enough to tell of a storm somewhere.

She stood up and pushed the stool away, stiff with so much sitting. Beside her, Ortmund dug at his eyes with his fists, and yawned. Holy Mother, but they were tired and

looked it. "Leave the tables," Emmeline told the journeyman. "We will set all to rights in the morning."

He smiled wryly. "Mistress, it is almost morning now."

They stood at the worktable to look down one last time
at what they had done.

The finished heart-shaped pendant in its collet of gold
filigree lay on a square of black cloth, its gold chain spread
out above it. They had put out most of the candles but the
remaining tongues of light set the polished, faceted crystal
to shimmering. It did not look so gaudy now. It was, in fact,
a perfect replica of the one Gervais Russel had showed her.

Being jewelers, their eyes searched at once for the tiny
hairline crack of the flaw. And found it.

They both sighed. "It will not be noticed," Ortmund assured her.

"Let us pray to the Holy Virgin." Emmeline crossed herself. God's Mother was a woman; she would understand
these things. After all, as the chancellor said, they were
trying to preserve a marriage.

And I am trying to save myself, and my boy, she thought.

"The chancellor will reward you," the journeyman murmured. "And the queen herself—surely she will be won-
drously grateful."

Emmeline could only nod. Ortmund gave her the keys
to the shop to close up, and went out. She looped the crystal heart about with its chain and put it in a pocket in her
skirts. Then she blew out the rest of the candles and took
up the small lantern. When she turned, she found the Lord
of Morlaix, sound asleep in the high-backed chair with little
Tom in his arms.

She approached him quietly, shading the lantern's light
with her hand.

He slept with his long legs sprawled out before him,
booted toes turned up, clasping the apprentice draped across
his lap. A strong man and well-made, broad shoulders in a
good red wool jacket trimmed with silver thread and silver

buttons—his court clothes—worn with tight-fitting black hose. He slept with his head back and his mouth slightly open like most men, his dark lashes shadowy crescents against his cheekbones. Dark red hair tumbled about his face. He looked young, handsome, his mouth gentle and soft.

It was an illusion. But that face made her sigh, remembering the young knight she had known.

No matter, he would be rewarded, too, Emmeline told herself. If what they had done this night went well, Niall fitzJulien's favor with Queen Eleanor would be immeasurable. Not to mention that all-important man, the king's chancellor, Thomas à Becket. King Henry was already indebted to him; Niall had once saved his life.

He had everything he wanted now, Emmeline told herself. He did not need her anymore. He had her fortune, her manor house, her goldsmithing shop. With all of that he should be content, and let her go.

Without thinking, she bent over him and smoothed a red strand of hair back from his face. He stirred, and opened his eyes.

He saw who it was and his face changed and hardened.

Emmeline said, "Wake up, the jewel is finished. You must now take it to the queen."

TWENTY-FIVE

The feast began in late afternoon with a continuous meal of legs of beef, mutton, veal and venison, capons, ducklings, chickens, rabbits, hundreds of eggs, wine and ale by the barrel, cheeses, roast boars' heads and swans in plumage, puddings, confections, pies, apples, plums and even sweet white grapes and oranges brought from France and Spain and rushed northward by couriers straight from the docks of London. There were also whole stags, but out of a sense of delicacy—or perhaps safety—these were kept on their roasting spits outside in the ward, and only haunches and loin cuts were brought into the hall.

Jongleurs followed the successive courses with music and singing. As soon as the spiced wine and wafers and fruit were served, Cadwallader's Welsh bowmen produced a dozen harpers and a chorus who entertained with Welsh songs until the acrobats and jugglers were brought in. The professional entertainment would last until midnight, when as was usual the tables would be dismantled and the guests take the floor to dance to the music of massed lutes, viols, and the small drums called tabors.

The queen and her ladies did not appear until after the serving of the first course. The king had seemed to be waiting impatiently for her to arrive. He drank heavily and kept glancing at the doors from time to time in spite of his animated conversation with Thomas à Becket and the Bishop of London.

All voices in the feast hall gradually trailed away as Eleanor of Aquitaine, her tall, exquisite figure showing no sign of her coming babe, and clad in a close-fitting gown of silver samite, cinched with a belt of silver rope studded with rubies, made her way through the doors and down the main aisle of the feast hall.

She wore a circlet of polished silver on her brow from which fell a short veil of transparent silk. Under it, her long, waving dark hair with its golden streaks was worn long and free to her elbows, like a maid's. Most enchanting of all, her luminous dark eyes were rimmed with charcoal, the lids touched with something silvery. As she walked, her slender body swayed, and her mouth curved with the faintest of smiles.

"God's wounds," Niall said under his breath.

The Lord and Lady of Morlaix were seated well down the table from King Henry and the swarthy Welsh prince, Cadwallader, Chancellor Becket, the Lord Archbishop Theobald, the justiciars, and England's earls, Hereford, Chester, and Salisbury.

They saw King Henry stand up, toss off the last of his cup of wine and vault the high table, barely missing the Abbot of St. Botolph's and other churchmen seated just below, and hurry his stocky, powerful body down the aisle to meet his queen.

Thomas à Becket leaned forward, hands gripping the table until his fingers showed white. The justiciar, de Lacy, turned to look at him.

"Where is it?" the chancellor muttered. "Where is the jewel?"

Emmeline could not see, either. The king approached the queen, his back blocking their view. Niall fitzJulien turned his head to her in that moment, and their eyes locked.

She was light-headed, she had had only a few hours sleep after the hectic night's work, but she was not mistaken. *They were in this together,* his look said.

In the middle of the feast hall, King Henry had taken the queen's hand. He turned, holding it high as though beginning a court dance, and started toward their table. He inclined his head and said something to her. The queen raised her eyebrows provocatively.

"God's face, what games now are they playing?" de Lacy murmured.

The young king and his queen never took their eyes from one another. Henry's ruddy face was filled with sardonic glee. With her catlike smile, his queen returned it. The passion, the challenge, the cross-grained fascination they had for one another was there for all the world to see as they continued their measured walk toward the high table. A few cheers broke out in the back of the hall, then swelled to a roar. Henry's grin grew wider.

Thomas à Becket accepted a cup of wine from a server and downed it in a gulp. De Lacy leaned to him. "You take these things too seriously, Thomas," he observed. "It will only bring you trouble in the future, mark my words."

The queen's silver samite gown was cut low in the French fashion, showing the cleft of her famous beautiful breasts. Nestled there was the gift the king had given her, a crystal heart set in gold filigree on a gold chain. The light of torches and candles winked on the surface of the jewel, and made shimmering sparks.

Servers, carvers, ushers, and stewards scrambled ahead of the king and queen as Henry escorted his lady to her seat. As Queen Eleanor stood by her chair he placed his hands on her shoulders and drew her to him and kissed her. Even more gallantly, he lifted the crystal pendant and placed his lips against it.

A kiss for the queen. A kiss for his token of love to her.

Emmeline looked down the table at Thomas à Becket, whose darkly handsome face was masklike. But his eyes betrayed him.

With a shock, she realized that once that clever and intelligent man, Henry of Anjou, had lifted the crystal heart in his hand he had seen the flaw, and known the truth.

"It doesn't matter," Niall said. He went down the tower stairs swinging his cloak over his shoulder.

"What do you mean, 'it doesn't matter'?" Emmeline hurried after him, clutching her morning gown to her body. She was not yet dressed because everyone was hurrying to catch up with the king, who was already on the road. Magnus and Joceran were waiting at the bottom by the open door, the squire holding the reins of the destrier, Jupiter.

He said over his shoulder, "You have already seen how the queen and King Henry settle things, haven't you? And did not Henry send Thomas à Becket here to secretly parley for peace with the Welsh, not letting his own marcher barons know of it?"

He was still bitter about that. Magnus threw himself on Niall to hug him, and he put his arm around the boy's shoulders.

She said in a voice the others couldn't hear, "But you warned he was vengeful!"

He shrugged. "If the king knows it is not the jewel he gave Queen Eleanor, I tell you it doesn't matter. He took her to his bed after the feast, and the servants say they stayed up half the damned night. And last night he slept with her again."

But afterward, Emmeline knew, King Henry had risen before dawn, breaking camp and riding away for Chester before even Earl Rannulf could know of it. It would be nightfall before all of the court could get itself on the road north. Even Prince Cadwallader had been roused in the middle of the night to bid King Henry goodbye. Now the camps were in the usual uproar, and the queen was said to be following the king to Chester at her own pace.

Niall fitzJulien had the king's order to go north with an

escort of fifty Morlaix knights in the vanguard of his titular liege lord, Rannulf, the Earl of Chester, and take his annual oath of fealty there before Henry. Joceran had packed his belongings, and in the absence of Walter Straunge would act as his squire. Magnus was staying behind, much to his loud dismay.

Emmeline thought: Thank God Henry of Anjou is not my husband. She felt as if a whirlwind had seized them. As indeed it had.

She followed Niall as he led his horse out into the ward. Knights and servants milled about loading wagons and saddling horses. She was thinking that what he had told her, that it did not matter if the king had recognized the crystal heart as a copy, made no sense.

And yet in a way it did. She was learning that everything that surrounded the king and queen and their court was not what it seemed. And even that changed constantly. That strange tableau at the feast, when Queen Eleanor had presented herself almost defiantly to her spouse—and he had reveled in it—would stick in her mind forever.

Joceran had been sent to look for something in the baggage. He came running back with a role of vellum and gave it to his lord, who was tightening the girth on his saddle.

Niall took it and turned to her. "I haven't had time to talk to you about this."

She knew that he had, and from the look on his face had put it off until the last minute. She took the role of vellum tied with red string, feeling it was something unpleasant.

Magnus tugged at her hand, begging, "Mother, Mother, may I saddle my pony and ride with them as far as the river?"

"It is the deed to the Neufmarche manor house in the town," Niall told her. "Becket had one of his clerks draw the writ for me so he would know what I was settling on you and the boy."

She turned the vellum over in her hands, not wanting to open it. She didn't want to read it, she told herself.

"And some money. We will go over it when I come back."

She looked up at him. He was traveling mailed and armed at the head of his knights and only lacked his helmet that Joceran was holding. Speaking to her, he was the perfect Norman knight, distant and implacable.

"Jesus God," he said, "why are you looking like that? I thought it would make you happy."

She whispered. "Why would this make me happy?"

Joceran handed him his helmet and he put it on, jamming it down on his brow. He looked out at her from behind the jutting steel nasal. "I never understand you. You will need income from the house and some money when you go to live with old Simon in Wroxeter. You wanted to be free, didn't you?"

Joceran and Magnus goggled at his words, mouths open. Emmeline herself could hardly believe what he'd said. He'd never mentioned the subject before.

Niall took the reins from the squire's hands and swung himself up into the saddle. Rannulf of Chester came cantering up from the bailey and reined in his horse beside him.

"There you are," the earl said. "I wondered if you would drag yourself out of a warm bed like the rest of us. Is this disorderly mob what you plan to take with you?" He touched his helmet to Emmeline, and made a pretty speech to her about her fine hospitality.

She stood clutching the thin morning robe to her while Magnus jerked at her hand. She thanked Chester, and urged him to come back. "No, you can't go," she hissed at her child.

The big men on their horses made their goodbyes. They

rode out into the crowded ward and through the arch to the bailey. Joceran went to get his horse and the pack mule with their baggage.

"I don't want to go live anywhere," Magnus yelled. "I want to live here!"

Emmeline let go his hand. He ran down into the bailey, calling out to Joceran to wait. She held the vellum role tightly to her as she made her way back over the trampled grass to the tower.

She could think of only one thing. *That he'd said she was free.*

It began to rain on the following day, the spell of bad weather they should have had in late summer. There was so much work to be done now that the court had left their camp in the meadow and the town, that every one was cranky and out of sorts. First they discovered there were women and children left behind, mostly camp followers of the court. The Cistercian fathers at the monastery took the women in and fed them and their babes until the rains stopped and they could take to the road again in search of their men.

Then the castle seneschal, Baudri Torel, took to his bed with an attack of quinzy, leaving the reeves and chambermaids free to be idle and gossip, and the cooks and kitchen staff to quarrel and fight as they always did given the chance. Gotselm the serjeant had gone to Chester with his lord, leaving Jiane, the lanky Provençal serjeant, in charge of the remaining garrison, which had grown slack in a remarkably short time. Several fights broke out at once over dicing debts.

Emmeline took Magnus to town to the manor house, as he was restless cooped up in the castle while the autumn rains continued. She'd thought he would like to work with Tom and Ortmund on some new orders for communion plates and cups that had come in. But Magnus loudly claimed he was not interested in goldsmithing work, was savage with young Tom, and wouldn't obey Ortmund. He wanted to spend his time in the barracks at Morlaix Castle, watching the gambling and wrestling, and listening to the knights' talk.

Ortmund told her to let him go. "The work's not in his head anymore, mistress," the journeyman told her. "But he don't need to give us the back of his tongue, neither."

She made Magnus apologize, and had him spend the rest of the day polishing brasses. The empty manor made her strangely downhearted. She knew she should be happy; she had the deed to it now and the promise of leaving, escaping a marriage she hated, to go live elsewhere. But as she walked through the spotless rooms Emmeline couldn't help wondering where Walter and Berthilde were, and how they were faring. With any luck, they should have made Walter's home in Normandy by now.

Had he been able to marry her? she wondered. Did he still want to? She found herself thinking of them much more than she thought of King Henry and his queen.

At night she lay in bed and tried to imagine going to live with her grandsire, old Simon of Wroxeter, who was in his eighties by now. She hadn't seen him since she was a small girl. How could one tell if the old man even wanted her and her boy? And now her coming babe?

Life was not easy for women who did not live with their husbands. Most were in convents. On the other hand, money and a good reputation were what mattered; if one had those one would not be bothered too much by priests and gossiping women. Still, she worried.

It would be strange to be alone again. Freedom was all well and good but she was not sure now how she could raise Magnus. The little that he had seen of a knight's profession, especially the few days with the king's court, had seemingly spoiled him for goldsmithing and a life of commerce. Dear Holy Mother, if worse came to worst she supposed she could send Magnus back to his father and let him train to be knighted there at the castle! It was something she'd never thought she'd consider. But then her life had changed so it was no longer easy to say what she would or would not do anymore.

I will set up a goldsmith's shop in Wroxeter, she told herself.

She thought of the Wroxeter guild, and how she would have to apply to them. There were already several prosperous goldsmiths there; if they had a bishop or abbot in the district who opposed women in trade, it would be even more difficult.

She turned over and tugged at the bedcovers, restless and inexplicably discontent. The bed seemed empty; she missed the warmth of a body next to hers.

I am a fool, Emmeline thought.

The rain finally stopped and a gusty wind tumbled gray clouds across a lowering sky. The earth dried out enough so that the villeins began their plowing for the winter crop of grain. The Lord of Morlaix sent two of his knights from Chester to fetch his jousting lances as King Henry and Earl Rannulf had decided to hold another tourney to challenge the king's Northumbrian barons. When Emmeline asked the young knights who had come for the lances how the king and queen fared, if they were still cordial with one another, they only gave her blank looks.

Then John Avenant came up from the town with some of his fellow wool guild members, bringing a letter from Nigel Fuller. Emmeline was astonished. The young fuller had disappeared so completely she'd thought him dead.

"Not dead, mistress," the wool factor told her, looking aggrieved. "But sent in chains to York as punishment by your lord for helping you, and then sold as a boundman to wool buyers from Bruges. Fortunately, as he is well-schooled and vigorous, young Nigel has recovered from his misfortune and has been taken in by a company of merchants of that city. This is what his letter is about."

Emmeline listened, fascinated, as the guild's clerk read the letter from the fuller. After a flowery greeting and wishes for everyone's good health and spirits and most particularly the happiness of the gracious Lady of Morlaix, it proposed the marketing of their local cloth in Bruges. Nigel offered a long-term contract with a substantial cash sum in advance, agreeing to a fixed-annual payment for the duration of the contract.

"But Flanders makes their own cloth in great quantity," Emmeline said, "that is why we sell them our wool. What little we make here has always been for our own use."

Much of their Morlaix clip was shipped raw and unsorted to the Flemings. Once they received it, an apprentice removed the damaged wool and divided it into three grades: fine, medium, and coarse. Then it was washed in lye to remove the grease, and laid on wooden boards to dry. Forceps in hand, the apprentices then got on their hands and knees and crawled about, removing bits of soil and other particles. The wool of carcass sheep used for slaughter was kept apart. It was considered an offense to mix it, and usually the factors did not bother to send theirs abroad.

Morlaix wool was known for its high percent of "fine" grading. But even then the local factors always kept back the very best, to remain in the town where, after it had been washed and dried, it was beaten, combed, and carded until the fibers were aligned. Then John Avenant and the wool guild consigned it to spinners, all women, who spun it into yarn with a distaff and spindle. Then it went to the weavers, who were nearly always men. Although a few specially skilled women did ply the trade.

Nigel the fuller had treated the Morlaix weavers' finished cloth at his fuller's shop, soaking and shrinking the fabric and rubbing it with fuller's earth, a thick clay that not only cleaned it and gave it body, but conditioned the cloth to take the dye.

Emmeline had passed by the shop many times to see the fuller and his assistants trampling the mixture in a trough with their bare feet in a process called waulking, or walking. Which also explained why some fullers were called Walker as well.

After the cloth was soaked again, it was hung up to dry on wooden frames called tenters and fastened by tenter-hooks so that the cloth was stretched to the right length and breadth.

She had always known Morlaix cloth was excellent. Which was why they kept most of it for their own and did not sell it. She liked to watch the final stage of finishing the wool cloth, when the nap was raised with teasels while it was still damp, and sheared when dry with great shears that were sometimes three or four feet long. The finest cloth was shorn and reshorn a number of times. In Morlaix the exact number was a secret, but most of northern England knew that their fine wool made extraordinary clothing. To have a Morlaix wool cape meant it was not only beautiful but nearly rainproof. One could wear it and hardly have a drop of wet come through.

However, it was a very ambitious plan to think of making the cloth in quantity, as they would surely have to do, to send on to Flanders to be sold. But then Nigel Fuller was a very ambitious young man. She couldn't help wondering if he still thought he loved her.

John Avenant had been watching her closely. "Ah, yes, mistress, the Fleming cloth trader who brought Nigel's letter says the young fuller asks after you most eagerly and wants news of you and your boy. Which I told him, so that he could bring it back to Bruges."

Emmeline folded the parchment and handed it back to him. "And, pray, what was that?"

The factor's eyes glinted. "That my wife Gaeweddan had told me you were carrying the lord's babe."

She gave him a cool look. "I am honored that you come to me with this proposal from Nigel Fuller, but I can do nothing. You must ask audience of the Lord of Morlaix, and lay it before him. It is the lord's permission you want, after all, to trade with Flanders."

There was a groan of disappointment.

"Nay, Mistress Emmeline, it is you we always come to," one of the clipmen cried. "Have you not lent us money and exchanged our coin and given us wise advice in the past? You have known our wool trade since you were a young maid wed to old Bernard Neufmarche." He crossed himself. "May God be merciful on his everlasting soul."

There was a flutter of hands as the others did the same.

Emmeline could not answer them, although all eyes were on her. She couldn't tell them that she would soon be leaving to go and live in a fairly faraway place. But sweet heaven, they *did* want to hold her there, she thought as she looked around. They wanted her to be their lady of Morlaix and their good angel and their banker and moneylender, too!

She suddenly had a feeling, strangely enough, that if she wanted to stay at Morlaix, Niall fitzJulien would not object.

It began to rain again as the woolmen rode out of the bailey and down the road to the town. The guildmaster and another wool factor rode mules, the others were on foot.

They would all get a drenching before they made their houses, Emmeline thought as she watched them from the portal gate. It was a blessing the September weather was still mild. In October they would feel not only the rain that lashed the slopes of the Welsh mountains, but the first bite of winter.

Geese and ducks came out to waddle through the puddles

in the outer bailey. They ran away squawking as Emmeline shooed them out of her path. She stopped at the kitchen house to send one of the little knaves to fetch Magnus from the knights' tower, and drank a cup of ale the cook got for her.

She sat a trestle table in the kitchen house in the midst of the steam and bustle of preparations for the evening meal, and told herself she could hardly remember Wroxeter. She'd visited there only a few times when she was a small child. Even then her grandsire was old, a tall, taciturn man with black eyes and graying black hair who'd been a warrior in his youth, a friend of King Henry the First, the Lion of Justice. And finally a scholar in his later years, far-famed not only in England but in France and Germany and other foreign lands. Sometimes, although she could not remember where she'd heard it, he was called Simon the Jew. Jewish blood ran in the family, someone had whispered.

When Magnus came in, dragging his feet and begging to be allowed to sleep with Jiane and the Gascon knights, she promptly sent him up to the lord's bedchamber and Hedwid after him to see that he had hot water to wash with before he came down for the evening meal. It was far too noisy in the kitchen. She left half her ale in her cup and went out into the rainy ward with some idea of visiting her mare, who was due to foal any day. But she stopped when she heard the hail of the guards stationed at the postern gate.

Whoever the visitors were, the knights passed them at once. Standing in the ward, Emmeline saw two riders approaching, rain streaming from their cloaks. It was only when the rider on the black destrier threw back his hood that she saw who he was.

He was not wearing a helmet. His hair was thick, curly, and black like his heavy brows, in contrast to the paleness of his skin. A handsome Welshman. One who would stand out in any gathering.

The rider was Prince Cadwallader. The other man, who also threw back his hood, was the one Emmeline knew as the gold courier.

TWENTY-SIX

He was holding her hand so tightly it hurt. Up close, she could smell his musky, travel-wet clothes. Prince Cadwallader's blue eyes were flecked with yellow streaks, like a cat's.

"Don't pull away," he warned. Jiane the knight serjeant had come to the door of the great hall and stood there watching them. Cadwallader lifted her captive hand to his lips. "Milady Emmeline, be sure you let your people see that you welcome me."

There were people all around them: kitchen knaves carrying refuse out to the midden pile, knights stabling their horses, all more or less watching them. But for the life of her Emmeline could not speak, could not do anything, she was so stiff with surprise and fear.

It has finally happened, she told herself. She saw the curly-haired gold courier looking at her with something like amusement.

"Lady Emmeline, you tremble." Prince Cadwallader's voice was soft. He let go her hand. "Is it the matter of the last gold that Rainald passed to you, and which you kept and did not forward to me?" She jerked around to look at the gold courier. Cadwallader nodded. "Ah, yes, but rest easy, what is done is done. We will let bygones be bygones. I am not so much concerned with what is owed now as with what is paid." Handsome as he was, his face was full of cruelty. "Like those payments I wish to make to that bastard Irish cur, your husband, which he so justly deserves."

At his words she tried to pull back from him. He knew she had stolen his gold from the courier. Niall fitzJulien had burned Cadwallader's fort, Glyn Cierog, with a terrible slaughter, and then bested him in the tourney before all King Henry's court. It was clear what the Welsh prince meant when he talked of payment.

She could not help it, she shuddered.

She'd foolishly never thought to see him there again. Even now she was reminded that she was alone with Magnus, that Joceran and Gotselm were gone, attending their lord with King Henry in Chester. She had only Jiane and the garrison knights.

She was suddenly, wildly, tempted to call them to attack Cadwallader and take him prisoner. In the next instant she knew she could not do that all unprovoked: the Welsh were now at peace with England and King Henry.

Out of the corner of her eye she saw Jiane start across the ward toward them. The prince was saying, "Do you have a place for us, out of the wet? We must beg your hospitality, dear lady, it has been a long journey."

She lifted her hand and wagged it to show Jiane she didn't need him. He couldn't help her, nor could any of the knights. She must needs take care of this herself.

Emmeline drew a deep breath and said, "Come into the feast hall then, milord. There is a goodly fire on the hearth where you may dry out your clothes. And my cooks can offer you hot food and wine and ale."

She started for the hall, but instead of following her Cadwallader took her arm. "We are not hungry," he said in her ear. "I desire a place more intimate, where you can properly entertain me. Take me to the lord's chamber."

For a moment her fright was like a fearful ringing in her head. Dear God, she was trapped, she thought; he had planned this before he came. It was proper enough to take

the Welshman to the lord's bedchamber and offer a change
of clothes and enough hot water to bathe in because the
prince was a sovereign lord. She would do no less for King
Henry.

But it was not the same. And he knew it.

She licked her lips, her mind racing. There was nothing
she could do now short of murder. It was within the Welsh
prince's power to ruin her—ruin all of them, for that matter.
All that was needed was for him to denounce her to King
Henry as a traitor for what she had done with the gold
from France for so many years. Prince Cadwallader himself
would not be blamed in this new time of peace; only those
who had smuggled the gold to him.

Helpless, she gestured toward the Old Tower.

They splashed across the ward in silence. Emmeline dug
her hands into her cloak, not wanting him to see how much
they were trembling. The guard knights at the bottom of
the tower stairs saluted them, faces full of curiosity.

Emmeline said, "My Lord Cadwallader, give me a moment, I must send my maids away."

He looked as though he would say something but she
raced ahead without giving him the chance. She took the
winding stairs two at a time, threw the door open and then
closed it behind her quickly. Magnus had bathed as she
had told him; the rushes were full of wet towels. Hedwid
had dressed him in clean clothes. He was sitting on a stool
pulling on his boots. Two of the other maids were straightening up the room.

She went quickly to Magnus, put a hand on his shoulder,
and clapped her other hand over his mouth. Hedwid turned,
swallowing a cry when she saw her face.

"Hush," Emmeline said to all of them. "The Welsh
prince is here. Go out together talking and chattering
loudly, and keep Magnus in the middle." She had a good
reason for not wanting Cadwallader to know her son was
there. "Hide him if you can."

She took her hand away from her son's mouth and looked down into his upturned face. She smoothed his red hair. He did not look at all frightened, only excited. "I need a knight's sworn quest from you," she said softly. "You must tell me if you can do it."

It was just what he wanted to hear. "Yes, whatever it is I swear it, Mother!" he squeaked. "Oh, I swear it!"

"Hush." She almost put her hand over his mouth again. "Keep your voice down."

She looked at the fearful women clustered around her, and told them what she wanted them to do. To Magnus she said, "You must ride your pony straight to Master Avenant's house in the woolmen's street." She didn't think anyone would take too much notice of a child on his pony. "You must not linger anywhere. Swear it now, like a knight."

His eyes shone as he lifted his hand and put it in hers and solemnly swore.

The two girls helped her quickly take down her hair. They raked it out over her shoulders and arms with their fingers. There was not time to do more.

Hedwid pulled off Emmeline's wet cloak, then bent to straighten her bliaut and overdress. "Oh, milady, whatever happens, the Morlaix people love only you," she whispered. "It's the Welsh they hate."

One of the girls grabbed her hand and kissed it before she could pull it away. She knew they feared what Cadwallader was going to do to her. She feared it herself.

She almost had to push them out onto the landing. The maids went down the tower stairs talking loudly with Magnus jammed between them, and left the door open. A few moments later there were footsteps on the stairs and Prince Cadwallader and the courier, Rainald, came in. The prince took off his cloak and put it on a stool by the fire. He looked at length at the tapestries on the wall, the inlaid tables from Outremer, the bed, and the two massive Flemish cupboards.

"Very elegant," he said at last. "This room pleases me." He sat down in the high-backed chair by the fire, the gold courier standing beside him. "I have heard you brought much wealth to this joining, Lady Emmeline. Even though it's no secret there's no love lost between you and Morlaix."

She went to the cupboard and brought out the wine and cups. "Prince Cadwallader, someone has misspoken. I am a dutiful wife to my lord and husband."

He smiled charmingly. "That is not what I said."

She poured one cup of wine for the prince and another for the courier and brought it to them.

After a sip the prince lifted his eyebrows. "Ah, this is fine wine." He lifted the cup in salute to her, silver armlets gleaming against his black clothes. He never took his gaze from her. "God be with us, Milady Emmeline. Sweet as the day and as fair, now that we meet after so long a time."

She had no idea what he meant although the look in his eyes was plain enough. "The wine is some of Chancellor Thomas à Becket's prized Burgundy," she told him, coming to refill his cup. "He favored us with some of it as a token of his stay here."

He seized her wrist as she bent over him. "And you will make my stay all the pleasanter, will you not?"

She struggled again to get away from him. "Milord, I do not know what you mean."

The courier hastily finished his wine and set down his cup. "Milord prince, milady, I beg you a good evening." He kept his eyes down as he let himself out, closing the door behind him.

"Where is he going?" Emmeline used her other hand to pry Cadwallader's fingers from her wrist.

"Merely outside." Using his strength, he drew her down into his lap. "He will guard the door."

Held prisoner against his hard body, Emmeline tried not

to struggle. She hadn't been mistaken; no wonder her first
thought had been to order the knights to carry this wolf-
eyed Welsh warrior and his toady down to the cells under
the cistern and leave him there until her husband, Niall,
could deal with them! The saints knew there was no argument about *his* hatred.

Yet even as she squirmed to break free she found herself
curious as to what he wanted of her. To sleep with her,
yes. But there was more. "Milord, release me. I have done
nothing to invite this attention!"

He laughed softly. He had her arms pinned while his hand
was busy unlacing the front of her gown. "Nay, dear lady,
you must pay what you owe me." He stopped and looked
into her eyes. "As for example, you will continue to receive
King Louis's gifts of gold from Rainald, but you will not
need to send them over the mountains, I will come for them.
I will tell no one of your help. But in return you will pay
for my silence in bed most sweetly."

She fought his hands that had pulled open the neck of
her gown. Her breasts spilled out from the laces, white,
lush, rosy-tipped. "Prince Cadwallader, my husband will
kill you for this!"

"Sweet lady, Morlaix has had his chances and he has
not done so yet, has he? Come, you regard this Irish
butcher as I do." After a long, appreciative stare he lowered
his head and nuzzled her flesh. "How I relish," he said,
his voice muffled, "cuckolding this Henry Plantagenet's
rough piece of offal!"

His breath felt strangely hot on her skin. She struggled
but he held her tightly, gripping her upper arms so that she
could not pull away.

"This is the payment I spoke of." He nipped at her breast
with his teeth. "That you will help me against King Henry,
and that you will give to me what you give to that Irish
gutter dog. But with more pleasure."

Emmeline jerked her body straight and literally slid off

his lap. Before he could grab her she was on her feet, her gown gaping open, her breasts thrusting out, the air touching the wet tips of her nipples where he had suckled them. She left it that way, murder in her heart, as his eyes devoured her.

She got the wine pitcher and crossed the room to him and leaned over him, breasts swaying temptingly in his face. She poured him another cup.

"Jesu," he growled. He reached for her, but she stepped deftly out of reach.

She had finally heard the Welshman's filthy scheme. In spite of the treaty of peace he had signed with King Henry, the great Prince Cadwallader wanted her to continue to be a traitor and pass the foreign gold to him just as she had stupidly done for years. She was not to give it to the shepherds to take over the mountains, she was to wait for the prince himself to come and claim it. At which time he would take his revenge on Niall fitzJulien by crawling into her bed!

Jesus God, Niall fitzJulien was a brave and honorable man, ten times Cadwallader's worth! He had proved that by whipping the Welshman both in war and on the tourney field. But to seduce another man's wife—that was what infuriated her. That, and that Cadwallader assumed she was slut enough to betray her own husband.

She turned away. Behind her, he began somewhat unsteadily to pull off his boots. When that was done, he stood up and began to untie the top of his hose.

Emmeline carried the wine pitcher to refill his cup. "Let me touch you," he muttered, putting his hand over her breast and squeezing it. He handed her his cup and she pretended to sip from it.

She let him do what he wanted, teeth gritted, a frozen smile on her lips. When he pulled the cup away and tried to kiss her, she held him off. Then she put down the wine pitcher and took him by the hand and led him to the bed.

The tall, swarthy Welshman had pulled off his tunic and undershirt and wore nothing but his hose. He stood by the bed and stripped these off. His shanks and backside were palest milky white but where he had hair it was pitch black, silky. He climbed the step up and turned around and sat down on the bed.

"Little golden minx, I will make you forget him." His words were a little slurred. "I have wanted you since the moment I saw you at the English king's tourney."

Stark naked, Cadwallader fell back among the pillows. "What a picture you make, with your gown opened like that," he said. "Take off the rest."

Emmeline wanted to give him more wine, but she doubted that he would take it. She pulled off her overdress, then her bliaut and stood there in her shift. She would run naked to hell and back if he asked, she told herself.

Prince Cadwallader, the great hero of the Welsh, lay on his back with his legs spread apart, his shaft almost erect, very long, and narrow. It stood up from a bush of black hair. His legs were covered with black hair as were his arms, and the lower part of his belly. He was not as gracefully made as her husband, for all Niall fitzJulien's size.

She saw his eyes droop and he muttered something. Then they closed.

Emmeline looked down at him. She would have stripped naked for him if that was what it took, and crawled into bed with him, but she was glad it had not come to that. When he stirred, she turned and ran to the door and flung it open.

Jiane was on the stairs with two Morlaix knights. By now Magnus was on his pony, headed for the town.

Jiane stepped over the body of Rainald sprawled on the landing. She held open the door for them. The knights started for the bed and the sleeping Prince Cadwallader. When they saw his condition, they exclaimed.

Jiane pulled at the bedclothes to wrap around him.

"There's no time," Emmeline hissed. "Take him as he is."

Her knees were beginning to shake from nerves and sheer tiredness. She suddenly had to sit down on the edge of the bed.

The two Morlaix knights hauled Prince Cadwallader out of the covers and slung his naked body between them. "It is all right now, milady," the Gascon knight told her. "We will take care of the rest."

They carried the Welshman across the room that way with his head dangling, his long black hair sweeping the floor.

Emmeline said, with what felt like the last of her strength, "And the one on the landing. Take him, too."

She heard Jiane grunt his assent as he closed the door.

TWENTY-SEVEN

Emmeline woke up, and screamed.

Her husband bent over her, candle in hand, so mud-spattered she hardly recognized him. Joceran and Gotselm, just as filthy, were in the shadows behind him.

"What happened?" His voice was hoarse with tiredness. "I have nearly killed a good horse getting here from Chester. Tell me what you have done now."

Beside her, Magnus bounced up in the bed. "Milord," he cried joyously, "you are back!"

Niall flung him a savage look. "I am not your lord, I am your father! And get out of this bed, you are too old to sleep here with your mother like a mewling babe!"

Emmeline sat up beside him, pulling up the bedcovers to her chin. "Holy Mother, have you lost your senses," she screamed, "to come storming in here saying things to Magnus like that?" In a quieter voice she said to Joceran, "Fetch more candles from the cupboard, and take Gotselm and leave us."

Magnus regarded Niall, wide-eyed. "Are you my father, milord?"

"No, he lies." Emmeline turned to her son. "He will say anything when he is in a foul temper, you know that."

With a snarl Niall turned and went to poke up the fire while Joceran fetched the candles. He took off his filthy cloak and flung it over a stool.

With his back to her, he said, "Chester's knights brought

the news that Prince Cadwallader has been found in the
market square in Morlaix, naked and drunk, with his cock
painted black."

"*Blue.*" Emmeline watched her son crawl out of bed and
go to stand somewhat timidly beside him. "And *dyed* blue,
not painted. It was not my idea, it was John Avenant's dyers
who did that. The wool people hate the Welsh."

"God rot it!" Joceran jumped and dropped a lighted candle into the rushes. As he scrambled to pick it up his lord
strode to bed and leaned over her, his face right in hers.
"Do you know how the Welsh hate being mocked? King
Henry has taken great care to tell me that satire is the
greatest punishment their bards inflict. When Welsh chiefs
are mocked and derided they give up their thrones, send
their wives to convents, disown their heirs, go into exile!"

She returned his glare, unflinching. "Mother of God,
would you have had me murder him? That would have
brought about war, would it not? Your wonderful prince
said he came here to cuckold you! That it was his revenge
for all that you have done to him!"

He stared at her for a long moment, then abruptly sat
down on the bed. "Tell me how Cadwallader came to be
naked in the market square."

Emmeline looked past him to the two knights and her
son. "First send Gotselm and Joceran away. And have them
put Magnus to bed."

He waved his arm, and Joceran pulled an unwilling Magnus to the door, Gotselm following.

"Milord!" Magnus cried. "Mother—"

Niall lifted his head. "I will talk to you later, boy. It is
time someone told you the truth."

Magnus fairly bounced up and down. "Milord, the knights
say—am I truly—?"

"Out!" Niall thundered, pointing. "Go with Joceran and
do what he tells you!"

When the door swung to Emmeline pushed the covers

away and sat straight up in the bed. "Cadwallader was not drunk, I gave him Gaeweddan's powders that I still had from your time with your bad leg. God's love, I gave Cadwallader so much wine I thought it would drown him! He still took enough of the herb to fell a horse before it put him to sleep. Then Jiane and the knights carried him through the passage under the cistern that leads out of the castle and down the hill to the river. I sent Magnus to town on his pony, and he carried a message to John Avenant and his guild. You must praise him, it was really a very brave thing for a little boy to do." She bit her lip. "Holy Mother, he will not understand if you tell him he is your son!"

"Hah. You heard what the boy said. Half the world guesses, anyway."

Emmeline sighed. "The woolmen came and got Cadwallader from the bank of the river and did with him what they thought best."

He never took his eyes from her. "Holy Jesus in heaven, there is a secret way out of the castle? Jiane and his knights carried the Welsh prince out through it?"

She shrugged, uneasy. "It is an old passage. I was going to tell you about it. The builders found it and took me to see."

"You were going to tell me about it." He ran his hands through his disheveled red hair. "And when were you going to tell me about the French gold?"

Emmeline's mouth dropped open. For a moment she could not breathe. The room spun around her dizzily, as though the world was coming to an end.

She shut her eyes. When she opened them the room no longer whirled. She barely managed to whisper, "You knew!"

He got up from the bed and paced to the fire. He stood looking into it, one hand on the mantel.

"The king had hoped to flush out Hugh Bigod and the rest of the French king's English friends who plot to do him so much ill," he said in a weary voice. "The gold that King Louis has sent for years to the rebellious Welsh is only a part of the scheming. But instead, thanks to my wife and her makeshift conspirators, we now have Cadwallader himself, naked and drugged for public view in my town square, his prick painted with woad. The French king is extremely pious; he will think a long time before sending any more aid to this sort of debauched princeling." Under his breath he groaned. "However, when he heard of it our own King Henry was peculiarly entranced."

Emmeline swallowed. *"Entranced?"*

"You are beautiful, dammit, and the king loves beautiful women, to his eternal folly. And Henry's spies have told him that you were but carrying out, like a dutiful wife, what your husband Neufmarche had first begun during the war between his mother the empress and King Stephen."

He turned to face her.

"But what dazzles most is that King Henry is greatly admiring of the way the Lady of Morlaix uses her food at royal banquets to fell those damned troubadours. And the clever way you replace lost jewelry—the king is a great admirer of cleverness, as you well know, or he would not stay with that bitch he has married. Of course, Henry is sorry he was not able this time to expose the traitors around him as he was eager to catch his great friend the Earl of Norfolk in his treachery. But the news of Cadwallader's blue-painted prick took the king's fancy as nothing has since your runaway roast."

She said, "You are mocking me."

"No, by all that is holy I am not. The king does not like Cadwallader, he thinks him a pompous barbarian. Henry's good humor now knows no bounds. Even Queen Eleanor received his unrestrained attention. After a great drunken roistering feast last night with many bawdy toasts to the tenderest parts of the Welsh alliance, he promptly took her to bed."

"I don't believe you!"

He sat down on the stool and lifted his leg and said, "Come help me pull off these damned wet boots."

She got out of bed and padded to him. Lifting her nightdress, she straddled his leg, and he put his other foot on her bottom and pushed.

"It is true enough. Henry loves us now for all the things I have mentioned, may God and the angels save us. He wishes you—*us*—at court, a condition I will devote my best efforts to see come to naught. I do not want the king anywhere near you. Here, help me off with my mail."

He bent forward, and she pulled the hauberk over his head. It was heavy enough to make her stagger. He quickly stood up and pulled her to him. With one arm around her Niall looked down into her face and lifted a hand to pull back her fiery, tumbled hair.

"I know that you want to be free," he said huskily, "and I have promised you that you will. But I have to tell you that King Henry has made that difficult so to do, as he will shortly make you a countess."

She could only stare at him.

He said, "Have you nothing to say to that? It will be a difficult task to live in Wroxeter with your grandsire and the precious heirs to Morlaix. So far from your husband, Niall fitzJulien, the great earl."

"No," she whispered. "Oh, no!"

He let her go, his tawny eyes hooded. " 'No' that you will have your freedom and go to live in Wroxeter? Or 'no' that I will not be a great earl?"

Emmeline turned and started for the bed, her long red hair swinging free down her back, her nightdress clinging to her shoulder blades and the soft curve of her bottom. "No, I don't want to be a countess! I never wanted any of these things. I do not like the court and the cruel gossip and those who fawn on King Henry and Queen Eleanor. I am a guildswoman, a goldsmith, I want Magnus to be a good man, I want him to be the same!" She climbed the step to the great bed and got in and pulled the covers up to her chin. "It is you who are ambitious for fame and glory. I want no part of it."

Niall shed his tunic and hose and followed her quickly under the bedcovers. He propped his head on his arm and rolled his big body against her. She pulled the coverlet over her head.

He prodded the covers gently with his finger. "Speak to me, wife," he told her.

She threw them back and looked up at him. "That night long ago," she whispered, "when first I saw you, I thought you a young and eager hero like those from the tales of Arthur the king. Remember how you wooed me in this bed? You were another—Gawain. Another Sir Lancelot," she said with a sob. "Ah, I was such a silly fool!"

He leaned over her and kissed her lightly. "I have never forgotten it. And the room and the candlelight and the rich hangings on the wall, and that I had eaten a full meal for the first time in days. If you were a silly lass, I was a raw young knight with not a penny in my pockets and when I saw you standing by this bed you were so beautiful I was near terrified out of my poor wits. I thought you a dread enchantress like King Arthur's Morgana the witch. And I knew I was lost. For I loved you from the moment I saw you."

Emmeline jerked up in the bed and turned to look down at him. "You have never told me that! Why have you never said anything to me like that?"

He put his arm behind his head and looked down his nose at her. "King Henry will make Magnus—*Julien*—my heir. We will petition Archbishop Theobald, who will then send to Rome to the pope. Some day the boy will be the Earl of Morlaix."

She sucked in her breath. "His name is Magnus, it will always be Magnus!" He was pulling her nightdress over her head; her voice was muffled. "I will never call him Julien. Ugh. Holy Mother, you can't call someone *Julien fitzJulien*—everyone will think it a jape!"

Both hands enclosed her breasts as she leaned over him. He touched his lips to their rosy tips. "Stay with me, Emmeline, dearling, I will give you anything you want, King Henry will not let me do less. You have your workshop and the deed to the manor house. Look, you may even have another brace of Beguines."

"No, I don't want that." She shuddered as he pulled her under him and thrust his body between her thighs. "Poor women. I wonder every day how Walter and Berthilde are faring."

"Umm," he murmured, kissing her deeply and passionately. "Fire witch," he growled. "You have not yet told me that you love me."

Emmeline looked up at the familiar blue hangings and gold tassels above them that had enclosed them that first night they loved one another. *And it was love. Through all these years,* she told herself, *we have never been able to forget.*

"Mmm, I will tell you later," she murmured, opening her body to him. And putting her arms lovingly around his neck.

Author's Note

A golden era began for England in the early years of the reign of Henry Plantagenet and Eleanor of Aquitaine who were, as a couple, exceptionally intelligent, admirably educated, and otherwise well-matched. The queen generously fostered a flowering of music, art, and poetry already influenced (through the Crusades) by the Mediterranean and Near East. Other women followed her example, notably Marie of France, one of many women musicians, artists, and poets largely unrecognized and unrecorded in the annals of the time.

Henry II was the most remarkable ruler of his century, a gifted king who encouraged commerce and expansion, and the law and governmental reforms started by his grandfather, Henry the First, the "Lion of Justice." But Henry's compulsive womanizing eventually alienated Eleanor, who turned to her sons and encouraged their bloody and costly rebellions against their father.

Within a few years the church had suppressed the Beguines, as well as women actively engaged in the trade guilds, encouraging talented women instead to enter convents, where many had brilliant if limited careers.

TODAY'S HOTTEST READS
ARE TOMORROW'S SUPERSTARS

VICTORY'S WOMAN (4484, $4.50)
by Gretchen Genet
Andrew—the carefree soldier who sought glory on the battlefield, and returned a shattered man . . . Niall—the legandary frontiersman and a former Shawnee captive, tormented by his past . . . Roger—the troubled youth, who would rise up to claim a shocking legacy . . . and Clarice—the passionate beauty bound by one man, and hopelessly in love with another. Set against the backdrop of the American revolution, three men fight for their heritage—and one woman is destined to change all their lives forever!

FORBIDDEN (4488, $4.99)
by Jo Beverley
While fleeing from her brothers, who are attempting to sell her into a loveless marriage, Serena Riverton accepts a carriage ride from a stranger—who is the handsomest man she has ever seen. Lord Middlethorpe, himself, is actually contemplating marriage to a dull daughter of the aristocracy, when he encounters the breathtaking Serena. She arouses him as no woman ever has. And after a night of thrilling intimacy—a forbidden liaison—Serena must choose between a lady's place and a woman's passion!

WINDS OF DESTINY (4489, $4.99)
by Victoria Thompson
Becky Tate is a half-breed outcast—branded by her Comanche heritage. Then she meets a rugged stranger who awakens her heart to the magic and mystery of passion. Hiding a desperate past, Texas Ranger Clint Masterson has ridden into cattle country to bring peace to a divided land. But a greater battle rages inside him when he dares to desire the beautiful Becky!

WILDEST HEART (4456, $4.99)
by Virginia Brown
Maggie Malone had come to cattle country to forge her future as a healer. Now she was faced by Devon Conrad, an outlaw wounded body and soul by his shadowy past . . . whose eyes blazed with fury even as his burning caress sent her spiraling with desire. They came together in a Texas town about to explode in sin and scandal. Danger was their destiny—and there was nothing they wouldn't dare for love!

Available wherever paperbacks are sold, or order direct from the Publisher. Send cover price plus 50¢ per copy for mailing and handling to Penguin USA, P.O. Box 999, c/o Dept. 17109, Bergenfield, NJ 07621. Residents of New York and Tennessee must include sales tax. DO NOT SEND CASH.